Entangled in Death

An Allyson Worthy Mystery
Book One

David Carlson

coffeetownpress

Kenmore, WA

coffeetownpress

A Coffeetown Press book published by Epicenter Press

Epicenter Press
6524 NE 181st St.
Suite 2
Kenmore, WA 98028

For more information go to:
www.Coffeetownpress.com
www.DavidCarlson.net

Note: *Entangled in Death* is set in 2020, when there was little hope that the war in Syria would end.

Cover design by Scott Book
Design by Melissa Vail Coffman

Library of Congress Control Number: 2026935964

ISBN: 978-1-68492-360-1 (Trade Paper)
ISBN: 978-1-68492-361-8 (eBook)

Entangled in Death *is dedicated to the Writers' Workshop, Three Lakes, Wisconsin; The Taos Mystery Book Club, Taos, New Mexico; Mind Chimes Bookshop, Three Lakes, Wisconsin; and Wild Geese Bookstore, Franklin, Indiana.*

Acknowledgments

I am grateful to so many who have supported my writing efforts. I remember fondly Mrs. Black, my eighth-grade Language Arts and Social Studies teacher, and Mrs. East, my high school Latin teacher, who were always encouraging and demanding.

In college, I had an English professor whose name I cannot remember. What I do remember was the Cs on papers when I tried to write what I thought he wanted. In frustration, on the next paper, I wrote what I felt about the topic. I received an A on that paper and learned a life-changing lesson.

I am also indebted to my wife, Kathy, for her daily encouragement, her incredible editing skills, and for the beautiful covers that she paints for the series. I also want to thank my agent, Sara Camilli, who has been with me all along the way and my editor at Coffeetown Press, Jennifer McCord, who is a wonderful critic and friend.

Main Character List

CIA and FBI

Allyson Worthy—FBI agent on loan to CIA office in Rome; works undercover in Caritas
Morgan Stamper—Allyson's CIA case manager
Chaz Eaton—CIA agent; ex-Navy Seal
Sally Patton—CIA agent; Allyson Worthy's roommate
Arnold Sanderson—CIA Bureau Chief, Rome Office
Braylen Manners—CIA agent
Khadija Mubarak—CIA agent; works undercover in Caritas Refugee Camp
Gianni Treni—Chaz Easton's contact in the police

Caritas Refugee Camp

Seppe D'Angelo—Sant Anselmo Aid Worker in Caritas
Fatima Rasul—Young Syrian refugee in Caritas
Hasan Kadir—Syrian elder in Caritas
Daliyeh—Young Syrian mother in Caritas
Asha Malik—Young Syrian refugee in Caritas
Jameela Malik—Young Syrian refugee in Caritas; sister to Asha Malik
Sabia Terek—Leader of criminal group in Caritas
Father Sal—Seppe D'Angelo's confessor and spiritual mentor

PROLOGUE

June 22, 2020

DESPITE TRAFFIC SOUNDS, ALLYSON Worthy awoke refreshed on this, the Monday that would begin her third week in Rome. The weather could not have been better, seventy degrees and sunny. Out her apartment bedroom window, she could see the top of the Church of St. John the Lateran's white façade, where statues of saints looked out across the city. Allyson, however, wasn't a pilgrim interested in Rome's churches, nor was she a tourist. She was an FBI agent on loan to the CIA Rome office.

Allyson knew that she wouldn't have received the opportunity to serve with the CIA if it hadn't been for 9-11. That tragedy had exposed the cost of US intelligence agencies working in silos, the CIA, FBI, NSC, and even the Secret Service too often competing with one another rather than working cooperatively. Now, twenty years after that wake-up call, agents who could work across agency lines were valued highly and were often promoted ahead of schedule. Allyson was a four-year veteran of the FBI who'd garnered from previous cases high marks for focus on mission, ability to adapt under pressure, and creative problem solving. She also knew that it was her near fluency in Italian that allowed her to leapfrog over other agents when the CIA came looking for an agent to work with their office in Rome.

Allyson would have accepted the assignment—to work undercover in a refugee camp, on the lookout for criminals and potential terrorists—even if it were just a smart career move. The truth was that Allyson had loved Italy for more than a decade and, in a sense, she credited the country with saving her life.

When Allyson was a junior in high school, her mother had, without warning, announced that she wanted a divorce. Until that moment, Allyson thought her parents' marriage was, while not great, at least secure. Her mother and father would disagree, especially about her father's irregular work hours, although no more than Allyson's friends' parents. Looking back, Allyson could see that her mother had been more distant in the weeks before the demand for the divorce, with everyone in the family, not only Allyson's father.

Little made sense to Allyson in the weeks that followed: her father, Detroit's most awarded homicide detective, stopping by the house almost weekly to remove more of his clothes and belongings, her mother refusing to go to couple's therapy, or her younger sister, Amy, pretending the divorce wasn't happening. Everything for Allyson came to a head a month after the divorce was finalized, when Allyson came home from school to find her mother and father sitting over coffee together in the kitchen as if nothing had happened.

She ran away that night with a bag of toiletries, a suitcase filled with clothes, and one book—a book of photos of Venice. The book had been a lifeline for Allyson, Venice becoming a dream city where she imagined she could flee to if she wished hard enough. Reality proved otherwise. She'd lived over that summer in an apartment over a schoolmate's garage, returning home two days before the start of her senior year. She'd never told her parents where she'd been, and she'd never regretted running away. She'd even delighted in knowing that her famous father, renowned for solving difficult cases, had been unable to solve the mystery of his own daughter's disappearance.

Consequently, being offered an internship in Venice in her third year of college had been a dream come true. Venice hadn't disappointed. When friends in the States asked her for her opinion of the city, she'd replied that Venice was the only place she'd been—and who knows, maybe the only place in the world—that was more beautiful than the best photos of it.

However, her current assignment was in Rome, and Rome was far different from Venice. Venice was quiet, often eerily so at night; the noise in

Rome was constant. Venice was not just a city of canals, yet a walker's city. Rome was a city of buses, trains, taxis, and scooters—thousands of scooters. If Venice was more beautiful, Allyson acknowledged that the assignment in Rome offered a better chance of benefitting her career. Her goal for the case with the CIA was the one she always set for herself, to exceed the expectations of her supervisor and end a case with a glowing assessment of her contribution.

Now starting her third week on her assignment in Rome, Allyson knew that achieving her goal wouldn't be without challenges. Rome's CIA office might have wanted someone with her language proficiency and previous experience in the country, but that didn't mean that they didn't treat her as an outsider. The case manager and Allyson's superior was Morgan Stamper, an eighteen-year veteran of the CIA. Stamper had initially been a bit standoffish, yet she'd impressed Allyson with her no-nonsense approach to the refugee camp assignment. Allyson was unimpressed, however, with Chaz Easton, the only male on the team, who'd been with the Agency three years. He'd pulled rank on Allyson from their first encounter, when, after letting her know that he'd graduated from Brown University, he'd asked what university she'd attended. When she'd replied that she'd graduated from Franklin College, he'd frowned as he asked, "Where the hell is that?"

Before she could stop herself, she'd replied, "It's in Indiana. Maybe you've heard of it. It's that state between Ohio and Illinois?" In their team meetings, Allyson felt Chaz's critical eye on her whenever she offered something, and he relished whenever Stamper pointed out where CIA procedures were different from the FBI's.

Allyson was consequently surprised when Sally Patton, her roommate and a relatively new CIA agent, asked Allyson if Chaz had hit on her yet.

"No, thank God. Actually, I'd say he's decided to hate me."

"That's not the impression he gave me," Sally said.

"What do you mean?"

"He stopped by my desk a couple of days ago and, after saying he thought you're cute, asked if you're gay."

"What?"

Wincing, Sally said, "Hey, don't get mad at me. I'm just the messenger. You have to understand that Chaz feels it's his duty to hit on every women under thirty in the office."

"That would include you."

"Hey, I'm not that desperate. Not yet, anyway. Did he tell you that he graduated from Brown?"

Allyson shook her head. "Oh yes, Mr. Ivy Leaguer. Have you noticed how he carries himself—that stiff way like he's getting ready to mow somebody down in front of him. I saw the same thing in college, with some of the football players."

"You have noticed Chaz, then."

"Only because we're on the same team, and I can't avoid him. I'm just glad we have different assignments. I work in the camp, while he's in the liaison with the Italian authorities and works in the city."

Afterwards, Allyson thought back on what Sally had said. She admitted to herself that she could have handled her first exchange with Chaz better. Yet, she suspected that if she'd been polite instead of sarcastic, Chaz would have become a different kind of problem.

There was more to her reaction to Chaz than what she'd shared with Sally. She'd dated widely in college, although never very long with any one guy. If she were to try to explain why that was the case, she'd confess that she was always waiting for men to disappoint her. That hesitation, that tension, continued on through her training period in the FBI and then onto her first assignments as an agent.

She'd sworn to herself that she wouldn't let her parents' divorce be the defining moment of her life, yet to this point that had sadly been the case. No man had come into her life that she clicked with. Chaz Eaton was just the latest example.

Over the past week, however, she'd wondered if an aid worker in the refugee camp, Seppe D'Angelo, might prove to be the exception. He was handsome and tall for an Italian, with dark hair and an open smile. She'd also noticed, perhaps because it was such a contrast to Chaz, that Seppe eased into a room as if he didn't want to disturb anyone. Best of all, he hadn't tried to impress her. Just as she began to hold out hopes that Seppe might be the exception to her previous relationships with men, he'd told her that he was contemplating becoming a priest. *Just my luck,* she thought, *to be attracted to a guy whose dream is to be celibate.*

CHAPTER ONE

Caritas Refugee Camp
June 23, 2020

Fatima Rasul hadn't slept well since the funeral. Not that sleeping soundly was ever possible in Caritas, one of the refugee camps outside Rome. Yet now it wasn't the restless sounds of others or their snoring that disturbed her. It was rather raw fear.

She had known the dead man, Hasan Kadir, because they both worked in the camp's school. Like many older men she'd known in Syria, Hasan was soft-spoken, not offering advice unless asked. His advice was usually wise, causing a majority of the Syrians in Caritas, facing numerous problems in a foreign country, to ask Hasan to be the go-between with camp authorities.

Because of that, Hasan Kadir's prominence in the camp made his murder all the more disturbing. Also, with the Muslim practice of burying someone on the day of death, now only a week ago, the fear among the camp residents hadn't diminished.

Hasan had been stabbed, his body found in the early-morning hours inside one of the men's bathrooms. It was unusual for the Syrian community not to know more specific details about his murder, given the Muslim custom of having men, in Hasan's case, prepare the body for burial. Instead, when the community had received the body, it was already shrouded. The community was assured that an imam from Rome had supervised the body's preparation, yet that didn't stop rumors from spreading, one that Hasan had also been castrated and another that his tongue had been cut out.

In her journey from war-torn Damascus to Turkey and eventually Italy, Fatima became familiar with death. Although the only deaths occurring in Caritas in her nine months there were all from natural causes, refugees and migrants described other camps as being crime-ridden. Some people told stories of residents, especially children, disappearing; others told tales of torture. Rapes were so common in some of the other camps that authorities did little when victims reported that crime.

Since Fatima had survived the civil war in Syria, the death of a fellow refugee, especially an elderly man like Hasan, wasn't what frightened Fatima. Instead, it was what he had whispered to her the day before he was killed, asking her to meet with him to discuss "a serious matter from home." At the time, she wondered if the comment meant that Hasan Kadir was also from Damascus. Then she thought he might have contacted her because she'd been chosen by camp authorities to represent the Syrian youth on the camp's educational committee. Hasan's death the next night had given her more disturbing thoughts. Had the elderly leader wanted to talk to her about something more serious, something that got him killed and might now put her in danger?

Fatima's daily routine began with prayers, then a shower in the women's bathroom. Some of the Syrian women showered much less frequently, yet water had been so scarce in Damascus in the last weeks she lived there—if one could call hunkering down in fear of airstrikes really living—that the morning shower, the hot water cascading down from her hair to her feet, was her way of celebrating her survival. She then went to the women's dining hall where her celebration of life continued with her tray of orange juice, muesli, and a pastry. From there she walked to the camp's school.

Fatima was enrolled in three classes: English, Italian, and Introduction to Religion. She was one of nearly forty students in the two language classes, yet was one of only nine in the religion class. Had her parents survived the bombardment of Damascus and the long journey to Turkey and finally Italy, they, especially her father, would have forbidden her to take such a class. There was only one valid religion, Islam, and to study others would only open her to confusion or, worse, draw her away from Allah.

Fatima's parents hadn't survived. Her father was killed a year before

Fatima managed to leave, as he was returning home with a precious loaf of bread. Despite this, her mother insisted on staying in Damascus with her two sisters, who were also widowed by the war.

The low enrollment in the religion class was no doubt proof that her father's fear about studying religion was shared by most in the camp. She was, in fact, one of only two in the class from Syria, the other a middle-aged merchant who was Zoroastrian. Despite being curious as to why Allah would allow other religions to exist, Fatima hadn't immediately signed up for the religion class. The course, unlike the two language classes, was hardly practical, although she remembered hearing of Christians and people of other religions in Syria. The schools in Syria, however, did not offer an opportunity to study those religions. It was only in reading the camp pamphlet listing the courses being offered that Fatima saw the chance to satisfy her curiosity.

Her progress in Italian and English was steady, although it was her religion class that most intrigued her. Perhaps she was fascinated because the course was considered taboo, or perhaps she enjoyed the class because the instructor, a retired Italian professor, had lived in Cairo. Thereby he was nearly fluent in Arabic, treating every religion surveyed in the course with respect. On the first day, Professor Napolitano apologized that he had been unable to find a textbook on the subject written in Arabic. The class would be using a textbook written in Italian—basic Italian, yet still Italian. The reading assignments were therefore tedious for everyone. Fatima embraced the challenge mainly because the class's struggle with the textbook in the afternoon and evening was rewarded the next day with an approach new to her—open discussion.

Religious education in Syria was restricted for boys, and where girls were allowed, the curriculum consisted mainly of cooking and sewing along with reciting the Qur'an. Good students were those who pleased Allah by mastering chapter after chapter of the text, not questioning or discussing what they memorized.

Professor Napolitano did not require memorization. Instead, he encouraged students to summarize what they'd read before listing questions they had. He even encouraged disagreement, which Fatima found both frightening and thrilling. Fatima asked the most questions, which at first, she could see, scandalized the Muslim men in the class.

That morning, the professor asked the class to compare how Jesus was viewed in Judaism, Christianity, and Islam. Instantly, one of the men who'd spoken little in the class, asked, "Christians, how can they deny what the Holy Qur'an says, that Allah has no son? Why do they not say Jesus, peace be upon him, is a prophet?"

The room became instantly silent at that point. Professor Napolitano had never said he was a Catholic, although that was what Fatima had always assumed. He was an Italian professor, after all. The student's question challenged both the professor's authority and the legitimacy of Christianity. She wondered if the professor would rebuke the student.

Instead, Professor Napolitano smiled and replied that his question was a good one. "Would anyone like to offer an answer?" he posed in Arabic.

No one spoke for several minutes, before Fatima raised her hand. The professor smiled again and nodded in her direction. "Religions have different scriptures," she said. "As a Muslim, I read the Holy Qur'an. Yet if I'd been born in Italy . . .," she paused, wondering if she were about to insult Allah, "I'm not sure I'd be Muslim."

The room remained silent again until the Zoroastrian member of the class said, "The Avesta is our scriptures. Don't I follow them because my parents and their parents did as well?"

Rather than answer, Professor Napolitano wrote on the board: "Does a person's religion depend on where he or she is born?"

Fatima felt a stirring in the class, perhaps because the question, which could be taken to either question or support Allah's control of a person's fate. Professor Napolitano turned slowly around to face his students. He was silent for a moment as he scanned his class. Finally, he said, pointing to what was written on the chalkboard, "For tomorrow, write a one-page response to this question. I want your own thoughts."

Fatima walked slowly back to her dormitory, wondering if her comment had prompted an assignment that some might interpret as questioning Allah's will. Inside the women's bathroom in her dormitory, Fatima studied her face in the mirror. From the outside, she appeared to be the same person, only healthier, who she was when she arrived at Caritas. Her gray hijab still encircled the same face, her dark eyes gazing out at the world. Her hands still showed faint traces of the henna tattoos that were common among Muslim women from Syria.

What the mirror couldn't reveal was the changes that were taking place within her, day by day, as she adjusted to her new life in Europe. She knew that many refugees in the camp tried to live as if they were still in their home villages and countries. They looked at, although refused to really see, the brick barracks of the camp, the hill towns surrounding the camp with their medieval walls and churches, and the Italian flag that waved above the administration building of the camp. For them, living at Caritas was a dream—some parts good, some parts bad, yet all parts foreign—from which they would one day awaken to find themselves back home.

Fatima chose a different path. She knew she would always be Syrian, yet she no longer expected to return to the land of her birth. Where she would live the rest of her life was an unknown that excited her and had prompted her to learn both Italian and English.

From the bathroom, she returned to her assigned space in the dorm, where she opened the second drawer of her pine dresser to remove the clothes that she reserved for her afternoon work. That was when she saw the neatly folded tan piece of paper. Knowing that she possessed no paper that color, she wondered who had sent it. Written in shaky Arabic script were the words "Danger coming from Damascus and Aleppo." Below the single line were the initials "HK."

Fatima sat down abruptly on her bed, realizing the note was from Hasan Kadir. How had it gotten into her dresser? She was sure the note wasn't there the night before when she put away her work clothes. Someone, who had to be another woman, had entered Fatima's dormitory during the night or earlier that morning to hide the note.

Neither the words nor the appearance of the note itself made sense to Fatima. If she hadn't recognized Hasan Kadir's handwriting from an earlier memo that he sent out to co-workers in the school, she might have doubted that this cryptic message was from him or was meant for her. Also, the timing of the note bothered her. Hasan's death took place a week earlier.. Someone must have hidden the note away for those days before delivering it. If that was the case, why the delay? Or, had someone in authority in the camp found the note in Hasan's effects? If that were the case, how did that person know to deliver it to her?

For a brief moment, Fatima was tempted to throw the note away. It was likely that only one other person, the person who put the note in her dresser, knew of the note's existence. The brief note asked nothing of her, not explicitly, anyway. Yet everything within Fatima told her that the message was connected to Hasan's death. The note might well be his final thoughts, she reasoned. That brief message was likely his last will and testament.

What, however, should she do with the message? Damascus was a bombed-out city from which the blessed ones, like her, had escaped. What "danger coming from Damascus and Aleppo" was Hasan talking about?

Even as Fatima worked at her afternoon assignment supervising the young children's playtime in the school, she had trouble focusing on the games being played. What she realized, and what caused her such uncertainty, was that she had to talk to someone about the note and its possible meaning. But who? The logical choice would be to talk with camp security, yet she immediately realized that if Hasan had wanted the authorities to know about his concern, he would have gone to them himself instead of sending the note to her. The bizarre thought then struck her that if Hasan were alive, she'd go to him.

She thought of other elders among the Syrian community in the camp, but, there again, they weren't a feasible option. The leaders were all men, and they were the same camp residents who'd made it clear that they disapproved of her taking the class in religion. Of course, there were numerous Syrian widows in the camp, some with children and some without. Most of them looked askance at her as she walked from the dormitory to the administration building with her textbooks in hand.

Fatima was stunned to realize how much, by her choices, she had distanced herself from the wider Syrian community. Only with the school children did she have an easy and natural relationship, yet the children were clearly not an option.

By that evening, she realized there was only one person in whom she could confide—Professor Napolitano. The professor could, of course, decline to help. Yet somehow, she sensed he would help if he could. He would at least know where she should take Hasan's cryptic note.

After class the next day, she spoke with the professor, who agreed to meet after his last class of the day, which ended at nine p.m. That evening, Fatima carried the note with her as she walked in the deepening darkness back to the school. All the children had been brought into the tiny family apartments for the night, and, except for two women who were carrying plastic baskets of clothes from the laundry, Fatima saw only men sitting on the benches lining the sidewalk. Some were smoking, yet all interrupted their conversations to stare at her as she passed. She hadn't been out alone this late at Caritas, and though she walked as quickly as she could, she felt as afraid as if she were back in Damascus.

An hour later, she began her return to her dormitory, feeling relieved. Professor Napolitano had been the right person to share her secret with. She hadn't known that her professor, along with his teaching at Caritas, was also on the board of oversight for the camp. Although they talked about Fatima's hopes for the future as well as the class, they always returned to the note. While he had no more insight into Hasan's intended message than Fatima, he agreed that if Hasan hadn't brought his concern to the head of camp security, he must have had a good reason.

Toward the end of their conversation, the professor shared that the camp, in addition to having a department of security, was also "watched over" by Italy's Ministry of Defense. He promised, if Fatima would trust him with the note, that he would pass it along to a contact he had in that ministry. The initial relief that Fatima felt as she continued toward her dormitory came partially from being able to do just that—hand the note over to someone else.

I did my part, Fatima reasoned, even as the thought did not rest easy with her. She couldn't imagine that Hasan or the person who'd hidden the note among her clothes intended her to simply pass the note on to someone else. If that were the case, however, she thought Hasan and the messenger expected too much from her, a seventeen-year-old student with no influence in the camp.

A sound off to her right, in the dark space between two buildings, forced Fatima to stop. She wasn't sure what to make of the sound of something hard hitting something soft until she heard a barely audible woman's voice call out for help in Arabic. Fatima instinctively ran toward the sound, yet when she entered the dark corridor and called out, the space was eerily quiet.

Fatima sensed more than heard the person behind her and started to run farther into the darkness. She had only taken a step, however, when she felt a sharp pain on the back of her head. At the same moment, she felt herself floating and her body becoming numb. Brilliant white stars floated across her vision, and, in the next second, everything went black.

CHAPTER TWO

June 25, 2020
Rome, CIA Headquarters

"Allyson, please stay behind for a few minutes," Morgan Stamper said as the Friday morning team meeting came to a close.

Allyson Worthy remained seated, as the other agents—mostly male—headed with quickened pace for the door and the beginning of the weekend in Rome. Before the meeting began, two of the men and one of the women had asked Allyson about her own plans for the weekend. She skirted the question by responding vaguely that she intended to head out to the beach at Ostia. It wasn't a complete lie, as her plans did include Ostia, yet she intended to visit the ancient Roman ruins rather than the bars of Ostia's modern beachfront.

"Who with?" Chaz asked as a follow-up. From someone else, the question could have been totally innocent. From Chaz, Allyson wasn't sure that any question was purely curious.

"I'm going with a couple of girls from my apartment complex," she replied, a pure lie. She had no intention of sharing that she was headed for Ostia in the company of Seppe D'Angelo.

"Locals?" Chaz asked. There it was, that claustrophobic feeling Chaz gave her. Allyson had given Chaz no encouragement, hoping to ward him off. She thought of herself as cute by Midwestern American standards, though certainly not beautiful. Based on her internship experience in Venice, Italy, five years before, however, she knew that her strawberry blond hair, fair complexion, and height—she was five eight—caught the attention of Italian men. Why Chaz even noticed her, with so many women of Rome who could pass for models, made no sense to her. She hoped her description of her weekend plans as being with local girls from her apartment complex would further his suspicion that she was gay.

Chaz can't imagine a straight girl, especially from humble Indiana, finding his company unctuous, she thought as she watched him holding the door for Sally Patton, Allyson's roommate. She thought she had few worries about Sally, a tanned figure straight out of a California travel poster. Surely the two of them made Chaz the butt of too many jokes for either of them to fall for his line.

Her ruminations ended when Morgan Stamper took the chair next to her. Despite her case manager having been in the Rome office for the past six years, Morgan showed few signs of being influenced by Italian styles. To Allyson, she was the type of woman featured in before-and-after commercials, someone who could be stunning with a new hairstyle and make-up, but in everyday life looked normal. Today, Morgan was dressed practically in slacks, flats, and a pale blue blouse.

"How are you finding Rome, Allison?" Stamper asked. The question was yet another one that was innocent on the surface yet was, Allyson thought, the prelude for something more pointed.

Allyson decided to play innocent in her reply. "I'm from Detroit, which means I'm used to big cities. And I'm beginning to like Rome, the fact that I can't walk more than half a block before I come across a plaque commemorating something."

"Well, if you like history, this is the place for you," Morgan said. After a pause, she added "Your living situation is acceptable?"

"No complaints there," she said, wondering if that sounded like she had complaints elsewhere.

"Listen, Allyson, we're happy to have you with us. As I've said before, the way the FBI does things can be different from how we function in the CIA. I'm happy to say that your reports so far have been fruitful."

Allyson said nothing, sensing there was a "however" coming.

"It's just that in the last two team meetings . . . well, other than your comments about the conditions in the camp, you've been unusually quiet."

Allyson tried not to show her surprise. She always prided herself on being not just ambitious but mission-focused, traits she knew she'd inherited from her famous father. Now Morgan was implying that she was too soft-hearted.

"You're sure everything is okay. No, romantic troubles back home?" Morgan asked.

Allyson almost laughed. Her romantic troubles were that she felt allergic to romance.

"No, ma'am, no romantic troubles," she said

"It's Morgan or Stamper, not ma'am. Look, Allyson, I read in your file about your internship in Venice five years ago. I also read that your father, Lt. Christopher Worthy, worked on that case with you, along with a family friend, Father Nicholas Fortis. Here, you're on your own."

"Ma'am . . . sorry, Morgan, I'm the last person to feel homesick. My father was in Venice for a total of four weeks; I was there on my own for three months. And if you want to know the truth, I didn't want my father there," she said, hearing the clipped tone of her own voice.

"Have you met someone here who's interfering with your . . . your focus?" Stamper asked.

This interrogation isn't going to end until I throw her a bone. I'm certainly not going to tell her about Seppe, however, who is, at best, a friend, Allyson thought. "I'm sorry if I come across that way," she said. "Someone in one of the other apartments is in a garage band. They're not very good despite practicing until about two a.m. I'm getting used to that, so I'm sleeping better."

All that was another lie, as the case manager could easily discover if she talked with Sally, her roommate. Yet Allyson knew that if she shared even Seppe's name, Morgan would haul out the orientation handbook and turn to the section on why romance with locals was taboo for agents, like Allyson, assigned to work with the CIA. Allyson had already heard the repeated reminders of the dangers of blackmail.

Her relationship with Seppe could hardly be described, at this point, as a romantic one. Two or three times a week, Seppe and she sat together as they interviewed new refugees in the camp. Of course, there was a major difference between them. Seppe was part of the Sant Anselmo community, a lay Catholic movement committed to refugee relief efforts, while Allyson's aid-worker role in the camp was her cover.

Yet, Morgan was suggesting that she was doing more than playing at being an aid worker. She wondered if Seppe's priorities had rubbed off on her, Seppe being the type of aid-worker who remained in Caritas until the last refugee who wanted to talk to him were able to. Not surprisingly, Seppe had become one of the leaders, both of the Sant Anselmo community and of the aid workers assigned from various charities to Caritas.

When Morgan reiterated Allyson's mission being to identify potential terrorists and criminals among the refugees, Allyson felt herself blushing. While she had no intention of ignoring the living conditions of the residents of Caritas, she vowed to keep her feelings in check and certainly hidden from Morgan and Chaz.

CHAPTER THREE

Allyson's Apartment

At outdoor newsstands in Rome, Allyson had seen an amusing calendar that displayed sexy young Italian priests. Based on the priests who were everywhere in Rome, she was convinced that the men in the calendars were male models dressed in Roman collars.

On a recent break from their interviews with incoming refugees in Caritas, Seppe had repeated that he was considering the priesthood, as if he wanted to make sure that she didn't misunderstand their relationship. In thinking about the priest calendars again, she realized that Seppe could have been included; he was that good looking. He was physically as handsome as the models featured in the calendars. However, it was his luminous smile and ease with people that made him such an asset to Caritas. When Seppe spoke, whether in aid meetings or before TV cameras—his English was as excellent as Allyson's Italian—he came across as unaffected and believable.

That night, as she felt sleep coming on, Allyson wondered again if she'd had accepted Seppe's invitation to visit Ostia if he hadn't told her that he was considering the priesthood. *Am I pretending to be open to a romantic relationship but really just playing it safe?* she asked herself.

June 26
Corpus Christi Hospital

It hadn't taken Professor Napolitano much effort to convince Fatima Rasul's medical team to accept him as the closest thing that Fatima had to a relative. Her condition hadn't changed—she was still in a coma—yet it hadn't gotten any worse. Daily, the professor brought Italian children's books and read to her. The nurses had also heard the most recent medical findings that some comatose patients were able to hear and process what was said to them.

It was hard for the professor to connect the inert figure lying in the hospital bed with the energetic and eager learner who'd been in his class. He wondered if people in a coma dreamt, and, if they did, what they dreamt about. He also wondered how much of the night of the attack Fatima would remember.

The professor had taught many refugees in Caritas and before that in another refugee camp in Sicily. Few were as hungry to learn as Fatima. When he'd asked the attending staff if Fatima could have lingering brain damage from the attack, they told him that it was impossible to tell until she regained consciousness.

Part of what troubled him was wondering if the attack on Fatima was related to her coming to his office that night and entrusting him with Hasan's note. That was the other reason he visited Fatima almost daily. Once awake, Fatima would undoubtedly be interviewed by the police, the camp's security officers, and even the media. Depending on how much she remembered of her attack, Fatima might let it slip about her meeting with him and her trusting him with Hasan's note. If that happened, the police and the camp's security officers would certainly wonder what part he might have had in Fatima's attack. He couldn't afford for them to poke into his role in Caritas and his past, especially at that delicate moment. That was why he had to warn Fatima, as soon as she awoke, to say nothing to anyone about their meeting just prior to her attack.

He had to be concerned not just about the police, camp security, and the media, but Fatima herself. Upon awaking, she might think back and realize that her attack and her visit to his office could be connected. That would mean that everything he'd worked for carefully and secretly in his time in Caritas would be blown.

JUNE 27, 2020
ANCIENT RUINS OF OSTIA

"WHAT'S THE MOST IMPORTANT thing I should know about Ostia?" Allyson asked as they approached the city of ancient ruins.

"That's easy. Keep your eyes on the road," Seppe replied with a laugh, pointing down at the street. "These cobblestones will break an ankle in a second, but, if I'm serious, it's Ostia as a whole that impresses me, no matter how many times I've been here. Pompeii is great and obviously important. Ostia, however, gives a better feeling of the past."

Allyson thought it a gross understatement to describe the road as "cobblestones." The pavement was made up of chiseled stones the size of large bread loaves. They both paid attention to where they were walking, even as Seppe pointed to ruts in the pavement left by ancient Roman chariots and wagons.

"I know Pompeii was buried under ash. Is that what happened here?" Allyson asked.

"No, Ostia was the original port for Rome. The Tiber flowed into the sea just there," he said, pointing to his right. "We'll come to the marketplace in a few minutes. The city must have been a noisy and bustling place."

"Why did it fall into ruins?"

"The river channel shifted, which meant that Ostia was no longer where goods, soldiers, and prisoners landed," Seppe explained.

The two continued in silence until Allyson said, "I can't imagine what it's like to grow up surrounded by this much history. I mean . . . does it ever feel heavy, like a weight?"

Seppe didn't answer for a moment. Finally, he said, "I'm not sure I can answer that. You see, Rome is all I've ever known. That doesn't mean I take its history for granted, although most modern Romans, if they're honest, will confess that they drive past the Colosseum without noticing it."

Allyson realized she hadn't expressed herself well. "Yet doesn't a place like this make you feel insignificant? All the Caesars and popes, I mean."

"I suppose it depends on the person. Rome must be hell for someone whose ego demands fame and power. Think about it; how can such a person compete with all the greats, especially as you say, the Caesars and popes, not to mention the saints who've lived and died here? It's something

I hadn't thought much about until you asked. I think Italy, and especially Rome, encourages a kind of humility in people, and I don't just mean Italians. If the city could say anything, I think it would remind us that our lives are short, and there is the bigger scheme of things."

"Well, the 'big scheme of things' in American terms is twenty years, not twenty centuries. Does that mean we view the refugee issue differently?" Allyson asked.

"Maybe, yet it's vital that Americans are involved. The refugees deserve people of action. Italians can talk something to death and still not make one significant change."

Allyson thought about that comment and had to admit that Italy was often a country of endless red tape. Just getting a parking permit near the apartment she shared with Sally had taken three afternoons of visiting one office after another.

"Seppe, you describe Americans, and I suppose that includes me, as people of action. I'm not sure that's always good. Someone said that Americans confuse activity with progress. That isn't what I want to ask you about. You also said that Italians tend to 'over-talk' things and don't get around to acting. That's not how I see the Sant Anselmo community. Your group does a lot more than talk."

"Maybe it's not surprising that our community was started by a teenager back in the late sixties, when a lot of young people were tired of all the talk. They wanted action, not just posturing."

For a moment, Allyson could picture Seppe as one of those students from the sixties.

"Is Sant Anselmo named after the founder?" she asked.

"No, Anselm was a famous saint in the eleventh and twelfth centuries. He's our model, though, our inspiration."

"I have to confess I don't know much about the saints. I mean I know almost every church in Italy is named after a saint."

"Is your family not religious?" he asked.

"We did go to church until my parents divorced. My grandfather was a minister, however."

"Your grandfather was a priest? How is that possible? Oh, wait; I forgot. Protestant ministers can marry, right?"

Allyson laughed. "Yes. In fact, it's considered odd if they don't."

Seppe laughed as well. "What is odd for one is normal for the other. For us, priests are celibate."

Allyson wasn't sure whether or not to ask the question she was most curious about. Then she thought, *Nothing ventured, nothing gained.*

"Why is that? Why can't Catholic priests be married?" she asked.

"Oh, it sounds hollow to say it's tradition, yet that's the truth," he replied. "Your Greek Orthodox friend, the monk, is celibate, isn't he?"

"Father Nick? Yes, that's because he's a monk. I asked him about it once, and he said Orthodox priests can be married."

"Ah, yes, I think I knew that," Seppe said. Allyson thought she detected sadness in his voice, yet before she could ask any more, Seppe stood and said, "Please, I want to show you my favorite part of Ostia. It's not far from here."

After walking along a back street of ruins for another five minutes, Seppe asked Allyson to stop and stand where she was. He walked farther, and after disappearing for a minute, appeared behind what appeared to be a marble counter.

"Would you like vino or beer?" he asked with a smile.

"What is this?" she asked, taking in the structure.

"This was one of Ostia's taverns. Come around the back side, and I'll show you."

Allyson let Seppe take her by the hand and lead her farther into the shop.

"These are the wine cisterns," he said, pointing to large clay pots set into the floor. "And back here, in this open area, was a quiet place where customers would sit. Please," he said, pointing to a stone bench along the side of the wall.

Allyson sat down even as Seppe took off his backpack and opened it. With fake ceremony, he withdrew a bottle of red wine and two plastic tumblers.

"We must join my countrymen who drank wine in this same spot two thousand years ago."

"You've come prepared," she said, then immediately blushing, as she recalled what "coming prepared" in American college circles meant.

Seppe didn't appear to know the reference. "You see, Allyson, we Romans, yes, we have history around us all the time, but Rome is a city, not a museum. We Romans believe we can have fun with history, too." He poured wine into two glasses and handed one to her. "Salute, Allyson."

"Salute," Allyson replied and took a sip of the wine. "This is nice," she said, not sure whether she were referring to the wine or to the two of them sharing the wine.

After she commented on how few tourists they'd met within the ruins, Seppe cleared his throat. "There is a reason I wanted us to sit here in quiet, Allyson," he said, before pausing.

Oh, no, Allyson thought, *please don't say what I think you're going to say.* She knew some Italian men had a reputation of pledging love and devotion as a way to get women into bed, yet hadn't she assumed she'd be safe with Seppe?

Seppe had difficulty continuing, which made Allyson all the more uneasy. She pictured the awkward train trip back to the city, the two of them not knowing what to say.

"I have something I want to ask you, Allyson. You can say no."

What does that mean? she thought.

"You said your father is a detective, yes?"

Allyson felt relieved, then, to her surprise, disappointed. What did her father have to do with anything? She rearranged herself on the bench, sitting up straighter and feeling defensive.

"Yes, he's a detective."

"I looked him up on the Internet. He's quite famous, isn't he?"

"Maybe. It's hard for me to say because he's my father," she said, no longer interested in the wine.

After an awkward pause, Seppe said, "I don't know if you've heard about what happened in Caritas. Last week, an older refugee from Syria was stabbed to death while another refugee, a young woman, was attacked and is in a coma."

Allyson forgot her irritation for a moment. "Oh, my God, that's awful, Seppe. What do the police say?"

"They say little."

"Do they think it's someone in Caritas, maybe another refugee, or someone from outside?"

"Allyson, that is what we all want to know. All the camp's security office says is that they continue to work on the case even as they wait for the woman to regain consciousness."

"What do you want me to do?" she said, hoping Seppe wasn't asking her to invite her father to Rome to investigate the case. Five years before, she'd struggled when she worked with her father in Venice, and although that ended well for both of them, she had no desire to repeat the experience.

"I know I'm asking a lot, but I'm hoping . . . I'm hoping you've inherited his talents," he said in a pleading voice.

"Oh," Allyson said in surprise. "You want me to look into the attacks?"

Seppe sighed. "I'm sorry, Allyson. I see now how ridiculous is what I'm asking. Forgive and forget, please."

"No, no, not at all." *How crazy,* she thought. *Here I am in Rome working undercover for the CIA as an aid worker, in search of criminals and terrorists in the camp, and now I'm being asked to look into a murder and an attempted murder.*

"You would do this with me?" Seppe asked, the smile returning to his face.

Allyson took another sip of wine, which once again tasted delicious. "I'll be happy to help if I can, although I don't know how much I've inherited from my father."

Seppe leaned over and hugged her. "Thank you, thank you. I am relieved."

Allyson didn't resist the hug and, to her surprise, found herself returning it. *He's not a priest yet,* she thought.

June 29, 2020
CIA Headquarters

"Of course, the attacks in Caritas interest the Agency," Morgan said after Allyson shared what she knew about the crimes. "But the CIA has to be careful, Allyson. We don't want to advertise our presence when we're working in other countries. That just stirs up anti-American feeling and makes our work more difficult. In addition, we'd want to look into the case without ruffling the feathers of the local authorities." After a pause, she added, "I do think, however, that you're ideally placed to look into the matter in your cover role as an aid worker. You should have help, and besides whatever assistance I can give you, I think I know who I should pair you with. Although this isn't public knowledge, he's an ex-Navy Seal."

"Oh?" Allyson asked, trying to think who in the office had that background.

"Yes. I see you working well with Chaz Eaton."

CHAPTER FOUR

June 30, 2020
Campo de Fiori, Rome

ALTHOUGH EVERY CELL IN her brain rejected Morgan's suggestion of Chaz, Allyson could think of nothing concrete to counter the suggestion. If being a "lech" disqualified someone from serving the greater American cause, then Allyson figured half the politicians in Washington would be out of a job. No, the value of Chaz's training as a Navy Seal meant that the Agency would expect her to handle the personal side of their relationship and handle it with finesse. Yet she did wonder why Chaz had left the Seals. Or had he been thrown out? she wondered.

The more immediate concern to Allyson was the challenge of working with Seppe and Chaz simultaneously without either of them finding out about the other. As she thought about this, she realized that Chaz would be the simpler of the two men to deal with. The Chaz Eatons of the world didn't understand that their coming on strong was, in fact, their greatest weakness. No, the harder challenge would be Seppe, for the challenge with him went beyond maintaining her cover as an aid worker. The truth was that she increasingly felt attracted to Seppe—as a friend, she told herself—and nobody enjoyed lying to a friend.

As she breakfasted on espresso and pastries outside one of the cafes lining Campo de Fiori, she wondered if deception was a matter of degrees. Seppe knew her as a fellow aid worker, which wasn't a total fabrication. Her desire to see an improvement in the treatment of refugees pouring into Europe and North America was more than a cover; her concern was genuine. Also, she rationalized that NGOs working with refugees would want terrorists and criminals hiding within the ranks of the genuine asylum seekers to be weeded out. Her working on that potential danger while assisting with humanitarian help was a level of deception she was comfortable with.

To investigate a homicide and an attack at the refugee camp, however, while pretending she was simply an aid worker would take deception to another level. It felt like a lie within a lie.

Today, she wouldn't have to solve that puzzle. She would spend the morning with Chaz and Morgan setting out a plan for the investigation. Morgan's presence should guarantee that Chaz would remain professional, and she had to admit that she was curious about what his training could mean for their partnership.

From Campo de Fiori, Allyson walked to the Europa Spec offices. The outer door buzzed as she waved a pass card and went into the building. As she walked by the receptionist's desk, she glanced at a signboard listing the building's occupants, all companies that were covers for various U.S. and E.U. agencies that operated surreptitiously in Rome.

The sense of pride and purpose she felt when she'd first walked into the building weeks before still burned within her. Although all US agents in the building were committed to the fight against terrorism, their motives were likely to be different. Some, and she wondered if Chaz with his Navy Seal background was in this category, saw terrorism through the eyes of 9/11. To uncover terrorism anywhere was to potentially protect the U.S. from another attack and to demonstrate love of country.

Allyson's war on terror was more personal, and she doubted that she was alone in this sentiment. She considered the leaders of terrorist organizations to be cowardly in their recruiting of the most hopeless to attack the most vulnerable: often women and children. The attack on the two Syrian refugees, an old man and a young woman, was a perfect example of both gross injustice and cowardice. It wasn't love of country for Allyson. It was the deaths of such innocents who'd led her to agree immediately to Seppe's request for help.

As she walked the two flights of stairs up to her office, she found herself shaking her head as she recognized that in this as in other ways, she was like her father. Christopher Worthy's supervisors in Detroit considered his one glaring flaw to be his disregard for the politics of a case. He offered neither deference nor rudeness to powerful people whom he met in the course of an investigation. He cared only about what the person could tell him that might help with the case. If one of those people who helped him happened to be a local politician or business leader, he left it to the department's public relations head to send a note of appreciation or recognition.

As she opened the door to her office, she realized that her father wouldn't think of the Ivy Leaguer Chaz Eaton any more highly than she did.

July 1
Rome, CIA Headquarters

"Let's recap," Morgan Stamper said, as the meeting drew to a close. "Allyson has regular access to the list of everyone living in Caritas. Using that list, we should be able to see if Hasan Kadir and Fatima Rasul have any family in the camp. Let's also remember that we can't assume the attacks are the work of another camp resident. Whether the attacker is from the camp or outside, we must look into security arrangements in Caritas as well as other crimes linked to the camp. That's your job, Chaz. Any questions?"

Allyson waited for Chaz to respond first. He had sat across from her in the conference room and had looked over at her a number of times. She assumed he wanted to play the role of an alpha dog and speak first. With his freckled complexion and dressed in a blue oxford button-down shirt and khakis, Chaz would never pass for an Italian. He could be a German, Scandinavian, or North American, Allyson thought, as she realized her own complexion and hair color also shouted "American."

"I can work on all of that from my office," Chaz began. "And while Allyson visits the camp in her aid-worker role, I think we should put one of our people inside the camp as a refugee."

"Ah, I see what you mean. Allyson, how frequently do new refugees arrive at Caritas?" Stamper asked.

"According to my contact in Sant Anselmo, it isn't regular. It's more like whenever a new group arrives."

"Who's your contact?" Chaz asked.

The question took Allyson by surprise. "Another aid worker. I think it's best that he remain anonymous for the time being," she replied.

Chaz raised an eyebrow, and Allyson guessed that she'd violated one of the CIA's procedures.

After an awkward silence, Morgan said, "In the CIA we always want to know who we're dealing with. As you say, Allyson, that's only for the time being."

Meaning, the Agency will want to dig into Seppe's past and do a thorough background check, Allyson thought. For some reason Allyson felt a desire to protect Seppe, to distance him from people like Chaz.

Morgan gathered her papers as she said, "If we can insert someone into the camp, that person reports to me."

Allyson nodded her agreement, even as Chaz offered a hearty "hear, hear."

As she left the conference room and thought about the exchange about Seppe, Allyson felt disheartened. How had he beat her at her own game?

CHAPTER FIVE

July 2
Freiburg, Germany

As Khadija Mubarak stepped off the bus and looked down at the text message, she felt a tightening in her stomach. *Your bicycle is ready to be picked up in Munchen. Call to make an appointment.*

The reference to "bicycle" meant she should communicate with the CIA office in Munich, 125 miles east of Freiburg, where she worked, as cover, as an Arabic translator for an academic publishing firm specializing in Middle East history. Her past year in Freiburg had been uneventful—her secret life consisting of a bi-monthly meeting with her handler over coffee—that she forgot most of the time that she was anything more than an Arabic translator with proficiencies in German, English, and Italian. It was only when she received a check and breezy greetings in Arabic each month from a fictitious sister in Brussels that she had cause to remember her other self.

Khadija immediately tried to guess what the message was about. She'd been careful to observe all precautions and meet all deadlines for translation work that she knew were important to the Agency. She was sure the quality of her work would not be in question, because she had a facility with languages going back to her first days as a grade-school refugee in Brixton, outside London. Picking up languages quickly had been a matter of survival in the playgrounds and schoolyards of the tough suburb.

No, her worry was not about her work, but about a question that her German handler, Felix Grunemeyer, had asked her in their last meeting.

"You look like you've lost more weight," he'd said as he sat back and stared at her.

She felt a wave of panic at the time and avoided answering by taking a sip of coffee. She knew the large German across from her at the table, the rings on his hands pinching his fingers like tight waistbands, would know little about eating disorders and would have even less sympathy.

"I've just gotten over bronchitis," she lied as she gave what she hoped was a credible imitation of a healthy smile.

"Huh," Grunemeyer had replied. "You look more like you've had intestinal flu."

"No, nothing like that," she'd said. "With the coughing, I lost my appetite. I'm better now." She'd forced herself to stop at that point, remembering what she learned in the Agency's training, that many women explain themselves in unnecessary detail and thereby draw attention to themselves.

Grunemeyer had nodded, as if he understood, yet now Khadija wondered if he'd sent along a concern to the office in Munich. The knot in her stomach tightened even further when she remembered that Grunemeyer had said "you look like you've lost *more* weight," not simply "you look like you've lost weight." *He's noticed my weight before,* she thought.

Her mind raced with what she feared was a demand that she come to Munich for another medical exam. She looked critically at her reflection in the window of the coffee shop before remembering that bulimics never "saw" themselves accurately. *How would I know if I'm too thin, when I've never thought I was thin enough?*

She knew that shame always accompanied bulimia, yet she had reason to feel a double dose of that. Her mother had always chided her, saying that any Palestinian refugee fortunate to grow up in England should be proud to carry a few pounds. "Look, world, I'm not starving" was what her mother would often say as she stood over the stove preparing the family dinner. Khadija knew that trying to educate her mother on the difference between dieting and bulimia was a hopeless exercise, She would just eat what her mother put in front of her before sneaking later into the bathroom or out beyond the back fence of their yard in Brixton for her private ritual.

As she entered her apartment, she thought of what awaited her in the kitchen. There, like a sentry keeping watch sat the blue notebook, the log of her daily calorie intake. She knew it made no sense, yet she couldn't help keeping track of the calories she ingested.

What she would do tonight because of the message from Munich was as much a part of her ritual as the logbook and the bulimia. She would binge on French fries, tapioca pudding, and ice cream, then force herself to remain on the couch watching TV until she fell asleep. In the morning, she would awake, a heavy feeling still in her stomach, giving her the illusion that others would see her for the rest of that day as normal.

Allyson's Apartment

Allyson gazed at Sally, her roommate, in disbelief. "I can't believe you've changed your mind about Chaz."

"I'm just saying I think we prejudged him," Sally replied from where she was sprawled on the couch.

Allyson stood in their kitchenette with a glass of ice water in her hand. "Just listen to yourself. He calls himself 'Chaz!' Who calls himself Chaz except a prig like . . . like Chaz?"

"Look, where I come from, 'Chaz' isn't that odd a name. There was a guy in my high school named Corky. I don't mean Corky was his nickname; that was his real name. And we also had a Buffy; you know, after the TV show," Sally said.

"You do know that Chaz's real name is Chatsworth, don't you?" Allyson asked.

"And do you remember that he was *given* that name at birth. It's not his fault, Alli. You're blaming him for something he couldn't control. Look, if your name was Chatsworth, what would you call yourself?"

"I'd change my name. I'd call myself Ernest or . . . or Liberace. Anything but Chaz," Allyson said with a laugh.

"You know what you are, Alli? You're a snob."

"Me? Don't you have it backwards? The snob is Chaz."

"No, you're a Midwestern snob. Either that or you secretly have a thing for him," Sally said, laughing.

"No, no, don't try that on me. You're the one who started this by agreeing to go out for a drink with Chaz, and that's after we both we're warned about his reputation at the Agency."

"He's a red-blooded American ex-Navy Seal stationed in Italy. At least I'm not a snob, and I'm not looking for a saint. In fact, I wouldn't go out for a drink with a saint. I'd be afraid he'd change my wine into water."

"I think it's the other way around, Sally, but I see where this is headed. You're going to smile your flirty smile over the table at the bar and pretend what he says is oh so clever. Just promise me you won't bring him back here."

"Why? Will your priest boyfriend be here?"

"He's not a priest, and he's not my boyfriend!" Allyson said as she balled up some tinfoil from the kitchen counter and threw it at Sally.

"Hey, that was close. You must have a thing for this guy."

"No, I don't," Allyson said, knowing that wasn't the complete truth. "I'll make a deal with you. I won't say anything about Chaz and you have to promise that you'll never say anything about Seppe to Chaz. Is that a deal?"

Sally looked puzzled. "Why? He's just an aid worker, isn't he?"

"Look, all I can tell you is that he's another aid worker, and he's a friend. Also, I don't trust Chaz. I'd really like to know why he left the Seals."

CHAPTER SIX

July 3
Munich, Germany

When Khadija inquired through the proper channels about the purpose of her upcoming meeting, she was given only the date and time when she was to report to the CIA's Munich office. In the intervening days, she'd played out all the possible scenarios she could imagine, and most of her fantasies involved being confronted on her health and being censured for failure to control her disorder.

Control. How could she explain to the Agency that her eating disorder was not a failure to control her life? It was instead a manifestation of control gone amok. She imagined a courtroom setting where she was ordered to step on a scale by five, ten, or twenty—the number increased the more she fantasized about her upcoming ordeal—plump Germans. She imagined being shamed by a roomful of people who'd never seen a pastry they didn't crave.

The day of the meeting finally came, and she arrived by train two hours early. The taxi ride to the CIA's Munich offices took another forty-five minutes, which left over an hour before her appointment. She sat on a bench in the park across the street from the Agency's fictitious business and tried to steady her breathing as pigeons encircled her.

"You picked on the wrong person," she said to the birds. After strutting around her for nearly ten minutes, the pigeons got the message. As the birds flew off, she imagined them frowning at her.

Well, at least they didn't shit on my shoes, she thought. *I wonder if the Agency will be that kind.*

With ten minutes to spare, she crossed the street and entered the building. At a reception desk, she handed over her I.D. card. After a call was made, Khadija was directed to a second-floor office.

She wondered if the meeting, one that could determine her future with the Agency, could have been avoided if she'd dealt with Grunemeyer differently. If she'd bought him a box of chocolates occasionally, would he have been too preoccupied with the sweets to notice her weight? Or if, at their first meeting nearly a year ago, she'd accepted his invitation to join him at one of Freiburg's beer halls, would he have viewed her in a more favorable light? Her "what ifs" regarding Grunemeyer didn't stop until she'd imagined buying bigger clothes and stuffing a pillow under them. No such disguise, she realized, could hide the hollowness of her cheeks and the prominence of her teeth behind her narrow lips.

Her teeth. Yes, they were the giveaway. The more weight she'd lost, the larger her teeth appeared, and she remembered reading that anorexics and bulimics often contracted gum disease. To avoid the taste of corrosive bile when she vomited, Khadija had tried to re-channel her eating disorder with laxatives. That strategy hadn't worked, and if she were ever forced to offer an explanation, she would say that method simply didn't satisfy her need.

As she rode the elevator up to the second floor, she thought of the pigeons' disappointment in her. Perhaps, she thought, the birds had offered a preview of what she'd experience next. She whispered a hasty "Inshallah," whatever Allah wills, as she stepped from the elevator.

Inside an office marked "Europa Spec Exports," Khadija was met by Erika Gunther, her mentor during orientation.

"Khadija, it's good to see you again," Erika said, shaking her hand. "Your trip was good?"

"Yes, very good," Khadija lied, even as Erika's smile helped her relax. *Perhaps I completely misunderstood the summons,* she thought as Erika ushered her into an inner room. Khadija was grateful to see the room was empty, with only two chairs on opposite sides of a small table holding two cups and a coffee urn.

She remembered liking Erika from orientation, and now Khadija wondered if there could be something else to bind them. Erika was thin, not thin like Khadija, but thin like someone who was perhaps a committed runner.

"We have a new assignment for you, Khadija, one that should prove a bit more exciting than translation work. It will also be significantly more challenging."

Khadija felt lightheaded as her fears of exposure evaporated. "That sounds interesting," she replied, aware of how lame that sounded.

Erika opened a folder. "If you agree, you'll be transferred to Rome for a special assignment. In your file I have your scores in the Italian language test. They are quite impressive."

Rome instead of Freiburg? Yes, yes, Khadija thought. "I've been to Milan but never Rome," she said, shocked again at the vapidity of her response. "What I mean is, I am definitely interested in a transfer."

"Let me give you the details before you agree," Erika said, no longer smiling.

"Of course, of course," Khadija replied quickly.

"You'll be working out of the Europa Spec office in Rome, although you won't actually be working in the office." Erika paused and studied Khadija.

Khadija felt her face redden. *She's wondering if I'm healthy enough for the assignment. Look healthy, silly.*

"Your proficiency in Italian will be helpful. However, you can't let anyone know that you understand the language," Erika said. "It's your native language, the Arabic, that you'll be speaking—always."

Khadija tried to look professional as she hid her curiosity. "I'll be speaking Arabic in Rome, then," she said, trying to make her words sound like a statement, not a question.

"You'll be living outside of Rome, and" Erika said, pausing again, "you'll be living in a refugee camp."

Khadija was unable to mask her quick intake of air. "Oh," she finally said. "What is my assignment, then?"

"The refugees in this camp are from the Middle East and North Africa, most from Syria and most are Muslims. We want an agent in the camp because two Syrian refugees, an elderly man and a young woman, have recently been attacked. The man was killed, the woman is in a coma, and her recovery is uncertain. The attacks might suggest the work of a crime ring."

Khadija cleared her throat. "I see," she said. "Actually, I don't think I do see. What role will I have in the camp?" she asked, even as she hoped she wouldn't be placed in the kitchen.

Now it was Erika's face that reddened. "I'm sorry. I thought that would be obvious."

They were both quiet until Khadija sat forward with a start. "Please tell me why I have been selected."

Erika also had had time to compose herself. "It's your weight, Khadija. You will pose as a refugee most recently living in Syria. We have to have someone who looks . . . who looks malnourished."

As Erika's words hung in the air, Khadija looked down at her hands. A pewter ring that had once been snug was loose enough to slide from her finger. *That's what I look like,* she thought with shame. *I look like an emaciated refugee.*

CHAPTER SEVEN

July 4
CIA Headquarters

CHAZ STUDIED THE POLICE reports of the two attacks in the Caritas camp. From prior research, he'd discovered that homicides, while not uncommon in other refugee camps in Europe, hadn't occurred in Caritas until now. The death of the elderly Syrian man had happened a little more than a week before, and the file contained so few updates that Chaz assumed the Agency wouldn't have become involved had a second attack on a teenage Syrian girl not occurred.

Knowing little Italian, Chaz was relying on the Agency's translated copies of the police reports. Other than one contact that he'd made in the Italian police, he wasn't impressed. As far as he could tell, the police in Rome were mainly good at three things: driving their Alfa-Romeos with lights and sirens flashing at top speed through the city's narrow streets; smoking one cigarette after another as they stood guard outside government buildings; and producing more bureaucratic paperwork than the U.S. Navy and the CIA put together.

The enormous amount of paperwork meant that Chaz had spent most of the morning reading and then discarding over half the contents of the files. He was consequently in a bad mood when Morgan stuck her head in the door of his cubicle.

"Do you have a couple of hours this afternoon? I'd like the two of us to pick up the agent who's going to be undercover in the camp."

He looked at his watch. It was already eleven in the morning, and he just started reading the forensics about Hasan Kadir. To stop now would mean two things: the rest of the day would be shot, and his evening date with Sally Patton could be jeopardized.

"If I do that, you won't get my report on the two victims until tomorrow," he said, hoping Morgan's need for the report was greater than her desire to have company when picking up the new agent.

Morgan motioned for him to come with her. "I don't see how another day will matter. Let's go, Chaz."

"No problem, then," he said. "Where are we going?"

"Khadija Mubarak is coming in from an airfield we use north of Rome, just outside of Orvieto. Have you been up that way?"

"I've been to Orvieto," Chaz said, frowning as he remembered that his one visit to the city was a disaster. Six months before, he drove to Orvieto with a date, another CIA agent assigned to Rome. She'd been a graduate of Wellesley, which led him to assume, wrongly, that she would share his passion for the finer things, like Italian art and architecture. Yet after only fifteen minutes in the city's impressive cathedral, his date complained of being tired. She told him he should stay in the church. She would be across the square in a bar she'd spotted earlier. For the next hour and a half, he tried to block out his disappointment while studying the cathedral's altarpiece, the famous Capella del Corporale side chapel, and the glittering gothic façade. His disappointment with the day didn't peak until he found his date sitting at the bar with two empty bottles of Orvieto's famed white wine, and a third half finished. The capper of the day had been when he was forced to pull over to the side of the autostrada twice when his date became sick. He hardly noticed her transfer a month later to Lisbon and couldn't even remember her name now.

"If you like wine, Chaz, we can stop in Orvieto. They have a terrific white," Morgan said as they pulled out of Europa Spec's parking garage.

"I think I'll take a raincheck on that, if you don't mind. I have some work I want to get to tonight," he said, hoping she wouldn't press him for details.

"No problem. A lot of agents are into Italian wines."

"Yeah, I've noticed that," he said as he looked out the window at they drove along Via Lungatevere. Rome was his second placement with the Agency after leaving the Navy Seals because of botched replacement surgery that had left him bitter. He'd found Rome to be a mixed bag. He couldn't deny that Rome was arguably one of the best cities in the world for anyone interested in architectural history, and the fact that Florence was a quick ninety minutes away by train and Venice no more than four hours away excited him when he was first offered the placement in Rome.

After visiting Florence, Siena, and Venice, however, he found Rome disappointing. Rome's incomparable architectural history existed within a city whose noise was constant. In addition, he found the city dirty, especially when compared to his first posting in Switzerland.

What frustrated him the most about Rome was its cacophony of languages. Perhaps if he'd grown up in New York City instead of in the Berkshires in upstate New York, he wouldn't have found Rome so disorienting. Living in Rome, and especially being charged with identifying terrorists, was like watching a multiplicity of foreign films simultaneously and trying to make sense of all of them.

"What's your impression of Allyson?" Morgan asked, breaking into Chaz's reverie.

"Frankly, I'm not sure what to think. She wasn't exactly forthcoming in our last meeting."

"About not revealing her contact? Yes, I found that puzzling too. Maybe that's the way they operate in the FBI."

"Why are we using someone from the FBI, anyway?" he asked.

Morgan signaled and changed lanes to pass a truck from Romania. "Get used to it, because you might end up working with the FBI in the future. Poor communication between intelligence agencies was an easy scapegoat for 9/11. Ever since then, politicians have tried to shut the barn door after the horse got out. That means when our agency became aware of an FBI agent like Allyson with proficiency in Italian and previous police work in the country, the higher-ups saw an opportunity of relieving some of the pressure from Washington."

"Politics. Why am I not surprised?"

"Here's the thing, Chaz. Assuming our relationship with the FBI works in this case and we get results, we can use that to our advantage. The Agency will have proof that we can cooperate, and when the Agency looks good, Congress will show their gratitude."

"How will they do that? Send us more FBI agents?"

"Don't be cynical. What I see down the road is this: if Allyson works out well here, we'll be able to cash that in on our next appropriations request. Think of Allyson as a meal ticket. That's why you're supposed to do whatever it takes to work with her, make her look good."

Chaz felt the beginning of a headache coming on. "Look, Morgan, I've reached out to her. Allyson hasn't reciprocated."

Morgan coughed, and Chaz wasn't sure if she did that to stifle a laugh. He didn't doubt that she knew his reputation.

"I have one suggestion, Chaz. For the time being, respect her wishes. Don't try to find out who her contact is in the aid agencies, the one who alerted her and us to these attacks at the camp."

"Who says I was going to do that?"

"Oh, come on, Chaz. We both know—"

"Okay, okay," Chaz interrupted. "Allyson can keep her little secret for now."

"Good. Now let me brief you on the woman we're picking up." Morgan turned toward Chaz and gave a sly smile. "Maybe she'll respond better to your charms."

CHAPTER EIGHT

On the Road Back to Rome

NOTHING IN KHADIJA'S WEEK of preparation for her new assignment made her as uncomfortable as being trapped in the car with these two American CIA agents. She'd often wondered if the straight teeth, toned bodies, and self-confidence of American movie stars were exaggerations, yet the two agents sitting in the front seat had all those features. The more Agent Stamper tried to engage her in conversation, the smaller and more insignificant she felt. Eventually, she apologized, saying she was tired from the flight, and pretended to sleep.

With her eyes closed, she listened to the conversation between the two agents. Once they realized that they'd both played lacrosse in college, they engaged in a spirited debate about which version, women's or men's lacrosse, was superior. Although Khadija wasn't sure if she'd ever heard of the sport, she listened for how the two related. Humor came easily to both of them, the kind of humor that was expressed in jabs and insults, and Khadija was happy to pretend to be asleep. As a Middle Eastern girl wearing a hijab in Brixton, she'd experienced enough harassment to last a lifetime.

When the male introduced as Agent Eaton asked Morgan Stamper, the case manager, if his request for vacation time in December had been approved, Khadija realized that he was the woman's subordinate. That was something she didn't remember from American movies. Before answering the man's question, the woman asked what his vacation plans were. When he shared that he wanted to return to a ski resort in Switzerland, Khadija felt as if she were in one of those movies. She'd never known anyone rich enough to go skiing, and that made her wonder at the time if lacrosse was also a sport played only by the wealthy.

Then a comforting image came to mind. Of the three agents in the car, she was the only one who wouldn't stand out in the refugee camp. The very Americanism of the two, their all too obvious health and confidence, made them appear like gods from another world.

In the refugee camp, she wouldn't be the Middle Eastern girl sitting shyly in the back of a classroom filled with English teenagers. She wouldn't be that Muslim in a hijab in a sea of Christians and secularists, and she wouldn't be that "too-skinny-to-be-normal" Muslim girl in Brixton. *Yet, what does it say about me,* she thought, *that I have to be in a refugee camp to finally feel free?*

Caritas Refugee Camp

In Caritas, Allyson and Seppe listened through a translator to the pitiful stories of the new refugees to the camp. All were from Syria, and most had been orphaned by the war. Two of the new arrivals were teenagers and siblings, and, although other refugees might envy their coming together, the two grieved for a younger sister, who'd been killed in an air strike.

Allyson tried to see the new refugees through the lens of the CIA. Could any of them be terrorists? Certainly, most refugees had witnessed enough carnage and experienced enough neglect by the world's developed nations for the seeds of terrorism—humiliation and alienation—to fester and blossom in them. It was easier to wonder what Caritas looked like to new arrivals. Did they see the camp as a safe haven from war and terror, or did they see Caritas as a holding tank, a different kind of prison, where their future was still determined by others?

The issue of terrorism in Caritas was the second reason Seppe and she were in Caritas that day. Hoping to get clues about the two attacks on Hasan Kadir and Fatima Rasul, they headed for the main administrative building that housed the office of camp security. As they walked across the dusty patch that served as a playground, children, both African and Middle Eastern, left their games of soccer or tag to beg for money or candy. From previous visits, Seppe and Allyson knew to bring small pieces of candy to pass out.

Although adults sitting on benches along the perimeter of the playground didn't approach them, Allyson could see that they were studying them. *I wonder what we look like to them,* she thought.

"What's the current number here in Caritas?" she asked.

"The last number I saw was about a thousand, although Caritas isn't supposed to hold nearly that many."

"Is that both refugees and migrants?" she asked.

Seppe frowned. "I'm sure the government keeps records of that. Sant Anselmo, however, doesn't make that distinction. We believe everyone should be served." Glancing over at her, Seppe added, "I'm sure you've gathered that everyone here has a story, and all those stories are filled with pain. Yes, some here in Caritas are classified as refugees because they're fleeing persecution or war. What about the people who are here because they fled drought or because their children need medical care? Are they any less worthy?"

Yet it's a distinction that the CIA considers important, Allyson thought. It was a poorly guarded secret in the Agency that its concern about terrorists masked the deeper concern of European and North American governments for the rising tide of migrants and refugees coming from south to north, east to west. Closing a border or forcibly returning migrants and refugees to their countries of origin didn't upset the consciences of citizens in the developed world if terrorists were rumored to be among them.

"Do you worry about politicians who claim Europe can't absorb any more people?" Allyson asked as they approached the main administrative building.

"Whether Europe should accept more refugees and migrants depends on whether we view the situation as a political or moral question. That's what Sant Anselmo believes is the most important question to answer. Right-wing politicians say the refugees threaten Europe's so-called Christian heritage. That's a smokescreen. How can a heritage that turns away desperate people be considered Christian? For us at Sant Anselmo, the right question to ask is if European countries could welcome more people seeking a new life than they do. We say, 'yes.'"

Inside the building, more refugees sat in clusters outside offices, talking in their native tongues. Seppe asked a young Middle Eastern man sitting at a reception desk where they could find the security director of the camp. In faltering Italian, the young man pointed down a hallway and then gestured to the right.

"I should have used English," Seppe said as they walked in that direction. "English opens up more countries, more job prospects. Besides Americans like you, who speaks Italiano outside of Italia?"

"On the other hand, I wish I knew Arabic," Allyson replied, as they came to a door with *Direttore de Sicurezza* painted neatly on it. After Seppe knocked on the door, they heard "*Pronto*" from within.

Allyson and Seppe entered an office overrun with filing cabinets and stacks of papers. Rising from behind two stacks balanced precariously on a desk was a short, balding man in his forties, Allyson estimated, who introduced himself as Giancarlo Prazzi.

Imagining that it might be difficult for female aid workers to be taken seriously by Mr. Prazzi, Allyson let Seppe lead the way.

When the director of security heard the name "Sant Anselmo," he smiled and complimented the organization on their work in Caritas. When Seppe explained that Allyson was an aid worker representing Europa Spec, the director looked puzzled before confessing that he wasn't familiar with the name.

"We usually work through other agencies, like the Red Cross, and sometimes Sant Anselmo," Allyson explained. That partially-true explanation appeared to temporarily satisfy the director, who scooted around the desk to remove stacks of papers from two chairs and gestured for Seppe and her to sit down.

Seppe leaned forward. "Sant Anselmo knows about Hasan Kadir and Fatima Rasul," he began. "We're hoping you can tell us about Fatima Rasul's condition and what progress has been made on her case."

"And what is the interest of the American in this?" Mr. Prazzi asked, glancing at Allyson.

Europa Spec doesn't fool him, Allyson thought. *He knows I'm an American.*

"I invited her," Seppe explained. "She's not only an aid worker. She comes from a family of famous detectives."

A family of detectives? Allyson let the exaggeration stand when she saw that Mr. Prazzi was impressed. He looked back to Seppe as he replied, "We don't know if her case and Hasan Kadir's case are connected, and Fatima Rasul remains in a coma. The doctors do not know if she will recover."

"Does that mean that she hasn't said anything since the attack?" Allyson asked, obviously surprising Prazzi with her Italian.

He shrugged and shook his head at the same time. "Not a word."

"Do you know why she was out that night?" Seppe asked.

Mr. Prazzi raised both hands. "It is unusual, yes, and we don't know why she did that. Her body was found about two hundred meters from her dormitory."

"Do you think she was going to meet someone?" Allyson asked.

"Or coming back from having met someone?" Seppe added.

"We have no witnesses, and no one has come forward," Mr. Prazzi answered. "She does not appear to have made many friends here."

"Yet Mr. Kadir and Miss Rasul knew one another, right?" Seppe asked.

"Yes, yes. Both worked in the school."

Seppe looked over at Allyson as if to ask if she had any more questions.

"Can we get a copy of Mr. Kadir's and Miss Rasul's camp files, please?" she asked.

Mr. Prazzi scratched his beard as he grimaced. "It is irregular, but, as you are a detective—an American detective maybe like Columbo, yes?—I will allow it." As he stood, he picked up two folders from his desk and exited the room.

"What do we do now?" Seppe whispered in English.

"I think we go to the hospital."

"Even though she's in a coma?" Seppe protested.

Nodding, Allison said, "The least we can find out is who's visiting her."

Mr. Prazzi returned to the room and handed a folder to Seppe. "Please, this is just between us. Don't let anyone know I gave this to you."

Seppe thanked him even as he opened the file for Allyson and him to read. The first document showed a photo of Hasan Kadir, with a date underneath it from two years before. Allyson thought that the man looked tired and discouraged. *Probably like a lot of refugees who wonder where they are and what happens next,* she thought.

"Did you know Hasan?" Seppe asked Mr. Prazzi.

"Yes, yes, certainly. He was a community leader among the Syrians. He came to see me a few times, mostly about installing locks in the dormitories. Hasan was easy to like. He always tried to understand my position, about my difficulties overseeing the whole camp."

"To your knowledge, was anyone jealous of his position?" Allyson asked.

"I don't think that's likely. Hasan was a volunteer. He received no money, and if he benefitted from the black market, I never heard about it. And truthfully, I don't think Hasan would have been involved in that."

"Residents have told me that the black-market deals mainly in cigarettes," Seppe said.

"I don't understand," Allyson said.

"Refugees receive a certain number of cigarettes from the Italian government. If a person doesn't smoke, he or she can use them as a kind of currency," Seppe explained.

"To buy what?" she asked.

"Anything you can think of," Mr. Prazzi explained. "Tampons, maybe a newer blouse or shoes for the women. For the men, lottery tickets or alcohol if they aren't religious."

Mr. Prazzi said that they would have to excuse him because he had another meeting. As Allyson and Seppe walked in the direction of the parking lot, Seppe asked, "Did we learn anything?"

"I don't believe he gave us everything from the files. He knows more than he's sharing; I'm sure of that."

Once they were in the car, Seppe said, "Did you learn that from your papa, about knowing when someone hasn't told the whole truth?"

"Not in the way you're thinking," Allyson said before asking herself if she wanted to say more. In the end, she stared out the car's windshield toward the camp's dormitories and said, "My folks separated and then divorced when I was in high school. I didn't see it coming, and I didn't really understand why. Not at all. That's when I first realized that people rarely tell the whole truth."

"I hope you don't see me that way, Alli."

"No, no, I'm definitely not talking about you," Allyson replied, feeling a pang of guilt for her own compromise with the whole truth with Seppe. "Mr. Prazzi was 'blowing smoke' as we say in the States." When she saw that Seppe didn't understood, she asked, "Do you know what a tell is, Seppe?"

"A tell?"

"A tell is when a person does something with their body, and especially their face, like an unconscious gesture, that reveals that they're hiding something."

"And Prazzi has that—a tell?"

"Oh, yes. Several times, he looked down to his left. That can be an indication that the person is lying."

"This 'tell' only shows a person is lying? It doesn't show the truth?"

Allyson smiled as she looked over at Seppe. "That's asking too much, Seppe. On the other hand, we did learn something from Mr. Prazzi. We know that Fatima was meeting someone that night. We have to find out who that was."

In a Restaurant in Trastevere

Although Allyson worked with Seppe three days a week in Caritas, she was pleased when Seppe asked her out for dinner. She realized that he hadn't invited her to Ostia the week before simply to ask her to look into the attacks in Caritas with him.

That Friday afternoon, Seppe took her first to a Mithraic Temple that had been excavated beneath one of Rome's oldest churches. Seppe played the role of tour guide with a light touch, not offering too much information and most often letting placards instruct instead of him. After the visit, Seppe took her to a restaurant in the medieval neighborhood close to the church. Allyson was happy to hear only Italian being spoken and was also pleased that the restaurant didn't offer the ubiquitous tourist menu. *This is where locals eat,* she thought. Then, without any warning, another thought came into her head. *This is where Seppe and I would eat if we lived together.*

She felt herself blush but didn't try to suppress the thought. The afternoon at the excavation and now the dinner were a welcome break from the tensions and sorrows of Caritas. Somehow, both of them, without saying anything, agreed to forego talking about the camp, which included not bringing up Hasan Kadir's and Fatima Rasul's names. That freed Allyson from worrying about protecting her secret. She also noticed that Seppe didn't once bring up the issue of the priesthood.

We're just two friends who could be slowly falling in love, she thought.

IN A ROMAN BAR

THE TRUTH WAS THAT the drive up and back to Orvieto with Morgan and the new agent that afternoon had exhausted Chaz. He'd been the one to suggest placing an agent inside Caritas, yet if he'd hoped the new agent would be a "Bond girl," he couldn't have been more mistaken.

From as far back as he could remember, Chaz was never comfortable in the presence of women he considered ugly or poor. In the co-ed preparatory school he attended before Brown University, Chaz had been in classes with others who came from wealth, from "old families," or from both. He knew that wealth by itself didn't make a person beautiful. Yet money offered numerous ways of masking what would otherwise be taken as plain.

As he drove back to Rome from Orvieto, he could see in the rearview mirror the new agent pretending to sleep in the backseat. Each time he glanced back and saw Khadija, he felt more depressed. He was repulsed by her scrawniness, her grey hijab, and her lack of makeup. He wouldn't have been surprised if she'd said, "I apologize; I know how I must look to you," and maybe, now that he thought about it, she'd managed to convey that message without words. The longer the return trip to Rome had taken, the more the woman's ugliness filled the car and settled within him as a pounding headache.

A memory of his female relatives came to mind. His mother and one surviving grandmother had always been described as "classy," and his female cousins were all stunners. "Good genes like the Kennedys" was what Eatons always said when they gathered for the yearly family photo.

Now, as he sat at a bar outside the Pantheon, he tried to forget about the new agent and concentrate on Sally Patton. She'd done her best to attract his full attention by wearing a low-cut linen top and tight jeans. She would occasionally lean forward, revealing the curve of her breasts. However, the headache from the afternoon blocked his hormones.

Chaz had to remind himself to smile as he tried to sound clever and charming. When Sally let her foot rest against one of his legs, he surprised himself by instinctively drawing back. *What's wrong with me?* he wondered.

He covered the awkward moment by complimenting Sally's choice of perfume, even as he told himself to get a grip.

"I assume from the way Allyson's been acting, that she has somebody in her life. A man, I mean," he said.

The smile on Sally's face evaporated.

"And maybe you do as well," he quickly added.

"Me? Didn't you know? I'm married with five kids back in the States," she said as she took another sip of wine.

Forcing a laugh, Chaz said without thinking, "Right, and I'm gay." Immediately, the pounding in his head intensified as he wondered if Sally Patton would report him for violating Agency policy on inappropriate language.

Sally only laughed. "I think it's more likely that I have five kids than that you're gay."

Chaz swirled the wine in his glass, regretting the way Chianti would add to the pain centered between his eyes. His goals for the evening quickly narrowed, and sex with Sally Patton wasn't one of them. He yearned to end the date as soon as possible without damaging his reputation or a chance for raincheck sex with Sally. His second goal, given that he wouldn't be able to end the date for another thirty to forty minutes, was to discover what he could about Allyson Worthy. From Sally's reaction, his first mention of Allyson was obviously too much of a frontal assault, and he tried to find a way to approach that topic differently.

"I understand Rome isn't your first assignment with the Agency," he began. "Where was it—Madrid?"

"Barcelona," Sally replied.

"Ah, Barcelona. I've always wanted to see that city. In case I get reassigned there, what's the Agency like?" he asked.

"How do you mean?"

"Good folks to work with? Assholes for colleagues? I'm interested in your impression."

"It was my first placement, which means I took everything as normal. My boss was a male, and he was an asshole. Everything by the book."

"It sounds like our situation is better here with Morgan," he said, beginning to see how he might steer the conversation around to Allyson.

"Without a doubt. I expected that, though. I mean, for a woman to get to her level, she has to be better than a man, right?"

"I never thought about that. I suspect you're right." The first part of his answer had been the truth; he'd never wasted his time wondering if women had it tougher than men. The second part of his answer, however, was a lie. If he thought anything about Morgan's status in the Agency, it was that she'd benefitted from Congress's gender equality goal.

"Who do you like working with here in Rome?" he asked.

Chaz waited, hoping that Sally would bring up Allyson's name. Sally listed several agents, although Allyson's name wasn't among them.

Chaz leaned across the table to whisper, "I heard you're working narcotics."

Sally smiled. "Whispered like a real spy."

"They've got me working on refugees and migrants," he said. "I suppose you already know that."

Sally nodded again. "Yes, Alli told me that you were working together."

"I wouldn't say we're working together. For some reason, she's put up a barrier between us."

Chaz tried to look hurt as Sally responded, "Have you talked to Morgan about it?"

Chaz wanted to answer with care. "No, it's probably nothing serious. It's more a vibe she gives off. I did find out her father is a decorated homicide detective. I wondered if that could make her . . . I don't know, a bit standoffish."

"Well, Alli is on loan from the FBI."

"Right, right. You think that might explain it?" Chaz said with a slight frown.

"I just meant that Alli's future isn't with the CIA, Chaz."

"Good point. Good point. If I look at it that way, yes, I can see that might explain her detachment. Yes, that's a good insight." He forced himself to empty his glass before adding, "I thought she might have told you—her roommate—if she had a problem with me. I'm thinking of our careers, you see. I want our relationship . . . our working relationship to go smoothly."

"By 'our,' I take it you mean your relationship with Alli," Sally said in a tone that Chaz thought was on the brusque side.

"Oh, I'm sorry, Sally. No, no, of course I want my relationship with you to be . . ."

"Smooth?" Sally offered.

"Exactly," Chaz said as he felt his face redden.

There was a moment of awkward silence as Chaz looked down at the table.

Sally put her hand on her purse. "Chaz, I've developed a headache all of a sudden. And I have a full schedule tomorrow."

Chaz knew he should be relieved that the evening was over early and he no longer had to pretend to be enjoying himself, but, as he paid the bill and they walked out of the bar, he was irked. Sally had as much as accused him, Chaz Eaton, of being a bore.

CHAPTER NINE

July 5
Caritas Refugee Camp

THE AGENCY GAVE KHADIJA three nearly identical outfits to wear in the camp. She donned the first, a ragged robe or chador and a hijab, in the Agency's offices and now looked at her reflection in a mirror in her dormitory in Caritas. The woman who stared back looked as her could have been her mother when the family first arrived in England.

Khadija's experience that first day in the camp bore out Morgan's warning that she'd probably be exhausted and confused. From morning to late afternoon, she moved from table to table to fill out endless forms before being assigned to a dormitory. Because she was self-conscious about her command of Arabic—she'd translated the language in Germany not spoken it—she was at first halting, but those who were interviewing her didn't act like they noticed. *Perhaps,* she thought, *I sound like other refugees, still in shock after washing up in a foreign country.*

She recalled the stories her parents and other Palestinian refugees in Brixton had told her. The stories were both similar and wildly different. What was similar was the pain of being evicted by the Israelis from their villages and ending up initially in tent cities in Jordan. A second similarity was the conclusion that most of the Palestinian refugees came to, that staying in Jordan was to settle for a bleak future. What was different in the stories was the tearful accounts of who and what they'd left behind.

Khadija's initial worry was that she'd be unable to pass for a Syrian refugee. When she pointed out to her trainers in Germany that she spoke Arabic with a Palestinian accent, the Agency told her to identify herself as a Palestinian who'd married a Syrian engineer and moved to Syria six years before the civil war began. They told her to say that her husband had been killed a year ago when he served in the "White Helmets," the brave Syrians who risked their lives to recover people trapped in bombed-out buildings.

Khadija thought it possible that she would encounter refugees in Caritas who really were from Damascus. Therefore, she'd spent her last days in Freiburg studying maps of Damascus and reading accounts by refugees who fled the city. If she were questioned by a genuine refugee from Damascus, she could account for her limited knowledge of the city by saying that her husband, being traditional, had restricted her movements outside the home.

That left only one part of her personal myth for the Agency to construct. If she were to meet and question Hasan Kadir's relatives in the camp without raising suspicion, she should explain that Hasan's relatives were relatives of her husband.

On her first day in Caritas, she was asked if she preferred to work in the camp's food services or in the school. She quickly chose the school, even as she knew work in the dining hall would expose her to more residents. She knew, however, that she'd be sickened at the sight of hundreds of refugees who, having arrived at Caritas malnourished, would be relishing every bite of food three times a day. *Yet another layer of shame,* she thought.

That was the moment when she realized that the longer her assignment in Caritas lasted, the more her safety would be threatened. For two or three weeks, she would look like nearly every other newcomer to the camp. The problem was that if she continued to look pale and thin after a month, she would stand out. Khadija felt her stomach, empty as it was, turn as she thought, *I have escaped nothing.*

July 6
Corpus Christi Hospital

In her written report to Morgan, Allyson shared her belief that Mr. Prazzi, Caritas' head of security, knew more about the attacks on Hasan

Kadir and Fatima than he was prepared to share. She didn't mention that Seppe accompanied her to the interview and would go with her to visit Fatima in the hospital.

I'm being stupid, she thought, as she sat on the bus taking her to the hospital and tried to recall when and why she'd first decided to withhold Seppe's identity. Finally, she could see that the deception began a week ago, when she lied to Chaz about her weekend plans to visit Ostia.

Am I really in this bind because of Chaz? she wondered. As she exited the bus and saw Seppe waiting for her, she saw her true motive more clearly. To tell Morgan and Chaz about Seppe would be admitting that she was spying on him. If Seppe couldn't know about the Agency, she felt that she'd achieved a kind of balance by making sure the Agency didn't know about him. As Seppe looked up and smiled as he watched her cross the street, her heart sank, as she realized that this balance could not last. When Seppe and Stamper found out about each other, she knew that she'd lose the trust of both of them. "For the time being," to use Morgan's phrase, she'd lead the double life that let her be *almost* honest with Seppe when they were together.

Once inside the hospital, Allyson and Seppe understood immediately that the doctor overseeing Fatima's recovery wasn't hiding her concern. "Fatima is young and quite strong. However, we can't predict how the brain will respond."

"When will you know, Dottore?" Seppe asked.

The doctor frowned as her hand clutched the end of the stethoscope around her neck. "With this type of injury, recovery depends on stopping the brain bleeds that she's experiencing. Until then, we don't dare wake her."

"My friend," Seppe began, nodding in Allyson's direction, "tells me that reading to someone in a coma, maybe even holding the person's hand, can help. Do you agree?"

"Yes, I've read that too. You should know that Fatima already has someone who comes every morning to read to her. An older man, Italian. I think he's from the camp. He comes every day with his briefcase full of books."

As Allyson and Seppe started to leave the room, the doctor caught Seppe's arm. "Please know that we're doing everything we can." Seppe bowed slightly as he thanked her.

Outside the hospital, they sat on another bench. "I think Fatima's visitor could be important, especially because he's someone from Caritas," Allyson said. She knew that the Agency with its resources could spit out the man's name in a few seconds. Seppe, however, couldn't know that. Even if she waited a day or two to share the visitor's name, Seppe would likely want to know how she'd discovered it. She settled on another way.

"Why don't we come back tomorrow morning and wait for the man to show up?"

Seppe agreed and walked beside Allyson toward the bus stop. Nearly there, he abruptly stopped and made the sign of the cross.

"I just realized that the Church of Sant'Agnese is just behind this wall. Have you heard of her?"

"No, who was she?"

"An early martyr, but that's not the only important part of her story. St. Agnes protects young women—like Fatima. I take that as a good sign."

CHAPTER TEN

July 6
CIA Headquarters

As Chaz walked to his cubicle the next afternoon, he sensed that Allyson and Sally were both avoiding him. For Allyson, this wasn't unusual. The only time Allyson made eye contact with him was when Morgan called the team together for a case update. Sally, however, who usually greeted him, ignored him despite his calling out his usual, "Afternoon, fellow spies" to the entire room.

All because I didn't cancel the date when I should have, he thought, as he opened the police file on Hasan Kadir. He looked at the photo of the old man taken when he arrived at the refugee camp. He wondered if refugees ever smiled. That brought back the painful memory of the new agent, what was her name—Khaja something? How was he supposed to keep track of all these foreign names—Fatima, Hasan, and now the new agent? That also thought brought back the memory of the headache that had spoiled his date with Sally.

He shook his head to clear it and focused on the file. To his surprise, he discovered that Hasan Kadir had been a civil engineer and ran a company in Damascus before the war. Chaz's own father headed up an engineering firm in Connecticut, which led Chaz to imagine—for just a second at the most—his father and Hasan Kadir changing places. He felt dizzy as he tried to picture Kadir living in Greenwich and driving a Mercedes E class, while his father was in a refugee camp.

He studied Kadir's file in more detail, looking for anything that might shed light on the Syrian civil engineer's death. On one form, dated five months before Hasan's death, Chaz read that he'd been elected as one of four Syrian representatives to the camp council. He made a note to look further into that, even though he suspected that representatives to the camp council did little more than pass along complaints from other refugees. That, he reasoned, wouldn't get someone killed.

Turning more pages, he found a list of Hasan Kadir's relatives in the camp, a brother and his family. Chaz considered this potentially significant, especially if Kadir's family had a history of conflict in Syria. Vendettas, he reasoned, crossed borders as easily as birds.

On the last page of the file, Chaz found something that made him forget his rotten evening with Sally. It was a copy of a commendation with an English translation attached. Flowery scrollwork and a golden seal decorated the document that read: *This is to acknowledge the compassionate work that Hasan Kadir has contributed to the care of Syrian orphan children in Caritas, 2019-20.*

Leaning back in his chair, he sensed that the commendation might suggest a deeper reason for Kadir's death. Rising to bring his suspicions to Morgan's attention, he saw Allyson already in the case manager's office. Then he saw Morgan gesturing in his direction, beckoning him to come to her office.

For a moment, he felt a wave of panic before he realized he'd done nothing to warrant being reprimanded. He strode casually to the case manager's office, trying to project a look of confidence.

"Chaz, I thought the three of us should check in with one another," Morgan began, as she took the chair behind her desk and nodded for Allyson and Chaz to sit down.

"Something new to report?" he asked.

"Allyson was in Caritas yesterday and talked briefly with the director of security, a Mr. Prazzi."

Chaz bristled. "I thought that's why we embedded our new agent—what's her name?—in the camp."

"I was there in the camp," Allyson explained slowly, as if she were talking to a child, "for intake interviews. I thought as an aid worker that I had a right to ask about the attacks. It was just about killing two birds with one stone."

Deciding to back off, he leaned forward and feigned interest. "And you apparently discovered something."

Allyson nodded. "I think I did. I managed to learn what hospital Fatima is in, and I visited there this morning."

Are we meeting to applaud Allyson? he thought. "The girl is still in a coma, right?"

"Yes, and her doctor isn't optimistic."

Which you could have gathered from a phone call, Chaz thought.

"I'm going back tomorrow morning. Fatima has a regular visitor, an elderly Italian from the camp who reads to her most mornings."

"Sounds like a do-gooder to me," Chaz said.

"Maybe he is," Allyson conceded. "The problem is that as far as I know Fatima doesn't have close friends in Caritas. I'm hoping he can tell us something."

Morgan asked, "And what have you found out, Chaz?"

Chaz crossed his leg and tried to look relaxed. "I've been focusing on Kadir's police file. A couple of things caught my eye." For the next five minutes, he looked solely at Morgan as he shared the news about Hasan Kadir's relatives in the camp and the man's position on one of the camp councils.

"There's something else I want our inside man . . . woman to work on. Hasan Kadir received a commendation for his work with Syrian orphans, children, I mean."

He waited for Allyson to throw the "He sounds like a do-gooder to me" line back in his face. Allyson, however, said nothing. It was Morgan who asked, "What are your instincts on that, Chaz?"

With his best look of concern, he replied, "Anytime children are in the mix, we have to consider the possibility of trafficking. Given that Kadir worked in the school and was attacked for some reason, we have to consider possible inappropriate conduct on his part."

Morgan sighed. "I suppose you're right. There might be a slight problem with our agent inside, however."

Ask me if I'm surprised, Chaz thought, remembering how the woman repulsed him.

"From the layout of the camp and how refugees spend most of their time sitting outside and watching one another, Allyson thinks any attempt by her to make contact with Khadija will look suspicious. That means we have to come up with a way for Khadija to smuggle her reports out. Any ideas, Chaz?"

Chaz took a fountain pen out of his shirt pocket and studied it. *My talisman,* he thought, as he looked at his reflection in the Mont Blanc's shiny lacquer surface. When his grandfather gave him the gift on his admission to Brown, the old man had put his arm on Chaz's shoulder and said, "Always remember, son, this is a Mont Blanc Meisterstuck 149. Having such a pen will always set you apart from the rabble."

In his four years at Brown, he discovered that simply holding the pen in his hand reduced his stress. Whenever he was asked a question for which he didn't have a ready answer, he took a breath, reached into his pocket for the pen and held it in his hands, sometimes twisting the cap on and off to reveal the gold nib. Inevitably, the person who questioned him and anyone else in the room would follow his gaze and focus on the pen, and the Mont Blanc was a fountain pen that spoke volumes.

"Well," he said, holding the pen between his two hands, "I have one suggestion. Tell me what you think." With a smile, he said, "Morgan, I think you'd agree that our new agent looks pretty wasted. What if we added to her cover story that she has to have regular treatment at a hospital, something more serious than the camp's medical staff can deal with? That way, we can arrange for her to be picked up for hospital appointments here in Rome, when actually she'll be brought here."

Morgan looked in Allyson's direction. "What do you think?"

"I think it could work," Allyson replied.

"Good. Then we're agreed," she said, smiling broadly as she made a note and closed a file. "Now, all we have to do is create a false health report and get that delivered to the camp, which shouldn't be too hard. It can't be unusual for medical information to arrive after the refugee does."

Chaz stood, pleased with how the meeting had turned out. Allyson may have gotten her licks in first, yet he scored the winning punch. Just to emphasize the point, he stopped at the door and turned to face the women. "Maybe Allyson can figure out how we get the word to our new agent."

July 7
Corpus Christi Hospital

More each day, Fatima felt she was surfacing into a blackness filled with watery echoes. All her energy was consumed with what was the most important question in the world—were her eyes open or closed? If they were open, then maybe she was floating in outer space or at the bottom of the ocean. If they were closed, maybe she'd already died and was awaiting paradise.

She waited in the darkness, at times hearing a sound far away, at other times nothing. She wondered how long she'd been dead or left in this darkness. Was it a minute, a day, a month, or part of a lifetime?

She had been visited by her dead father. She felt his cool hands on her forehead, yet was confused when he talked in a language she didn't understand. More than once, she heard her dead brother's voice down by her feet, then a sensation that he was sticking the soles of her feet with something sharp.

Then, one day or night—she couldn't tell—she heard someone calling her name in Arabic. She sensed the voice belonged to an older man and assumed that Hasan Kadir had come to pray for her departed soul and Allah's forgiveness.

"Fatima . . . please . . . co . . .back . . . us. Fatima . . . you . . . live. Fatima . . . don't . . . give . . .," the voice said, its volume rising and then falling into silence.

How she longed for even the faintest light. There were moments when she suspected someone was drawing back her eyelids, which was followed by the briefest feeling of warmth. The intensity of the darkness, however, never varied.

Hasan, where are we? Hasan, is Allah here? Hasan, what did you want to tell me?

CHAPTER ELEVEN

July 8
Caritas Refugee Camp

"KHADIJA, WHY DIDN'T YOU tell us about your condition?" one of the camp nurses asked in an angry tone through a translator.

Khadija looked down, pretending she didn't understand Italian and hoping she'd hidden her confusion. She tried to trace the question backward, to what must have occasioned it. How had her eating disorder been discovered this quickly? She'd forced herself to eat at least half of her meals and made it obvious that she wrapped up the rest in napkins, as if she were a food hoarder. She was sure no one had seen her flush the stashed food down the toilet.

Somehow, someone had detected her secret. She thought that the Agency might pull her from the camp or at least insert a poor performance review in her permanent file.

"I don't understand," she finally said.

"You should have told us when you arrived," the nurse said.

Khadija fought back tears. "I don't think you know much about my condition if you think I'd just broadcast it."

The nurse's face softened, and Khadija could tell from the tone that something had changed. "Having stomach cancer is nothing to be ashamed about," she said, even as she reached across the table and touched Khadija's hand.

Stomach cancer?

She cleared her throat and said, "I'm afraid I don't understand," this time meaning it.

Another exchange occurred between the nurse and the translator, before the translator said, "The clinic has to know about your treatments, you see."

"My treatments," Khadija answered, offering her words as a statement, not a question, to bide for time.

"Yes, we received a physician's note from your previous camp, describing your cancer and your radiation treatments. The camp doesn't have that technology. That means you'll have to be taken to a hospital in Rome."

The picture cleared for Khadija, as she realized what the Agency had arranged and why. "When is my next treatment?" she asked.

Even though she understood the Italian nurse's response, she waited for the translator to tell her in Arabic that her trip to Rome was scheduled for the following day. "The cancer must make eating a chore at times," the translator added without prompting from the nurse.

Oh, brilliant, she thought. *The Agency must think of everything. Now even my eating disorder has a cover story.*

July 9
Corpus Christi Hospital

ALLYSON TOOK THE BUS to meet Seppe and was relieved when he passed the Church of Sant'Agnese without commenting. Any attraction she felt toward him was quickly dashed by his frequent mention of his considering the priesthood. Of all the problems she had with Chaz, she could count on the two of them never discussing religion.

When they arrived at the hospital and Seppe held the door for her, Allyson thought, *God, if you exist, take Chaz. There's something wrong with a religion, something selfish, that takes all the good men for itself.*

Arriving on Fatima's ward, Seppe asked her doctor if anyone had visited Fatima that morning.

"No, the man from the camp doesn't usually arrive for another half hour. You're both free to wait in the lounge."

It wasn't more than fifteen minutes before a short, thin man in his late sixties or early seventies, with a shock of gray hair, approached the nurses' station. Allyson and Seppe both watched as he bowed respectfully to the nurses and talked quietly for a few moments before shuffling across the hall and entering Fatima's room.

The fact that the man didn't look in their direction suggested to Allyson that the nursing staff hadn't alerted the man to their presence. Better, she thought, to introduce themselves after the man had visited Fatima, when they could invite him for coffee.

While they waited, Seppe said, "Allyson, tell me about Europa Spec."

The request took Allyson by surprise, and even though she'd memorized her cover story, she hated that she would be lying to Seppe.

"I don't know everything the company does except that it's focused on pharmaceuticals and medical equipment. I work on the philanthropic side of things."

"I wish more companies showed concern for refugees. Sometimes I think my father's business cares only about profit margins."

"Your father is in business?" Allyson asked.

Seppe's face turned red. "My family has been in banking for over three hundred years." Seppe paused to look at her. "I can see that surprises you."

"Yes, it does."

"My brother, Leo, is already in the family business. Even though I'm older, he'll head it up when my father retires."

"Does that mean your father wants you in the business as well?" As Allyson said that, she realized that she was hoping the answer might be yes.

Seppe looked down at his hands as if they held the answer. "In his own way, yes, although he'll never try to force me. It's Leo who reminds me constantly that there's no profit in human suffering."

"Family gatherings must be rough," Allyson responded.

"They can be. Most the time, what I'm doing with my life and what I might do in the future doesn't come up."

"Does your mother understand?"

"She tries to," Seppe said, smiling at Allyson. "She still makes cannoli for me. I don't expect Leo to ever understand, especially if—," Seppe broke off as he glanced toward Fatima's room. "There's Fatima's visitor. Let's catch him before he leaves."

PROFESSOR NAPOLITANO ACCEPTED THE invitation to coffee in the hospital's cafeteria. He listened as the young man introduced himself and his friend and explained their concern for Fatima's well-being.

The professor explained that Fatima was bright, independent, and a voracious reader. "For a Muslim young woman, she's quite vocal. If her Italian were better, she wouldn't be out of place in a university class. Now I just pray she recovers."

"We understand you read to her regularly. Have you seen any change, positive change, I mean?" Allyson asked.

The professor shook his head slowly. "Some days, I see what looks like eye movements behind her eyelids, and once I saw her fingers twitch. That raised my hopes, but her doctor said those movements were probably involuntary responses."

"What do you read to her?" Seppe asked.

Allyson thought the professor looked embarrassed. "I read children's books in Arabic. I suppose I want her to hear—if she can hear—simple stories. And I make sure that the endings are always good ones. No sad endings."

"When was the last time you saw Fatima before the attack?" Allyson asked.

"Actually, she came to see me the night she was attacked. The next morning, I heard that she'd been found unconscious."

"Was that unusual, Fatima coming to see you in the evening?" Allyson asked.

Allyson thought she saw the professor's face twitch. After a pause, he said, "She had questions about a paper that I'd assigned for the next class. Fatima was very conscientious, you see." After a pause, he added, "Of course, I feel guilty. If she hadn't come to see me that evening, she wouldn't have been attacked."

Allyson let the thought hang in the air. Seppe broke the silence by asking, "Did she ever mention having any problems in the camp? Any enemies?"

An ambulance, sirens blaring, passed the hospital on the street below. The professor watched as a police car followed at high speed before saying anything. "Fatima is an unusual refugee, especially for a young Muslim woman. I asked her once if she had relatives in Caritas, and she said no.

You see, if her father or brother were in the camp, I don't think they'd allow her to be as independent, as involved in camp life."

"What about friends?" Seppe asked.

"I've never seen her with anyone, except in the school. Fatima loves children."

Allyson pondered the irony. After reading that Hasan was similarly described as loving children, Chaz immediately thought of child abuse. No one would accuse a young girl like Fatima of that.

"Twice you've described her as independent," Allyson said.

"Have I?"

"Yes. Do you think someone might want to punish her for that?"

"I hadn't thought of that. When she recovers, I don't expect her to be any different. Fatima has gone through too much for someone this young, and she survived. I pray she'll survive again."

CHAPTER TWELVE

July 10
CIA Headquarters

A TAXI COMPANY USED BY Europa Spec delivered Khadija to CIA headquarters the next morning. Wearing one of the three outfits that she'd been given, she wasn't surprised when others stared at her as she was escorted to the elevator. Once she'd arrived on the second floor, she was escorted to a conference room where Chaz and Morgan were waiting along with a woman she didn't know.

After greeting Khadija, Morgan said, "This is Allyson Worthy, another one of our agents. She works closely with aid agencies in Caritas, which means you'll probably see her there."

When the agent stepped forward and shook her hand, Khadija immediately felt ashamed. Allyson Worthy was tall and obviously healthy, neither too thin nor stocky. *What must I look like to her?* she thought.

"Thank you for taking this assignment," Allyson said. "And don't worry about my blowing your cover. If we see each other in Caritas, we can pretend we've already met."

Khadija returned the smile. Was it just her imagination, or was this agent completely different from Chaz?

"Please have a seat," Morgan said. "Would you like coffee or tea? Maybe water?"

She could feel Chaz's eyes on her. *He's wondering if bulimics avoid drinking as well as eating,* she thought. "I'd like tea, please," she said.

"Hot or iced?" Morgan asked.

"Oh," she said again, feeling herself flush. "I've never had cold tea. Yes, I'd like to try. Thank you."

Morgan pushed a button on her side of the table. In a few seconds, a young man stuck his head in the door.

"A pitcher of iced tea and four glasses," Morgan said. Without a word, the young man disappeared.

"I'm sorry that we couldn't warn you about the change in contact arrangements," Morgan said. "Was there a problem, any suspicions raised, when you heard about the new cover story?"

"I was confused at first, although I don't think anyone noticed."

"Excellent. We'll use the same system until it becomes a problem—same days and time. Chaz, why don't you bring Khadija up to date?"

Khadija watched as Chaz reached into his shirt pocket and removed a large black pen. Once he'd unscrewed the cap, Khadija realized he was holding a fountain pen. One of her teachers back in Brixton had had a similar pen, though not as large or shiny.

"Absolutely," he said, though she noticed his eyes remained on the pen instead of her. "We know that you're just getting acclimated to the camp. It's time we explained your assignments. Do you understand?"

Only with the last word did the man look up and meet her gaze. Before she could answer, there was a knock on the door followed by the young man bringing in the iced tea on a tray.

Agent Worthy poured the first glass and placed it in front of Khadija, before pouring the other three glasses. Khadija took a small sip and found the temperature of the drink colder than she expected. It wasn't until the second sip that she tasted the tea.

"Yes, I understand," she said.

"Good, good," he said, looking down at his notes. "First of all, make contact with Hasan Kadir's relatives in the camp," he said, passing a sheet of paper across the table. "This is a list of their names."

"Second assignment: find out what Hasan Kadir's position was on the camp council. Is the council looking into anything . . . anything the Agency would be interested in?" He paused before asking, "Good so far?"

"Yes, yes."

"Third and maybe most important, Kadir received a commendation for his work with orphan children in the camp. We shouldn't be too quick to assume that was all above board. Given that we don't know the motive for his murder, you must find out all you can about that. Anything else, Morgan?"

Khadija thought she remembered Chaz addressing their case manager by her first name on the car ride from Orvieto, yet it still surprised her.

"I can't think of anything else. What about you, Allyson?"

Allyson waited a moment before she asked, "What are your impressions of the camp, Khadija?"

"The camp is overcrowded, which I understand isn't unusual. Everyone has a daily work assignment, but that still leaves a lot of time with nothing to do. Most of the residents sit outside in the afternoon and evening until it gets dark."

"There's probably a rule about the amount of work the Italian government can ask for," Morgan said.

"Of course," Khadija agreed hastily. "What I'm saying is that the residents have to have something besides their work to keep them occupied."

"What do they talk about when they're sitting around?" Chaz asked.

"Mainly family members who've died or who are still back in Syria."

"That's not good," Allyson said.

"It's to be expected after trauma. Focusing on the past, that is," Morgan commented.

"Just as long as they're not talking about hating the US or how to build a bomb," Chaz offered.

The room felt as cold as the iced tea to Khadija, and she saw that she wasn't the only one in the room who was shocked by the remark. Across the table, she saw Allyson's face redden.

"Oh, come on, don't look at me that way," Chaz said in a louder voice. "All I meant was, why should their sitting around yakking about the past matter to the Agency?"

Khadija was sure she heard Allyson say under her breath, "Apparently it doesn't to all of us."

Morgan sat forward. "If you're asking if what Khadija has noticed should concern the Agency, the answer is yes and no. No, the Agency is obviously not in a position to affect camp conditions much—even if we wanted to. However, it's a well-known fact that idleness breeds a lot of problems."

Khadija waited to see how Chaz would react to the rebuke. All he did was take a sip of his drink and say nothing.

"Allyson, anymore from you?" Morgan asked.

"What Khadija is saying might provide a link between Hasan and Fatima. Although we don't know yet how well the two knew each other, they're atypical. Neither was living in the past, as you put it, Morgan. Hasan was elected to the camp council, and Fatima was enrolled in several classes. They were thinking about the future—Hasan with the future of the camp and Fatima with her own future."

Chaz snickered at Allyson. "You're not honestly saying they were attacked because they were ambitious."

Khadija's heart raced. *He attacks like a scorpion,* she thought, although she could see that Allyson wasn't cowed.

"Think about it, Chaz," Allyson said. "If you're consumed with the past, you're probably not going to be too aware of what's going on around you. You're still drowning in grief. If you're thinking about the future, you're going to notice all the obstacles standing in your way. You're paying attention, and you might be trying to do something about things that aren't right in the camp."

In the silence that followed, Fatima sensed that everyone was waiting to hear Morgan's position. In that moment, Khadija felt sorry for the case officer. She'd experienced similar tension in the Munich office, and these two American agents, Chaz and Allyson, were oil and water or, worse, gasoline and a spark. Eventually, Khadija thought, there would be an explosion.

"Allyson is right," Morgan finally said. "Hasan and Fatima were clearly not ordinary camp residents. It's possible that they both noticed something amiss, something other residents didn't see or didn't want to see. We just have to hope that Fatima wakes up and tells us what that is. Until then, Khadija, you are our eyes and ears in Caritas."

Morgan closed the file in front of her and stood. As soon as Chaz and Allyson left the room, she approached Khadija. "If there's anything you need, let me know. And one other thing. With a killer in Caritas, I'm sure I don't have to tell you to be careful."

Allyson's Apartment

Allyson's first impression of the new agent was that a strong breeze could blow her away. Even compared to real refugees in Caritas, Khadija looked fragile. Immediately, Allyson had felt protective of her, and by the time the meeting was over, she worried if Khadija could, on the one hand, handle what the camp would throw at her and, on the other hand, be able to stand up to Chaz.

The gulf between Chaz and her was widening, and Allyson wondered how much she was to blame. Sally's comment that she was a snob, a Midwestern snob, had struck home with her. Perhaps in reaction, she'd pretended interest in Chaz by asking Sally how her date with him had gone. Her roommate had only shaken her head. "Don't ask. The guy's a bigger tool than you said he was."

"Why, because he made a play?" Allyson had asked.

Sally stopped brushing her blond hair and looked at Allyson's reflection in the mirror. "Believe it or not, he didn't try to come on to me, yet he still managed to make the night a total bust."

"Ouch. Oh, well, I still predict he'll try again."

Sally put the brush down. "Why does Chaz have to be the only good-looking young guy in the office? My plan is to pretend he's invisible."

"Well, good luck with that. Chaz works hard to be noticed."

Now, sitting at her desk after the meeting, Allyson concluded that Chaz's bad luck was continuing. Chaz had not only been rebuked by Morgan. He'd alienated himself from the new agent, Khadija. If Allyson felt a modicum of pleasure that Morgan sided with her in the meeting, she hadn't forgotten that Morgan still expected her to find a way to work with Chaz. That he would want to be the alpha dog made the task daunting, as he was trying to best her before Morgan, and Allyson was unwilling to give him that leverage.

She thought of her father, her "famous father," as Seppe had referred to him, who'd told her more than once that jealousy came with the territory in police work. Was that what Chaz felt toward her—jealousy? Jealous of what? Rome was the first time she'd been loaned by the FBI to the CIA, and she'd come with few other talents than previous experience in Italy and a facility for the language. Furthermore, once this assignment in Rome was over, Chaz and she would never see one another again. *Then why do I threaten him, and why do I get the feeling that he wants to destroy my career?*

The worst part of her situation was that she could think of no one to confide in. Not Stamper, who made it clear that she expected Allyson to be the bigger person in working with Chaz. Her roommate, Sally? Well, Allyson was certain that Sally, if desperate enough, would change her mind and meet Chaz again for drinks and whatever would follow.

The one person she knew who would listen to her and help her see a way forward was Father Nick, her father's partner in detection. He, however, was back in his Ohio monastery. Allyson knew she could email him, even text him, but because she was an FBI agent working with the CIA, there was too much about her dilemma she couldn't share.

The thought of Father Nick, however, reminded her of Seppe. Yes, if she were careful how she described her problem, she knew Seppe would listen as attentively as Father Nick, and the realization that she could be at least partially transparent with Seppe comforted her. *One less lie,* she thought.

CHAPTER THIRTEEN

July 11
Caritas Refugee Camp

PROFESSOR NAPOLITANO SAT IN his empty office in Caritas and thought about the two aid workers who'd cornered him at the hospital. He wasn't troubled by the lie he'd told because he didn't feel he owed the two nosey aid workers the truth. Yet he was troubled by the possibility that the aid workers would know, once Fatima recovered consciousness, that he'd lied.

I must be there when Fatima wakes up, he thought. *That way, I can warn her to say nothing about Hasan's note.*

The professor didn't know Hasan, and he wouldn't have expected an older refugee to take his class, especially one on world religions. He had, however, read the newspaper account about the elderly man's death. The unsolved murder, coupled with the attack on Fatima, had led to a spate of rumors in the camp. Some blamed the attacks on ISIS while others suspected the long reach of Assad's regime. So far, camp administrators were content to repeat the police theory, that the two attacks were either random or part of preexisting clan tensions in Syria.

All that would change, he knew, when camp administrators found out about Hasan's note.

CIA Headquarters

Chaz knew he needed a comeback. He bristled at the memory of the meeting with Morgan, Worthy, and that new agent, whatever her name was. If the ratio in the room had been three to one, male to female, instead of the reverse, he knew he'd have come out of the meeting without a scratch. Instead, the way the three women reacted to his comment about the refugees made him look insensitive.

Anyone in the Navy Seals would have reacted as he did, and any female desiring to be accepted into that elite group would be judged on her toughness, her grit. *Why the hell wasn't the same true for the CIA?* he thought, and again he wished his knee had healed properly so that he could have stayed in the navy. The Agency's mistake, he realized, was assigning three female agents to deal with the mess in the camp.

From his point of view, the sole importance of refugee camps was their connection with terrorism. The CIA in his opinion should be making sure refugees remained a European concern, which meant that agents should support the political parties in Europe that were "standing up" to the problem. To him, Italy's approach was a disaster, its leniency and misguided compassion offering refugees little chance of becoming productive members of Italian society. As far as he could determine, camps like Caritas were little more than holding tanks.

That was why he saw the recent attacks in the Caritas camp differently from Allyson, Morgan, and the new agent. The attacks should awaken Italy to the threat their so-called humanitarian policies posed to the country's economy, social services, and security.

CIA training mandated that agents refrain from becoming directly involved in the politics of foreign governments. Chaz saw that rule for what it was: useful language to quote when the Agency was caught doing exactly that—meddling in another country's policies. If the Agency were honest, the rule would read, "Agents should refrain from being caught meddling in the politics of foreign governments."

As Chaz reflected on this, anger rose within him. He should have been commended, not censored, for reminding his fellow agents that the conditions in the camp weren't the CIA's concern. It should have been Allyson who was confronted by Morgan for misunderstanding her assignment.

She was assigned to *pretend* to be a humanitarian aid worker; compassion for the refugees was simply to be part of her cover. Instead, Allyson's bleeding heart was clearly influencing the group, not to mention leading him to be publicly shamed. His anger led to clarity and certainty, as it often had in the past. *In the end,* he thought, *Morgan will realize her mistake about Allyson, even as Italy will eventually realize its mistake.*

IF CHAZ THOUGHT ALLYSON would be gloating after the meeting, he was mistaken. As Allyson sat at her desk, she was worried. Chaz's nasty side, now shown openly, made cooperating with one another even less likely.

That night, sitting with Seppe at an outdoor café overlooking the Tiber River, she explained her problems with an unnamed male colleague in as much detail as she could. On the river below, a racing shell shot by, the rowers graceful, pulling together. *Why can't Chaz and I work together like that?* she thought.

Seppe, as Allyson had expected, listened attentively until she finished her account. He sat without commenting for a moment before saying, "We think of the world as round. It's not; it's layered. At the bottom are the poor, the migrants, the refugees, all those suffering and powerless. That's the layer Fatima, Hasan, and the others at Caritas live in." He raised a hand over his head. "At the top, so far above that they don't even know what lies below, are the few who hold the reins of power. These are history's one percent, the Emperors who built the Colosseum and the popes who built St. Peter's. Stroll around the Spanish Steps and you'll see people carrying Gucci and Armani bags as they walk to their Ferraris. Am I right in thinking that this is your colleague's world?"

"Yes, that's a fair description," Allyson agreed. "It makes me wonder what I am. I'm far from poor. I'm a Midwestern American who worked summer jobs, managed to attend college—though with a lot of student loans—and isn't too proud to buy cheap clothes from street-corner vendors here in Rome. And you, Seppe?"

Seppe grimaced. "I envy you being in that middle layer. I think it's only those in the middle who can see who's above them and who's below. As I already told you, I grew up in the same rarified atmosphere as your colleague."

"Except the two of you couldn't be more different," Allyson said.

"I hope that's true, although I haven't completely shed my life of privilege."

"Seppe, you know about the poor and the powerless—and you care about them."

"Then I don't owe that to my family. It was Father Sal, my spiritual confessor, who opened my eyes to what the world calls 'those below.' And to be honest, I hated Caritas the first time I went with him. I remember feeling dizzy. Later, I realized that the reason the rich ignore the poor is that when we see beggars in front of churches or in the subways, we realize, deep down inside, that we might someday fall that far."

The sun was setting over the Janiculum Hill, and the lights of the city were blinking on. "You said 'we' but I know you're not like that, Seppe," Allyson said. "What did your friend do to help you change?"

"The change started when he told me something that sounded crazy. He said that once he stopped pitying the refugees in Caritas, he realized how much they had to teach him. As I said, that didn't make sense until I began to wonder if the disgust I felt in Caritas meant that I was missing out on something, something important." He gazed again at the river. "After that, every time I went to Caritas, a refugee said or did something that showed me what dignity really looks like. I could see it in their eyes."

Seppe reached over and touched Allyson's hand. "That's what your colleague needs from you, Alli."

A jolt passed through her. "Believe me, Seppe, this guy isn't going to take anything from me."

"Maybe not immediately. I'm hoping you'll show him the same sympathy that Father Sal showed me, a sheltered university student. I bet a month ago, your colleague hardly knew places like Caritas existed. I was the same. As I said, for those of us with lots of money, meeting refugees for the first time is like looking over the edge of an abyss. I thought if I didn't get out of Caritas those first few times, I'd fall over that edge. It wasn't until later that I realized God is found among the poor, not the rich like me."

Allyson sat in silence, wondering how the word "God" rolled off Seppe's tongue so naturally. She also wondered if Seppe ever asked himself why a loving God would create a world this unequal, this unfair, a world of mansions and refugee camps.

"It's getting late, and we're going back to the hospital tomorrow to check on Fatima," Seppe said as if he were waking from some spell. "Let me walk you back to your bus stop."

As they strolled along the sidewalk alongside the river, Seppe offered his arm for Allyson to take and said, "I talk too much. I'm sorry."

"It's okay. It's just a lot to think about."

"I suppose it's because I know something of what your colleague is experiencing. And you, Alli—how did you describe yourself, a Midwestern American girl?—you're probably the only person who can help him look over the edge and see what's really down there."

JULY 12
CORPUS CHRISTI HOSPITAL

FATIMA REMAINED TRAPPED IN a landscape without shape, without borders, without a floor, without a ceiling, but something was changing. The blackness of her world had periods when the color shifted to gray, and she could hear muffled sounds, like voices under water.

Even without being able to see images, Fatima knew she had been visited again by the dead—her father and Hasan. Yet when the grayness left, her father and Hasan left her as well. Muffled sounds swirled around her as she felt first cold, then a burning, and finally a sharp pricking somewhere below her. *I must have legs,* she thought, even as she tried to scream.

Then, without warning, she saw as much as heard the words "ana huna Fatima," Arabic for "I am here, Fatima," fly over her in a streak of green and then depart, only to come again, and again. *Someone is here with me. Who?* she wondered.

At times, the streaks of green flashed like strange lightning in her gray world. Yet someone just spoke her name, and that someone was "here," wherever here was.

A few seconds later, as clear as the first message had been, she heard a second phrase in Arabic: "Tell no one about the note."

The note! Yes, I was given a note. Why can't I remember what it said? The phrase "Tell no one about the note," shot through her grayness on another green streak, was repeated, and then repeated a third time.

In the background, Fatima thought she heard words as if from down a

long hallway, words that she didn't understand yet were somewhat familiar. *Italian,* she thought. Then she recognized one of the voices as Professor Napolitano's.

Professor has my note, she remembered. *He's telling me to say nothing about the note. Why?*

She felt an odd sensation of her left arm being raised, raised by someone or something else, not by herself. The same happened to her right arm, followed by her left leg being elevated and finally her right. *I have a body,* she thought, even as she felt a burning on her back.

The space surrounding her changed from gray to tan to white as she heard a scream. She screamed in return before realizing both screams came from her. Other voices, all speaking Italian, now surrounded her as she felt herself rising, rising into the light.

Just when Fatima thought she could rise no farther, her eyes opened.

CHAPTER FOURTEEN

July 13
Caritas Refugee Camp

As Khadija made her bed the next morning, she reviewed the assignments that Chaz had given her. She had to make contact with Hasan's relatives, check into the work of the camp council, and look into Hasan's work with orphans. The first task, to speak with Hasan's relatives, might reveal something in his past in Damascus that would explain his murder. The second task, to check into Hasan's role in the camp, might uncover something in Caritas that he'd stumbled upon, something so serious that it got him killed. The last task was darker, to determine if Hasan had abused the children he worked with.

Deciding to begin with Hasan's relatives in the camp, she returned to the building where she was processed just days before. There, she was relieved to see a woman on the other side of the desk who could have been her relative. She introduced herself before saying, "I'm hoping to make contact with one of my husband's relatives. Before I escaped Damascus, someone told me he could be here."

The woman, who'd introduced herself as Aaeesha, replied in a soft voice, "You have to remember that there are other refugee camps in Italy. Please, what is his name?" she asked as she turned on a computer.

"Hasan Kadir."

The official's face, full of sorrow, looked up at Khadija. "I'm sorry. You must not have heard. Hasan Kadir is dead."

Khadija bowed her head and offered a prayer for the man. *Just because I already knew that, it doesn't mean I can't pray for him.*

The woman reached across and placed her hand on Khadija's. "I'm very sorry."

Khadija nodded. "Was he sick long?"

The official's face showed even more pain. "He was killed. I'm sorry," she repeated a third time. "Please, sit here for a moment. Can I get you some water?"

Khadija sat down and shook her head. "Thank you, no." After what she thought was a suitable pause, Khadija asked, "Is it possible Mr. Kadir had other family members in the camp?"

The woman's face brightened a bit. "I'll be happy to check." She hit a few keys on the computer before retrieving a list from the printer. "Ah, this is good. He has a brother, Faisal; a sister-in-law, Atama; and a nephew, Mahmoon. Here are their camp addresses."

"Thank you," Khadija said and rose from her chair.

"Would you like to bring the families a small gift, perhaps some candy?" the official said.

"Yes, yes, I would, but I have little money," Khadija said truthfully.

Aaeesha shook her head as she rose from her desk and went to a cabinet. "That isn't necessary," she said as she returned with two small boxes. Offering a hug, she said, "Khadija, come back to see me, and please take care of yourself. Do anything you can to avoid illness."

Khadija understood that Aaeesha was reacting to her appearance. "I promise I will," she said, aware as she left the office that even in a refugee camp, she was an object of pity.

She found Atama, Hasan's sister-in-law, mending a well-worn shirt in the family's two-room apartment. The woman appeared to be in her late thirties or early forties, although with one eye drooping above a scar that ran from her jaw to her cheek, she looked twenty years older, When Atama talked, Khadija could see that most of the teeth on one side of her jaw were missing.

After Khadija identified herself, expressed her condolences, and handed the small gift box to the woman, Atama asked Khadija to wait while she called her husband. She walked with a limp out to the second-floor landing, from where she called her husband's name.

In a few moments, a short, balding man with a thick moustache entered the room. As was the traditional custom, he nodded to the female visitor instead of offering to shake her hand. He took the one remaining kitchen chair and positioned it to the side, letting his wife know she should carry on the conversation.

"Khadija's late husband is related to you and Hasan," Atama said. "And one of the camp officials told her about what happened to Hasan. She has brought us candy."

Faisal nodded and accepted the box from his wife, yet he didn't look at Khadija.

Atama went to a kitchen counter, nearly bare, and brought back two photos. "This is Hasan," she said simply. "Does he look like your husband?"

Khadija studied the two pictures. In one of them, someone who looked like an older version of Faisal was sitting formally next to a woman in a professional photo. "That was taken on Hasan and his wife's fiftieth wedding anniversary," Atama explained.

"Yes, I see. They look very . . . very unworried."

"It was before the war," Faisal said. "My brother was a civil engineer."

Khadija nodded before turning to the second photo, this one of a smiling Hasan standing behind a row of children. Caritas's school was in the background.

"Hasan is . . . Hasan was like a grandfather to the orphans," Atama said, her voice little more than a whisper.

"He looks very happy here," Khadija observed.

Faisal cleared his throat yet said nothing. Instead, Atama said, "The children liked Hasan to tell them stories. He did that every day."

"The children must miss him terribly. Such a tragedy," Khadija said.

"It is Allah's will," Faisal said.

"Inshallah," his wife added, again in almost a whisper.

"Inshallah," Khadija said. After a pause, she said, "I understand Hasan was a member of the camp council."

"Hasan was very well respected. Many people, not just Syrians, looked up to him," Atama replied.

"Did his role on the council have something to do with his engineering background?"

"No, no," Atama said. "He was not an engineer here. Hasan was most interested in protecting the orphans."

Khadija wasn't sure how many questions she could ask before arousing suspicion. After Faisal took a piece of candy and passed the box back to his wife, Khadija said, "My late husband was also involved in local politics—before the war, of course. The two were then alike, concerned about others."

Neither Faisal nor his wife replied, leading Khadija to say in as casual a way as she could, "I didn't know the children needed protection. Isn't the camp safe?"

Khadija felt something in the room change as Atama glanced at her husband and then looked down.

"We know nothing about that," Faisal said. His voice, flat and distant to Khadija, did not invite a further response. "Now, please, we have work to do."

Khadija stood, knowing she'd knocked on a dark door and received no response.

Trattoria in Rome

Chaz sat across from Gianni Treni, his contact in the police, at an outdoor table. They'd finished their first beers, and now it was Gianni's turn to pay for the next round.

When the Agency had given Gianni's name to Chaz, they described him as a respected police officer who spoke excellent English. Chaz had met with Gianni weeks before to share non-confidential information of mutual interest. This, however, was the first time he would ask a favor of his counterpart. When Chaz broached the subject of Gianni looking into police files for him, Gianni played dumb. It wasn't until Chaz suggested the Agency could put in a good word to Gianni's superior, highlighting his valued assistance to the Agency, that the policeman's pose faded.

When Gianni returned with two more beers, Chaz offered the clincher. "Perhaps I can promise a training opportunity back in the States with the Agency, the kind we conduct for various police forces."

Gianni took a sip of his beer. "Why would I want more training?"

Chaz smiled. "Because the training will be in Las Vegas, and there will be plenty of free time."

Gianni set his beer down and stared at Chaz. "Seriously?"

"Seriously."

"Let's say that interests me. What do you want from me?"

"I want anything more you have on a refugee named Hasan Kadir."

"What's special about him?"

Chaz leaned forward. "He was murdered in the camp a few weeks ago."

"And the CIA's interest is what?"

Chaz shrugged. "He's a person of interest to us."

"Anything particular that you want me to look for?"

"We're curious about what Kadir was involved in in the camp."

"Do you suspect drugs?"

Chaz shook his head. "It's unlikely. What we do know is that he served on the camp council and worked with orphans."

Gianni nodded. "I think I understand. When do you want this?"

Chaz smiled. "This is the CIA, Gianni. We'd like that info no later than yesterday."

Gianni looked across the street in the direction of two young women talking outside a bakery shop. "Can I bring my wife?"

"Pardon?"

"To Las Vegas. Can my wife come along?"

"I don't know whether to admire you or feel sorry for you, Gianni. Most men don't want to bring their wives to Vegas. That cuts down on the possibilities, if you know what I mean."

Gianni grimaced. "I didn't say that I wanted to bring my wife. I asked if she could come. Everyone knows about Las Vegas, including my wife. If I go, she has to come along."

Chaz laughed. "If that's what it takes, I'm sure I can arrange it. Back to business. When can I see the file?"

"Day after tomorrow. Meet me here."

"Let's make it that morning. I want to bring whatever you uncover to a meeting later that day. My gut tells me there's something."

JULY 14
CARITAS REFUGEE CAMP

KHADIJA DECIDED TO VISIT Hasan's nephew as soon as possible. Not knowing how close the Kadir family was, she didn't want Faisal and Atama giving the nephew prior warning. If, as she suspected, Faisal and Atama had held something back, she hoped the visit to the nephew would fill in the gaps.

The nephew, Mahmoon Kadir, lived as she did, in a dormitory for unmarried refugees. As a woman, she couldn't enter the men's dormitory, which meant she had to ask one of the older men sitting outside the building to help. After a few minutes, the man returned with a younger man who resembled both Faisal and Hasan.

As she handed the box of sweets to the nephew, she explained her husband's connection with Hasan. The nephew was less furtive than Hasan's brother and sister-in-law, which she took as a favorable sign.

"You are from Damascus, then?" Mahmoon asked.

"Not really. My husband was from there. I'm Palestinian. We lived in Damascus when the war started."

"I did not know your husband," Mahmoon said.

Fatima accepted that the comment could stem from genuine curiosity or from suspicion. "He was a distant relative, I believe."

"It is important in the camp to have family, even if they are not close relations," he said.

"Thank you. My husband was part of the White Helmets, and he died in an air raid. I am alone."

Mahmoon looked to the older man. "I accept her as family. Let anyone know who asks."

The older man nodded.

"I have a great respect for the White Helmets. Anyone who would go into a bombed building to find those still alive is one of Allah's chosen," Mahmoon said.

Khadija accepted the condolences by glancing down. "That is why I wanted to meet your uncle. I heard he was a humble man who loved Allah. Then I heard of his tragic death."

Khadija decided to leave out the details of Hasan's death, in the hope that Mahmoon would reveal more than she already knew.

"Hasan was a good man and, yes, a holy man. The one who killed him will burn in hell. Hasan is in paradise."

"Has anyone been arrested for the crime?" she asked.

"No, to the Italians, Hasan was just another refugee. They think they knew my uncle. They did not. Hasan was a respected engineer in Damascus.

He gave me a job and trained me as well." Mahmoon paused and sat up straighter on the bench. "Hasan was our family patriarch and, as I said, a holy man, a man utterly trustworthy. He would never do anything to shame his family." Fatima thought the tone was bitter, yet she knew she had to be careful pressing for further details.

"Of course not," she said. "You must miss him very much. Do the police have any idea why someone would want to kill him?"

At this, Mahmoon's face changed, and Fatima saw the same guardedness that she saw on the faces of Hasan's brother and sister-in-law.

"The police tell us nothing, nothing. There is no reason why anyone would want to kill my uncle. He was . . . he was a holy man," Mahmoon repeated once again.

I may have been accepted as a family member, yet no one trusts me with something they know, she thought.

CHAPTER FIFTEEN

July 14
Corpus Christi Hospital

Allyson's first thought when she returned to the hospital was that something terrible had happened. Doctors and nurses were running down the corridor before turning into Fatima's room. There was so much commotion that Seppe and Allyson were able to approach the doorway to the room before anyone noticed them.

Inside, Fatima jerked wildly on the bed while she was both screaming and choking. Allyson at first feared that she was witnessing a seizure before she noted that Professor Napolitano and a nurse were leaning over Fatima from opposite sides of the bed and talking to her in Arabic. From behind, two nurses pushed Seppe and Allyson aside as they wheeled in a cart of medical equipment.

At a doctor's direction, the nurse closest to Fatima inserted a syringe into an intravenous tube, and Fatima slowly began to calm. The professor and the nurse stepped back as the doctor moved in to shine a light in Fatima's eyes. After a moment, Fatima lay still, her eyes open.

"Explain to her where she is and what happened to her," the doctor instructed Professor Napolitano and the nurse. When the nurse rested her hand on Fatima's forehead and spoke softly to her, Fatima studied her face and said something back.

"She said 'It was dark,'" the nurse relayed to the room.

"Good, that means she's been coming to consciousness slowly," a second doctor said. Turning to one of the other nurses, he said, "Keep the lights low for the next twenty-four hours and the curtains drawn. Over the next two days, bring the lights up slowly. We don't want her to go into shock."

The doctor addressed Professor Napolitano. "Can you stay with her for a bit?"

"Of course, of course."

"What about these two?" the doctor asked, gazing in the direction of Seppe and Allyson.

The professor shrugged. "They're aid workers hoping to talk to her, I think."

The doctor turned to Seppe and Allyson. "Even if you were from the police, you couldn't question her. Not for a day or two. I don't want anything to bring back what happened to her until she's ready."

Seppe edged forward and addressed the professor. "Can we speak to you again when you're free?"

The professor hesitated before nodding.

"We'll be in the lounge," Seppe said, gesturing down the hall.

An hour later, the professor appeared in the lounge. "Fatima is resting." He sat down heavily in one of the vacant chairs and wiped his forehead with a handkerchief.

"Deo gratias," Seppe said.

Professor Napolitano nodded. "Yes, thank God, indeed."

"Did she say anything—about what happened?" Allyson asked.

"The doctor was very clear. I have to let her determine the conversation. She asked if she were in Damascus, if she'd been wounded in an air strike. That was my first clue that she didn't remember much."

"Is there anything we can do?" Seppe asked.

The professor shook his head and looked from Seppe to Allyson before looking back at Fatima's room. "The truth is that for the next few days there's probably little any of us can do. I'll stop by after my class and sit with her. The doctor said that the more Fatima recognizes my face, the more memories of the camp and the assault will come back."

Allyson saw Seppe's expression, and she thought he might have caught the professor's evasive glance away as well. "We'll come back in a couple of days and see how she's doing," she said. "Our agencies will want an update."

The professor shrugged. "If you prefer, I can let you know how she progresses. I assume I can reach you through the Sant Anselmo office," he said, looking at Seppe.

"It's no problem. We'll be happy to come back," Allyson said.

"As you wish," the professor replied before he walked slowly down the hallway to the elevator.

"Ever since you told me about the 'tell,' I've been watching people more carefully," Seppe whispered. "Did I read him right that he was being evasive?"

"I agree, although he's been through a shock." Allyson was still looking down the hallway as the professor entered the elevator. "I think there might be a way for us to find out," she said, as she started to walk down the hallway. When they got to the nurses' station, Allyson caught the attention of the Arabic-speaking nurse.

After explaining Seppe's and her connection with Caritas, Allyson asked if Fatima had said anything about her attack.

The nurse hesitated, then said, "I thought she said something to the professor about a note. Then again, the poor girl hardly knows where she is."

"A note?" Allyson asked. "Did she say what the note was about?"

"No. The professor said she was just rambling. I think the doctor would agree."

Rambling? I'm not convinced, Allyson thought, even as she knew what she must do next. She'd use the Agency's resources to discover who Professor Napolitano really was.

CIA Headquarters

Chaz walked back from his morning meeting with Gianni Treni, knowing he'd struck gold. Morgan and Allyson may have swallowed the camp's portrayal of Kadir as the wise elder dedicated to orphans. He, however, had been wary from the beginning. Wasn't that a lesson he learned early, that anyone with a spotless reputation must be hiding something?

Chaz recalled his feeling of humiliation in the last meeting. Given what Gianni shared with him, however, the only thing that mattered was that everyone in the office would soon view him in a new light, as an agent who could be counted on to focus on facts, not be swayed by sentimental emotions.

He entered the conference room to find one other person present, the new agent. In his previous encounters with her, he'd felt awkward. Her appearance was revolting, her thin body like a sickly child's. He was afraid, and he wasn't sure the fear was irrational, that she could already be carrying disease from her time in Caritas.

Given what he'd brought to the meeting, a feeling of vindication overshadowed his unease. In fact, the glow that he felt throughout his body made the sickly agent nearly invisible. After he nodded in her direction, he was content to sit with his secret.

After a few moments, in which the new agent rubbed at a stain on her robe, Morgan and Allyson entered the room together. For a second, Chaz was bothered by the closeness that was obviously growing between them. Then he remembered that in a few moments, Morgan and Allyson would both be forced to treat him with more respect.

Morgan began by asking the new agent to report on what she'd discovered in the camp. Chaz listened with half an ear until she described her feeling that Hasan's relatives were hiding something.

They sure as hell are, Chaz thought. He knew he could jump in at this point and score his victory, yet he waited, letting the woman's doubts hang in the air.

"What do you make of their evasiveness?" Morgan asked.

Khadija was quiet for a moment before saying, "Maybe Hasan's family is just frustrated. They are convinced the authorities don't care about finding the killer. I think they're also trying to protect the family's honor."

I owe you, Chaz thought. *No one is going to doubt what I've uncovered now.*

"Good work, Khadija," Morgan acknowledged, as she wrote herself a note.

"Who wants to go next?" she asked, looking from Allyson to Chaz.

"Let Allyson go ahead of me," Chaz said with a smile in Allyson's direction.

Allyson looked at him oddly before describing the turn of events at the hospital and what she wanted to know about the professor.

"What makes this interesting is that the professor was probably the last person to speak with Fatima before she was attacked," Allyson said.

"Do you think the professor might have been her attacker?" Khadija asked in a soft voice.

"I'm not sure," Allyson said. "I'm convinced he knows something about a note that he isn't sharing." Closing her file, she looked at Morgan and said, "That's it for me."

Morgan turned her attention to Chaz. "You're awfully quiet. Chaz. Anything to contribute?"

Chaz opened the file he'd brought and ceremonially passed out copies of his report. "I think you'll find this interesting." As the women read the damning one-page report, Chaz took out his Mont Blanc fountain pen and studied it. Yes, this was a moment his grandfather would relish.

Morgan sighed. "Damn it. When was the accusation made?"

Having memorized the memo and researched all the variables, Chaz said, "Two days before his death."

"And it's just the one accusation?" Allyson asked.

"You're missing the point. The accusation that Kadir was a pedophile is supported by convincing evidence."

Morgan sighed. "You're saying someone who worked with him in the school walked in on Kadir with a boy in a bathroom. Kadir acted strangely, as if he and the boy had just done something."

Chaz was pleased to note that Morgan called him Kadir, no longer Hasan. "Notice she also reported that Kadir offered her money not to turn him in."

"Did the authorities confirm that she'd actually received the bribe?" Allyson asked.

Chaz smiled. "Yes, they did. She showed them a twenty Euro note. That much money isn't exactly floating around in the camp."

"Did camp authorities begin an investigation?" Morgan asked.

"They were gathering other statements when Kadir was killed. They did, of course, remove him from working with the children."

"At the bottom of this," Allyson said, pointing to the document, "the report states that Hasan denied all charges."

"The guilty usually do, don't they?" Chaz countered, relishing the moment.

No one said anything as the three agents re-read the report. Finally, Morgan removed her glasses and rubbed the bridge of her nose. "You trust your source, Chaz?"

"My source is a police lieutenant," he explained, smiling again at Allyson.

"Did your source say anything about the police following up on the charge?" Allyson asked brusquely.

"Look, somebody, probably a relative of the boy, killed him. Case solved."

"That's hardly true if Hasan is innocent," Allyson argued.

Chaz realized the exchanges were now between Allyson and him. *Fine by me,* he thought.

"Why the hell would the girl lie?" Chaz asked.

"God, Chaz, I can think of several reasons," Allyson shot back, her face red.

"Such as?"

"Maybe her job performance was poor, and she went on the offensive, accusing him of the worst thing she could think of."

Morgan intervened, "I suspect Khadija can check that out—"

"No, Morgan," Chaz said, cutting her off. "Allyson just said there could be several reasons why the girl lied. She's only offered one. I'd like to hear a second."

Before Allyson could answer, Khadija said in her soft voice, "Perhaps the girl's family and Hasan's have some sort of feud, either in the camp or back in Syria."

Chaz stared at her. *You just lost an ally,* he thought.

"Or," he said in a louder voice, "we can quit acting like we're Kadir's defense attorney and admit the old man was just what he's charged as—he was a pedo."

Stamper raised both hands to silence the room. "Okay, okay, these are all good points. Chaz, see if you can find out anything more from the police. The one fact that we know is that Kadir was killed two days after the accusation was made. That fact leads to three possibilities. One, as Chaz suggests, Kadir's death was an honor killing by the boy's family. If that's the case, then there's no connection between his death and the attack on Fatima Rasul. Two, there is a link between Kadir and Rasul that we still have to find. Allyson, your investigation into this professor could shed some light on that. That leaves us with a third possibility—that the two attacks were simply random acts of violence, which is not something unheard of in refugee camps. Khadija, talk with the other residents. Get a sense of how concerned they are about security at Caritas."

"Or, we could save time and ask security," Chaz suggested.

For a second, Chaz saw Morgan's eyes flash at him. "If safety is a problem at the camp, then the last person who's going to admit that would be the head of security." After an awkward pause, she added in a milder tone, "Chaz, good work with the local police. Keep that channel open."

The praise felt like an afterthought to Chaz, much less effusive than what he deserved. He knew he was the only one in the room who wasn't playing "what if." No, he alone had hard evidence, evidence from an unimpeachable source, and it made Kadir look damned guilty.

JULY 15
CARITAS REFUGEE CAMP

THE NEXT MORNING, KHADIJA presented herself at the school in Caritas to volunteer. That way, she'd be where the accusation against Hasan was made and maybe be near the woman who made it.

As she'd returned to Caritas the previous evening from her supposed medical treatment, she reviewed the meeting with the other three agents in Rome. During the meeting, she found herself wanting to side with Morgan and Allyson and defend Hasan. In the taxi, however, she realized that she'd taken that side of the issue for two reasons that might not be sound. One, because Hasan was a trusted Muslim leader in the camp, she wanted him to be innocent of such a grave sin. And two, Chaz, who'd acted arrogantly in the meeting, intimidated her. She shivered when she remembered the look he gave her after she spoke up.

I have to keep an open mind, she thought. For all his arrogance, Chaz's stance on Hasan at least had solid backing.

Maryam Abdullah, the supervisor of the children's program, was pleased to welcome Khadija as a volunteer, especially when she discovered that Khadija understood basic Italian. Humility, however, wasn't the only reason Khadija downplayed her facility with the language. She thought the Italians who worked in the school might speak more openly if they thought she didn't understand them, yet it was the Arabic-speaking women working in the school who most interested Khadija. Unless Hasan's accuser was no longer at the school, she would be one of the five Syrian women who worked in the school.

Mrs. Abdullah appeared to be in her fifties, a woman with an open face beneath her hijab. She was the age of the children's grandparents, and as she gave Khadija a tour of the facilities, she projected an air of authority. At the end of the tour of the classrooms, she looked Khadija fully in the face as she asked, "Are you a flexible person?" and "Are you willing to admit when what you're doing isn't working?" With both questions, Khadija tried her best to return the woman's eye contact and assure her that she was.

Over tea, Mrs. Abdullah handed Khadija over to one of the other teachers, Daliyah, who worked with the children ages three to five.

With a warm smile, Daliyah said, "I'm relieved to have some help. We've lost three volunteers recently. Please, sit here with me. We'll keep an eye on the children."

Daliyah's hijab was one of the more modest kinds, covering all her hair. Her eyes were bright, and she spoke softly. "I don't know how much Mrs. Abdullah told you. This isn't like schools in Syria," Daliyah explained. "As you can see, girls and boys are in school together, and there is no difference in how or what they are taught. The biggest difference from Syrian schools here, however, is the approach."

"This approach, is it difficult to learn?"

"Not if you're willing to unlearn," Daliyah said.

"I don't understand. What does 'unlearn' mean?"

"Where are you from originally?" Daliyah asked. "You don't sound Syrian."

Khadija blushed. "I'm Palestinian. My husband was from Damascus, though. I lived there before he died."

"I'm sorry. I wouldn't have asked if I had known."

Offering the grieving face of a recent widow, Khadija looked down at her hands. "Thank you," she said. After a pause, she repeated, "What does unlearning mean."

"It means forgetting how you were taught in Palestine—that is, assuming you were allowed to go to school. In most Middle Eastern countries, children are taught by memorizing the Qur'an. The teacher recites a line, and the students repeat it back until they pronounce the words correctly."

"Yes, that's how I was taught," Khadija lied.

"You won't see that here," Daliyah said. "That's what we all had to unlearn to work under Mrs. Abdullah. She's lived in Italy for ten years and has a university degree, you see."

"Ah," Khadija said, the information explaining Mrs. Abdullah's ease in authority.

"Here, everything is different. We don't stand at the front of the room, and the children don't parrot back what we say to them. The children themselves choose what and how they want to learn.

Khadija thought back to what she observed on the tour with Mrs. Abdullah. In every room, the children clustered around a variety of tables, all built at an appropriate height for their ages. She assumed the children were having "free time," a break from their schoolwork. Now she realized she was seeing children learning on their own.

She remembered her own schooling in England, which was based on the opposite belief that children have a natural desire to avoid learning.

"That's what on the tables, tools?"

"Yes, tables have puppets, crayons, chalk, plastic blocks. With the government not giving us much money, we do what we can with what we have. Or maybe the child will stand by one of the easels where there are finger paints and brushes. For example, this morning I read a story to the children about going fishing with a grandparent. After the story, the children chose what table they wanted to go to. That invites them to respond to the story in the way they want."

"What if they did something else at the tables," Khadija asked, "something that had nothing to do with the story?"

"Oh, I like your questions," Daliyah said. "You already see how this works, don't you? Well, if a child uses the tools for another purpose, we believe that's what the child needs to work on. Our main role is paying attention to what the child is trying to learn. We try to help the child achieve that goal—their goal, not ours."

Khadija liked what she was hearing, even though it left her regretting the education she'd received both on the West Bank and in Brixton.

As if Daliyah read her mind, she said, "What we do here has rubbed off on me. Some days, the children teach me. I'm sure I'm a better mother because of it, and my own children are in one of the other classes."

"What does your husband thinks of the program?"

Daliyah looked away for a moment. "Like you, Khadija, I'm a widow. My husband was a hospital administrator in Aleppo. Because of all the wounded, he felt he had to go to work every day, despite the danger. Then, Assad's people gassed the place. The chemical weapons killed nearly everyone inside the hospital."

After they watched the children playing at the tables, Khadija said, "I'm sorry."

"We're all sorry," Daliyeh said as she wiped tears from her eyes. "And thank you for not saying 'Allah's will.' I struggle to believe that Allah willed that my husband and everyone in the hospital should die."

Khadija accepted the risk that Daliyah had taken by sharing such a thought, one Muslim to another. Such honesty could cost Daliyah a lot, and she wished she knew what to say to assure Daliyah that she wouldn't judge her.

"Have I shocked you?" Daliyah said, breaking the silence.

"No, I think people sometimes blame Allah for what they don't understand," she replied. "And that makes me wonder if that doesn't offend Allah rather than praise Him."

Daliyah looked over at Khadija and offered a slight smile. "I think we're going to be friends, Khadija."

Khadija returned the smile, feeling Daliyah was seeing her as someone other than an emaciated refugee. Trying not to be too curious, she said, "I'm puzzled; why would three volunteers leave such a wonderful place to work?"

Daliyah shook her head and sighed. "You must be new here. Some terrible things have happened recently in Caritas. One of our volunteers died and another one is in the hospital. And the third one, her I don't miss. She liked to gossip, and now she's disappeared. Maybe she was transferred to another camp. I don't know, and I don't care."

Khadija assumed Daliyah was describing the worker who accused Hasan. "Was she sent to another camp as a punishment?"

For the first time, Daliyah glanced suspiciously at Khadija. "Help me with the snacks, Khadija, will you?"

CHAPTER SIXTEEN

July 16
A Bar in Trastevere

CHAZ AND HIS POLICE contact, Gianni Treni, sat in at a bar across from the church of Santa Maria in Trastevere. The sun was setting beyond the roofline of the ancient church, and families with their children began strolling by the fountain in the square's center. As if on cue, men from Africa and Southeast Asia appeared, approaching parents and children as they hawked cheap toys.

"When is the seminar in Las Vegas?" Gianni asked.

For a moment, Chaz was confused before he remembered their last meeting. "I'm still checking on the dates," he said, making a mental note to find out when the CIA was in fact offering the next anti-terrorism seminar in the U.S.

"My wife, she is thrilled. She wants to see Penn and Teller. You know them?"

Chaz frowned. "No, are they singers?"

"Magicians. The one is about seven feet tall and does all the talking. The other one is shorter than me," Gianni explained. "He doesn't talk."

"Most men don't go to Vegas for the magic," Chaz said.

Gianni blushed as if he'd been caught out. "Don't forget that my wife comes with me. Her father was a magician, something of a smalltime Houdini."

As long as he was lying, Chaz added to what he promised last time. "You know, it's possible for your wife to see the magicians while you and others from the seminar attend a different kind of show. I am talking about Vegas, after all."

Gianni laughed. "Shh, my wife has spies everywhere."

"Got it. I'll get back to you on the details. Now, what are the police doing about Kadir's death—anything?"

Before answering, Gianni looked around, this time as if he feared their conversation was being overheard. "We're still looking into the connection between his death and the attack on another Syrian a bit later."

"That would be Fatima Rasul," Chaz said.

Gianni looked surprised. "How do you know that? It's not in the file I gave you."

"Hey, I'm in the CIA. There's not much we don't know," Chaz bragged. "Now, back to the investigation. Any link between Kadir and Rasul?"

"With both of them working in the school, they had to know each other. In addition, they both came from Damascus. The second victim is still in a coma, which means we haven't been able to talk with her yet."

Although Chaz knew that Fatima had surfaced from her coma, he didn't think he had an obligation to pass along information that the police would know within a day.

"Okay, Gianni, here's what we should do next. I want you to arrange an interview with the girl who accused Kadir of child abuse. She must know the Rasul woman if they worked in the school. I want to be there for the interview, although I'll be in the background."

Gianni looked around again and sat forward. "Not possible, Chaz, she's gone."

"What do you mean, 'gone?'"

"Just that," Gianni said with a shrug. "Refugees get shifted from one camp to another, or maybe she ran away."

Feeling frustrated, Chaz said, "To go where? You're not telling me that a girl who speaks only Arabic can just walk out of a camp and survive in Italy."

"Maybe she had help," Gianni said. "It's easy for traffickers to lure girls out of the camps. They make big promises—money, jobs, or gifts."

Promises like going to Vegas, Chaz thought. Instead, he said, "You're saying prostitution?"

Gianni shrugged again. "Maybe. Unfortunately, she could be anywhere, maybe no longer in the country. Why does it matter? She turned Kadir in, and now he's dead."

Chaz knew what that meant. The local police weren't going to invest anything in finding the girl. His motivation, however, was personal. He wanted the girl to share the details of what she saw Kadir and the boy doing. That would give him the opportunity to throw what he learned in the faces of Allyson, Morgan, and Khadija.

"Can we at least interview the boy who was involved?" Chaz asked.

Again, Gianni shook his head. "The girl who reported it said she didn't know the name of the boy. Anyway, we didn't need the boy. The money Kadir gave her was enough proof for us to investigate. Unfortunately, Kadir died before we got any further."

"It sounds like you have nothing for me," Chaz said as he sat back and looked over at a family being approached by a balloon seller.

"Just a minute, Chaz. Please, I beg you. I still have something," Gianni said.

Chaz turned back to Gianni, who looked as if his Las Vegas junket were about to fly away like one of the balloons.

"I'm listening," Chaz said without warmth, wanting Gianni to squirm.

"The girl who accused Kadir, she has a sister in the camp. We can question her. Maybe she knows where her sister is."

Chaz took a sip of his beer and thought about the offer. "Or maybe she told her sister about Kadir. Okay, set the meeting up, and we'll hope she knows something. The Agency has to have something concrete, Gianni."

Gianni exhaled as if he had barely passed some test.

Chaz's Apartment

Later that evening, Chaz watched the AC Milan and Roma match on TV while his brain bounced back and forth between two issues. One, it'd been weeks since anyone shared his bed. His problem was that the pickings were slim in Rome. Despite beautiful women being everywhere, he knew only enough Italian to order drinks and read maps. In addition, Italian women knew nothing about Brown University, lacrosse, or summer homes in the Berkshires. That left him being just an English-speaking male, attractive by American standards, yet no competition for local male competition.

He'd sampled the bars frequented by the numerous American college students studying in Rome for the chaperones, not for the college-age females. To his dismay, he found those women either too old or too preoccupied with worry for their young charges. Only once had he hooked up with an American who came to Italy in the hope of a romantic fling away from her dull married life at home. Even with her, he felt her fantasy was for an Italian stud, a Fabio, rather than another American.

That left the pool of women attached to the Agency as his best bet. The divorcees tended to pursue him in such a needy way that he had no interest. He preferred to pursue, not be pursued. Morgan came across as a career woman, meaning she'd do nothing to jeopardize her prospects for advancement. He figured if she had an active sex life, she restricted it for men in the Agency above her on the ladder.

That was what made his relationship with Allyson frustrating. When he first met her, he predicted that they'd hook up within a week, two at the most. He found her attractive by American standards and intelligent, though too serious. He assumed that when she looked at him, she'd see him as he saw himself—an Ivy League preppy with money and a desire to spend it having fun abroad.

The situation should have been perfect, which only made Allyson's coldness more frustrating. Because he could think of nothing wrong with his approach, he felt she was deliberately withholding something he had a right to expect. She also projected the feeling that she was interested in someone else, someone she wouldn't talk about. That only added to his slow burn.

That left Sally, Allyson's roommate. She was less frosty toward him in the office over the past two days, and he wondered if it was time to try again. Besides the opportunity for regular sex, sleeping with Sally was bound to irritate Allyson. With a grin, he pictured coming out of Sally's bedroom in the morning and running into Allyson in the kitchen. "Oh, hello. Fancy meeting you here," he'd say with a smile.

AC Milan was up by two goals, and Chaz could see that Roma wasn't their equal. That gave him time to consider the second issue on his mind, an issue that could also achieve his goal of frustrating Allyson.

Gianni's hunger to escape Italy for Las Vegas, even with his wife tagging along, made Chaz feel certain that the policeman would arrange the interview in Caritas. To be included in that meeting meant that he had to get Morgan's permission to enter Caritas. As he pictured himself making that request, he imagined Morgan replying that Khadija was better positioned to make the contact.

Chaz's training as a Navy Seal taught him respect for the chain of command, yet it also encouraged initiative when unexpected opportunities arose, and wasn't that the situation now? His relationship with Gianni must be preserved, and what harm would it do for him to be inside the camp for two hours at the most? From the size of Caritas, he knew that his chances of running into Khadija were minimal. He could enter the camp, participate in the interview, and leave without anyone in the Agency ever knowing. When he updated Morgan, Allyson, and Khadija, he would present the findings as the police's.

The added bonus of his plan was that he'd have the satisfaction of operating as an agent capable of working on his own, an agent with initiative. If he presented proof of Kadir's crime, that would crush Allyson's bleeding-heart support for a child molester.

CHAPTER SEVENTEEN

July 17
Allyson's Apartment

ALLYSON AWOKE THE NEXT morning from a troubling dream in which Chaz and Seppe were both arguing over her. Chaz was yelling at Seppe, claiming Allyson was a tease. Seppe was calmer—*of course, why wouldn't he be*? Allyson thought—replying that Chaz didn't really know Allyson. To that, Chaz replied, "Whose fault is that?"

Whose fault is that, indeed? Allyson thought, as she sat up in bed and heard Sally in the kitchen. She knew what had prompted the nightmare—Seppe's belief that she was the only person who could help Chaz understand the plight of refugees. What Seppe didn't understand was that anything she might say to Chaz would likely backfire. Chaz would misconstrue her interest in him, leaving her wide open again to his slimy advances.

In the kitchen, Sally looked up from her bowl of muesli to say, "Do you know you talk in your sleep?"

Allyson looked at her. "No, I don't . . . do I?" Trying to look unconcerned, she opened the fridge and, with her back to her roommate, said, "What did I supposedly say?"

"'Supposedly' nothing. You kept saying over and over again, 'No, no,' and 'I can't, I can't,'" Sally replied. It sounded like you were being . . . you know, assaulted. I was wondering if—"

Allyson turned to stare at her roommate. "It wasn't a flashback, if that's what you're getting at. I've never been assaulted, although we both knew guys who tried to go too far. I was probably dreaming about your spaghetti. I was saying 'no, no' and 'I can't,' meaning I can't eat any more."

"There was nothing wrong with my spaghetti," Sally said. "Remember, I'm the one who makes an effort to cook. You'd order out for pizza every night if you could."

"Don't you think it's a crime to cook when some of the best food in the world is all around us?"

Sally shrugged before saying, "Chaz asked me out again."

Allyson stared at her roommate.

"What's that look supposed to mean?" Sally asked.

"It's nothing," Allyson lied. It wasn't bad enough that she'd dreamt about Chaz. Now, when she was barely awake, Chaz had as much as barged into their kitchen.

"I thought you were going to upchuck there for a minute," Sally said. "It's only for drinks."

"Only for drinks," Allyson repeated. "I'm pretty sure that's not how Chaz will see the evening."

Sally brought her breakfast dishes over to the sink and began to rinse them. "Look, Alli, you and I are never going to agree on this. If Chaz were the last man on earth, you still wouldn't sleep with him. Whereas for little old me, Chaz *is* the last man on earth . . . to ask me out. I mean honestly, Allyson," Sally said, as she squared herself to look at her roommate, "are you telling me, when you were assigned to Rome, that you never thought of hooking up with a hot Italian?"

Allyson placed the back of her hand on Sally's forehead.

"What's that for?" Sally said.

"I'm just checking if you have a fever and are delusional. You're confusing Chaz with a hot Italian."

"Very funny. Your 'hot Italian' prefers celibacy. Given the choice, I'll take Chaz for a one-nighter anytime."

"If I knew how to pray, I'd pray that you'd wake up, Sally."

"Don't worry about that. I'll wake up tomorrow. It's just a question of where I'll wake up."

Caritas Refugee Camp School

At ten-thirty every morning, the children in the school were offered snacks, usually fruit juice and either bread and peanut butter or cookies. By her third day at the school, the twenty children in the class began to treat her as if she'd always been there. They called her Khadija, pronouncing the Muslim name far more accurately than her schoolmates back in England, and pulled on her ankle-length chador whenever they wanted something.

The school's current rule mandated that an adult be in the room with the children at all times. Khadija wondered if the rule had been put into place because of the accusation made against Hasan.

What Khadija dreaded was the expectation that she sit with the children during snack time. Her stomach knotted as she tried to smile as the children stuffed cookies into their mouths and guzzled fruit juice.

It was what happened on the second day, however, that disoriented her. At the small table where she sat with four of the children, a five-year-old girl rose from her tiny chair and presented, almost as a gift, a cookie to Khadija. Khadija declined politely, yet the girl was adamant. Before Khadija could stop her, the little girl had pushed the cookie into her mouth.

"Make it disappear, make it disappear," the girl said, clapping her hands and laughing. *Oh, I can make it disappear,* Khadija thought, before she remembered that her identity in the camp as a widow from Damascus wouldn't refuse the cookie. She chewed the cookie and swallowed it, even as she lied by saying, "Hmm, that's good."

When Khadija was a child, her mother had set food in front of her and said, "Eat, now; you have to eat" as she sat across from Khadija and watched her intently. In primary school, she sat alone in the cafeteria, the girl in a hijab who "ate crazy Arab food," according to her classmates. When her eating disorder picked up momentum in her teens, meals became a time of suspicion, whether she was at school or at home, a test she could never pass.

Yet this cookie had been given to her by a child, a five-year-old who treated cookies as a gift. To the child, eating was a magical act. Food was never magical in Khadija's family. Rather, food was the family's proof that they'd escaped the poverty of the West Bank and the refugee camp in Jordan.

Today, her third day in the camp, she feared the child's game would spread to other children. Her fear was realized when another child put a piece of bread with peanut-butter into Khadija's mouth and, laughing, told her to make it disappear. Overcoming the urge to choke, she chewed the morsel until she could swallow it, while the children at the table laughed again and clapped.

"They quite like your game, Khadija," Daliyah said, sitting at another table. "Ask them to do magic with their own snacks."

This is not me, Khadija thought. *This is another Khadija, a widow from Syria who has no eating disorder and who can even encourage others to eat.*

Not that the children's game changed her behavior in the camp's dining hall. There she continued to barely touch her food and purge after meals in the secrecy of a bathroom in her dormitory. This was the only Khadija she'd ever known, the girl and young woman who could never look at food without seeing the sneers of schoolmates, or worse, her mother's accusing face. She remembered her mother gripping the sides of her plate whenever she ate, as if someone could wrench it from her hands if she let down her guard.

Somehow, however, that wasn't how Khadija felt with the children's game. For the first time in her life when she was in the presence of food, she wasn't watching herself. Instead, she was only aware of the delight on the children's faces.

Asha Malik's Apartment, Caritas Refugee Camp

Later that day, Chaz left the CIA offices early, explaining that he had a meeting with his police contact. There was nothing untrue in that explanation, yet what he left out was that he would accompany Gianni to Caritas for the interview with Asha Malik, sister of Jameela Malik, the woman who'd reported on Kadir and had now disappeared.

Not knowing what to expect in the camp, he was unprepared for the children mobbing Gianni and him as they walked through the gate. Chaz hadn't gone more than ten yards before children as young as five or six and as old as eleven or twelve pulled on his pant leg or sleeve asking for candy and money. He looked over at Gianni, who was handing out change to the younger ones and shaking off the older ones.

The hands touching him first on one leg or sleeve, then the other, irritated him, and he quickened his pace as if he could leave the discomfort behind. More children, however, came from all directions as he searched his pockets for loose change. The children somehow knew that Gianni was Italian and the American was a mystery, for he heard "per favore" from those surrounding Gianni and "please, mister" and "candy" from those hovering around him.

At the thought of germs assailing him with every touch, he used both arms to swat away the hands. As he swatted, one of the smaller boys fell to the ground, which brought loud calls and gestures from older residents watching from nearly benches. For a second, he felt dizzy as if he too would end up on the ground. Guiltily, Chaz stooped down and helped the boy to his feet, the child running tearfully away in the direction of the adults.

Seeing what happened, Gianni told Chaz to head for the big, white-washed building ahead of them as he appeased the children by handing out coins before he too moved in that direction.

"You should have warned me," Chaz said after they reached the administration building.

"I thought you knew what these camps are like," Gianni said, also panting.

"My first visit," Chaz explained, even as he promised himself it would be his last. He had never liked crowds because they made him feel small, and he'd found crowds of children even worse, because he always struggled to know what to say to them. These children, who knew only the phrases "please, mister" and "candy," had given him no space to breathe, their grubby hands touching him all over.

Beggars, that's what they'll grow up to be, he thought, as he pictured the olive-skinned kids joining the gangs who pickpocketed outside Rome's tourist attractions and pleaded for money in the subways. Again, he felt dizzy as he thought, *They'll keep coming and coming, and every nation welcoming them is going to sink beneath their weight.*

As a Muslim woman rose to meet them, Chaz nodded, not bothering to catch her name when Gianni introduced him. Chaz's one request—no, a demand—was that they avoid the swarms of children milling about in the open area outside.

Chaz's face reddened when the translator stared at him as if he were a new species in a zoo. His embarrassment turned to anger as he thought of how ineffective and pointless camps like Caritas were. In offering just enough food, shelter, and medical care for refugees to stay alive, these camps perpetrated the lie that the world cares about them. No, the best future these refugees could hope for would be working in the worst jobs, living the life of bottom feeders.

Gianni and Chaz followed the woman out the back door of the facility and moved along the periphery of the camp until they arrived at a series of apartments. That morning, Chaz had studied the photograph of Jameela Malik, an eighteen-year-old who looked healthier than he'd expected. He read that Jameela and her sister, Asha, were originally from a Syrian village near the Turkish border and had been in two camps before coming to Caritas. He also noted that the sisters had been removed from their last camp because Jameela had gotten into several fights. *Does that make her accusation against Kadir less credible?* he thought. Remembering how much the children had reminded him of rats, he thought fighting couldn't be that rare in camps such as Caritas—and given that the photo of Jameela revealed an attractive girl, with a smiling face and no hijab, he thought it probable that the fight was over a man.

On the way to the apartments, the translator cautioned the two men that Asha, as a good Muslim, wouldn't shake their hands. Instead, the men should bow politely in the woman's direction and not expect the woman to even make eye contact with them.

The young woman who opened the door, however, was clearly not shy. Without a hijab, Asha Malik's black hair glistened, and unlike the translator, Asha wore both eye shadow and lipstick.

Chaz forgot the grubby children, finding himself aroused as Asha, looking both men full in the face, invited them into her apartment. On a low table, Asha had already set out a tray of tea and simple crackers. When Gianni introduced themselves and offered his appreciation for Asha's willingness to meet with them, the woman replied in a strong voice. The translator looked surprised by what the woman said, and it wasn't until she translated her words into English that Chaz realized why.

"Visitors break the boredom of the camp, and I like meeting Americans," Asha had said, smiling at Chaz. He smiled back at her and imagined having drinks with Asha that evening instead of with Sally. Yes, he sensed the two of them wouldn't require a translator to understood each other.

Gianni was also impressed by Asha as, stammering, he began to ask his questions. "Do you know where your sister is now?"

Asha shrugged, and after she spoke to the translator, the translator said, "Maybe in another camp. Maybe she ran away."

"How could she run away? Did Jameela know anyone in Italy outside the camp?"

Asha smiled. "Jameela is a friendly person. She likes to meet Italians who come to the camp."

"Do you mean aid workers?" Gianni asked.

"Yes, sure. Also the men who bring deliveries."

The translator's tone told Chaz that she did not approve of Asha's forwardness. Chaz, however, approved of Asha very much.

"Did your sister tell you about the accusation she made against Mr. Hasan Kadir, a fellow worker at the school?" Gianni asked.

Asha took a sip of tea as she listened to the question being translated. "Yes, she told me about that dog," she said.

Gianni nodded. "Did your sister tell you what she saw?"

Asha started to answer before the translator had completed the entire question. "That man was evil, and he deserved to be arrested."

Chaz leaned forward. "May I call you Asha?"

The translator shook her head at the inappropriateness of the question, yet Asha apparently understood a bit of English. "Yes, please, mister," she said, smiling.

"Asha, did Jameela leave the camp before or after Kadir was killed?" he asked, studying her face.

The question was apparently too complicated for Asha. After it was translated, she replied, "He deserved to die."

Chaz asked the translator to repeat his question, pointing out that he wasn't accusing Jameela of the murder. Instead, he wanted to know when Jameela left Caritas.

A long back-and-forth between Asha and the translator followed, and finally the translator said, "Jameela left two days before the man was killed. Asha says she couldn't have killed him."

Chaz nodded in Gianni's direction. Gianni referred to his notes and asked, "Did Jameela tell you the name of the boy involved in the incident?"

"No, Jameela said the security officer told her that she shouldn't tell anyone the name of the boy. She just told me the name of Kadir."

Gianni nodded when Chaz asked him if he could ask another question. "Does your sister Jameela usually tell the truth?" he asked.

While Chaz could see that the translator again disapproved of his question, he wanted to challenge Asha and insisted that she relay the question as he'd stated it.

Asha Malik's eyes flashed when she understood the question. In a strident voice, she offered a long reply.

"She asked who said her sister is a liar," the translator said.

"Tell her that I'm not calling Jameela a liar. I just want to know if her sister told the truth this time."

After another exchange that was equally heated, the translator said, "Jameela told the truth this time and at all times. She asks, why would her sister lie?"

Chaz continued to hold Asha's gaze. "Did Jameela show you the twenty euros that she said came from Kadir?" he asked.

Once the question was translated, Asha Malik laughed before answering.

"Twenty euros? It was two hundred euros," the translator said.

Chaz exchanged a glance with Gianni and then asked, "Kadir gave her two hundred euros to be quiet?"

"Jameela showed me the money. Yes, it must have been from Kadir."

Although Chaz knew that the answer was an assumption, not a proven fact, he let it go. Where would Kadir get that kind of money except through crime?

On the return trip to Rome, Gianni and Chaz spent most of the time talking about Asha. Both men noted that with her sister gone, Asha had somehow been allowed to remain in the two-bedroom apartment instead of being moved to a dormitory.

"Two hundred euros. That sounds like serious hush money," Chaz said.

"That's assuming Jameela told her sister the truth, and I don't just mean about the bribe," Gianni replied. "Of course, the money would have made her running away from the camp more likely."

Chaz agreed. "If Jameela is like her sister, she could have convinced a delivery guy to help her. We both know she's not on her own," Chaz said. "Any chance you can trace her?"

Gianni shook his head. "I can't see my department doing that. Wandering away from camps like Caritas isn't unheard of."

Exiting Gianni's car, Chaz was still picturing Asha's face when a jolt of panic ran through his body. He slapped at his shirt, his hand understanding what it had taken his brain a few more seconds to register. He reopened the car door and scanned the seat and the floor.

"What is it?" Gianni asked.

"My Mont Blanc. I don't have my Mont Blanc."

"What's a Mont Blanc?"

"It's a fountain pen. It's a gift from my grandfather. It's my . . . I can't explain."

While Chaz swore as he continued to search under and behind the seat, Gianni looked in the space between the passenger seats and then on the floor of the car.

"Sorry, I have to go, Chaz. It's just a pen, right?" he asked.

Chaz groaned as he stood by the side of the departing car. "If you only knew."

CHAPTER EIGHTEEN

Corpus Christi Hospital

THAT SAME AFTERNOON, AS Allyson and Seppe walked together to the hospital, she said, "A colleague of mine in Europa Spec has a drinking buddy in the police. He found out that Hasan's accuser is someone named Jameela Malik. He also learned that she's no longer in the camp."

"You *are* a detective," Seppe said, obviously impressed.

"Just lucky to know someone who knows someone," Allyson replied, "although I'm not saying we should assume the accusation is true."

"True or false, it could still explain why he was killed," Seppe said.

"Now who's talking like a detective?" Allyson said, smiling at Seppe. "And you're right, especially with Hasan's death coming only two days after the accusation was made. Until Fatima talks to us, we won't know if her attack has anything to do with his death."

Seppe paused outside the entrance of the hospital. "Does your colleague know how the police are viewing Hasan's death?"

Allyson didn't respond immediately, wondering how much to share. Remembering the advice given to FBI agents, that it's safer to tell as much of the truth as possible, she said, "From what I was told, they're treating Hasan's death as an honor killing."

"That makes sense, although that rules out a connection between the two attacks," Seppe said, sounding disappointed. "Let's see what Fatima can tell us."

Allyson walked into the reception area of the hospital, feeling nervous after the brief conversation with Seppe. *How long before I slip up and Seppe discovers he's put his trust in the wrong person?* she thought.

July 18
Caritas Refugee Camp

I saw him. I'm sure I saw him. Khadija tried to make sense of who she saw outside the dorm window—Chaz Eaton walking with two others toward the apartments.

She wondered if she missed something in the last case review session that would explain why Chaz, the agent who frightened her, would be in the camp. Although she knew that Allyson came to the camp several times each week to conduct intake interviews, she couldn't believe that Morgan gave Chaz permission to enter the camp.

Her mind reeled with the possible "what-if" consequences of such exposure. A man had been killed in the camp; another refugee had been nearly killed. The attacker was probably still in the camp and would be on the lookout for anything out of the ordinary. Did Chaz know he was putting her in danger?

How do I know he hasn't already blown my cover? she asked herself as her breathing caught in her throat. If she trusted Chaz, she might not be concerned. He clearly tried to intimidate her in the meetings, and he succeeded. Not knowing what brought him to Caritas, Khadija feared the worst, that the wrong people in Caritas knew that she a spy, not a refugee.

July 18
Chaz's Apartment

The Mont Blanc pen that disappeared in Caritas camp was not, as Gianni had put it, "just a pen." The pen was a link to his grandfather, Rhys Pendarvis, a Cornish immigrant who settled in Maine in the 1930s. A miner in Cornwall, he came to America to make his fortune any way he could, as long as the work was above ground—and he had made a fortune, first as a stunt pilot during Prohibition, flying low along the coast up to

Nova Scotia to pick up cases of whisky and gin, and later transforming the makeshift airfield he'd created into a prosperous regional airport.

When Chaz was admitted to Brown University, his grandfather took him aside and gave him the Mont Blanc Meisterstuck 149 fountain pen. "This isn't a dog-eat-dog world, Chaz," he told him. "It's a wolf-eat-deer world. It's even a wolf-eat-wolves world. Now, this Mont Blanc is the finest fountain pen in the world. It was given to me when they named the airport in my honor. They didn't give me this pen or name the airport after me because they loved me; no, they did that because they respected me, and yes, feared me. I'm now giving you this pen. However, what I'm really giving you is an edge. When you hold this pen—even when you simply look at it—remember that you're only safe if you're the top wolf. Always attack the other wolves before they attack you."

Now, as Chaz dressed for his date with Sally, he pictured the Mont Blanc somewhere in the camp, being passed around, played with, and ultimately destroyed by the kids who couldn't keep their hands off him. The more he thought about it, the less he blamed himself. No, what had happened was no accident, no careless misplacing of the pen. Because he'd brought no candy to distribute, one of the orphans had intentionally robbed him.

He felt his grandfather's anger joining his own as the pen was probably lost forever. Such a treasure shouldn't have such an ignominious end, in a refugee camp of all places. He wasn't sure where to place his anger—all the faces of the children blended together. Eventually, he decided to blame Allyson. Had she accepted the obvious, that Kadir was a pedophile, there would have been no need for him to sneak into the camp, no need to be surrounded by a swarm of filthy kids, and no need for him to meet Asha Malik, whose beauty was fading quickly as he grieved and seethed.

Chaz knew his grandfather wouldn't want him to waste his anger. No, Rhys Pendarvis would want his grandson to make good use of the rage. Chaz would see to it that Allyson was humiliated before she returned to the FBI, and he would try, even if the odds were against him, to somehow get the Mont Blanc Meisterstuck back.

July 19
Corpus Christi Hospital

Fatima looked up to see two young people enter her room along with the Arabic-speaking nurse, Miriam. The man looked vaguely familiar, while the woman's robust health made her look foreign, American, she guessed. Drawing the bed sheet up under her chin, she thought, *Why are they visiting me?*

The pain in her head was easing with every day, and she was getting used to the nurses spoiling her. Because the dressing on her scalp was changed daily, she was without her hijab. That had initially made her feel exposed. Now she wondered if she'd wear the hijab once she was released from the hospital.

When Miriam introduced the two visitors as aid workers from Caritas, she remembered the man with the gentle smile and relaxed a bit. The face of the woman was also kind, and Fatima wondered if the two were a couple.

"Given what you've been through, you look remarkably well," the man named Seppe said, as he brought chairs to the side of Fatima's bed.

"You're an aid worker at Caritas, aren't you?" Fatima replied.

"Ah, you have a good memory. And this is another aid worker, Allyson Worthy."

"Have I seen you in Caritas too?"

"I don't think so," Allyson replied.

"I was attacked," Fatima said, as much to herself as to her two visitors.

"Yes, you were," Seppe said. "Thank God you made it through."

"Inshallah, it is Allah's will," Fatima replied. She had a vague sense she should be careful what she told the two aid workers, yet she had no clue why she felt that way.

"Have they given you any idea when you'll return to Caritas?" Seppe asked.

Do I have to go back there? Fatima thought as she clutched the bed sheet.

"It's too soon to tell," the nurse answered.

Seppe nodded that he understood.

Allyson leaned forward and, with a smile, asked, "We won't stay long, Fatima. We want to know if you remember Hasan Kadir."

Fatima felt a twitch near her head wound. *Hasan Kadir. Hasan Kadir. Yes, I remember him. He was attacked. I was attacked. He died. I only thought I died.*

"Hasan and I worked together at the school," Fatima said.

"Do you remember Hasan being dismissed from the school?" Seppe asked.

"No, no," Fatima said, yet sensing that wasn't true.

"Do you remember another worker named Jameela Malik?"

"Is Jameela okay?" she asked.

"We don't know. Jameela left the camp," the woman replied.

"Why would Jameela leave?" Fatima asked.

"We don't know," Allyson said.

"Jameela worked with Hasan, right?" Seppe asked.

Didn't Jameela hate him? Why did she hate him? Fatima thought. "I can't remember," she said, closing her eyes.

Miriam said something to the aid workers that caused them to stand.

"One more question," Allyson asked. "Did someone give you a note, or maybe you gave someone a note?"

Danger, danger! Don't answer that, Fatima heard a voice in her head. *Yes, there was a note, and I did give it to someone. I wonder who.*

"No, I don't remember a note," Fatima said, her eyes still closed.

"Okay," Seppe said. "Rest and be well. We'll stop back when you're feeling better."

CHAPTER NINETEEN

Restaurant in Rome

EVEN THOUGH CHAZ HAD lost his fountain pen, he was determined to push through the evening with Sally. He had an image to preserve, after all, and that meant impressing the woman across the table. Sally once again wore a low-cut top, which he took as permission to admire. His mind had other ideas, however, as he found himself wondering where his treasured pen was at that moment. He felt as if a part of him, an important part of him, was imprisoned in the camp.

"You look a million miles away, Chaz."

"Huh? Sorry, my bad," Chaz said, raising the bottle of Valpolicella to top up Sally's glass, then his own. "I was just thinking how tired I am of this whole damned refugee thing."

"Well, investigating Mafia links with drug lords in the U.S. might sound romantic. Let me tell you, it's not. Most days, I spend my time studying shipping manifests," Sally said.

"Oh, come on. You must have moments when you stop a shipment or uncover names. What's frustrating about this refugee business is that there's nothing the Agency—any agency—can do to change anything. No matter what I do or any of us do, they'll just keep coming and coming."

"It's funny; Alli says she likes it," Sally said.

Alli. The last time he sat across the table from Sally, with her breasts thrust toward him as now, he tried to steer the conversation to talk about

Allyson. Tonight, Allyson was the last person he wanted to think about.

"Allyson should have been a social worker. Sometimes I shake my head, wondering what the FBI was thinking when they chose her," he said, immediately aware of how bitter he sounded. "I'd appreciate it if we kept that between the two of us, Sally."

Sally smiled as if she enjoyed keeping the secret, then leaned forward even more. "Everything must feel boring after the Navy Seals."

Chaz gazed at the crystal pendent hanging between her breasts. *She wants more wine, a good dinner, a bunch of war stories, and then . . . to bed we go.* However, the question, "Is that what I want?" wasn't one he normally asked himself. He always desired the chase, the attention, and the ultimate reward for his effort. Then why was the thought of all that nauseating tonight?

Caritas Refugee Camp

That same evening, Khadija was invited to Daliyeh's one-room apartment for dinner. Khadija made a habit of declining invitations that included food, yet this night would be an exception, because Daliyeh might share what she knew about Hasan, Fatima, and Jameela if Khadija wasn't too obvious. Thankfully, Daliyeh had prepared a simple meal of cucumber salad, hummus, and pita bread along with tea.

Also making the evening less threatening were Daliyeh's children, Mikal and Karina, twin six-year-olds, who Khadija knew from school. In fact, the evening had the same safe feeling of the school, so much so that when Karina picked up an olive from her plate and danced around the table to put it into Khadija's mouth, Khadija was able to laugh. Apparently, the twins had heard about the game played with the snacks in their mother's classroom. *Is it wishful thinking to imagine that my eating disorder would loosen its grip if a smiling child with no judgment fed me every day?*

After supper, the twins vied with each other for Khadija's attention to their toys—few, though obviously well-loved. Karina proudly showed Khadija the small white house with red shutters that she'd made with Lego blocks. Mikal, more passive than his sister, tugged at her chador until she opened his Italian pop-up picture book and read to him.

An hour later, with the twins finally in bed, the women returned to the kitchen for more tea.

"If you don't mind," Daliyeh said, "let's not talk about the past, how we got here. It's always a tale of pain and death, or an account of how good life was in Syria before the war. For my children and me, this is now home. I don't want Karina and Mikal to spend the rest of their lives chained to a past they can't change."

"That's wise," Khadija said, relieved that she wouldn't have to relate the Agency's cover story yet again.

"Tell me what your plans are for the future, Khadija."

Khadija felt a wave of panic, as she realized the previous moment of relief was just that, a moment. The Agency had never constructed a fictitious future for her, meaning she'd have to think of something off the top of her head. She took a deep breath and realized that the way through her predicament would be to share her actual dreams for life after the Agency.

"If I learn more languages, I can open up a translation business," she said, hiding the fact that she'd already completed many of those studies.

"Here in Italy?"

"Somewhere in Europe and certainly not back in Syria. As you said, this is home now."

"And marriage?" Daliyeh asked.

Khadija felt her face redden as she shook her head. "Men aren't interested in me." She expected Daliyeh to object, to repeat what her mother always said, that the right man would come along. Yet Daliyeh just nodded.

"What about you?" Khadija asked, happy to shift the focus.

Daliyeh pursed her lips as she looked down on the small Lego house and the pop-up book. "It's hard to say when a dream is impossible, isn't it? What I know for sure is that I want my future to be what I want, not what someone else is willing to give me. I've thought about being a seamstress or running a laundromat. That way the twins and I can have a place of our own."

"Here in Italy?"

"That's my plan, although the language is hard for me." Daliyeh paused for a moment. "My plans will take money, which means there are decisions," pausing again as she looked down at her hands, "I have to make."

Khadija was silent, hoping Daliyeh would explain what she meant.

"Do you know what I'm talking about?" Daliyeh asked, in little more than a whisper.

"No, sorry."

Daliyeh sighed as she slowly shook her head. "People think everyone in Caritas is poor. That's not true. Think about it, Khadija. You have a bed in a crowded dormitory, and I live in this tiny place while the girl you're replacing at the school lived in a two-bedroom apartment with her sister. Why is that? I know a man in camp who has no job at all here, yet he always has at least a hundred euros in his pocket. Do you see what I'm saying?"

Khadija had noticed that some of the school children wore newer clothes than the others, and one boy bragged of having a new soccer ball. She'd assumed, however, that this was related to the different levels of poverty in Caritas.

"Tell me about the girl I replaced, the one with the apartment with her sister," she asked.

Daliyeh took a sip of tea. "Her name is Jameela. She knew what she wanted, and she was prepared to do whatever it would take to get that. Although I didn't like her, I respected her. I remember when I first realized that she had more money than me. I looked down and saw her shoes. They were new, and I mean brand new, not the castoffs we're given here. Then one day I saw that she had a watch, and it was a nice one, a woman's, not some used man's watch. And I thought, how did she get a watch?"

"Did you ask her?"

Daliyeh nodded. "One day, when we were in the bathroom together, I saw her take the watch off before washing her hands. When I asked where she got it, she just smiled and said, 'You just have to know the right people.'"

Daliyeh paused, as if to let that picture sink in before she continued. "Of course that made me think about my kids and this tiny place. I said, 'Can you introduce me to these people?'"

Khadija knew that every camp had a black-market system, yet there was a big difference between a few more cigarettes and a watch and a two-bedroom apartment. "Did Jameela do that—introduce you to these people?"

Daliyeh shrugged. "She introduced me to someone who knew the right people. It was a woman, and I recognized her as someone others in the camp are afraid of. She asked me, 'What do you want, and what are you prepared to do to get it?' She said it just like that. I told her I was trying to save up money to open a business when my family got out of Caritas. I thought she'd laugh in my face. Instead, just smiled and said, 'We can help you.'"

"What did she say about what you were prepared to do?" Khadija asked.

Daliyeh sighed. "I was afraid she was going to tell me I'd have to offer sex. I wondered sometimes if Jameela might be doing that. She talked about how rich the Italian government is, and how the government sends all this money to Caritas for food, for building dormitories, and for all the staff. I couldn't figure out what this had to do with my saving money for a business. Then I understood. Some people in the camp have found a way to steal some of the government money."

Khadija sat silently as the picture became clearer. "How did Jameela and her sister fit into the picture? Italians run the camp, not us."

"All I can tell you is that the woman showed me her rings, three of them. Then she said, 'Do you think we're stupid just because we're refugees?'"

Khadija tried to put the puzzle pieces together. "Did the woman say anything else?"

Daliyeh shook her head. "She repeated what she said before, that the people she knew could help me start my business."

As she looked around Daliyeh's tiny apartment and her children's meager toys, she said, "You said no to the offer, right?"

"I did, and I'm still saying no. When the war broke out in Syria, gangs and sometimes the military came to our home demanding protection money. The twins were newborns, which meant we had no option except to pay what they demanded. How I hated that some people were making money off the war." Daliyeh looked out the kitchen window to the dusty playground below. "It isn't that I'm afraid of being caught. I could tell that this woman and Jameela didn't worry at all about that. I don't want Mikal and Karina finding out one day that their momma was a thief. And there's something else, something my father taught me. He said, 'If a room has an entrance, make sure it has an exit.' That was his way of saying I should never join a group that I couldn't break free from.'"

CHAPTER TWENTY

July 20
Allyson's Apartment

A SCENE OUT OF A nightmare greeted Allyson the next morning when she shuffled into the kitchen. There sat Chaz, shirtless and maybe less than that, given that the table blocked the lower half of his body. He was eating cereal—*her* cereal—at *her* kitchen table.

It took Allyson a moment to make sense of the scene. Had Sally not understood that whatever she did with Chaz had to be done somewhere else?

Dressed only in a T-shirt and panties, Allyson turned on her heel without saying a word and retreated down the hallway to Sally's bedroom.

"Hey, don't go away mad," Chaz said with a laugh.

Allyson didn't bother to knock as she barged into Sally's bedroom and shut the door behind her.

"I can't believe you did this," she hissed as she approached Sally's prone figure beneath a sheet.

"Did what?" Sally said, peering up with only one eye open.

"Get him out of our apartment, right now," Allyson ordered.

Sally slowly sat up, revealing she was naked. "He's still here?"

Allyson pointed to Chaz's clothes draped over a chair. "Does that look like he left?"

Sally flopped back on the bed. "Have some pity. My head aches."

"Pity? That's what I would expect from you. I walk into the kitchen in my undies, and Chaz is sitting there eating a bowl of my cereal."

Sally moaned and she closed her eyes again. "Can't you tell him to go?"

Allyson reached down and shook Sally's arm. "If you still want to share this apartment with me, you have five minutes to get him out of here. And if you really intend to sleep with him again, you have to go to his place, to some sleazy hotel, the street, I don't care. Never here again. Don't you understand that you've violated not just me, but Agency rules?"

"What do you mean?"

"Chaz and I are on the same team, which means we have to work together. To act professionally toward him—not that that's been easy—I've had to put up a wall. What you've done is allow him to break down that wall."

"You're overreacting, Alli. You've got clothes on."

"I could have been naked, and for all I know, he's sitting naked in our kitchen—my kitchen!"

Sally sat up slowly and swung her legs off the side of the bed. "Are you going to report me?"

"I don't see why I wouldn't. This is harassment, and it's your fault. It's not as if Chaz is going to let me forget it."

"I don't suppose it will change your mind that the sex wasn't that good." After sitting silently for a moment, Sally rose and headed for the door. "I think I'm going to be sick."

"Then be sick and get him out of our kitchen. I'll be in my bedroom. Knock when it's safe for me to be in my own apartment."

As Allyson sat waiting for Sally's knock, she shivered. She was sure Chaz had pulled the stunt to show her that he was fit, to show her that he was proud of what he'd done, and to show her that he didn't have to have her permission to invade her space.

JULY 21
CIA HEADQUARTERS

THE FOLLOWING MORNING, KHADIJA was keenly aware of the iciness in the conference room as she, along with Chaz and Allyson, waited for Morgan to appear. Khadija was nervous herself, not having slept well the previous night. After learning of the crime ring in Caritas and then seeing Chaz in the camp, she had been both puzzled and afraid. Yet the tension in the conference room made her own nervousness pale by comparison. Both Chaz and Allyson were staring so hard at the papers in front of them that Khadija felt those papers could burst into flames at any moment.

Khadija was on the verge of excusing herself and leaving the room when Morgan entered carrying a coffee cup and a folder.

"I think we're making progress," Morgan said, as she sat and opened a folder. "I have a lead that I want to share with you all. Someone sitting at a bigger desk than mine has formally requested that the police use its resources to locate Jameela Malik. If she's still in the country, there's a chance we might be able to interview her."

Morgan paused and looked up at the three of them. "No one besides me finds it something to celebrate that someone above my pay grade is taking an interest in our case? What's with you people today?"

Her question was greeted with a silence so awkward that Khadija coughed to break the spell.

Sighing, Morgan asked, "Khadija, what have you uncovered in the camp?"

Khadija didn't know whether to begin with what she'd learned from Daliyeh or with confronting Chaz on showing up in Caritas. She decided on the former.

"I'm volunteering in the same school where Hasan, Fatima, and Jameela worked. I'm trying not to appear too curious, just keep my ears open. The few times Hasan's name has come up, the conversation shuts down immediately. It's a different story with Fatima. Mrs. Abdullah, the head teacher, told us all that Fatima had regained consciousness," Khadija said, looking in Allyson's direction. "Everyone at the school is excited about her coming back."

Morgan looked over her glasses as Khadija. "Have you heard anything about Jameela Malik, the missing woman who accused Hasan?"

"I'm pretty close to one of my co-workers, and she had quite a bit to say about her." Khadija shared the news about Jameela's and Asha's two-bedroom apartment and the fancy watch, then what Daliyeh had learned about how the crime ring in Caritas operated.

"Fraud in refugee camps is pretty common," Morgan said after a pause, "although it's usually small-time stuff. Did your co-worker suggest there's a connection between Jameela Malik's extra goodies and her accusation against Hasan?"

"Daliyeh didn't say, yet I think it's possible that Jameela accused Hasan before he could accuse her—of the crime, I mean," Khadija said.

"And now Jameela is gone. I wonder what that means," Morgan said.

Chaz finally raised his head and entered the conversation. Looking from Morgan to Khadija, he said, "Hold on a minute. The two of you can't both be right. If what you're saying is true," he said, now focusing on Khadija, "that Kadir knew about Jameela Malik's part in the crime ring, then it makes no sense," his gaze now shifted to Morgan, "for us to link the attacks on Kadir and Fatima."

"Why not?" Allyson asked.

Chaz glared at Allyson. "It's all about being logical. This is what we know: Jameela Malik went missing *before* this Fatima girl was attacked. That means if Kadir was killed because he knew of the crime ring—which there's no evidence for, by the way—Jameela could have had nothing to do with the attack on Fatima, and that's what I've always said. There's no connection between the attack on the pedophile and the girl."

Morgan, however, was not cowed. "Where you see no connections, Chaz, I, and the suits above us here in the Agency, see too many coincidences to overlook."

Khadija watched as Chaz's hand moved to his shirt pocket before dropping back to the table. He cleared his throat noisily before looking up at the ceiling. When he next spoke, Khadija detected an edge in his voice. "With respect, Morgan, the police have looked more closely into this case than anyone in the Agency, and the police agree with me. Kadir was a victim of an honor killing."

Khadija waited anxiously for what Morgan would say. Chaz was questioning not only the wisdom of the Agency's superiors. He was questioning Morgan.

The silence continued until Chaz said in a milder tone, "Despite what Italians say, the police aren't stupid, and they aren't closed-minded. And here's the proof. I know that they've covered their bases by going back to the camp to interview Jameela Malik's sister."

They've gone to the camp? Khadija thought. *What about you going to the camp?*

"Well, that's interesting," Morgan conceded, her tone also milder. "What did they hear?"

"Right after my contact returned from the camp, he called and told me what he'd discovered. The sister, Asha, hinted that Jameela might have run off with one of the delivery men who come to the camp. She gave me the impression that Jameela makes friends easily, if you know what I mean."

Khadija stared at Chaz, trying to understand how anyone could lie so boldly. Then it dawned on her. *In his mind, I don't exist.*

CORPUS CHRISTI HOSPITAL

WHEN FATIMA AWOKE FROM an afternoon nap, sunlight was streaming through the window and falling on the book of tourist sites in Rome that Professor Napolitano left for her. The more pictures she looked at, the poorer she felt. She'd lived in Caritas camp for almost a year, yet she hadn't seen even one of the sites in the book—not St. Peter's, not the Colosseum, not the Forum, not the Pantheon, and not her favorite site in the book, the Trevi Fountain. Although she was in a refugee camp not far from Rome, the Rome shown in the book seemed thousands of miles away.

She was thinking about Caritas' isolation when nurse Miriam entered the room with the two young aid workers, Seppe and Allyson. They took her by surprise, as she was expecting Professor Napolitano. Once again, she instinctively pulled her sheet up.

"They would like to talk with you, Fatima," Miriam said as she came around the side of the bed.

Her gaze shifted from Miriam's face to Allyson and Seppe standing at the foot of her bed. Seppe's smile again appeared kindly and open, while Allyson looked at her as if she were studying her. *What do they want from me?* she thought.

After an awkward silence, Allyson said, "We're here to ask for your help, Fatima."

Fatima waited for the translation, although she understood the woman's Italian.

"I don't remember much about being attacked," Fatima said, not offering the complete truth.

"We understand," Seppe said. "We're hoping you can help us with some questions we have about Caritas."

Her gaze returned to the sun shining through the window. *What do I know that aid workers don't?* she thought.

"Last time, we asked you about Jameela Malik. Now we're wondering if you remember anything about crime in the camp. We think Jameela might be involved in that," Seppe explained.

Fatima couldn't understand his complicated Italian, and even when Miriam translated, she was unsure what the man was referring to.

Are they accusing me of something? she wondered. "I don't understand. What crime?"

Allyson replied, "Have you noticed that some people in Caritas have possessions or privileges that others don't have."

Fatima nodded. She'd noticed that, yet she never thought to ask why. "I don't want extra cigarettes. I don't smoke," she said.

"This isn't about cigarettes," Seppe said. "We're talking about bigger apartments, new shoes, perhaps more food. Did you notice that Jameela had a new watch?"

Fatima relaxed. No, the two aid workers were accusing Jameela, not her. "Yes, I did. Did she steal it?"

Seppe explained that the watch, new clothes, and new shoes were things Jameela had been given for helping others in the camp steal money from the Italian government.

Fatima shrugged, struggling to understand what the man was telling her. "I don't take much notice of things like that. All I want is to get an education and, if Allah wills, leave the camp behind," she said. Before she could stop herself, she asked, "Was that wrong?"

Why am I trusting them? she wondered.

Allyson shook her head. "No, that makes perfect sense. That's what I would want if I were in Caritas. What would you like to do when you leave?"

After the question was translated by Miriam, Fatima hesitated as she weighed how much she should share. Yet there was something about the two aid workers that led her to say, "I want Italians to know that not all

Muslims are refugees. I want to become a tour guide for Arabic-speakers when they come to Rome. That's why I'm studying Italian and religion."

For the first time, Fatima saw Allyson smile as Seppe asked, "Why religion?"

Fatima shook her head. "Please, don't misunderstand. I am Muslim and will always be Muslim. However, Professor Napolitano told us that Rome has mosques, synagogues, and temples, not just churches. I want to be a guide who helps Muslims see that people of different religions can live together."

Now it was Seppe who smiled. "I'm sure that the agency I work for, Sant Anselmo, would be interested in your goal. Part of our mission is to promote spiritual friendship between people of different faiths."

Spiritual friendship. The two words reminded Fatima of something she learned from Professor Napolitano—that religious people do not have to hate other religious people just because they worship differently. With that memory of the class came another memory, however, that of the professor telling her not to say anything about the note—the note she'd remembered had come from Hasan and which she had given to her teacher.

As if Allyson could read her mind, she said, "Fatima, we know there was a note. What we don't know is who gave you the note or what it said."

Fatima felt her throat constrict. Was that what was behind Seppe's offer of help? She looked from Allyson's face, which she couldn't read, to Seppe's, whose face bore the same kindly expression it had when he made the offer. *Unless this man is a devil and his smile and his soft voice are lies, he wants me to trust him.*

Keeping her focus on Seppe, she asked in a faint voice, "Is the note important to finding out who attacked me?"

Seppe glanced briefly at Allyson before saying, "Yes, and the note might also help us understand why Hasan was attacked."

Fatima looked down at her hands and realized she was no longer clutching the sheet.

"The note, yes, there was a note," she began.

"Where did it come from?" Seppe asked.

They already know about the note. Should I trust them with more?

"I found it in my dresser, in the dormitory."

"What did it say?" Allyson asked

Even with Miriam translating the conversation and giving her a chance to think, Fatima felt she was in a train that had crested a hill and was gaining speed as it went downhill. Would she know when to stop?

"The note said 'Danger arrives from Damascus. More on the way.' I think Hasan sent it, although he was already dead when I found it. Someone else must have left it for me."

"Did you find the note the same day you were attacked?" Seppe asked.

"Yes."

Allyson waited before asking, "What danger do you think the note referred to?"

"I don't know. Do you think his warning was what got him killed?" Fatima asked, a tremor in her voice as she realized the person who attacked her had wanted her to die as well.

"Yes, we do," Allyson replied. "You said you worked with Hasan. If he knew about crime in the camp, would he have done something about that?"

"Yes, he was a very religious man, a devout Muslim. He led the children in the noontime prayers."

"Did you know that Hasan was accused of abusing one of the children?" Seppe asked.

"What? When?"

"Two days before he was killed," Seppe answered.

Fatima's heart raced. "I can't believe anyone would accuse Hasan of such a sin."

"Jameela Malik did," Allyson said.

For a moment, Fatima didn't know what to say; the idea was preposterous. "When he wasn't at school, I wondered what happened." After another pause, she added, "No, no. no. Hasan wouldn't have done that. Jameela is wrong."

Seppe nodded. "We agree with you."

"One more question, Fatima," Allyson said. "What happened to the note?"

Fatima felt herself close down, remembering that Professor Napolitano was due to arrive at any moment. The last thing she wanted was for him to hear what she was sharing with the aid workers.

"I don't know what happened to it," she said, looking down again at her hands. "Maybe my attackers took the note."

Seppe nodded. "You're probably right. Do you remember what you intended to do with the note, who you wanted to tell about it?"

Fatima shook her head, knowing one lie was now leading to another. "I didn't know what to do with it."

On their way back to the bus stop, Allyson and Seppe discussed what they'd learned and what they hadn't.

"Fatima doesn't know what we know," Allyson said, "that nurse Miriam overheard the professor mention the note to Fatima. That means that despite what she said, Fatima talked to at least one person about the note."

Allyson stopped walking. "Let's think this through. Fatima finds the note. Then she tells the professor about it, shows it to him, or maybe even gives it to him. Almost immediately, she's attacked. If that's not a coincidence, then what does that mean?"

"It might mean that the professor ordered her attack," Seppe suggested.

Allyson nodded, remembering that Khadija had suggested the same possibility. "Or, someone else knew Fatima had the note. Jameela had already left the camp. That means maybe someone like Jameela," she added, thinking of Jameela's sister, Asha.

Professor Napolitano was not happy when he entered the hospital and even less happy when he left thirty minutes later. After he left Fatima's room, he looked out a window in the corridor and saw the two aid workers walking to the bus stop, clearly discussing something.

His thoughts raced, wondering what Fatima could have told them. He remembered that the man worked with Sant Anselmo, a bona fide organization. That hardly explained why aid workers would be interested in Fatima's attack. They weren't showing compassion; they were prying.

During his visit, Fatima had been evasive, hardly looking at him. After only minutes, Fatima complained of being tired. Although he couldn't prove it, he felt certain that the change in Fatima had been caused by the aid workers' visit.

He stopped at the nurse's station and asked for Miriam before hearing that she'd gone off-duty a few minutes before. Now he felt even more frustration.

What had the aid workers said to Fatima, and, more importantly, what did they know?

CHAPTER TWENTY-ONE

July 22
Fountain Pen Shop, Rome

CHAZ WAS ALSO FEELING frustrated as he walked out of the pen shop near Piazza San Marco in Rome's business center. The shop carried a wide assortment of fountain pens, even a Mont Blanc Meisterstuck identical to the one that had been stolen from him.

Without hesitation, the owner had opened a bottle of ink and with the grace of a surgeon wielding a scalpel, dipped the nib a half-inch into the ink, no more, before handing the pen to Chaz. Up to this point, everything about the visit had been great. The black color and lacquer of the pen's resin were even more lustrous, the feel of the barrel in his hand was the same, and the nib floated over the page much as his own had.

Chaz told himself that in a matter of days, this pen would make him forget about the one he'd lost. Despite all his efforts to convince himself, he handed the pen back—the feeling that his grandfather's pen gave him simply wasn't there. As he left the store and the disappointed owner, Chaz, without thinking, tapped his empty shirt pocket with his hand. It was like losing the pen all over again.

As he walked down the steps to the nearest metro station, he felt both numb and adrift. His grandfather's words that had accompanied the gift—"Always remember, son, this is a Mont Blanc Meisterstuck 149. Having such a pen will always set you apart from the rabble"—tasted bitter in his mouth.

In that numbness, he wasn't sure what happened next, except that within thirty seconds, he was surrounded by angry Italians. Trying to recollect the scene later, he saw the filthy Romani woman with her baby move toward him, a begging cup in her hand, demanding money. The surprise of her gesture shocked him, and he remembered staring at her as if she knew who'd stolen his pen. When her hand touched his chest, not far from his shirt pocket, he reacted without thinking, shoving the woman so forcibly that she fell, her baby shooting out of her hands and rolling like a bowling pin down the steps.

What Chaz remembered next was Italians, men and women, surrounding him and shouting words he didn't understand. The baby, now screaming, was returned to the woman, even as the people surrounding Chaz began to push him hard enough that he felt close to falling. At the last minute, he steadied himself, turned, and ran up the stairs to the street above. He didn't look back until he was nearly a half mile away.

Later in his apartment, his hands shook as the scene replayed in his mind. He poured a tall whiskey and sank into his couch. Head down, he tried to steady his breathing as he thought, *I hate this damn city, I hate the damn gypsies, I hate the damn refugees, and I hate my damn job.* For a moment, he thought of quitting or requesting a transfer. Then the thought faded as he heard his grandfather's voice, "Not without the pen, Chaz. Not without the pen."

JULY 23
CIA HEADQUARTERS

CHAZ'S UNAUTHORIZED VISIT TO the camp operated like a powerful drug on Khadija as she waited for the next Agency briefing to begin. The two previous meetings, especially the start of the last one, had left her in agony. Now, she felt no dread as she waited for the others to enter the room.

Khadija hadn't decided when or how she would confront Chaz on his unauthorized visit to Caritas, yet she knew it was just a matter of time until she would do that. Her work for the Agency in the camp, not to mention her own safety, would be jeopardized if he ever again barged into the camp, and their paths crossed. Chaz's repeated dismissal of her work and her life stirred a desire within her to come out of the shadows and expose him.

The shadows. That was where she'd lived as a Palestinian immigrant in Britain, through university, and even into her first assignments with the CIA. She imagined how her Agency file described her. "Agent Mubarak is self-effacing and blends easily into a background where Muslims or others from developing countries congregate. Use accordingly."

Until the past few days, Khadija always told herself that her ability to appear invisible was her strength. It had taken Chaz to expose her shadow life for what it was—the life of a wraith, someone who exists in two dimensions and therefore someone who doesn't matter.

"Good morning, Khadija," Morgan said as she and Allyson entered the room.

Khadija returned the greeting and, for the first time, found herself noticing how the two other female agents were dressed. Both wore slacks, Morgan's brown with a tan top, Allyson's blue with a light blue sweater. Khadija had bought a similar ensemble in Freiburg, with the intention of venturing out in public without the long flowing chador and her hijab. She'd imagined blending in and not being stared at, yet when she made the experiment, she'd felt even more self-conscious, as if every stranger she passed were thinking, "Why isn't that Muslim girl wearing her hijab?"

Now, she thought she would try the outfit again, for weren't the chadors given her by the agency and her hijab the garb of a refugee in Caritas? If she could convince herself that her traditional dress were only her cover, might she begin to see who she was underneath?

Thoughts of her wardrobe were broken by Chaz entering the room. For some reason, he looked angry, and for a moment Khadija felt herself sink into her hijab and chador. Then she remembered what she had on Chaz and looked up, studying him as he sat down heavily with an audible sigh.

"Good to see everyone. I've read your updates," Morgan said, looking from Allyson to Chaz. "However, for Khadija's benefit, why don't you go first, Allyson."

Allyson looked mainly at Khadija as she shared what Fatima had told her about the note. Khadija paid careful attention, a task not difficult as Allyson never intimidated her.

"Khadija, I don't know if you've found out anything about Professor Napolitano. I still think he's our best lead for now," Allyson said. "He's probably the last person Fatima talked to before she was attacked, and his insistence on Fatima not telling us about the note is definitely suspicious."

"I've only heard about him from my friend Daliyeh," Khadija replied, "and her only comment was that he's been in Caritas as long as she."

"That doesn't preclude him being into something dicey," Morgan said. "For now, what do we know about the professor, Allyson?"

Allyson turned over a page in her notes. "Before he came to Caritas, he was a teacher in one of the refugee camps in Sicily. I know Sicily must be tired of being associated with the Mafia. However, that doesn't mean that some connection like that couldn't be true."

"The problem is that we have nothing at this point to connect the professor with either Kadir's death or crime in the camp," Morgan added. "Chaz, can you ask your friend in the police to look into the professor?"

Without saying anything, Chaz wrote down the professor's name. Khadija sensed that something was both new and wrong about him, and then she realized he wasn't using the big black fountain pen he'd had in their other meetings. Then she dismissed the thought. It was only a pen, after all, and she couldn't think why she'd even noticed.

Morgan turned to Chaz and said, "Okay, bring us up to date on what you're working on."

Chaz repeated what he'd said at the last meeting, that he was reviewing the police's notes on their interview in the camp with Asha Malik, Jameela's sister.

"Putting together what . . . what you said last time," he said, looking in Khadija's direction, "about Jameela's fancy watch and new clothes with how my friend described the larger apartment shared by the Malik sisters, it's pretty certain that she's involved in whatever's going on in the camp. Given that, I'd like permission to accompany my police contact to the camp to re-interview the sister, Asha."

The room became silent, and Khadija was uncertain who should respond. Finally, Morgan said, "That decision is yours, Khadija. The Agency never recommends one agent going onto someone else's turf. There are too many risks."

"I beg to differ. I can't see that there'd be a problem here. The chances of me seeing her," he said, nodding at Khadija, "in a camp the size of Caritas is minimal, and, of course, we'd arrange it so you," he said, smiling now at Khadija, "would know when I'm coming."

The words poured out of Khadija's mouth before she realized she was speaking. "Do you mean like you notified me last time?"

The smile on Chaz's face disappeared. His hand went to his shirt pocket then dropped to the table, even as Morgan sat back and cursed.

For a moment Khadija saw the face that Chaz must have shown when he, as a Navy Seal, cut an enemy's throat, before he said, "What the hell are you talking about?"

"You were in Caritas three days ago, with someone who I assume is your police friend. You didn't read his report; you were there. Yes, I saw you, and yes, you put my life in danger."

"What I did is called initiative, in case there's no Arabic for the word," Chaz said, his eyes still glued on her as if he were deciding where his knife blade would go.

Morgan glared at Chaz, her face turning red. "No, that's called stupidity and a serious breach of authority. How dare you put Khadija's life and the mission in jeopardy."

"Are you serious?" Chaz retorted. "What does it matter that she saw me? If we'd seen one another, I'd have ignored her."

"You mean as you do here?" Khadija asked, surprised to hear her voice again.

"You really think the rules aren't for you, don't you, Chaz?" Allyson said in a low voice. "It's called a tell, Chaz. Whenever a person unexpectedly meets someone he or she knows, the face, even the body, registers. Anyone observing you crossing paths with Khadija in Caritas would see in a second that you know one another."

"What's this have to do with you?" Chaz shot back. "And where'd you get that from anyway—in some beginner's manual for FBI agents?" he added.

Morgan leaned across the table, her face no more than a foot from Chaz's. "You just condemned yourself, you arrogant prick. It *is* in the beginner's manual—the CIA manual. Remember reading that?"

Chaz raised his hands in mock surrender. "Look, no harm's been done. If it's an apology you want, okay, you have it."

"The apology goes to Khadija," Morgan said. "What I want from you is a commitment to rein yourself in, cowboy. If that's too much to expect from you, then you're off the case. Do you hear me, Agent Eaton?"

For a moment, Khadija thought Chaz would stomp out of the room.

Instead he sat back in his chair. "No problem, no problem," his voice just above a whisper.

Morgan sat back herself even as she slammed her palms down on the table. "The word is 'team,' people, 'team.' When will we begin to act like one?"

The question went unanswered as it hung in the air. Finally, she said, "From this moment on, you are all going to act like professionals. Chaz, just so you get my memo, you're going to address Khadija as 'fellow agent Khadija Mubarak' until you prove to the rest of us that you actually remember her name and that she's a fellow agent. If you think I'm joking, you're greatly mistaken."

"Fine, fine," he replied in the same low voice.

"Let me remind you how professionals act. Khadija, do you see any way that you could conduct this second interview with Jameela's sister in Caritas? Forget your personal opinion. I want your professional assessment."

Khadija tried to picture a scenario in which she could naturally interview the sister. Shaking her head, she said, "I'm more likely to compromise my cover."

"Good. I appreciate your perspective. You lie low while Chaz asks his contact what the police know about the professor," Morgan said. "That leaves you, Allyson. Do you want to interview the sister?"

Chaz squirmed in his chair and breathed noisily. "Okay, everyone knows I already met her. And I tell you the honest-to-God truth, the sister and I, well, we already have something of a relationship that I can use. Allyson would be starting over."

"As I think I made myself clear," Morgan said, her voice icy, "I addressed my question to Allyson."

Allyson shook her head. "No, Chaz is right. He already has an in with the sister. I agree that Khadija has to know when Chaz is coming and he must stay clear of the school. He should do the interview and get out of the camp immediately."

Chaz's lips were closed tightly. He said nothing.

"All right," Morgan said. "I appreciate both of you," she said, looking from Allyson to Khadija, "keeping any personal feelings out of it. Chaz, can you do what Allyson suggests?"

Chaz mumbled another barely audible "no problem," as he rose and walked out of the room.

CHAPTER TWENTY-TWO

July 24
Caritas Refugee Camp

GIANNI AND CHAZ ARRIVED the next afternoon at Caritas and walked through the gate. Chaz had done as he was instructed, coordinating his visit with Khadija, making sure she stayed clear of Asha Malik's apartment while he stayed clear of the school. Although the reprimand from Morgan was bitter to swallow, he had reasons for not objecting, which he kept to himself.

When Chaz told Gianni that he wanted to re-interview Asha, Gianni protested, saying that even if Asha knew something, she probably wouldn't tell them. However, Chaz insisted, and Gianni, perhaps thinking about Las Vegas, eventually agreed.

This time, when the children in the camp saw the two men walking across the camp's open play area and ran toward them, Chaz fended off most of the searching hands by tossing small coins to his left and his right, as if he were feeding pigeons. Even with that strategy, he had to remind himself not to react when some of the smaller and dirtier children touched him. He didn't want a repeat of the incident with the Romani mother and baby in the subway, a memory that still filled him more with horror than shame.

This time, Chaz was delighted to see that Caritas had provided a different translator, a younger woman, as they approached Asha's apartment. Asha had obviously been forewarned of the visit, for she stood boldly in the open door of the apartment. Still wearing no hijab, her hair cascaded freely down her shoulders, and her dark mascara made her eyes look even blacker. She smiled at both men as she invited them and the translator into her kitchen and dining area, where cans of Coca-Cola and sweet pastries were already set out.

This time Asha began the conversation, saying through the interpreter, "Do you have other questions?" The way she said it and the look she gave Chaz hinted that she wouldn't be surprised if the two men had come for other, more personal, reasons.

Chaz remembered how Asha and he had flirted on their previous visit. He felt no desire this time. To achieve his goal for the visit, however, Chaz pretended to be flattered by Asha's glances in his direction.

Initially, he let Gianni lead the conversation, who first asked Asha if she'd heard from her sister. When the translator spoke to Asha in Arabic, Asha frowned as she said, "I was hoping you came to see me." Again, she looked in Chaz's direction, and he faked a knowing smile.

"Jameela sent me this," she finally said as she reached for a postcard on the end table. Instead of handing it to the translator or to Gianni, she handed it to Chaz, as if he could read the flowing Arabic script on the back. The front was a picture of the coastline in Calabria, one of Italy's southern regions, although Chaz noted that it had been postmarked in Rome.

He handed the postcard to the translator who took a moment to read the message before translating. "Jameela writes that she is well and for Asha not to worry. She also says she is not in a camp and is happy. At the end, she writes she will never come back to Rome."

"When did you receive the postcard?" Gianni asked.

Asha shrugged even as she smiled in Chaz's direction rather than the policeman's. "Two days ago," she replied.

Gianni looked at Chaz, to invite him to question Asha. Chaz, however, decided to wait.

"We notice you still have this big apartment," Gianni said. "How is that?"

When the comment and question were translated into Arabic, Asha didn't look embarrassed. Her smile remained as she replied vaguely, "Not all refugees are the same. I work on an important committee, you see," she said, as if that explained everything.

Chaz could tell that even though this translator was younger, she was still offended by Asha's brashness in front of the two men. That was when it dawned on him that the first translator might have refused to work with Asha again.

Gianni cleared his throat. "Are you aware of crime occurring in Caritas?"

When Asha understood the question, her sensual smile disappeared. "Are you talking about the crime of losing my family, my home, my business in Syria in a war the world doesn't care about?" she asked in a harsh voice.

"She's not going to answer that question," Chaz said in a low voice to Gianni. "Let me ask one."

"Yes, please," Gianni replied.

"Asha, you must want to get out of Caritas. What would you like to do when that happens?"

Even as the translator began to speak to Asha, Gianni gave Chaz a puzzled look.

Asha's attentive smile returned as she understood the question. Chaz, in turn, smiled back as he was sure he heard a word that sounded like "perfumery" amidst the Arabic.

"Asha made perfumes and sold them in Syria," the translator said. "Her dream is to live in a big city in Europe and work in a perfumery. Eventually, she wants to open her own shop."

"If we have your cooperation, the company I work for might be able to help you, Asha," Chaz said.

Her answer came quickly, as if his carrot was something she expected. "What is your company, and what kind of help can you deliver?"

No information comes cheap, he thought, as the two continued to study one another.

"My company prefers to remain anonymous, yet if you tell us what you know about crime in Caritas, I can promise you a reward."

"I want five thousand euros. I will also take dollars," she said with a smile.

"We can talk money later. First, you have to prove that you know something of value," he said. Gianni was now following the interchange with his mouth open. "Did Jameela and the director of security here know one another?" Chaz asked.

Asha looked bored. "We all know that lazy dog."

Another dog, Chaz thought. "How about Professor Napolitano?"

Asha's eyes narrowed, and the look of boredom disappeared. "If I tell you what I know, I won't be safe in the camp. For five thousand, I can take you to Jameela."

Even as Gianni groaned at the unexpected boast, Chaz raised a hand to signal the policeman to let him continue.

He removed a piece of paper from his shirt pocket and unfolded it. On a brochure that he'd picked up at the pen store in Rome was a photo of a Mont Blanc fountain pen.

"You'll get money from my company under several conditions," he said, as he handed the photo to her. "First, the meeting with Jameela has to be in person. If you can arrange that, you'll get four thousand."

"I said five thousand," Asha replied through the translator, ignoring the paper Chaz handed to her.

"There's another condition. What you're looking at is a picture of something that's mine. It's a fountain pen, and it's somewhere in the camp. When I was here last, one of the orphans stole it. You'll get the last thousand if you bring me that pen."

Gianni looked lost as he stared at Chaz. Asha's eyes grew wide, although likely for a different reason.

"Such a pen is worth that much?" she asked.

"It is to me."

Asha studied the photo with more interest and shrugged, even as she gave Chaz the answer he was hoping for. "I have friends who might know."

"Good," Chaz said, feeling a wave of relief.

"Now, no more talk. Next time, bring the money," Asha said.

July 26
CIA Headquarters

Allyson waited two full days for Khadija and Chaz to gain information about Professor Napolitano. When she asked Chaz that morning if he'd learned anything from the police, all Chaz said was "I'm working on something more important." She just stared at him, wondering what could be more important than investigating the last person Fatima talked to before being attacked.

She started to call the head agent in the Sicily office before she realized she would be repeating what Chaz had done: disrespecting the boundaries of a fellow agent. Instead, she peeked her head in Morgan's door and asked, "Do you have a minute?"

Morgan looked up from her computer and over the top of her reading glasses. "What is it?"

Allyson hesitated, not knowing if that was an invitation to come into the office or Morgan's way of letting her know that she had interrupted something important.

"Sorry, yes, please come in, Alli," Morgan said, removing her glasses and turning her chair away from the computer. "It's been a helluva week, that's all."

"It has been that," Allyson agreed, as she shut the door behind her.

"Sit down, Alli. Sometimes I think I should have stayed in police work," Morgan said, rubbing where her glasses hit on the bridge of her nose. "I thought working for the Agency would be such an advancement in my career. Now, handing out parking tickets in Morehead, Minnesota, seems like heaven in comparison."

"How long ago was that?"

"Twelve years, can you believe it? You were probably a happy teenager back then."

Allyson tried to smile, even as she remembered her teenage years as anything but happy ones.

"I want your advice. Or, maybe it's fairer to say I'm asking for your permission," Allyson said.

"Well, it looks like I have one agent who knows what protocols mean."

Allyson nodded that she understood. "That's what brings me here. I want permission to investigate the professor in the camp. My problem is—"

"Your problem is that I gave that task to Chaz, right?"

"Yes, ma'am."

"Did you run this by our Mr. Eaton?"

"Not exactly. I asked if he'd talked with his contact in the police, and he blew me off. To be fair, he said he was working on something more important."

"I wonder what that could be. Anyway, what do you have in mind?" Morgan asked.

"I was thinking of contacting the CIA office in Sicily. We know the professor taught in a refugee camp down there before he came to Caritas."

"Yes, I remember. That makes good sense to me. And I'd say Chaz's more important business, which is probably Asha Malik, gives you the green light to do that. As a courtesy, email him that you have my permission and then forward a copy to me. Actually, that's an easy call for me to make. I thought you were going to complain about Chaz again." she looked back at her computer screen. "That's what I'm working on right now, a report for his file. You probably don't know that for every negative statement I write about an agent under me, I'm required to write a paragraph on what I did or didn't do that might have contributed to the problem. My dilemma is that I don't know if Chaz will take direction any better in the future, at least from a female." Morgan sat back in her chair. "Tell me Alli, if you were in my position, would you give him another chance, or would you vote for me to transfer him?"

A wave of anger surfaced in Allyson's mind as she remember Chaz ogling her in Sally's and her kitchen. Chaz had violated her space, and she knew that he'd done that deliberately. She thought how much simpler her life would be if Chaz were transferred. The tension she felt with her roommate, Sally, would evaporate, as she'd be spared having to tell Morgan anything about Sally's part in that kitchen scene. She also knew that she could be transparent with Morgan and let her know about Seppe. There was something else that became clearer as she weighed Stamper's question. She realized that she hadn't given Rome a chance because Chaz had been the agent who'd picked her up at the airport. Before she saw even one ruin in the ancient city, she already had a negative reaction because Chaz had leered, rather than looked, at her.

Now, by simply agreeing that Chaz should be sent packing, the cloud and headache that he represented would lift. Might Rome begin to sparkle, might she look forward to coming into the office, and might the case in Caritas also proceed more smoothly?

As Allyson was about to share her thoughts, she remembered what Seppe had told her, that she had to help Chaz if he were ever to see refugees as human. It wasn't the first time she heard the echo of Father Nick's voice in Seppe's words.

Later that might as she struggled to fall asleep, the thought came back to her, and she decided that talking with Father Nick was exactly what she needed. Father Nick wasn't just her father's partner in solving crimes but someone she counted on for wise advice. Sitting up in bed, she called his number at St. Simeon's monastery in Ohio.

Good heavens, is Allyson really calling me?"

"Yes, it's me, Nick.

"Where are you, my dear? The last time you called, you were in New Jersey."

"Actually, I'm in Rome. I'm on a case, so I can't tell you much, but I can say that I'm working with refugees. The thing is, I need your advice."

"Of course. How can I help?"

"I've got a colleague who's anything but collegial. If you'll forgive my language, he's a prime asshole."

"Yet unavoidable, it sounds like."

You got it. I've tried to keep him at a distance, but last week he stayed overnight with my roommate. I walked into the kitchen the next morning in my underwear and there he was. He was sitting at the table, but he might not have had any clothes on. He was gloating, Nick. I mean, what he and my roommate did broke all kinds of company rules. She was just stupid, but he was harassing me. Then, yesterday, my boss gave me the perfect opportunity to nail him. No surprise, the guy broke another rule in the company and Morgan, my boss, asked if she should transfer him. Nick, I was this close to telling her to send him packing."

"Yet, you decided to call me."

"To explain that, I need to tell you something else, but it's complicated."

"My dear, I've found that life is rarely simple."

"Here's the complication. There's a man I've let into my life, Nick, which you know isn't something I'm prone to do. His name is Giuseppe, Seppe for short, and we work together at a refugee camp. The thing is, he's religious, but, like you, he's not judgmental. In fact, he's the opposite. I told him about the jerk I work with, and his response threw me. He said I might be the only person who can help this guy change."

"Ah, I see. Allyson, you know I won't tell you what to do."

"I know that, Nick, but can I ask what you'd do if you were in my place?"

"Allyson, I know myself well enough to know the difference between my first reaction and what I come to realize is the right step to take. When I was young, I was like most Greeks, prone to let my emotions—what the Early Church Fathers called 'the passions'—control me. I was known to have a sharp tongue."

"I would never accuse you of that, Nick, but I've been told I have one too," Allyson confessed.

"I haven't completely conquered those urges, but life here at St. Simeon's has taught me the wisdom of tasting my words before they leave my mouth. You have to understand that living in community with thirty-five other men is difficult perhaps in the same way that you find working with this colleague."

"You sound like Seppe."

"Which might not have been what you were hoping to hear. For me, when I feel the desire to confront someone, I try to remember that what would feel good for me is rarely what will help the other person."

"So you and Seppe are saying I should just grin and bear it."

"No, no, Allyson. All that will do is lead you to silently keep track of every negative thing this person says and does. That kind of silence stokes anger. I think your friend and I are saying you should treat this person you're having a problem with as someone with a disease. If you tell your boss to transfer him, will that help him become better or just make your life easier?"

CORPUS CHRISTI HOSPITAL

TWICE A DAY, ONCE in the morning and once in the afternoon, nurse Miriam held Fatima's arm as they walked the corridors of the hospital. At first, Fatima walked as slowly as an elderly person, and she struggled to accept how quickly she tired. Even though she walked more quickly each day, Fatima continued to wake in a cold sweat from dreams of being back in Caritas and being chased by a shadowy figure.

The source of her nightmare was what Professor Napolitano had told her, that neither camp security nor the police had any leads on her attacker. *Was her attacker waiting for her to return to Caritas to finish her off?*

When she asked her doctor when she could be released, her doctor appeared to sense her anxiety. *Anxious, yes, I'm anxious*, she thought, *just not in the way everyone thinks.* When she first arrived in Caritas, she'd adjusted quickly to being on her own, striking out in her own direction by taking courses and volunteering in the school. Now, the thought of doing anything, going anywhere in Caritas alone, petrified her.

She assumed her attacker was young, which meant that she required someone also young to protect her when she returned to the camp. She thought of the other students in her classes, especially her language classes, before dismissing the thought as she hadn't grown close to any of them.

The next day, when she was allowed to sit in a chair and look out at the bustling city from her hospital room, she came up with what she hoped would be a solution to her problem. Wouldn't the two aid workers who visited her, Allyson and Seppe, know camp residents her age who she could count on?

She was ready when nurse Miriam came into her room for their afternoon walk. "Do you remember the two aid workers who came to see me?"

"Of course. If they're bothering you, Fatima, I'll tell them to stop coming."

"No, no, I want to see them. Do you know how to contact them?"

"Are you sure Professor Napolitano would want you to do that?" Miriam said in a low voice, as the two stepped out into the corridor.

Fatima looked over at the nurse. "Why do you say that?"

"Yesterday, after the professor visited, he asked me about the two aid workers."

Fatima, still struggling with her balance, was grateful for Miriam's firm hand on her arm. "What kind of questions?"

"He asked me to repeat everything the aid workers said to you on the visit."

Fatima didn't say anything for a moment. "Did you do that?"

Miriam offered a smile. "My loyalty is to you, Fatima. You're my patient, and I'm here to help you heal. That's why I pay attention to all your visitors."

They walked to the end of the hall and stood before a window. Outside, Fatima could see people walking by the hospital, leading normal lives.

"Miriam, what did you mean when you said you pay attention to my visitors?"

Miriam relaxed her hand on Fatima's arm. "Can you balance without my help?"

“I think I can.”

“Good. What I mean is, when the two aid workers came back the last time, I could tell that you had decided to trust them. I feel the same about them.”

“And Professor Napolitano?”

Miriam shook her head. “At first I asked myself, why is he asking me about the aid workers instead of asking you? And then I realized he must have asked you those questions, and you decided not to tell him. If you didn’t want him to know, then I didn’t want him to know either.”

CHAPTER TWENTY-THREE

Caritas Refugee Camp

THAT EVENING, IN THE safety of Daliyeh's apartment, Khadija was tempted to take her friend into her confidence and reveal her true identity. Then a phrase from her training came back to mind: "A source is most valuable when the source doesn't know he or she is a source." As Khadija sat on the floor with Daliyeh's children, she thought of another reason to withhold the truth. Telling Daliyeh about crime in Caritas could endanger her or her children. Whoever killed Hasan and attacked Fatima was probably still in the camp.

Yet Khadija knew that Daliyeh was the one person who could name the woman who'd offered her the chance to join in the fraudulent scheme. As Daliyeh called her children and Khadija to the table, Khadija realized the challenge ahead—to allow Daliyeh to tell her about the woman without Daliyeh knowing that she was doing anything more than carrying on idle conversation.

The meal was like the last one Khadija was invited to by Daliyeh, pita bread and hummus, along with a salad of cucumbers and feta cheese. Only this time, Khadija knew from the smells emanating from the kitchen that lamb was included.

In the center of the table was a slim patty of meat, and Khadija couldn't imagine the four of them splitting it. As Daliyeh cut the patty down the middle, she said, "I hope you don't mind that I let the children have the lamb."

Khadija shook her head. "Please don't apologize; you're only doing what's right. Mikal and Karina are still growing," she said, smiling at the two children.

"Mama made rice pudding. Did your mother make rice pudding?" the little girl asked.

Khadija tried to block the memory of her mother coming into the room. Despite the effort, she remembered her mother's words: "No pudding until you eat everything on your plate."

"My momma made pudding sometimes," Khadija said, trying to smile, even as her stomach tightened. "Not often, though."

"We're having pudding because you're here," Mikal said as he ate a morsel of the lamb.

"Now don't tell Khadija all our secrets," Daliyeh said with a laugh. Turning to Khadija, she said, "I should warn you. They expect you to read them a story after dinner."

"Now who's telling Khadija a secret?" Karina said.

Daliyeh raised her hands in surrender. "You're right. I did a no-no."

"Will you read us a story?" Mikal asked.

"Not just one; I'll read two," Khadija said, happy to be talking about something besides food.

Karina and Mikal smiled at each other, as if they had pulled off a magic trick.

Daliyeh, however, turned the conversation back to food. "Families here aren't given much of a food allowance. I'm not ashamed to say I've brought a few snacks home from the school." After a minute, she added, her voice low, "That's not true. I am ashamed of that. It makes me no better than the others who steal in the camp."

"Like that woman you told me about last time—the woman with the gold wristwatch and the rings?"

"Yes, like her. I don't know much about her, except that her name is Sabia Terek. A friend said that she wore the jewelry from the first day she was in the camp." After hesitating for a moment, Daliyeh added, "I keep telling all the children in the school, including my own, that Allah always watches us. Those who do bad things are known by Allah. And I believe that, yet sometimes when I see how hungry they are," she said, looking at the twins, "I can't stop myself."

"Snacks are a lot different from gold watches and fancy rings," Khadija said.

"Hasan said the same thing," Daliyeh said, looking down at her hands. "He was like a grandfather to me. I never kept anything from him. When I told him what I did, he said something wise, I think. He said taking extra snacks home would be okay until I no longer felt guilty about it."

Khadija saw her opening. "Yes, that is wise. I wish I could have known him. Daliyeh, do you think Mr. Kadir knew about the watches and rings?"

Daliyeh stopped eating and thought for a moment. "I don't think he could have missed Jameela's new shoes and her watch, yet I don't know if he said anything to her."

"Has Sabia said anything more about how they make money here in Caritas?"

"I haven't seen her since the night she came to see me," Daliyeh confessed, before looking up in alarm. "Why? You're not tempted to work with her, are you?"

Khadija paused, trying to decide the right answer to give. If she said she was interested in the crime going on in the camp, she'd lose Daliyeh's respect and friendship. If she said she wasn't interested in what was going on, then she'd have to explain why she was interested in Sabia.

"No, not really. I'm just curious about what goes on in the camp," she said. "I've always been nosey."

"Yeah, I can understand that. Gossip is the best way to relieve the boredom of this place. My guess is you might see Sabia in the dining hall."

"How would I recognize her—besides the gold watch and the rings, I mean?"

"Oh, she stands out. She's tall and her hijab doesn't cover her hair in front. That's not quite the same as the younger girls who no longer bother with the hijab. My guess is that Sabia thinks she looks modern. Oh, and she likes to wear dangling earrings. Maybe they're gold as well."

"Does she come to the mosque for prayers?" Khadija asked.

"I don't remember ever seeing her there."

It wasn't until Daliyeh served up dessert and let the children take their bowls of rice pudding over to their toys that Khadija brought the subject back to crime in Caritas.

"You must wonder what the people in the camp are doing to get the new clothes, shoes, and jewelry," Khadija asked.

"I do and I don't. Mostly, I don't want to know."

"And no one has complained to security?"

Daliyeh paused for a moment and sighed. "Some say security is part of whatever is going on." Whispering, she added, "Please, Khadija, don't ask me anymore. It's not safe to be too curious."

July 27
Corpus Christi Hospital

Allyson pondered the choice that Morgan had given her, to recommend Chaz's transfer to another CIA office or to keep him on the team. She had asked Morgan to give her twenty-four hours before she gave her answer, even as a voice screamed within her: *Tell Chaz to go to hell.*

Hell. That was what was on Allyson's mind as she sat with Seppe in the hospital lounge. It was the first time that she felt resentment toward him. Yes, his talk about religion and his vocation got on her nerves, yet it was his advising her to give Chaz another chance that left her wishing she hadn't brought the problem to him. Feeling a desire to sting him, she turned toward him in the hospital lounge and said, "Here's what I don't understand, Seppe. How can an intelligent person like you can believe in hell?"

"I wish I didn't believe in hell," Seppe said.

She laughed. "Then don't. I certainly don't. Anyway, if God is loving and wants to give everyone a chance to change, why does there have to be a hell?"

Seppe didn't reply for a moment, and Allyson hoped that she'd ruffled him a bit. Then he said, "I think God wishes there weren't a hell too. Hell must be God's greatest sorrow."

She felt her jaw set. He wasn't going to get off that easily. "All that business about a devil with pitchfork, flames, and eternal suffering—you honestly believe all that?"

Seppe shook his head. "I think hell is a much *worse* punishment than that. Hell is where people never change. They remain the same guilty, angry, and fearful people they were here, only now they're alone with themselves."

It was now Allyson who didn't know what to say, even as she realized that her wish to make Seppe uncomfortable had backfired. "You make it sound like some people are in hell right now."

Seppe sighed heavily as he looked out the lounge window and down to busy traffic flowing by. "I do. Hell and heaven start in this world. I think humans are like everything else in nature—we're meant to grow. The problem is that some people refuse to change. Because of guilt, fear, anger, or maybe just willfulness, they refuse to grow. And that's the beginning of hell."

Allyson heard an echo of Father Nick in Seppe's words. Both men believed that everyone deserved the chance to change, even someone as arrogant as Chaz. Did she believe that? Did she *want* to believe that?

FATIMA WAS SITTING UP in a chair when Seppe and Allyson entered the room. She returned their smiles as they sat in the other two chairs, while Miriam sat on the end of Fatima's bed.

Allyson said, "Wow, you look a lot better."

Fatima decided to get right to the point. "That's why I wanted to see you both. The doctor says I can return to Caritas at the end of the week."

"Are you okay with that?" Seppe asked.

"Would you want to go back there, if you'd almost been killed?"

Seppe winced. "No, I understand. Have you thought about asking to be sent to another camp?"

"I have another idea," Fatima replied.

Allyson's eyebrows rose. "We're listening."

Fatima frowned. "I don't have many friends in Caritas. In fact, other than Mrs. Abdullah and another volunteer in the school, my only close friend is Professor Napolitano."

"Who can't protect you, right?" Allyson asked.

Fatima nodded, glad that the woman understood her concern. "I know you can't protect me either. I'm hoping you know someone in the camp, someone my age, who I can count on."

"Count on how?" Allyson asked. "Do you mean a bodyguard?"

Fatima shook her head. "I don't want any more attention drawn to me. I'm thinking more of a friend."

As she heard the nakedness in her words, Fatima feared how Allyson and Seppe would react. They knew as well as she that a person can't place an order for a friend. Allyson, however, responded almost immediately. "I think we can help. I came across the profile of a new resident this week. Actually, she's volunteering in the school and is about your age. She's what we Americans call 'gutsy.'"

"Then I'd like to meet her," Fatima replied, feeling relief, before another thought came to mind. Why did she have the feeling that Allyson's offer had come too quickly, as if she came that day for just this purpose?

JULY 29
CARITAS REFUGEE CAMP

KHADIJA COULDN'T REMEMBER A time when she sat in front of a plate of food and didn't feel the eyes of everyone on her. She realized, as she sat in the dining hall on the lookout for Sabia, the mystery woman, that the roles were reversed. However, two days of sitting in the dining hall for both the noon and evening meals produced not a glimpse of the woman, leading Khadija to wonder if Sabia, in addition to the golden watch and rings, had her own cache of food.

It wasn't until the evening meal when a woman matching Daliyeh's description entered the dining hall with two younger men, both hardly out of their teens. The woman looked neither to the right or left while the two men scanned the room. She was tall, a fringe of her hair protruding from beneath her hijab, and walked in a stately manner to the line of trays and silverware.

Khadija could see that she wasn't the only resident watching the woman's entrance, and she was amazed that the woman did nothing to disguise her privileged status. "Queen of the camp" is what came to mind as Sabia approached an occupied table with her entourage and stood there until the residents sitting rose and moved to another table.

It was obvious to her that the woman desired the attention she was receiving and had come to the dining hall not to eat as much as to impress and recruit. *How then can I make her interested in me?* Khadija thought. If Jameela still worked at the school, Khadija could subtly show her interest in the girl's jewelry. With Jameela gone, however, Khadija saw no one else in the school who showed signs of sudden wealth.

Sabia, meanwhile, was eating without talking to her companions.

When an older man and a middle-aged woman approach her table, her two companions shooed them away like flies before they could even speak to her. That meant any frontal assault, any attempt to catch the attention of the woman in the crowded dining hall, was out.

Khadija watched Sabia until she motioned for one of her bodyguards to remove her tray. She walked out of the dining hall in the same stately manner that she'd entered it. All eyes, except those of children, followed her.

Back in her dormitory, Khadija wrote down her impressions of the woman: bold, unafraid, regal, and proud. How could someone like herself, powerless and insignificant, break through walls of iron?

I must become someone else in this woman's eyes, she realized that night as sleep slowly crept into her brain.

Even as her eyelids closed, a plan came to her. If the Agency provided an expensive watch and ring or two, it wouldn't take long for the woman and her partners in crime to notice the jewelry. They would ask, "Who's the new woman with the swag, and, since she didn't get the jewelry from us, where did she get it?"

As she stared up at the ceiling, she turned the plan over and over in her mind, probing for its weaknesses. It was the plan's inherent danger, however, that made her pause. For perhaps the first time in her life, she would step out from behind the walls that had always protected her. She would be deliberately putting her life at risk.

CHAPTER TWENTY-FOUR

July 30
CIA Headquarters

MORGAN LOOKED AT HER watch, hesitating to make sure she would arrive for the case review five minutes after everyone else did. She wanted Chaz, Allyson, and Khadija in their seats, feeling the tension, the anger, the jealousy, and whatever else was getting in the way of their working together. Hadn't both Khadija and Allyson asked her, rather than going to Chaz, if they could pursue leads that she'd assigned to Chaz?

That made her meeting with Allyson the previous afternoon puzzling. Allyson had stopped by her office to say she thought Chaz should be kept on the team. It wasn't really Allyson's words that changed her mind as it was something else she'd heard in Allyson's voice that convinced her to reconsider.

Of the three agents waiting for her in the conference room, Allyson was the one who Morgan would have liked to have taken into her confidence. For some reason, however, Allyson was still keeping her secret, even though Morgan had discovered days before Allyson's relationship with Giuseppe D'Angelo, an aid worker with the Sant Anselmo community.

What puzzled Stamper was that she could see no reason for Allyson to keep Seppe's identity a secret. The only red flag that cropped up in his file—the Agency had files on all the aid workers in Caritas—was his relationship with a priest named Father Salvatore Grammchi who was considered a radical in some circles. What she found more interesting was Father Salvatore was known in Rome as a "dog-collar recruiter," someone who encouraged young men like Giuseppe D'Angelo to consider a priestly vocation. That made whatever relationship Allyson had with D'Angelo even more puzzling. It troubled Morgan when she didn't understand her agents, especially the relationship they had with people outside the CIA. Was that another secret of Allyson's, that she was religious?

Also on Morgan's mind was Chaz's preoccupation with Asha Malik. What was his game plan there? Did the police consider the sister someone of special interest, or had Asha become Chaz's personal obsession?

With both Allyson and Chaz keeping secrets, she wondered if Khadija were doing the same. Given Chaz's unannounced visit to Caritas, Khadija might well have decided that she couldn't trust anyone in the group. It was time for all of that to change.

"Thanks for your patience," she said, as she came into the room. As before, Chaz sat alone on one side of the table, while Allyson and Khadija sat on the other side with two empty chairs between them. Again, Morgan felt tension in the room as the agents looked up from their notes.

Sitting at the head of the table, she looked from one agent to another. Had none of them said a word to the others?

"I'm sure we all remember our training, that part about not stepping on the toes of fellow agents and not poaching other agents' sources. That's a good rule. The problem is that this approach isn't working for us. Today, we're throwing that rule out the window. Put bluntly, we have to function as a unit if we're going to get to the bottom of whatever is going on in Caritas. And we aren't even close to being a unit."

She paused to gauge the effect of her opening salvo. Chaz stared at his notes, his jaw set, while Allyson glanced at Khadija for a moment. She'd half expected Allyson to object, stating that there were no problems between Khadija and her, yet the two empty chairs would make such a claim hard to believe.

Morgan rose and approached the whiteboard where she wrote-"Crime in Caritas: murder and fraud" and beneath that, the names of Hasan Kadir and Fatima Rasul. Below that she wrote Professor Napolitano, Jameela Malik, and Asha Malik, followed by Sabia Terek, recruiter.

Stepping to the side, she said, "Caritas is the case *we're* working on. Not each of you individually. From now on, no one in this room *owns* any name written on the board. We share the work, and we communicate with each other. That way we don't get into anyone else's way.

"Khadija, we're changing your cover story. Your cancer has progressed, and you now you will be coming into Rome twice a week for treatments. That will give Chaz and Allyson the chance to tell you when they expect to be in Caritas. Allyson and Chaz, I want your daily updates going to each other, not just to me."

Morgan returned to the table. "It's time for us to play 'show and tell.' No more secrets, no more uncoordinated actions, no more coming to me for permissions you should be working out with one another. I'm leaving the room for the next thirty minutes. When I return, I expect each of you to tell the rest of us everything you're working on and," she paused as she looked directly at Allyson, "every contact you've made, every source you're using."

July 31
Church of Santa Prassede

Seppe knelt in the church of Santa Prassede and prayed for his upcoming meeting with his brother, Leo. The day before, Leo had asked to meet for lunch and told Seppe to choose the place. After a moment's thought, Seppe invited his brother to come to Santa Prassede before going to the nearby pizzeria.

Leo approached faith and the church much as Seppe had three years ago. Leo too had been an altar boy, though parish priests more than once had to shush him during the Mass. Not surprisingly, when Seppe announced the church as the meeting place, he heard Leo pause before agreeing.

Why did I ask him to come here? Seppe asked himself. As he rose from his knees, he knew part of the answer. He would share with Leo, the brother who always tried to beat him at everything, that he was seriously considering the priesthood. In his family's view, he'd already thrown his life away with his decision to work for Sant Anselmo. If he became a priest, they'd realize that they'd lost their son and brother for good.

His thoughts were interrupted by Leo entering through the side door.

In his cashmere sweater and leather coat, Leo looked like a model, which Seppe knew was his intention.

Leo removed his designer sunglasses, spotted Seppe, and smiled. "Why here, Seppe?"

"It's a place I come to . . . to think," Seppe said. "Plus, the mosaics are some of the oldest in Rome."

Leo offered the briefest of glances around the church before saying, "I keep forgetting you majored in art."

"Art history."

"Well, show me what I should pay attention to, in case there's a test." He offered Seppe a mischievous grin. "Oh, wait a minute, there'll be no test. Hallelujah."

Seppe forced a smile before taking Leo into the side chapel, a small space completely covered with mosaics. He put a euro into a light box to illuminate the space, causing the bright colors of the tesserae to pop from the walls.

Leo, however, gave the mosaics only a glance before pointing to a stone column on display within a glass enclosure. "What's this supposed to be?"

"Some say it's the pillar that Jesus was tied to when he was whipped before the crucifixion."

"And I bet others say it's something dug up from somebody's backyard."

Seppe bristled. "Does it matter if it helps people pray?"

"Oh, yeah, I guess there's that," Leo replied, yawning.

Seppe decided that further exploration of Santa Prassede would serve little purpose. *How did I think my brother would respond?* Seppe asked himself.

Fifteen minutes later, the two brothers sat outside the pizzeria, Leo with a glass of wine, Seppe with a beer.

"Very tasty, Seppe. How'd you find this place?" Leo asked, as he took a bite of his pizza. "I thought your office is in Trastevere."

"It is. Father Sal offers morning Mass at Santa Prassede. When we get together, he usually brings me here for lunch."

"Father Sal, Father Sal. Didn't you bring him to Sunday dinner once?"

"Yes, that's him," Seppe said.

"I tell you what I remember about that guy. He's way too smart to be a priest. I mean, what a waste. He'd be great in sales, anything in customer service, you know?"

"Father Sal is in customer service," Seppe said.

"Ha. Good one, Seppe. Face it, Father Sal's like you. Good with people, I mean. A person can make a fortune knowing how to deal with people. That's old wisdom that now has scientific proof. I've been reading about something they call 'emotional intelligence.' And Father Sal has it; that's all I'm saying."

Seppe couldn't argue with that, although he wondered why the notion of emotional intelligence was attracting such attention when the older term "compassion" meant the same.

"You said you wanted to see me about something, Leo."

"Two things, Seppe. One, Chiara and I are taking my new boat out this weekend. She's moored next to papa's near Ostia. Chiara said I should invite you to come out with us, maybe bring a woman friend, if you have one. For some reason, Chiara thinks you're sweet. Anyway, we're thinking Saturday. Lunch down by the beach, then out for a sail. Chiara will be disappointed if you say 'no.'"

For a moment, Seppe imagined the joy of sailing again, especially with Allyson along. Then he pictured Leo posturing in front of both Chiara and Allyson. The old rivalry between the two brothers, rather than emotional intelligence on either of their parts, would be on full display. He wondered if he could keep from getting sucked into that.

"I'll check my schedule at Caritas and give you a call tomorrow, Leo. I think it might work, and yes, there is someone I can bring. What's the other thing you wanted to talk about?"

Leo smiled broadly as he looked at his brother. "Okay, here's the big news. Papa found the Porsche from the early sixties he's always dreamed about. It's being shipped down from Germany as we speak. He actually bought it from just looking at pics on the internet. Pretty cool, huh?"

As Seppe listened, he wondered why the news interested Leo. Then it dawned on him. "That means he's decided to let the Alfa Romeo go."

Leo's smile widened. "It's up to us to work out which one of us inherits it."

Seppe pictured the Alfa-Romeo Spider from the early eighties that his father had owned from the day it rolled off the assembly line. Even as young boys, Seppe and Leo took turns sitting in the driver's seat and pretending they were at Le Mans. As long as their father owned the car, the two of them had argued about who would one day own it.

Seppe studied Leo's face, his brother wetting his lips the way he always did before a sailing race or even over a Monopoly board. *He wants me to fight him for it,* he thought, as he looked down the street to the massive basilica of Santa Maria Maggiore and thought how fitting it would be to see the Alfa, the Porsche, or any other classic sports car parked in front. Yet a sports car would look out of place beside Santa Prassede, as much out of place as if it were parked outside Caritas.

"The Alfa doesn't fit my life now, Leo. You should have it."

The grin disappeared from Leo's face. "You're not going all St. Francis of Assisi on me, are you, brother?" Seppe saw clearly that his response wasn't what Leo wanted from him. Besides wanting the Alfa, Leo wanted to attain it by somehow defeating him.

"I don't get you, Seppe. It's like you're walking away from us all—the family, I mean."

"Why, because we don't compete about everything anymore?"

"Is that so bad? Tell me some of the best days of your life weren't when you beat me at sailing."

The two brothers sat silently, as Seppe had to acknowledge that Leo was right. "I'm not interested anymore with making money," he said.

Leo's face reddened as he sat forward and glared at his brother. "You say that as if making money is some sin. Look, our family has worked hard for every euro we have. Don't expect any of us to follow you down this poverty road."

Seppe felt an unexpected wave of calm enter him. "I'm not asking you to follow me," he said.

"The hell you're not. You sit at the table every Sunday for family dinner, and you don't think we notice that you're wearing the same baggy sport coat week after week? We know exactly what you're doing. You're looking down on us as if, sitting there in our nice clothes and eating off mama's best china, we're beneath you."

Seppe felt pity for his brother. "You don't get it, Leo. I work with refugees, but it's not just a job. The refugees have taught me a lot. I can't live in two different worlds; no, two different planets. That's how far apart Caritas camp is from our family."

"God, Seppe, you've become such a . . . what? Such a pious loser. Where's your fight?"

Now it was Seppe who leaned across the table. "My fight's in the camp, Leo."

"And your refugees wouldn't love to sit at our Sunday dinner table?"

Seppe sat silently for a moment. "You're right, Leo. They'd love that, but we both know they'll never sit at a table like that. The Syrians in Caritas have lost everything. Now they're stuck in a camp that's so much like a prison that it makes me physically sick sometimes. And if they manage to be released—what kind of jobs do you think they'll get in Rome or Naples or wherever?"

"Yet you think you'll change anything by wearing old clothes from when you were at university and driving that old Fiat? You just admitted that your refugees will never sit at our table. Why then throw your life away on something that's never going to change?"

CHAPTER TWENTY-FIVE

August 1
Caritas Refugee Camp

PROFESSOR NAPOLITANO STUDIED THE package left on his desk in the Caritas classroom. The weight of the package suggested a book, perhaps two, even though he didn't remember ordering any in recent weeks. Yet, publishers sometimes sent him unrequested books for his review. He also knew that sometimes his superiors sent details of a mission through the mail, inside a book.

A new mission? With Fatima returning to the camp any day now, he hardly thought his current mission was over. It was no secret that his superiors blamed him for failing to protect Fatima weeks before, and there were many nights since the attack on Fatima when he'd wondered why he hadn't walked her back to her dorm. Part of him knew, however, that escorting Fatima would probably have resulted in both of them being attacked. He was old enough and experienced enough to know that hindsight was rarely clear sight.

He was frustrated by the way the Italian intelligence agency he worked for had reacted to the attack on Fatima. He had served faithfully for nearly a decade, supplying valuable information about organized crime in the camp in Sicily and now, sadly, in Caritas. His contributions, however, had apparently been cancelled out by Fatima's plight. Two days before, he received a coded message outlining the new and improved plan for

Fatima's security. Upon her return, Fatima's security would not be solely in his hands. Someone else, someone who would remain anonymous for the sake of further security, would keep an eye on Fatima on an hour-by-hour basis. Fatima would be informed of the new arrangement by others, who would discuss the matter with her before she left the hospital.

Even as Professor Napolitano recognized that his abilities to keep an eye on Fatima had always been limited by his role in Caritas' educational system, he couldn't help but take the memo as a vote of no confidence.

Not that he had any doubt about who would supply the added security. From their first visit, the professor suspected that the two people who visited Fatima were more than aid workers. By himself, the young man connected with Sant Anselmo might have fooled him. The American woman, however, never fooled him.

Of course, his first thought had been that the two visitors shouldn't be trusted. That was why he asked Fatima never to tell them about the note. Now he understood that the two saw him in the same way, a suspect rather than an ally.

He shook his head, once again aware of how much valuable time would be saved if different nations' intelligence agencies shared intel and strategies. Would not the four of them, including Fatima, have uncovered the criminal infrastructure in the camp if they'd worked together?

With scissors, he cut through the thick wrapping on one end before realizing the contents were wrapped within more thick plastic. If there was a new mission contained within a book, he predicted that it instructed him to take orders from the woman named Allyson. What was it Americans said about better late than never?

As the powdery contents of the package were released into the air, Professor Napolitano felt something like a steel band tighten around his chest. He could neither inhale nor exhale, and he slumped from his chair to the floor as his brain registered what was happening. The package didn't contain a new mission. Instead, he realized before losing consciousness the meaning of the moment: either the killer who'd attacked Hasan and Fatima had penetrated his false identity, or someone, someone supposedly on his side, had betrayed him.

CIA HEADQUARTERS

ALLYSON'S HEART WAS POUNDING as Morgan returned to the Agency's conference room and took her seat at the head of the table. Allyson knew that she had no choice. She had to reveal Seppe's identity, and yet, now that the time of reckoning had come, she blamed herself again for protecting Seppe in the first place.

Morgan cleared her throat. "The next half-hour will likely determine if the four of us will solve what's been going on in Caritas. The onus is on you three, even as I'll hold you accountable if I detect anyone is still withholding information. Each of you will share what you're working on, who you're working with, and what you need from the others on the team. Is that understood?"

After the agents nodded their agreement, Morgan turned to Allyson. "It's only fair that you go first."

Allyson kept her eyes on her notes. "As you all know, I've met with Caritas' head of security, and I've been to the hospital to see what we can do to build trust with Fatima. That last part has turned out better than we'd hoped. Just yesterday, Fatima asked if we could use our contacts in Caritas to find another resident her age who she could rely on for some protection. I immediately thought of you, Khadija. I think it's a perfect way for you to help Fatima as well as the investigation. I realize it's your decision, Khadija, and yours too, Morgan."

Khadija leaned forward. "If Fatima returns to the school, I'll have a natural connection with her."

"Although she didn't say, I believe the school is where she wants to be," Allyson said.

"Excellent," Morgan said, smiling broadly.

Chaz leaned back in his chair. "Allyson, you kept saying 'we.' Are you finally going to give us the name of your contact?"

"I was getting to that," Allyson said, feeling her face redden. "His name is Giuseppe D'Angelo. He's an aid worker with the Sant Anselmo Community, a Catholic lay movement. He's been working on refugee relief since he graduated from university, and he's one of the most influential and conscientious aid workers in Caritas. He's tireless." She took a breath and plowed on. "I met Seppe at one of the roundtable meetings of aid workers assigned to the camp. He doesn't know about my real identity, of course, but that's why I wanted to keep him anonymous."

Chaz said, "Come on, Allyson. That only explains why you kept your identity secret from him. Why the hell have you kept his identity secret from us? That is, unless you're not telling us everything."

Allyson paused, aware that her anger at Seppe had returned. Why couldn't he be a normal Italian in his twenties, a man with a past and secrets to hide?

"I kept his identity secret because . . . because I concluded that Seppe is the type of person the agency would probably misunderstand."

"And why's that, Agent Worthy?" Morgan asked. Allyson had never been addressed formally by her case officer, and she understood it wasn't meant as a compliment.

"All Seppe wants to do is help refugees. That's it. No other agenda, no big ego; he simply wants to help."

"I think this guy has taken you in," Chaz said.

Allyson's head snapped up. "Which is exactly why I didn't share his name from the beginning. There's got to be dirt on him somewhere, right?"

The room was silent for a moment. Khadija looked from Allyson to Chaz to Morgan.

Finally, Morgan spoke. "I'm with Chaz on this one. You've lost objectivity, and that's dangerous."

"Look, Seppe is one of the most respected and trusted aid workers in Caritas, and that respect and trust extends to his organization as well. Let's not forget that he was the one who brought the two attacks to our attention. He asked for my help, and you gave me the go-ahead, Morgan."

"All the more reason to assess his motives for bringing you and the Agency into play, Allyson," she replied.

Allyson sighed, feeling defeated. "Go ahead. Have at it. You're not going to find anything."

"We'll see, won't we?" Morgan replied. "I just hope you can accept what we find out about him."

Chaz reported next and looked energized by Allyson's comedown. He smiled as he shared that he hadn't, after all, ignored Allyson's request to investigate Professor Napolitano's time at the camp in Sicily. Gianni, Chaz's contact in the police, had phoned him the night before, implying more than stating directly that the professor was not a person the Agency should concern itself with.

"I asked if that meant the professor was one of their confidential informants, and my contact wouldn't say yes and he wouldn't say no. He simply repeated that the professor had nothing to do with the attacks in the camp."

No wonder Chaz looks so smug. He's been right all along, and Seppe and I have been barking up the wrong tree for days, Allyson thought. She'd only uncovered scanty information about the professor, just enough for him to be considered a suspicious person.

"Excellent work, Chaz, and kudos to your contact in the police. While it would have been nice to know about this before now, how could the police read our minds? The point is, it looks like we can definitely cross the professor off our list. Do you agree, Allyson?"

"Of course, but does that mean the professor knows about us, about the Agency's interest in the attacks?"

"If he does, he didn't get that intel from me," Chaz said.

Morgan added, "He's probably been as suspicious about you and your motives, Allyson, as you were of him. I think it's time to contact the professor and arrange for a show-and-tell session. Just keep your friend Seppe out of that, okay?"

Allyson nodded, her face burning as she absorbed the insult. Of course, she would keep Seppe in the dark. She didn't even want to think about how Seppe would react if he knew her true identity.

"Anything else, Chaz?" Morgan asked, smiling in his direction.

Chaz smiled back. "Okay, let me finish before you jump down my throat, Morgan. With the professor no longer a suspect, contacting Jameela Malik is more important than ever, right? For five thousand euros and two tickets to Milan, Asha will take me to her sister, and let's not forget that Jameela has all the answers to what's going on in Caritas."

The room became deathly quiet before Morgan spoke. "Chaz, you've got a helluva lot of explaining to do before I give you five euros, much less five thousand."

Chaz removed a fountain pen from his shirt pocket and studied it before answering. *I haven't seen the pen for a while,* Allyson realized.

"Frankly, I think five grand is a bargain," Chaz replied. "Asha knows how valuable contacting her sister is to us and the police." Chaz glanced up from his pen as he added, "I was actually able to talk her down from ten grand."

Nice tell, Chaz. I bet you don't fool Morgan either, Allyson thought.

"Even if we assume what you're saying is credible, why aren't the police coughing up some of the cash?" Morgan posed.

"Look, Morgan, I tried that out on my guy. He told me it'd take weeks before a request for that amount would be approved by his superiors. Besides, if the Agency pays for the information, then all the information is ours to do with as we decide."

To Allyson's surprise, Khadija asked, "Why Milan?"

"I thought that was obvious. Jameela is there."

"Then why don't we have our agents in Milan pick her up?" Morgan asked.

"Because Milan is a big city, and Jameela doesn't want to be found. If I show up with Asha, however, and convince Jameela that I'm not there to haul her back to Caritas, I'm betting she'll spill what she knows. Asha hinted as much."

"Are you aware that you're asking for the Agency to treat Asha Malik as a confidential informant?" Morgan asked.

"I'm fine with that label. And I'm happy to be her handler."

"Let's say Asha will take you to meet Jameela. Does Asha think that she'll be allowed to stay in Milan with her sister?" Allyson asked.

Chaz's tone was sharp. "Is that such a bad idea?"

"What Allyson is driving at, Chaz, is that your request has the Agency getting into the business of resettling a refugee," Morgan said.

"Don't we do that all the time with confidential informants?"

Morgan looked down at her folder. "Just to be clear. It won't be up to you or to me to decide if Asha and Jameela should be sent back to Caritas. If that's the Agency's decision, then our agents in Milan will do just that."

Chaz started to reply when there was a knock on the door. Morgan looked irritated at the agent who stuck his head into the room.

After scanning the room, the agent's eyes settled on Morgan. "We just heard. A package released some poison in the Caritas camp. Apparently there are several casualties, most minor. One person, however, was killed. He was some professor there."

CHAPTER TWENTY-SIX

Restaurant in Trastevere

It took only an hour for news of the bombing to reach Seppe at Sant Anselmo. Assuming that Allyson hadn't heard the news, he phoned to share what little he knew. Allyson could hear the grief in his voice, as he kept repeating, "I wish there was something we could have done."

They met that evening at a small restaurant on one of the backstreets of Trastevere. Police had already been to the Sant Anselmo headquarters to interview the aid workers who knew the professor, Seppe included.

"Have they questioned you yet?" he asked.

"No, not yet," Allyson replied, knowing that her interview would be much more thorough. "What did they ask you?"

"They wanted to know how we'd met the professor and what we talked about."

"What did you tell them?"

"The truth," Seppe said as if he were surprised by the question.

"What I mean is, did you tell them about the note and the professor trying to hide it?"

"Of course, and I told him that you and I had some suspicions at first about his relationship with Fatima."

"That must have gotten their attention," Allyson said.

"That's what surprised me, Allyson. I thought the same as you, that they'd ask me for details about what I meant. Instead, it was as if they already knew about Fatima and the note."

Which they did, Allyson thought. *Unlike you, Seppe, the police knew that the professor was one of their own.*

"Why do you think he was killed?" Seppe asked. "It must have something to do with the other two attacks, doesn't it?"

Allyson nodded, pondering how much to share with Seppe. She opted for a bit of deception. "If he was part of whatever is going on in Caritas, he might have become a liability to them."

"Oh," Seppe said, before becoming silent and making the sign of the cross.

"What?" Allyson asked.

Seppe's eyes were filled with fear. "Don't you see, Allyson? It could have been our digging into the professor's past that got him killed."

The jarring news of the professor's death ended the case review meeting before Khadija could share her new plan to make contact with Sabia. In Morgan's office later, however, she outlined her proposal.

The case manager sighed heavily when Khadija ended. "Khadija, you can probably guess what I'm going to say. Any proposal put forward isn't immediately approved or disapproved. Instead, any plan has to be evaluated in at least two ways. The first is to ask, 'What are the chances that the proposed plan will succeed?' You're suggesting that your plan will get the attention of those involved in crime in the camp. Tell me how that could happen."

Khadija was prepared for the question. "If you haven't been in a refugee camp like Caritas, it's hard to describe. No one has enough of anything—clothes, shoes, toiletries, toys, even pencils and paper. We walk around and see what little we have reflected in everyone we pass. When something sparkles in the sun, or someone is wearing something that doesn't look like it's been worn by ten people before, you notice. It's like Sabia shines when you see her. I imagine Jameela Malik did as well. And that's what I'll do."

"Okay, what happens then?"

"I assume that there's only one source in the camp for the jewelry and new clothes. Everyone who sees me with a shiny watch or rings will assume I'm part of the scheme."

"Except those who are actually involved in the crime that's going on there," Morgan said, frowning. "And that brings us to the second way the Agency evaluates every plan. What is the level of risk? Can you assure the Agency that your plan won't put you in danger?"

Khadija paused. The night before, when she first thought of the plan, she realized its danger. She looked Morgan fully in the face before answering. "Doesn't anyone who works for the CIA know that safety isn't guaranteed?"

"Think it through, Khadija. How will they come at you when they notice your swag?"

"I think they'll first want to know where my watch and rings came from. They'll also want to know if there's a new group horning in on their turf."

"And what will you say?"

"If I say that I'm part of ISIS or, better yet, a less well-known group like Al-Nusra, I'm betting Sabia's group will suggest our two groups join forces. They'll have to tell me how their scam works."

Morgan sighed again. "Look, Khadija, your entire plan is based on bluffing people who are fine with killing. Maybe Chaz could pull that off, but I wouldn't recommend even Allyson for the task. Beyond that, nothing in your file indicates you can do that, and, frankly, that's not how you've come across since you joined us. Are you capable? Yes. Are you good at fitting in? Yes. However, here you'd be playing almost the opposite role."

"That's why I have to do this, Morgan. That's exactly why I must do this."

The case manager leaned back in her chair and gazed out the window. "I'll give this some serious thought, and we'll have to get clearance from above. However, I can tell you one thing they'll ask me. What's your exit plan? How will we know when you're ready to be pulled? How will we know if your plan has thrown you into greater danger?"

"Trust me, Morgan, I have no death wish. The way I see it, what Allyson asked me to do in the meeting can work both ways. I mean about my being near Fatima to keep an eye on her."

"Explain that to me."

"If I'm going to keep a close eye on Fatima, then she'll be keeping a close eye on me as well. We'll be each other's safety net. If she goes missing,

I'll contact you right away. The same can go for me. If I don't show up some night in the dorm, Fatima will know to contact you."

"You're sure about this—about actually going through with the bluff?"

Khadija held her gaze and nodded. "Morgan, I have to do this."

CHAPTER TWENTY-SEVEN

August 3
Off Ostia's Coast

ALLYSON WAS LOOKING UP at the sails when Chiara yelled across the stern, "How you like Rome, Allyson?"

From how long it took Chiara to pose that question, Allyson realized that this might be the extent of Chiara's English. In Italian, she answered, "Enjoying Rome isn't hard. Are you from Rome originally?"

With obvious relief, Chiara replied in Italian, "Oh, I didn't know you're fluent in our language. My family is from Napoli. I moved here just two months ago, to be near Leo. Maybe that means you're more Roman than me."

"No, everyone can see she's an American," Leo said with a sideways smile that Allyson couldn't decipher. "Where from?" he asked in English nearly as good as Seppe's.

"The Midwest, actually."

"Chicago? Cleveland? Where?" he asked.

"Detroit."

"Where Cadillacs come from, yes?"

"I suppose that's true." *Cadillac? That says a lot,* Allyson thought. *I won't even tell him I drive a Corolla.*

"Seppe, you like my boat?" Leo asked.

Seppe's look shifted from the mast and sails to his brother. Allyson was relieved when Seppe had asked her to come with him on the outing. Seppe had initially blamed himself for the death of the professor, and at the professor's funeral he'd looked pale, reminding her that he was an empathetic aid worker, not some government agent. Today, she was glad to see that his color was better.

"I like the boat's lines," Seppe said, "and you've got the Genoa rigging you've always wanted. She runs upwind beautifully."

Leo nodded. "I thought you'd noticed that. Allyson, you sail in America?"

"Actually, my father recently bought a sailboat. He's restoring it . . . or her. I guess sailboats are supposed to be female. She's wooden, I think."

"Ah, a classic. Papa would approve," Leo said, looking at her with what appeared new respect. "He can sail in Detroit?"

"Yes, out on Lake St. Clair. I think he's been out on Lake Erie, one of the Great Lakes, as well."

"And what does your family do?" Chiara asked.

"Do?"

"The family business, I mean."

Allyson laughed. "We don't have a family business. Actually, we aren't a family anymore. My parents divorced. My dad is a police detective, and my mother is an intensive-care nurse."

"Oh, how exciting. A detective," Chiara said. "America, it has lots of killers, doesn't it? And your papa catches them?"

"He says his job is more paperwork than excitement."

"And you work with refugees, like Seppe," Leo said, not as a question.

Allyson felt uncomfortable, as Leo was clearly listening carefully to everything she said. She hadn't had much time to prepare for the outing, because Seppe had invited her for the Saturday sail only the evening before.

"That's right. We're both aid workers."

"Although not with Sant Anselmo," Leo said.

"Allyson works for Europa Spec," Seppe said. "I think she's their conscience."

"Ah, another evil company intent on profits and pandering to shareholders," Leo said, his eyes again on Allyson.

"Pharmaceuticals and medical devices," Allyson replied. "We've donated some of our products to the camps, although I work in the philanthropic wing of the company."

"If Seppe says you're their conscience, does that mean your company has a guilty one?" Leo asked. Allyson found the moment bizarre, pretending to defend a fictional firm's reputation and trying not to look at Seppe. *Am I giving off a "tell?"* she thought.

"Don't all corporations have a guilty conscience for one reason or another?" Seppe asked.

"Be careful, Allyson. My brother isn't a fan of capitalism, even though he likes my boat, and we both know where the money for this beauty came from."

Allyson felt her face reddening. She struggled to understand how these two brothers came from the same family.

"You should let your brother take you to Caritas, Leo," she said, pushing back.

After Leo guffawed, Chiara said in a quieter voice, "After I saw you on TV, Seppe, I wondered if I could visit the camp. Is it a very sad place?"

"You're both welcome any time," Seppe said. "Of course, even though refugees have a lot to be sad about, they're also grateful. Even happy, believe it or not."

"Pity doesn't help anyone," Leo said in what Allyson took to be a clear challenge to his brother.

Allyson glared at Leo, wanting to slap him across the face.

"That's where you and I agree," Seppe said calmly. "The refugees don't want pity. They just want a future. I hope to God Allyson and I aren't offering pity. Yet we do offer hope."

Nobody said anything for a few moments as Leo tacked, and the boat headed south from the Ostia marina.

"Come take the wheel," Leo said, looking at Seppe.

The man does like to give orders, Allyson thought. She wondered if the boys' father did the same.

Without responding, Seppe moved to the stern and took the wheel.

"Go ahead, put her through her paces," Leo again ordered. "Or don't you like sailing anymore?"

"Sailing doesn't have to be racing, Leo," Seppe replied, looking out to the horizon.

"Sure it does, Seppe." After a moment, Leo added, "Papa and I are going to trailer our boats down to Napoli this summer. We're going to sail around Capri."

"You mean you're going to race each other," Seppe said, glancing briefly at Leo.

"Sure we are. That's what we D'Angelos do; we race, we compete, we push ourselves. Remember?"

"Oh, I remember," Seppe said, leaving it there.

Allyson looked from Leo to Seppe and back again, sensing that the exchange offered an insight into the two brothers and what divided them.

Enroute to Rome

As Seppe and Allyson drove back from the sailing outing, Seppe felt for the first time in days that his mind was clearing. He had initially blamed himself for the professor's death, but had awakened yesterday feeling lighter. That was why he'd accepted Leo's invitation to sail and invited Allyson.

"You're awfully quiet. What are you thinking about?" Allyson asked.

"About the professor. Also about Leo."

"Ah" was all that Allyson said at first. After a few miles, she added, "It's hard to believe you two are brothers. Now my nemesis at work, Chaz, he could be Leo's brother."

"With everything going on this past week, I didn't tell you I had lunch with Leo. He said something I couldn't get out of my mind—until now."

Allyson turned in her seat to look at Seppe. "What'd he say?"

"He asked me why I'm throwing my life away trying to change something that's never going to change. That's why he got defensive when Chiara said she wants to visit Caritas."

"Wow, that's like something Chaz would say. What was your answer?"

"I didn't have one then. I think I have one now. Not that it would mean much to Leo."

"Care to share?" Allyson asked.

Seppe glanced over and offered a weak smile. "It's something that happened about six months ago in the camp. I visited the school, and I think that was when I first met Hasan Kadir. Although we only met briefly, I liked him. Anyway, I was there when the kids were having snacks. I was sitting with about four or five of the kids and without my understanding what was happening, one of the kids came around and put a cookie into my mouth. I guess it's a game they play. It affected me at the time, refugee children who'd known hunger sharing a cookie. It wasn't until we were out on the water today, when you put a cookie in my mouth while I had the wheel, that something else struck me."

"I guess I did do that. What did it make you think of?"

"Both times, the cookies being put in my mouth reminded me of receiving communion in the Mass. It felt like some great truth."

"Huh," Allyson said slowly. "I wouldn't expect Leo to understand that, and I'm not sure I do. How do those two cookies help you answer your brother's question? I mean, I ask myself all the time if we're doing any real good in Caritas."

Seppe drove in silence for a few moments. "In one respect, I think Leo is right. What we offer refugees won't change anything until something else changes—the attitude of those of us, myself included, who have more than enough. The poor remain poor because we who are rich want to be even richer. It's like what we aid workers always say: there's enough for everyone even while many are dying with nothing."

Seppe felt Allyson's hand on his arm.

"I know you said before that you came from a rich family," she said softly. "Yet, it wasn't until we were stepping onto your brother's boat that I understood just how rich your family really is. And yet I know you don't want a boat or any of that."

"Don't I? When we were out sailing, my hands itched—I mean, they literally itched—to take the wheel and show Leo, Chiara, and, yes, you, that I'm a better sailor than my brother. And the worst part of it is that I knew what Leo was thinking, 'Do it, Seppe. Do it.'" Seppe took Allyson's hand and squeezed it gently.

"I saw that on Leo's face too," Allyson said, "and I wanted you to show him up. Then when you didn't, I realized how strong you must be . . . to turn your back on all that."

Seppe turned into a layby and came to a stop. He glanced down on their hands intertwined and felt a lump in his throat. "My family thinks I hate them for being rich and that I love being poor. I don't. I hate poverty. I mean, I really hate seeing people in camps like Caritas simply because they're on the wrong side of history. I hate that the children in the camp, if they're lucky, will end up cleaning the streets of Rome or making the beds in hotels that they can never afford to stay in."

As Seppe wiped away a tear, he felt Allyson kissing him on the cheek. "Yet, those same kids fed you cookies," she said.

Seppe could feel tears flowing freely as he looked over and, without hesitating, drew Allyson to him. "Alli, I . . . I can't promise . . ."

"Shhh," Allyson whispered, as they kissed.

CHAPTER TWENTY-EIGHT

August 5
U.S. Embassy, Rome

LEO BELIEVED IN LUCK, especially the kind he could take credit for later, and today was a day of luck that he would long remember. The luck began with something that appeared to be a misfortune, a traffic jam that made him late for work. Instead of joining in the Italian pastime of shouting and honking at the cars ahead, however, he spent the time daydreaming about his papa's classic Alfa-Romeo that would soon be his.

From thinking about sports cars, he let his thoughts drift to Seppe. He still couldn't make sense of his brother's choices, choices which he considered self-destructive. A noisy one-bedroom apartment, a job without a future, a future without sailboats and Alfa-Romeos. Really? Why?

Finally, after a long delay, traffic cleared as he turned onto Via Veneto, one of Rome's poshest streets. Employees at D'Angelo Financial Services had joked for years about having to compete for parking spaces with employees of the U.S. Embassy that was across the street. Leo had a reserved parking place waiting for him, which meant he drew closer to the embassy without really noticing it.

That morning, however, the traffic slowed to a sudden stop a hundred meters short of the embassy, and it was while Leo was waiting that he glanced across the street. There was Allyson Worthy, Seppe's girlfriend, escorting two women in long black robes through the outer gate of the embassy. On instinct, he lowered his passenger window and called out.

"Buongiorno, Alli. Alli, it's me, Leo," he shouted.

And that's when he experienced the height of his luck. Allyson stopped on the sidewalk and instead of returning the greeting, turned back to shield the Middle Eastern women as if from an attack.

As the traffic began to move again, it dawned on Leo that Allyson's reaction was both strange and suspicious. By the time he'd parked his car, he knew what he would do. He would call a contact, actually an old girlfriend, whose company interfaced with European and American companies in Rome and ask her what she knew about Europa Spec. During the sailing outing, he'd felt certain that there was more to Allyson than she let on, and he relished the thought that he might uncover something that Allyson was hiding from Seppe. Yes, that would be delicious.

August 7
CIA Headquarters

Over the next two days, Allyson waited for Seppe to call and ask her to explain why she was at the U.S. Embassy and why she'd reacted as she did to Leo. Her reaction to seeing Leo's face was instinctive, the two worlds she'd kept apart colliding without warning in that moment. When Seppe didn't call, she began to dread a call from Leo asking her to explain.

After days of silence, she contemplated calling Seppe to give her version of what had happened. She could say that she was taking two residents of Caritas to the embassy for a logical reason. However, what possible reason would that be? She could hardly tell the truth, although that was exactly what she wanted to do. What she wouldn't give to ask Seppe to meet her that night and when he asked why, she would say, "I have so much I want to share with you."

She didn't make that call. For one thing, the Agency insisted that the best sources never knew they were sources. Seppe was such a person. He shared Sant Anselmo lists of refugees with Allyson only because he assumed she was a fellow aid worker.

That revealed the second reason she couldn't tell Seppe the whole truth. As long as they were just colleagues, fellow aid workers, the possibility of exposure, of his finding out her true purpose in Rome, was an acceptable risk. If her cover or Europa Spec's cover were blown, the Agency would simply close down its office and open another one elsewhere in the city under a different name.

Yet, Seppe and Allyson were no longer just colleagues. They had acknowledged that they were more than friends, and now Allyson sat in her office in agony, wondering how, just days before, she'd been that naive. What had she imagined—that she'd get married, and then, maybe a year or two into their marriage, she'd tell him the complete truth? On what planet would a happy ending actually happen?

No, she now saw that the romantic notion that their love would overcome everything—her lies, deception, and using him on behalf of the American government—was pure illusion.

I can do nothing, she thought. *I can't tell Seppe the truth, and I won't tell the Agency that my cover might be blown. I'll wait and hope for a miracle. Otherwise, the future holds only one inevitable outcome—Seppe walking away from me forever.*

AUGUST 8

MORGAN STOOD OUTSIDE THE front doors to Europa Spec and frowned at the cigarette she'd just lit. "Well, I stayed away from you bastards for almost a year, but you got me back."

However, today, the day when the decisions came down from above about Chaz's and Khadija's separate plans, she'd stopped on the way to the office to buy a pack of cigarettes. Two days before, she accompanied Chaz to the offices above hers, where he convinced the suits to fund his request to use Asha Malik to take him to meet Jameela. As she watched him smooth-talk the men above her, she realized that Chaz with his Navy Seal and Brown University pedigree was their type of guy, their type of drinking partner, their type of agent. *Dammit, I'll probably end up working for him one day,* she thought as she took another drag on the cigarette.

The other plan approved by the higher-ups was Khadija's scheme to draw the attention of the ringleaders in the camp by showing up suddenly with shiny jewelry. The powers-that-be had even come up with a plausible cover story for Khadija to spin if she succeeded in getting the attention of people behind the attacks. The new story linked Khadija's wealth with one of Syria's lesser-known rebel groups, Al-Nusra.

Morgan crushed the remainder of the cigarette out on the sidewalk and looked out over the Tiber River. Her superiors had complimented her on the boldness of Chaz's and Khadija's plans. However, she knew that boldness masked the danger inherent in both plans. If either plan backfired, she, not Chaz and Khadija and not the suits above her, would be held responsible.

Well, I asked us to act like a team, she thought, *and it looks like I got my wish.*

CHAPTER TWENTY-NINE

August 8
US Embassy, Rome

After weeks recovering in the hospital, Fatima found the prospect of returning to Caritas worrisome. Yes, it was comforting to know she would have someone, an agent named Khadija, looking out for her, yet that comfort came with complications.

Fatima had been impressed by Khadija and the determined look in her eye when Allyson introduced her. That had been in the car when Fatima thought she was being taken back to Caritas. As Allyson went over how Fatima's and Khadija's relationship would work, Fatima felt her anxiety building, made worse by the car not taking them to Caritas, but to the U.S. Embassy instead. When Fatima turned and asked Allyson to explain, Allyson told her that everything would become clear once they were inside the embassy.

On the way into the building, Fatima heard someone call Allyson's name from across the street. She noticed that Allyson initially looked rattled, although by the time they were inside embassy, she appeared to be in control once again. The three women were immediately ushered into an office where two men, who looked like they could be American TV actors, were seated.

If Fatima expected the men to introduce themselves, she was mistaken, although they knew her name. As soon as everyone was seated, the older, balding American took charge of the meeting. "You're Khadija Mubarak, correct?" he asked, looking at Khadija.

"I am," Khadija replied.

"I understand you will translate if Ms. Rasul doesn't understand our English."

Khadija simply nodded.

"Good. My colleague and I are diplomats, assigned to the U.S. Embassy. In case you're worried, you're not in any trouble." He paused before adding, "Please pay close attention to what I'm going to say next."

Fatima's command of English evaporated as the man stared at her, and she turned to Khadija as much for support as translation.

"We're investigating the three attacks in Caritas—the murders of Hasan Kadir and Professor Napolitano and the attack on you," the man said.

After the statement was translated, Fatima looked down at her hands. Allyson said, "It's okay, Fatima," although Fatima wasn't convinced, and she wished that the other aid worker, Seppe, was in the room. *Why isn't he?* she wondered.

"I don't know who attacked me," she finally managed to say.

"That's what we intend to find out," Allyson assured her. "We already think we know why the attacks occurred."

Fatima didn't say anything and noticed that Khadija contributed nothing to the conversation except to translate.

"I am free to tell you this, Ms. Rasul. There is a crime taking place in Caritas called fraud," the other man said. "In this case, we believe a group has found a way to siphon off money from the Italian government that is meant for refugees. A lot of money. We think that's what Mr. Kadir was warning you about in the note."

"I never understood the note," she protested. "All I remember is that it said something about more bad things coming from Damascus."

"You have noticed that some people in the camp have more than others, right?" the man continued. "Jewelry and clothes, for example."

"Jameela did, but I heard she's gone."

The two men looked at one another before the bald man spoke again. "I understand that Allyson has told you about Khadija watching out for you once you reenter the camp. In addition, Khadija will be doing something in the next few days what could confuse you. That's why it's important that you know that she works for us."

"I don't understand. What will she do?"

"The day after tomorrow, she will begin to wear a fancy watch, rings, and earrings. That's to make it look like she's receiving cash and gifts from someone. We think residents who've been given jewelry, like Asha and a woman named Sabia, will notice. They will likely make contact with Khadija directly to find out where her wealth comes from. Or, they could approach you, to hear what you know about Khadija's clothes and jewelry."

Fatima felt a chill of fear run down her spine. "What am I to tell them? I don't know what's going on."

"What you do is more important than what you say." The other man reached across the table and placed a small packet of facial tissues in front of Fatima and a second one in front of Khadija.

"There's a radio transmitter inside each packet. If someone approaches Khadija directly and threatens her in any way, she'll push on these two corners, and that will send out a signal. If someone approaches you and scares you, you will do the same. If someone is just curious, however, tell them that you don't know where Khadija got the jewelry. Do you understand what we want you to do?" the bald man asked.

Fatima felt dizzy as she tried to process what she was hearing. Not knowing what to say, she turned to Allyson. "Do you work for these men as well?"

"Yes, I do, Fatima, and I know this is a lot to take in. Please believe me when I say that we're trying to stop the crime going on in Caritas. Khadija will keep tabs on you, and you will keep an eye out for her."

"And Seppe, the man who came to the hospital with you. Does he work for you as well?"

Allyson looked at the two men before answering. "No, he doesn't, and he know nothing about any of this."

"Why? I thought you were friends," she said.

Allyson sighed. "It's complicated. We are friends, but Seppe doesn't know about this part of my job. Seppe won't be in any danger as long as he knows nothing about our plan."

"Do I have a choice?" she said, keeping her eyes on Allyson.

The bald man cleared his throat. "You're free to say no, and if that's your decision, we will give you a new identify and send you to another camp. That's for Khadija's safety as much as yours. If you work with us, Fatima, we promise that you'll be released very soon and allowed to stay in Italy.

We'll also help out with expenses as you get settled. In other words, we'll help you begin the next chapter of your life. That's because we're convinced that we're close to identifying the people behind the crime and the attacks in Caritas. What do you say?"

Fatima said yes, and now, as she sat on her bed in Caritas, she tried to ready herself for tomorrow when Khadija would begin to attract attention with the jewelry and new clothes. She shivered, remembering how only a day before, she'd counted on Khadija Mubarak being her safety net in Caritas. Instead, the person she thought would protect her might be bringing more danger her way.

August 8
Fiumicino Airport, Rome

As Chaz drove to the airport to pick up the agent assigned to accompany him to Milan with Asha, he could hardly believe what was safely stowed in his sport coat pocket. On his last visit to Caritas to brief Asha on the details of his plan, she'd handed him his Mont Blanc Meisterstuck 149. He'd feared the pen would be damaged, a permanent reminder of his naïveté in dealing with refugees. To his relief, the nib, the most vital part of the pen, showed no signs of being used. He tenderly inspected the pen one more time and felt his grandfather approving his determination to get the heirloom back.

The return of the pen also buoyed his trust in Asha, his conviction that she would follow through on the plan—his plan—to contact Jameela. From his three meetings with Asha, he got the impression that she deferred to Jameela. Chaz thought of Asha as a pretty face, a very pretty face, yet not someone intelligent and scheming like Jameela.

Jameela. She, not Asha, was the woman whose jewelry first drew the attention of the authorities to something fishy occurring in the camp. She, not Asha, was the woman who accused Hasin Kadir of molestation. She, not Asha, was the woman who had all the answers to the attacks and the criminal activity in the camp.

If Jameela told him all she knew, the Bureau Chief in the Rome office had given him permission to offer Jameela immunity and protection. The alternative he would present would be arrest and incarceration. As the taxi weaved through Rome's morning traffic, he felt certain that Jameela would choose wisely.

He arrived at Fiumicino Airport a few minutes ahead of the arrival of Braylen Manners, a CIA agent fluent in Arabic and attached to him for the duration of the operation. The day before, Morgan showed him a picture of Manners, a woman as striking in her Nordic coloring as Asha Malik was in her Middle Eastern appearance.

They should make a movie of this, he thought, as he parked in an arrival line outside Lufthansa Airlines. *Three hot women, counting Jameela, and an ex-Navy Seal, now CIA agent, set for a rendezvous in Italy.* There was also, at least on his part, a feeling of competition with Khadija's plan, where she would attract the crime ring's attention by wearing jewelry. Allyson being assigned to work with Khadija and Fatima on the details of the other plan made the competition all the sweeter.

He listened to the sounds of planes arriving and departing and thought of the time in the not-too-distant future when he would be flying out. Rome wasn't the assignment that he'd imagined. While he wasn't naïve nor had he imagined that every assignment would be exciting or romantic, he had hoped his posting in Rome would have had some of the danger he faced as a Navy Seal. Consequently, when Morgan impressed upon him the risks in his plan, he probably appeared to be calm, even as his arms and legs were tingling.

The automatic doors opened, and Braylen Manners appeared, as tall and attractive in person as she was in the photo in her file. She wore a blue ensemble of slacks and blouse, stylish without standing out. His heart raced a bit as he thought of the days ahead.

Before he could even think of playing the gallant role, she spotted him and opened the passenger door. As she slid in, she turned and extended her hand to shake his.

"Braylen Manners, right?" he asked, feeling immediately stupid.

"Which makes you Chaz Eaton," she replied, not offering even the beginning of a smile. "And drop the Braylen; call me Manners."

As he pulled away from the curb, Chaz asked, "Is this standard for you—being brought in at critical moments on a case?"

"Lately it has been," she said, not elaborating. "Although this is my first time in Rome. You like it?"

"Not really. It's limiting, not knowing the language."

"Naturally. No thought of picking up Italian while you're here?"

"I don't plan on being here that long," Chaz said. After an awkward silence, he asked, "Did you fly in from the Middle East?"

"Northern Europe," she said, leaving it at that as she stared out the window.

"Yet you've worked on the refugee issue, I was told."

"Among other things," Manners said. They rode in more silence until she asked, "Anything I should know about your relationship with Asha Malik before we pick her up?"

"Like what?" Chaz asked, feeling defensive.

"What does she know about you, for example?"

"She knows I'm American, and she knows my organization has the power to get her out of the camp. She doesn't know she's being used by the CIA."

"Have you had sex with her?"

Chaz looked over, trying to decipher the expression on her face. Manners, however, was looking out the window. Was she trying to put him off balance?

"No, I don't have clearance for that," he replied, trying to sound casual.

"Yet you want to, right? I mean, I've seen her photo."

And maybe you've seen my file as well, Chaz thought. "Do you want me to say it's never crossed my mind?"

"No, I want you to be straight with me. By the way, your sex life isn't of interest to me. What I want is your assurance that we're going to focus on the plan, Agent Eaton, focus on the plan. I have no time for guys, Navy Seals, maybe like yourself—yes, I've read your file—thinking they can play me. I want to be in and out of this gig in hours, not days, so we don't have time for games. When you look at me, I don't want to see you imagining me naked on top of you in bed. I want you seeing the agent who has your back and that's all. Do you follow what I'm saying?"

"Yeah, I follow," Chaz replied, feeling that Agent Manners was flaying his skin from his body one strip at a time.

"Of course, it's great if Asha Malik thinks you're going to hit on her. We can use that, just so long as it's she who's losing focus, not you. What does she think she's going to get out of all this?"

"The same as any refugee—money and a ticket out of the camp. That way she can get on with her life."

"Makes sense. She wants to follow her sister. In the file, you describe Asha as the follower of the two."

"I'm sure of that. Too many times she's said, 'You'll have to ask Jameela.'"

Manners turned, as if allowing Chaz to look at her fully for the first time. "What part of the plan makes you the most nervous?"

Although Chaz thought of denying that he was even close to being nervous, he knew she'd see through that. "There's a couple of points where things could go south, which is true of every plan. In this case, I've made accommodations if they do. The first will come with the initial meeting with Jameela. We have to convince her to come to the rendezvous unescorted, preferably someplace public. If she's accompanied by any muscle, there's a chance of a firefight, and that's something the Agency wants to avoid at all costs."

"If I follow what you're saying, success is going to depend largely on Asha Malik being able to convince her more savvy sister," Manners said, keeping her eyes on Chaz.

"I'm sure she can do this."

"And the second point?"

"That's the moment it dawns on the two sisters that they can't stay in Milan. Jameela will undoubtedly see it first. Whether or not Jameela shares with us what she knows about crime in the camp, she'll know we can't let her walk out of the room. Both Jameela and Asha will have to be resettled and offered protection."

"And if one or both of them reject the deal?"

"Jameela will see that it's still a good deal. They get what they want, a ticket out of the camps."

"Assume the worst. Let's say they refuse."

"Then we'll give the signal for our agents standing by in Milan to waltz in and take them to a secure location for enhanced questioning."

"And you're sure Asha Malik hasn't thought about that?"

Chaz paused, for the first time wondering how confident he was about Asha. For him, the risk in the plan always centered on Jameela and her reaction. He'd known women like Asha before, always trying to prove they were attractive to men. "Yes, I'm sure," he said. "As I said, Asha is not what I'd call a deep thinker."

"We'll soon see, won't we?" Manners said, turning away from Chaz to study the passing scenery.

CIA HEADQUARTERS

ALLYSON WAS BATTLING NERVES as she sat at her desk. Morgan had assigned her to be Khadija's and Fatima's "wide receiver," the in-house agent waiting for a signal from an agent in the field. Khadija and Fatima were in place; Khadija had returned to the camp that afternoon from her supposed appointment with her oncologist; and Fatima was delivered to the camp three hours later.

With Khadija not donning the swag until tomorrow morning, no one expected the next fourteen hours would be eventful. To calm Fatima's worries, however, Allyson promised Fatima that she'd be awaiting a signal from the moment she walked through Caritas's gate.

The empty time meant that she found herself worrying about Seppe. She texted him that morning to say that she was required to attend an in-service seminar at Europa Spec and wouldn't be going with him to Caritas. Ever since she pressed "send," she wondered if Seppe already knew the truth about her. If he did, then her text message would be another nail in the coffin of their relationship, further proof that she only ever lied to him.

Whatever happened, she knew that such a conclusion was far from the truth. Her time with Seppe hadn't been a total lie, yet how would she ever convince him that he was the first man with whom she'd let her guard down, the one person who mattered to her more than anyone else?

She imagined sitting with Seppe alongside the Tiber River, two boxes in her lap. She would explain that one box contained all the lies she'd told him while the other box contained everything about their relationship that was the truth. She pictured herself throwing the box of lies into the river and it disappearing forever, yet the image gave her little comfort. There was so much that she'd said to him that fit into both boxes. *If I can't separate the lies from the truth, how can I expect Seppe to do that?* she thought.

Last night, as she struggled to fall asleep, she fantasized telling Seppe, Agency rules be damned, the complete truth. In the morning light, however, she realized that it was too late for total honesty.

CHAPTER THIRTY

August 8
Caritas Refugee Camp

WHEN THE WORLD TURNS *upside down, how does a person recover his balance?* Seppe asked himself as he drove to Caritas. He glanced over at the empty passenger seat and felt a sob catch in his throat.

At the last Sunday family dinner, Leo whispered that he wanted him to step outside for a few moments.

"Why?" Seppe asked.

"You don't want the family to hear what I have to tell you."

Outside, the two brothers walked toward the massive plane tree where they'd once built a treehouse. Beneath its shade, Leo offered Seppe a cigarette.

"No thanks.'"

"Okay, although I think you'll want one in a minute."

Leo then delivered what he discovered through a friend of his. Europa Spec was a company that set up shop in Rome in the winter of 2001. Public records indicated that Europa Spec had its European headquarters in Germany although it was an offshoot of a Washington-based parent company. What Leo's friend uncovered was that the parent company was founded the same month in the same year.

"My friend thought the set-up looked a bit dicey," Leo said. "And there's more. She talked to one of her friends in our government's regulatory agency and, well, brace yourself, Seppe. Her friend said that the regulatory agency had discovered that a number of companies based in the U.S. and Canada with spin-off companies here in Europe popped up out of nowhere in late 2001 and early 2002. In other words, in the months right after 9/11."

The words came out of Seppe's mouth before he could stop them. "What is this, Leo? Is my being happy with Allyson too much for you to take? Is it that hard for you to share the limelight?"

Leo said nothing for a moment as he took a drag on his cigarette. "I didn't know you were that serious about Allyson. Just remember, I told you to warn yourself. And there's still more, I'm afraid."

"Afraid? I bet," Seppe spat out.

"Look, Seppe, you're my brother and in my own way I care about you. I would never have questioned Europa Spec if something hadn't happened a couple of days ago." Leo then went on to describe seeing Allyson in the company of two Middle Eastern women entering the American embassy.

"I'm sure there are good reasons why Allyson might be at the embassy, but the thing is, she didn't want me seeing her," Leo said. "It's like I pulled back the curtain and saw what I shouldn't have. Plus, the soldier at the gate took one look at her ID and let them in. Do you follow what I'm saying?"

Seppe placed his hand on the plane tree for support. His first thought was that he had no reason to question Allyson about Europa Spec. Then, unwanted and troubling thoughts began to surface. How had Allyson found a companion in Caritas for Fatima that quickly? And hadn't he wondered when she saw through the camp's security chief too quickly, all that business about noting a "tell" that people gave away when they were lying? Out of his growing feelings for Allyson, had he failed to note the "tells" that she was showing?

For the next twenty-four hours, hours with little sleep, he reviewed everything Allyson and he talked about and did together. Why, he wondered, had Allyson never invited him to Europa Spec's offices to meet her colleagues? And why that morning, after Allyson had seen Leo and acted strangely, did Allyson text him that she wouldn't be accompanying him to Caritas?

At some point in the middle of the night, Seppe gave up trying to convince himself that Allyson was at the embassy for some logical and innocent reason. He admitted that the most probable explanation was precisely what he'd been warned about in his first days with Sant Anselmo. The memo was clear: *Be aware that not all aid agencies are legitimate.* He interpreted the memo originally as a warning against groups intent on fraud. Now he realized the memo also alerted aid workers to spies among them.

He laughed a laugh that pained him as he considered the irony of the situation. He was working with Allyson to defeat fraud in Caritas, yet if Allyson were working for an American intelligence service, wasn't she the bigger fraud?

CHAPTER THIRTY-ONE

August 9
Caritas Refugee Camp

Fatima watched everyone, including herself, as if from a distance when she entered the school and was embraced warmly by the other workers. Working for months in the school and then being in the hospital for nearly three weeks left her with the uneasy feeling that she was on familiar and yet unfamiliar ground.

Adding to the strangeness of the morning was Khadija arriving at the school wearing a shiny watch and bracelet. The children were familiar with Khadija and obviously liked her. Because of that, their failing to notice the bling didn't surprise Fatima. However, Fatima could see that some of the other volunteers were already whispering about Khadija's abrupt change of appearance.

Part of what made Khadija's appearance striking was that her gauntness and ashen pallor had suggested to Fatima that she was one of the poorest residents in Caritas. Only if Khadija showed up wearing a tiara would the contrast have been greater.

Fatima realized that the change in Khadija was more than wearing jewelry. In the meeting at the U.S. Embassy, Khadija had been quiet beyond her service as a translator. This morning in the school, Khadija acted outgoing and looked even taller. While she didn't go out of her way to flaunt the jewelry, she didn't hide it either.

Fatima studied the faces of the other volunteers assigned to the school. Was another school worker beside Jameela also part of the crime ring? Did one of the other school workers know who killed Hasan Kadir, who attacked her, and who was responsible for Professor Napolitano's death? As she patted the pocket of her chador containing the tissue packet with its transmitter, she wondered if the Agency's plan was a good one, or if Khadija or she could be the next victim.

D'Angelo Financial Services Office

Going against the traffic flowing out of Rome, Seppe drove to the one person he hoped would understand him—his father. As he turned onto the sycamore-shaded Via Veneto, he glanced over at the US Embassy. That was where Allyson, if that were even her real name, had been found out by Leo.

When he drove into the family business' parking lot, he was relieved to see his father's BMW SUV in its space, under the watchful and no doubt envious gaze of two security guards.

Seppe remembered coming here as a boy, walking into where his father, grandfather, and great-grandfathers worked, the family achieving aristocratic status by managing the fortunes of some of Italy's most illustrious families. For the first time in years, he noticed the massive brass-appointed wooden doors fronting the building and the doorman in charge of guarding the entrance.

Dressed carelessly for his work in Caritas, Seppe wondered if he'd be stopped and was relieved when the doorman smiled in recognition. *Here, they know who I am,* he thought, as he was greeted warmly by the receptionist while he hastened down the hallway to the elevator. It might be just his imagination, yet ever since he joined the Sant Anselmo community, he felt the people in the D'Angelo business welcomed him too warmly on one of his rare visits, as if they knew that one day they'd be reporting to him. That was the primary reason he'd avoided coming to the business over the past year. Now he thought, *Maybe they're right. Maybe this is where I belong.*

Exiting the elevator on the top floor, Seppe felt a jolt as his eyes glanced down the thickly carpeted hallway that led to his father's office. Instead of the burled walnut walls and chandelier catching his attention, it was the paintings that lined those walls. Here was the one thing that Seppe and his father, Massimo, shared—the love of fine Italian art. His father had stoked that passion in Seppe by his gifts at Christmas.

What was lining both walls was the real reason why he'd avoided coming to the family business. While he was working in Caritas, his father's art collection was a temptation stronger than stocks, bonds, gold, or silver, and his father knew that. Today, however, instead of forcing his eyes to look away, he stopped to admire paintings that wouldn't be out of place in some of Rome's finer museums and art collections. While some of the paintings were familiar, two or three were new. Was this collection, what had been the supreme temptation, now the door to a future, to a life as a fine art appraiser? Could his interest in art become, over time, if not a consuming passion, at least something to distract him?

In that moment, Seppe realized why he was always more comfortable with his father than with his brother. For Leo, everything was about money, influence, and power. His father's religion, however, was beauty, something ancient philosophers associated with the divine. Yes, that was it. These painting represented his father's deepest core, his spiritual life, and in that way Seppe knew he was more his father's son than Leo was.

Catarina Ruselli, the secretary who had been with Seppe's father from the time Seppe was in elementary school, came around her desk to rise on her tiptoes to kiss Seppe on both cheeks.

"Oh, my Lord, it's Seppe," she said, as she held onto both of his arms. "I've missed you."

"And I've missed you, Catarina," he replied, his voice quavering.

Catarina Ruselli paused, taking him in, before adding. "Is your work going well, Seppe?"

Seppe knew he could be honest with Catarina. Her salary and position as Massimo D'Angelo's personal secretary would tempt some people to look down on others. Catarina, however, was always just who she was, a woman from a small poor town in Calabria.

"To be honest, it can be a grind, Catarina, and, as everyone knows, the refugees just keep coming. It's hard to feel I'm making a difference."

"You are, Seppe. You've always had a good heart."

"I'm not sure anymore. I guess I finally let the numbness set in," he admitted.

She moved in closer to hug him again and whisper, "I don't worry about you, Seppe. I pray for you and for the refugees."

Seppe hugged her warmly back and tried to hold back tears. "That's why you're special to me, Catarina."

Catarina pulled away and shook her head. "There's nothing special about me, except maybe for my memory," she said as she returned to her desk, opened a drawer, and drew out a bar of chocolate. "I've saved these, just in case you came to see us. Is it still one of your favorites?"

Seppe made an effort to smile as he took the candy bar. "Yes, it still is."

"Then, sit down and let me see you enjoy it," Catarina advised. "Your father has someone in his office right now. I'll let him know you're here."

Seppe gladly did as Catarina asked as they talked about her family, especially her daughter, Claudia.

"She's had her second child, a boy, can you believe that Seppe?"

Seppe felt a pang of regret and guilt. It was no secret that Catarina had wanted Seppe and Claudia, who played like cousins as they grew up, to become something more for each other and for her. "I'm happy for her. Claudia deserves a big family."

Catarina raised a finger and shook it at Seppe. "What about you, Seppe? Do you have a special one?"

Seppe focused on opening the candy bar. "No, no one special."

Catarina sighed as she watched Seppe take a bite of chocolate. "Well, Seppe, don't rush things. The right woman is out there for you."

Seppe said, "Not that I can see," Seppe said, the words coming out of his mouth with a bitter taste.

As the door to Massimo D'Angelo's office opened to emit a tall man in a tailored suit, Catarina leaned across the desk and whispered, "Remember, I always pray for you."

In his own custom-tailored suit, Massimo D'Angelo smiled broadly as he stood in the doorway to his office. "Well, look who's my next appointment. Come here, Seppe, and give your papa a hug."

The two men embraced before father led son into his office. With the photos of generations of D'Angelos on the wall, the office had given Seppe a feeling of awe since he was a boy. It was as if he were looking into the family's future, not only the past.

And that's why I haven't come here for over a year, Seppe thought. The office always felt like a trap. Now he wondered if it weren't a window or doorway.

"On your way in, did you see my newest acquisition?" his father asked. "It's a Lavinia Fontana—not her best work, but quite good."

"I didn't know you liked her work. It's more religious than most of the other works."

"You know I prefer landscapes, yet with her, I bow to genius, especially her detailing of the Madonna's clothing. I fell for it as soon as I saw it on the market, and, to tell you the truth, I thought of you when I bought it."

Seppe took a seat on the room's leather couch while his father took an accompanying leather chair. "You thought of me?"

"Well, with you becoming more interested in faith, I thought someday you should have it."

Twisting a bit on the couch, Seppe wasn't sure how to respond. Forty-eight hours before, he would have taken the gesture for what it was, a kind of peace offering on his father's part. And now?

"That's generous of you, Papa," Seppe finally replied.

"Did you have a few minutes with Catarina? She's always asking about you. I think it irks Leo because it's clear where her preference lies."

"I did, Papa. She even had chocolate for me, just like when I was a boy."

"It wasn't that long ago you were sitting right there, your legs unable to reach the floor. Life goes by too fast," his father said.

There was a moment of silence as Seppe tried to think of where to begin. Finally, looking down at his hands, he said, "I'm feeling lost, Papa, about my future, I mean."

His father started to say something, then stopped. "I wasn't expecting to hear that from you, Seppe. Your mama and I accept that all this," he said, gesturing toward the room, "isn't something you want."

Seppe looked up and gazed around the room. "I thought that too, for a long time. Now, I'm not sure."

If Seppe expected his father to sense the opening and move to exploit it, he was mistaken. "I won't say we haven't been worried about you being at Caritas with the attacks and now this murder. However, we also knew that wouldn't deter you."

"It's not that, Papa. It's me. I no longer think we're making any difference. When new refugees come to camp, I listen to the most horrific stories. I never knew people could be that cruel. And what do I have to offer? A bed, a part-time job in the camp, and little else. They want a future for themselves and especially for their children, and they deserve it. The sad truth is, and I finally see it clearly, that we can't give them that."

"Look, Seppe, no one knows how the refugee situation is going to be resolved, if it can be. On the other hand, anyone can see that the camps offer the first safety many of them have felt in months, if not years." After a pause, he added "You should know that your mama and I, once we understood your desire to work in the camps, well, we realized how proud we are of the work that you do. Perhaps, we should have been clearer about that."

Seppe had always been impressed with how understanding his father was with people, yet he felt his choice to work for Sant Anselmo had created a gulf between them. Now, to his shame, he realized he was the one who had created the gulf.

"Seppe, do you remember your big announcement at the family Christmas dinner when you were six?"

Seppe nodded. "How can I ever forget with Uncle Maurizio reminding me every year?"

As if he hadn't heard Seppe, Massimo D'Angelo leaned toward his son and said, "You announced that when you grew up, you wanted to give petrol away free. And yes, your uncle teases you about that every Christmas. The truth is that your mama and I cherish that memory. Seppe, we cherish it deeply. It showed your heart, and it showed the family that a six-year-old could see that the world is very unfair."

"Does that mean that when I began to work in the camps, it wasn't a surprise?"

"Yes and no, Seppe. After we got used to your decision, your mama and I could see that your heart hadn't changed. I know we never talked about it—until now—although I think at some level I've always known you would never spend your life in this office."

Seppe felt the tears flowing freely now. "I just don't know if I can go back to the camp, Papa. I feel completely empty."

"Of course you do. That's only natural. You must remember that those refugees rely on you, Seppe. You must see that, if only through the same compassion in other aid workers."

Seppe looked up briefly and caught his father's eye. "Not all, Papa. Not all."

After a moment, Massimo asked, "What about the young American woman you've been working with? Leo said he met her and thought you two were closer than work colleagues."

Seppe lowered his head. "I guess Leo didn't tell you the rest of the story. It's over with Allyson. It didn't work out."

"I'm sorry, Seppe. The look on your face suggests it was painful."

Seppe just shook his head.

"Is that part of your decision to leave the camp?"

"It's the end of our working relationship, that's for sure. And yes, that's a big part of why I can't see my way forward."

Massimo leaned back in his chair. "Seppe, one lesson I've learned in business is that ending a relationship, especially one that has been a good one, should only be taken as a last resort. If you're asking my advice about the camp and your relationship with this woman, I'd say don't rush to make a decision."

CHAPTER THIRTY-TWO

August 10
CIA Headquarters

WITH SEPPE STILL NOT returning her calls, Allyson was wearily weighing her options. She felt she owed the Agency the truth, that she was now certain that her cover was blown. Yet, when Morgan heard how her visit to the US Embassy with Khadija and Fatima had led to her being recognized by the brother of her contact in Sant Anselmo, the case manager had shaken her head and said Allyson shouldn't blame herself. Allyson, she said, was simply in the wrong place at the wrong time.

Yet Allyson did blame herself, if not for the sighting at the US Embassy, then for everything else. On the one hand, she blamed herself for not honoring Agency policy forbidding personal and romantic relationships with sources. On the other hand, she blamed herself for not breaking Agency rules and trusting Seppe with her identity from the moment their relationship became serious.

"What's happened has happened. What we have to figure out is if the situation can be remedied without the Agency losing you in Caritas," Morgan said that morning.

"At least Khadija and Fatima can keep us informed about what's happening there, even if I can't," Allyson said.

"With Chaz's plan and Khadija's different plan now set into motion, I think we could be close to flushing out who's behind crime in Caritas.

That means we have to know if your source, Seppe, has let the camp authorities know about your real identity. I think it's critical that you meet with him ASAP."

Allyson shook her head. "He won't return my calls. I assume the worst," Allyson said.

"What was your trust level with him before?"

"Isn't the real question how low his trust is in me now?" Allyson asked.

"Look, I understand that you think that he no longer trusts you and maybe even hates you, yet from what you told the team, I assume you told Seppe as much of the truth as you could. In other words, not everything you said to him was a lie."

Allyson looked down, feeling her face blush. "No, not everything was a lie."

"Okay, Allyson, here's what you do. Somehow, before the day is out, you have to arrange to meet him. If it's what you fear, that he now sees through you, you might still have money left in the bank with him. What I mean is all you talked about that wasn't a lie."

"And if he thinks it's all been a lie?"

Morgan rose to look out the window at Rome's midday traffic flowing by. "Allyson, do you remember the first concern I had with you?"

"I don't know if it was your first doubt about me, but I remember what you first asked me about."

"I didn't say doubt, Allyson, but concern. I've never doubted your ability and commitment, but you're right if you remember that I was concerned in the beginning that you were losing objectivity. I worried that your concern for the refugees was getting in the way of your work for us in the camp. Now, if I felt your feelings for the refugees were personal, I'm betting Seppe felt the same thing. Because your concern for the refugees has always been genuine, hasn't it, Allyson?"

Allyson nodded. "Yes, it has, but Seppe isn't answering my calls."

Morgan turned and faced Allyson. "You can't just wait for him to do that. Think of where you might find him. With both of our plans now in motion, we have to know if he's jeopardized Chaz's or Khadija's safety. Do you understand, Allyson?"

Caritas Refugee Camp

After Khadija appeared in Caritas with a shiny watch and rings, Fatima was relieved that there wasn't an immediate reaction. Yes, two of the volunteers in the school whispered with one another as they looked at Khadija's jewelry, although their interest could have been idle curiosity. Yet, when she lay in bed in the dark that night, she felt as she had back in Damascus when the sirens warning of an airstrike began to wail.

In contrast, Khadija appeared calm, at least on the outside. Fatima's first impression of Khadija was that the woman must be ill to be so thin and so pale, even though she knew Khadija's supposed cancer was a cover story. It wasn't until Fatima joined Khadija in the dining hall that she noticed how little Khadija put on her tray and then how much she left uneaten.

Even though she wanted to ask Khadija about her odd behavior, she sensed that Khadija was self-conscious about her eating habits. It was only in the school, when one of the children played a favorite game of sneaking up to put a cookie into the mouth of one of the teachers, that Khadija looked unguarded.

Despite that, Fatima felt a strength and alertness in Khadija that she envied. Except in the dining hall, Khadija noticed everything around her, including the two volunteers in the school who noticed her watch and rings. All this gave Fatima the time and space to reflect on what the Americans had told her about crime in Caritas.

What was clear was that financial irregularities had occurred in Caritas, a skimming off of funds that the camp authorities received from the Italian government and the United Nations Refugee Relief Committee. However, the extent of the fraud, the precise method of how it was done, and the organization behind it were still unclear. In addition, being back in Caritas brought up the grief she felt for Professor Napolitano's death. He had given her hope that she could have a bright future. Now, that hope had been replaced by fear, fear that she was in as much danger in Italy as she'd known in Syria.

Danger arrives from Damascus. More coming. Whoever touched that note had been attacked, two of them killed, leading Fatima to accept that what Hasan uncovered in the camp was the criminal activity that the

Americans were concerned about. Fatima knew that she too had been meant to die. She also knew that the people who tried to kill her were still in the camp and therefore knew of her return. Did they still think that she knew what the note referred to?

CHAPTER THIRTY-THREE

August 10
Church of Santa Prassede

After receiving a desperate email from Seppe, Father Sal replied immediately, and they arranged to meet later that morning. Two hours later, when Seppe came through the door of the church, he noticed that Seppe walked with his head down. Then, as they embraced, Father Sal felt Seppe hang onto him.

In the sacristy, Father Sal saw Seppe look up to a crucifix on the wall before saying, "Something finally became clear. It's enough for me to say that I've felt betrayed by someone close to me. As painful as that was—no, as that is—I believe God has used all of that to help me see that I'm meant to be a priest."

Father Sal felt his heart clutch. He prayed for wisdom, and he hoped that Seppe would understand what he had to ask him.

"I can't deny that sometimes the call does come like that, Seppe. As your spiritual director, however, I have to ask you something."

Seppe looked confused as he said, "I thought you'd be pleased."

"Ah, well, if this is what God wants of you, of course, I will be filled with joy."

"But . . ."

"No buts, Seppe, just a question. Right before you felt this certainty about the priesthood, what were you thinking about?"

Seppe looked down at his hands, clasped as if he were still in prayer. "I was thinking about how this person who I thought was my friend—I even thought about marrying her—had betrayed me. That's when I realized that God is the only one who will never let me down."

Hearing those words, Father Sal caught a glimpse of Seppe's future as a priest. In a decade, maybe even less, Seppe would become one of those priests who found people, parishioners, as well as other priests and bishops disappointing or betraying him.

The Church in her wisdom knew what to do with priests like that. She sidelined them in places where they could do the least damage. Then the final blow would come. Forty, fifty, or sixty years down that bitter road, Seppe would arrive at the gates of hell. He would die feeling that God too had betrayed him.

"Seppe, as much as I wish that you have a vocation to the priesthood—and maybe you will in the future—I don't believe it's God who is making this decision right now. It's your wounded heart. That's what you have to deal with."

Seppe shook his head slowly. "I don't know how to do that, Father."

"What I will say next will sound impossible. It's your colleague, Allyson, you're talking about, isn't it?"

Seppe nodded.

"You owe her a chance to explain."

After sharing with Father Sal what Leo discovered, Seppe said, "Believe me, Father, I've tried to think of some way that she'd hasn't betrayed everyone in Caritas, not just me." Shrugging, he added, "I can't see what that could be."

"That's not the same as listening to her. You told me before that Allyson had real compassion for refugees. Do you really think she's been putting on an act this whole time?"

"I don't know," Seppe said. "No, it's not that I don't know. I agree; Alli isn't pretending in Caritas. She cares about Fatima, the woman who was attacked in the camp, and she cares about the other refugees. At the same time, Father, she was lying about who she is."

"All the more reason to give her a chance to explain before you judge. Will you promise me that you'll do that?"

WALKING VIA JULIA

TWO HOURS LATER, ALLYSON and Seppe walked in silence on the Via Julia. With their downcast eyes, they must have looked a sorry sight to the few people passing by on the quiet medieval street. They walked slowly, Allyson with her arms crossed and Seppe with his hands in his pockets. *It's like we're afraid to touch each other,* Seppe thought. The uneven cobblestone pavement of Via Julia brought back a memory to Seppe of their first walk together in the ruins of Ostia. That day, when Allyson and he were just beginning to know one another, seemed a lifetime ago.

"Maybe it's safer to talk about the camp," he said, to break the ice.

Allyson widened the gap between them as they walked. "You'd like to know why the organization I work for placed me in Caritas, right?"

Seppe let silence be his answer.

"I think I know what you think about me. You have to know, though, that when I was in Caritas, I was there as an aid worker. I'm not that good an actor, Seppe. My boss even accused me of caring too much about the refugees."

"That doesn't explain what your company's interest is in Caritas?"

"That's what I'm getting at. My organization and others we work with are trying to keep track of who's coming into Europe."

"You're looking for terrorists?" Seppe asked.

"That and criminals."

"I must have made your day back in Ostia when I begged you to look into the attacks in the camp. Here I thought that the relationship you have with your famous father could help. Is all that about your father real, about him being a detective, I mean?" Seppe wondered if he meant that to sound as bitter as it did to his ears.

Allyson sighed. "Yes, that's all true. My dad is just what you discovered."

"So tell me this. What were you getting from me?" Seppe pressed on, feeling he had a right to know.

"Names of those coming into Caritas, where the refugees came from, if they had a criminal record or any previous connection with ISIS, Al-Qaeda, Al-Nusra, or groups like that."

"Couldn't you have gotten all that from the police or Interpol?"

"Perhaps, but working with you I was able to judge for myself."

"It sounds like I was handy. I gave you cover; is that the right word?"

"If you want to see it that way, Seppe, there's nothing I can say that will change your mind. Yes, you provided cover for me, and through me, you provided cover for my organization. That's not the whole truth, though."

"What is the truth?" Seppe asked.

"That I care about the refugees. Fatima means something to me, and she's not the only one. It's up to you to decide if you believe that or if you think I'm lying again."

They walked without speaking for an entire block. Part of him was tempted to walk away from Allyson without saying another word. Another part of him, however, was no longer sure what he felt. They continued to walk, Seppe choosing to wait for what would come next.

God, tell me what to do, he prayed, as he looked over and saw Allyson staring ahead with her jaw clenched.

"I think I could forgive everything if I knew you had no choice," he said, his voice low.

Allyson stopped. "In the organization that I work for, we're told to never tell outsiders the truth, if that's what you mean. However, I won't use that as an excuse. I had a choice. Once I sensed that we were becoming more than colleagues and more than friends, I could have stepped back. Or, if that didn't work, I should have asked to be assigned elsewhere. I can see now that if I'd taken either of those paths, I wouldn't have hurt both of us."

Seppe locked eyes with Allyson. She moved back a step, almost as if she feared he might hit her. "Why didn't you do that?" he asked.

Tears welled up in Allyson's eyes. "Do you wish I had?"

Seppe shook his head. "That doesn't answer my question."

Allyson wiped the tears from her cheeks. "It wasn't only my training that told me to back away from you. You're Italian, and I'm American. Okay, that's not all that important. You have faith . . . and I don't. That is important. Maybe part of me has always known we weren't going to work."

Seppe looked down at the pavement. "I thought some of those same things myself."

"Then you had a choice, too," Allyson said, as she looked up at the sky. "My guess is that you and I both decided the same thing, then."

"And probably for the same reason," Seppe added.

"Yes, that's what messed everything up, didn't it? It should be rule number one in my organization: 'Don't fall in love with a local, especially a source.'"

"Is that what your organization thinks of me? I'm a local source?"

"I prefer to focus on the love part. That's what I've been afraid of for only God knows how long. Probably since my parents split up. You're the first person who made me feel that I don't have to be afraid to love."

Something in Allyson's words, those about her fear of love, cut through his last resistance. Hadn't that same fear been a big part of his desire to become a priest?

CHAPTER THIRTY-FOUR

August 11
Journeying to Milan

THE FOLLOWING MORNING, CHAZ and Manners had barely driven out of Caritas after picking up Asha Malik before she announced from the backseat, "You have to turn around. Jameela sent a message last night. She no trusts you. She make decision."

When Manners shot Chaz a look, he said in a low voice, "Take it easy; take it easy." In a louder voice, he said, "What are you talking about, Asha?"

"We not go to Milan in car. We go in train, the express in forty-five minutes."

"Pull over, Chaz," Manners ordered. "I thought you were calling the shots."

Even before Chaz had reached the curb, he'd thought, *No way I'm going to abort the mission.* After stopping, he turned and looked at both women, his gaze remaining longer on Asha. "Anything else?" he asked.

"Yes. You give me phones—now. You get them in Milan."

Before Manners could say another word, he said, ""Put yourself in Jameela's position, Braylen," he said, hoping she didn't mind his familiarity. "Jameela's worried about walking into a trap."

"She's worried about that? What about us walking into a trap?"

Chaz felt sweat forming on his brow and instinctively touched the fountain pen in his shirt pocket. "Look, Braylen, we don't need our phones until Milan. If we determine then that backup is necessary, I'll make that call."

Arriving at Termini, Rome's train station, they had just enough time to buy tickets and grab snacks before boarding the express train headed for Milan.

Once the train pulled out of the station and began to pick up speed, Chaz tried to relax even as Manners continued to stare at Asha. After thirty minutes, he felt calmer, and he credited Asha for that. She acted like a child on a field trip, consuming a bag of crisps and two cans of soda as she "oohed and aahed" at the countryside passing by outside.

"Look," she said, pointing to a medieval town perched on a hill. "Someday, maybe I live there," she said in Arabic.

Manners was hardly an enthusiastic translator. Yet, as Asha continued to gush at the scenery, she too appeared to relax.

Studying his ticket, Chaz was happy to note that the express train's only stop before arriving in Milan would be at Florence. *Everything's going to be okay,* he thought, telling himself that he would have taken similar precautions if he were Jameela.

Chaz imagined the mission's conclusion, when he would take the opportunity to emphasize the importance of being flexible to an uptight agent like Manners. The truth was that he, not Manners, knew Asha. He, not Manners, had interviewed her on numerous occasions over the previous weeks and knew both her wiles and her weak points. Even though Jameela would undoubtedly be stronger than her sister, he didn't doubt his ability to uncover her vulnerabilities.

Chaz's buoyant mood was broken, however, when he happened to look out the train window and recognized the hill town of Orvieto, the city where Morgan and he had met Khadija and brought her to Rome. He asked himself if he viewed Khadija differently now than he had then. She was still the most pathetic women he'd ever known, her sharp facial features, sickly pallor, and tiny hands reminding him of a rodent.

Now, Khadija and he were in competition to break this case open. To him, Khadija's plan was passive, while he'd taken the bull by the horns. As Orvieto disappeared from view, it dawned on Chaz that the difference between Khadija and him was culturally significant. Americans, at least those of his class, made things happen. He touched the Mont Blanc pen in his pocket and thought of his grandfather. In contrast, Khadija looked like the refugees in Caritas—those who wallowed in misery, waiting for something to happen to them. While he was travelling to Milan, Khadija was waiting for a phone call.

He glanced over and studied Asha's face. His attraction to her was based on more than her beauty. She, and no doubt her sister, Jameela, weren't typical refugees. Jameela turned Kadir in as a pedophile, a charge Chaz still believed was true. That took the kind of initiative he could respect. From his first meeting with Asha, he recognized that same initiative. Although Asha and Jameela might be part of the crime ring in Caritas, wasn't it admirable from a certain perspective that they refused to be helpless victims?

Caritas Refugee Camp

On the second day of wearing the heavy Rolex watch and rings, Khadija found a note beneath her pillow. Although other volunteers in the school had said nothing, Khadija was certain that they noticed the change in her appearance. Over the past two days, she'd also felt people treating her with greater deference, if not fear. *They probably think I'm part of the group behind the attacks,* she thought. Only the people who were, in fact, involved in the attacks in the camp knew she wasn't.

Even though some contact was what she and Fatima were both waiting for, she was unsure how Fatima would react. Since she returned to the camp, Fatima had clearly been nervous. Other workers in the school commented on how different Fatima was from the young girl who they remembered from before the attack. Back then, Fatima had been one of the most energetic camp residents, often seen walking briskly to one of her classes.

Now, Fatima didn't walk anywhere alone and, though Fatima ate everything on her plate at mealtime, her hands shook, and her gaze roamed the dining hall. More than once, Khadija leaned across the table from her own half-eaten food to whisper to Fatima to try to relax. Once, when Khadija awoke in the middle of the night, she found Fatima staring at her.

The note in Arabic that Khadija found under her pillow was brief. *School playground tonight at 11 pm. Come alone.* Although unsigned, Khadija was sure that Sabia, the mystery woman, had sent it.

After Fatima returned from her English language class, Khadija proposed a walk outside in the camp. There, she told Fatima about the note and reminded her of what the next twelve hours would demand of each of them.

To Khadija's surprise, Fatima accepted the news with obvious relief, and Khadija realized it was the waiting that was making Fatima anxious.

"Have you let Allyson know?" Fatima asked.

"Yes, Allyson and the Agency know that I made contact. Tell me again what you'll do tonight if there's any trouble."

"If you run into trouble, you'll activate the transmitter on your own."

When she didn't say more, Khadija stopped walking and looked at her.

"Fatima, I have to know that you understand what you have to do if something happens to me."

Fatima didn't look Khadija in the eye. "If you're not back to the dorm by one in the morning, I'm supposed to send a distress signal. But . . ."

"But what?"

"What if they take you out of the camp? How will anyone know where to find you?" Fatima said, in little more than a whisper.

Khadija put a hand on Fatima's arm. "I'm going into the meeting tonight with more than this jewelry on me. The agency gave me an advantage. It's known as a 'wire,' something standard for tricky meetings. I have it on under my bra. Look, I know what you're thinking, that they'll search me and find it. That's exactly what we want them to do. It's actually a fake device. I'll explain that the group I work for, Al-Nusra, insists that they don't remove it. I'll claim it's insurance guaranteeing my safety. Now, at that point, they'll either rip it off or let me keep it. It really doesn't matter because the whole purpose of the wire is to distract them. They won't even consider the pack of tissues with the real transmitter in it."

Fatima looked up, tears welling in her eyes. "You've done this before? You're not scared?"

"Of course, I'm scared. I'm no hero, but this is something I volunteered to do. If you haven't guessed why I'm doing this, I promise I'll tell you when this is all over."

CIA Headquarters

"Come to my office, Allyson. Another agent can handle the transmitter," Morgan said, sounding flustered on the phone.

Something's up, Allyson thought, hurrying to the case manager's office.

"Close the door," Morgan ordered as soon as Allyson stepped into her office. As Allyson did, she saw a man, vaguely familiar to her, standing by the window.

"Agent Worthy, this is Bureau Chief Arnold Sanderson."

Nodding, Allyson approached Sanderson, who was looking grim, and shook his hand.

Morgan, sitting at her desk, typed on her computer. In a moment, a video appeared on a wall-mounted screen.

"This is CCTV from Rome's train station two hours ago," she said. "You can see Chaz and his backup, Agent Manners, walking on each side of Asha Malik."

Allyson stood frozen. "The train station? I thought—"

"You thought what we all did, Agent Worthy," Sanderson said. "That's why it's taken us two hours to put the pieces together."

Oh God, Allyson thought, *Chaz jumped the rails.*

"When neither Chaz nor Manners answered the phone, we widened our search for them. Face recognition took us to the station's CCTV," Stamper explained. "The video showed that Chaz bought three tickets to Milan. That train arrived in Milan minutes ago, with our agents there to meet them."

"Except they weren't on the train," Sanderson added.

Nothing Allyson was hearing made any sense, yet she realized that even Chaz wouldn't have pulled a stunt like this.

"I think we all better sit down," Sanderson said. "We're waiting for CCTV from the train station in Florence."

"Florence?" Allyson asked, feeling she was in a nightmare that made no sense.

"The train they were on is an express, its only stop between Rome and Milan being Florence. Can you shed any light, Alli, on what in the world is going on?" Morgan said, and Allyson knew she was pleading.

"No, no I can't. It isn't like Chaz—"

"Cut the crap," Sanderson said. "Stamper's already filled me in on our Navy Seal."

"No, sir, not like this. Even Chaz . . . Agent Eaton wouldn't do anything this crazy. It would jeopardize the mission."

"Well, it certainly jeopardizes his career," Sanderson said.

"Just so it doesn't jeopardize their lives," Morgan said. She squinted to read a message on her computer screen. "Here's CCTV coming in from Florence from sixty-three minutes ago."

They watched the screen as some passengers exited the train while other passengers waited impatiently to board. For four nerve-wracking minutes, they studied the faces of everyone walking from the train into the station before spotting Chaz, Manners, and Asha Malik. Asha was walking ahead and talking with an unidentified woman, while Chaz and Manners were surrounded by four men, one on each side and two more close behind. From the way the two flanking men's coats covered their arms, it looked like both Chaz and Manners had weapons trained on them.

Hitting a few keys, Morgan put boxes around the faces of the people accompanying Chaz, Manners, and Asha. "I'm running these images through our databanks," she said.

"Run them through Interpol and Europol as well," Sanderson ordered. "While you're doing that, I'll get one of our techies to match their faces with everyone who boarded the train in Rome. This bunch must have gotten on there unless . . ."

"Unless what?" Morgan asked, clearly on edge.

"Unless the train arriving in Rome came from somewhere else," Allyson said, completing the thought.

It didn't take Morgan more than a minute to find the answer. "Shit, the train originated in Naples. They could have boarded there."

"We have to get CCTV from Naples as well as CCTV from outside the train station in Florence. It's clear that we're not dealing with amateurs here," Sanderson said. "Look at Asha Malik. She certainly looks pleased. What's that in her hand?"

Sanderson zoomed in on Asha's hand. "It's something small. She's showing it to the other woman. What is it? A knife?"

"Oh, my God," Allyson said. "It's Chaz's fountain pen, his prized possession. No wonder he looks lost."

CHAPTER THIRTY-FIVE

Caritas Refugee Camp

THAT SAME AFTERNOON, KHADIJA and Fatima sat side by side and ran through their checklist before Khadija's late-night meeting.

Fatima reached over and touched Khadija's arm above the watch. "Will you wear the jewelry tonight?"

Khadija held up her arm where the Rolex, too big for her tiny wrist, hung like a bracelet. "Yes, it makes a statement that I can't be intimidated."

"The authorities must have some idea what's going on here in the camp," Fatima said. "I don't understand why they didn't arrest Sabia weeks ago."

"If the Agency did that, we'd never know who's behind Sabia and the overall scheme. The Agency has to let matters play out. What we know is that Caritas hasn't had the problem other camps have—children as young as ten or eleven running away or disappearing."

"Traffickers?" Fatima asked.

"Has to be. Poor kids, especially teenagers, are promised something outrageous if they run away. Then they're sold as sex or sweatshop workers. As I said, Caritas has been spared this far."

Fatima shivered. "I wonder if that's what Hasan was trying to tell me with the note. That children in the school could be in danger."

"Well, you worked with both Hasan and Jameela. Could Jameela have been assigned to the school so she could identify the most vulnerable children?"

Fatima was now swaying back and forth, her hands twisting in her lap. "Maybe Jameela accused Hasan of abusing children because he found out what Jameela was planning. What I don't understand is why she disappeared?"

Khadija placed her hand on Fatima's. "Maybe by accusing Hasan, she drew too much attention to herself. Someone thought it was better to smuggle her out as soon as they could." Khadija saw no reason to tell Fatima that if Chaz's plan had succeeded, Jameela could already be in custody in Milan. If that were true and Khadija managed that night to uncover the details of the crime ring in Caritas, then by morning the Agency could move in and arrest everyone involved.

CIA HEADQUARTERS

ALLYSON AND MORGAN SAT alone in her office, each struggling to understand the confusing developments of the day. Bureau Chief Sanderson was somewhere in the building, no doubt conferring with those above him at CIA Headquarters in Langley, Virginia. Allyson didn't envy him as he tried to explain how the Rome office managed to lose contact with two of its agents.

Discoveries from CCTV over the past few hours were not encouraging. Only two of the five people who boarded the train in Naples were identified. Both had Mafia connections, which only added to everyone's concern. The Mafia never hesitated to eliminate opponents, even those in the CIA.

The CCTV from outside the train station in Florence showed Chaz, Manners, and Asha entering a small transit van with blackened windows. While the van's license plates were visible, a trace revealed that the plates were stolen.

Allyson felt that anything she might say would be pointless, and Morgan must have felt the same as neither had spoken for the past ten minutes. Finally, Morgan heard her phone vibrate. She read a message and looked across her desk at Allyson. "Sanderson texted. He wants to know if we should pull Khadija and Fatima from the camp."

With everything going wrong with Chaz's plan, Allyson had forgotten about Khadija's plan to meet with the people behind the crime in Caritas later that night.

"Part of me says 'yes;' it's too dangerous for Khadija now."

"And the other part of you says what?" Morgan asked, lighting another cigarette, despite company policy about smoking inside Europa Spec.

Knowing how much was at stake, Allyson paused to gather her thoughts. "The two plans—Chaz's and Khadija's—well, the good thing is that there's no overlap. What I mean is that no part of either plan depends on anything from the other. Asha has never met Khadija, and Fatima has never met Chaz. Assuming the worst in Florence, the only way that this could rebound on Khadija is if Chaz . . . well, if Chaz tells their kidnappers about her."

"Which our Navy Seal won't do, right?"

Allyson nodded. "I can't believe he'll tell them anything."

After another pause, Morgan said, "There's another issue. It won't be easy to get a message to Khadija. She transmits, while we only receive. That means we either pull Khadija and Fatima—which means shutting down everything in place in Caritas—or we let Khadija proceed with her plan."

Allyson felt Morgan's exhaustion as if it were her own. She knew her boss was going over and over her decision to okay Chaz's plan, wondering how it had fallen through. Allyson also remembered her meeting with Morgan just days ago, when they discussed Chaz's future with the Rome office. To Morgan's surprise, Allyson had recommended that Chaz be kept on the team. Now, given the threat to Chaz and Manners, Allyson knew that Morgan had to be second-guessing that decision.

As if she were reading Allyson's mind, the case manager said, "Alli, the worst thing we can do is obsess about what's going on with Chaz and Manners. We have to focus on Khadija's plan."

Allyson desperately wanted to fall into bed and sleep for a week. Just as desperately, she wanted to drive like mad to Florence. She could do neither thing. She had to remain clearheaded as she sat by the receiver awaiting any signal from Khadija later that night.

Allyson remembered what her father had once written to her, how he envied his friend Father Nick, who, when nothing was going right on a case, could pray. Thinking how Seppe had that same faith, she understood her father's envy.

Well, why not? she thought as she focused on her computer screen. She typed in "prayers for when your world is falling apart," imagining that the message would be "unknown." To her surprise, she found that she had her choice of prayers depending on the religion she chose. She scrolled down page after page, losing hope that she would find words that expressed what she felt. Then, just as she was ready to give up, she found a prayer written by the monk Thomas Merton that expressed how she'd felt for as long as she could remember. The prayer described feeling completely lost, not knowing which direction to take, and ended with the person admitting that he didn't really know himself.

Allyson reread the words, tears welling up. She knew that if she'd ever asked Father Nick how to pray, he would have suggested something similar. *Allyson, my dear, God is always ready to listen, as long as a person speaks the truth.*

On a pad of paper, she wrote down the words of the prayer, folded the paper, and stowed it in a compartment in her purse that held a few treasured keepsakes. One was a small picture of her father and mother kissing on their wedding day, a second was a spare key to the family lake cabin in northern Michigan, and a third was a tiny piece of bloodstained cloth, a piece of the blouse that she'd worn seven years before when she'd kept her head and saved Father Nick's life.

I guess I just prayed, she thought, wondering if she would throw the piece of paper away once the case was solved and she had a good night's sleep. Something told her that she wouldn't.

An Abandoned Warehouse Outside Florence

Their hands and feet bound with plastic cord, Chaz and Manners sat across the room from Asha and the armed men from the train. Being blindfolded, Chaz knew only that they'd travelled about twenty minutes from Florence's train station before being transferred to a smaller vehicle, an SUV. After another half-hour, they were led into a deserted warehouse.

Now, the blindfolds removed, Chaz could see through dirty windows that it was late afternoon, approaching evening in the Tuscan countryside. On a table sat two open computers, Chaz's and Manner's watches and cellphones, along with several automatic weapons.

Their captors spoke only Arabic and Italian, meaning that Chaz had to rely on Manners. He whispered, "What are they planning?"

From across the room, Asha said in clear English, "Ask me."

Chaz's jaw dropped. "What the hell?"

"Much you not know about me," she said.

"Jameela. Does she also speak English?" he asked.

"Ah, Jameela. You think she is smart one. You think I just pretty."

"Damn it," Manners said, shooting Chaz a look. "She played you."

Chaz struggled to understand. He stared at Asha as if for the first time, and she did, in fact, look like a different person, someone confident and in charge of the others in the room.

Asha crossed the room and bent down in front of Chaz. "I see how you look at me in camp. You think sex. Everything else about me is dirt. We lose our country, our home. You don't care. We kept in camp. You don't care." She paused, waiting for Chaz to say something, yet he remained quiet.

"You lose this," Asha continued, producing Chaz's fountain pen, "now you care. People have nothing in camp. You don't care." She retreated to the table before returning with Chaz and Manners' watches. Looking at Manners, she said "she have shiny ring. No problem. If I have nice watch, shiny ring, that is big crime, not allowed."

She put the fountain pen in Chaz's shirt pocket and turned as if to walk back to the table. For a moment, Chaz felt a surge of hope. She wouldn't destroy his pen, and she wouldn't kill them. As if she knew what he was thinking, she turned back and reached into his pocket and retrieved the pen. She placed it on the cement floor in front of Chaz. Chaz closed his eyes as her foot descended, and he heard the Mont Blanc being smashed.

"Open your eyes, Mr. American," Asha ordered as she stomped down on the pen a second time. Chaz watched as ink flowed onto the floor. Asha then took a step back and spat on the pen fragments.

Asha paused before setting a chair down in front of the two captives. Between her and Chaz and Manners, the ink flowed into cracks in the floor. "In Syria, we die every day, every hour. Like pen, we smashed to dust. Blood covers floor, street, school, hospital. There is no place where no blood in Damascus. America no care. Italy no care. For blood, you no care. For ink on floor, you care. Tell me, Mr. American, who is criminal—you or me?"

Anger surged through Chaz as he stared down at the pieces of the

Monte Blanc pen. He reminded himself that he was an Eaton, someone descended from alpha wolves and groomed to become one himself. He strained at his bindings and thought, *Damn it, I am the top wolf, a Navy Seal. This bitch will make a mistake, and I will pounce.*

CHAPTER THIRTY-SIX

Caritas Refugee Camp

THOUGH THE TEMPERATURE AT eleven p.m. was mild, Khadija stood huddled in Caritas's schoolyard. With the camp asleep, the open setting provided none of the security it offered in the daytime. She knew, however, that the rendezvous site hadn't been chosen for her comfort.

From the watch dangling from her wrist, Khadija could make out that it was five minutes past eleven. The weight of the Rolex and the awkward way it slid up and down her arm made her wonder why any woman would ever wear such a watch. Then she acknowledged that it was these same factors that drew the attention of others and reminded the wearer that she was special.

Her brief time in the camp posing as a refugee had brought back memories of her family's first months in Britain. Her mother had cleaned toilets in the Brixton train station, and her father had worked long hours in an upholstery shop. The little money the family managed to save was set aside for Khadija's and her sister's education. Yes, Khadija had a watch, but it was a lightweight, plastic Timex, a gift for her graduation from secondary school.

It was the shame of poverty that caused Khadija's mother to misunderstand Khadija's eating disorder. Khadija's mother pictured others viewing her daughter as a poor child from a poor family, not as a sick child. Dinnertime in the Mubarak home came with lectures and harangues about the scourge of poverty. Every Saturday until Khadija was old enough to refuse, her mother took her shopping. While groceries were the true reason for these treks to downtown Brixton, her mother's joy came from stopping outside nearly every shop's window and pretending to be deciding what she would buy.

Khadija always felt embarrassed when the shopkeepers snickered as they recognized the two women in chadors and hijabs. The shopkeepers knew that the women never entered their shops to buy.

As Khadija stood in the dark schoolyard, she wondered how her mother would react if she could see her. Would she be ashamed that Khadija, even as part of her career, was living in a refugee camp, or would she be proud to see a gold Rolex on her daughter's wrist? For nothing would please her mother more, Khadija knew, than to own such a watch—gold, heavy, and awkward, proof of some victory.

Her thoughts were interrupted by a flashlight blinking on and off from the other side of the playground. Taking a deep breath and offering a prayer, she walked toward the light. It wasn't until she came to within twenty yards that she saw a woman and a man standing behind it in the dark. She squinted, expecting to see Sabia. Instead, she saw the face of a younger woman without the hijab.

"Stand where you are," the woman ordered, and Khadija obeyed. As the man came toward her, she recognized one of Sabia's bodyguards. Without saying anything, he motioned for her to raise her arms as he came closer to her.

"If you're wearing some tracking device, it will go better for you if you tell us now," the woman said.

Khadija took another deep breath. "Of course, I'm wearing a wire. It's inside my bra."

The man's outstretched hands stopped in mid-air. He turned to the woman for instructions.

"What happens if we destroy it?" the woman asked, still standing where she was.

"Bad things if my people believe I'm in danger," Khadija replied. Even though her knees felt weak, she was thankful that her voice was steady.

Khadija could feel the woman studying her. *She doesn't know that being stared at doesn't scare me. I've been stared at my whole life,* Khadija thought.

After a few moments, the woman said to the man, "Let her be." Then to Khadija, she said, "Come with us."

With just a flashlight lighting the way, Khadija was led to the wire fence marking the perimeter of the camp. In a short while, they came to a section of the fence where a hole had been cut. Walking through the opening, Khadija fingered the tissue packet in her pocket. As she hoped, the mention of the wire had saved her from being searched. Now she had to hope that the Agency's tracking technology would work.

As the group came to a curb, a black SUV with its lights off pulled up. A man got out to open the back door and motioned for Khadija to enter before a cotton bag was placed over her head.

No one spoke for the next fifteen minutes, and Khadija resisted the urge to ask where they were headed. Finally, the vehicle came to a halt, and someone removed the bag from her head. She squinted to see the woman turn from the front passenger seat and stare back at her.

"They said you look sick, and they were right," she said. "What is it?"

Khadija's brain froze with the question, one she'd dreaded hearing most of her life. "I'm being treated for cancer," she replied, remembering at the last moment that a few in the camp knew of her arranged visits to the fictional oncologist in Rome.

The woman nodded, even as she said, "Huh. Anyone ever told you that you look anorexic?"

Khadija looked down. "With my treatments, I can't always keep food down," she said, hoping her words had fooled the woman.

The woman offered the beginning of a smile. "A tough one, even with cancer. I like that."

Khadija was ushered from the vehicle to the door of a warehouse where more men were waiting. The few windows were covered with drapes. The only thing Khadija was sure of was that she was somewhere within a half-hour of Caritas. Inside, someone turned a wall switch on, and Khadija found herself facing Sabia and a burly man. As her eyes adjusted to the light, Khadija watched as the young woman whom she'd just met on Caritas's playground took the seat on the other side of Sabia.

"Sit," Sabia said, gesturing toward a chair on the near side of the table. "I took the liberty of making tea."

Khadija sat down and smelled the fragrance of the tea. She had the odd sensation of entering a pleasant social gathering, the sensation only dispelled by the fact that two men remained standing along a wall, each with an automatic weapon held across his chest.

Khadija sat quietly, doing her best to steady her breathing as Sabia turned to the seated man. Her impression that he was Italian, not Middle Eastern, was confirmed by his response of "Si, si" to Sabia.

"It appears that two organizations have moved into Caritas camp," Sabia said. "Perhaps we can work out an arrangement, yes?"

Khadija tried to appear nonchalant as she replied, "I assume that's why I'm here."

In the quiet that followed, she could feel the people at the table studying her. Finally, the young woman said, "Have some tea. I assure you that it's only tea." After pouring three cups, she said, "We see that you wear the hijab. Is that a clue to the organization you work for?"

"And neither of you wear it," Khadija replied, looking now from Sabia to the younger woman. "Maybe that is a clue to the organization you work for."

Not knowing that Khadija understood Italian, the man in an angry voice said, "We have no time for these games."

The young woman sat forward in her chair. "Caritas is a business opportunity for us, nothing more. We have no religious connection. We are entrepreneurs, global entrepreneurs, in fact, not jihadists."

Khadija paused to consider the vague description. The words "business," "global," and "no religious connection," along with the Italian man's presence, led her to assume the worst, that she was in a room with someone with Mafia connections. What she still had to find out was what the "business opportunity" in Caritas entailed.

Remembering her cover story, she said, "We are servants of Allah. The West invades and destroys our countries. That is why there are these camps. We are here to do Allah's will."

Sabia translated her words into Italian, causing the man to ball his fist and scowl at Khadija. The young woman ignored this and asked, "Wearing expensive jewelry is Allah's will?"

"That was to get your attention. You can keep what I have on, if jewelry is important to you."

"Ah, then are you ISIS or Al-Qaeda?"

"Al-Nusra. We are here to avenge Allah's honor. There are many ways we are doing this. What you call 'business' is one of them."

Sabia spoke next. "As we already said, Caritas is a small camp. Two business enterprises in the camp won't work."

Khadija could not remember ever feeling as alert and focused. She felt she was watching the scene from somewhere above. Yet outwardly, she simply shrugged. "Maybe your business is not ours. Maybe we leave you alone, and you leave us alone."

Once translated, the words caused the man to turn red in the face. He slammed his fist down on the table. Khadija, however, didn't blink. Instead, she sipped her tea.

After the man whispered something in Sabia's ear, Sabia said to Khadija, "You talk about avenging Allah's honor. If you're talking about some act in the camp, such as a bomb, that could ruin our business."

Khadija shook her head. "No, not in the camp."

Sabia frowned, letting Khadija know that she'd picked up on the implied threat. "Somewhere in Rome, yes?"

"Rome, Paris, Milan, wherever Allah determines," said Khadija. "Now you tell me your business in the camp."

Sabia didn't reply immediately. Finally, she said, "Our business is to find where profits can be made in Caritas and other camps."

"How exactly? My organization won't know if we compete with you until we know how you are profiting."

"It is enough for you to know," Sabia said, "that we are placed wherever money flows into Caritas, and a lot of money does flow in."

Khadija thought of the offices in the camp that received money from the Italian government and international agencies, those devoted to health care, food services, and housing.

"You take a cut, is that it?" she asked.

"Hardly noticeable, but it adds up," Sabia said.

"Why do you draw attention to yourselves? The jewelry and the killings, I mean."

Now it was Sabia who shrugged. "Both have their purpose. The jewelry helps us recruit, and the attacks were necessary. We are close to being in control in Caritas, and anyone who threatens that will be dealt with. Anyone."

Khadija didn't miss the warning nor the new tension in the room. What concerned her more, however, were the words "close to being in control." Something else was in the works. What? Were those words referring to what Hasan meant in his note about "more trouble" from Syria coming to Caritas?

To force Sabia to be more specific, Khadija said, "It's not clear to me where our two organization are in competition. We are not in Caritas to make money as you are. There is no problem unless . . . unless you plan to expand in areas we are interested in."

Her words only increased the tension in the room. The people sitting across from Khadija rose from their chairs and retreated to the other side of the room, where they conferred in whispers.

Pretending to study the others in the room—the two men cradling their automatic weapons—Khadija strained to pick up anything Sabia and the others were discussing.

It was then that she heard an Arabic word spoken several times, a word that made her freeze in terror. The word was "children," and immediately, she saw the faces of Mikal and Karina, Daliyeh's children, as she grasped what Sabia and the people with her were discussing. The Mafia was going to use Sabia and others in Caritas to establish a trafficking network as they had in other camps. In that moment, Khadija understood what Hasan and Professor Napolitano had uncovered and what got them killed.

Her mind raced as she thought of what to say. "I heard you use the word 'children,'" she finally said.

They stopped their whispering and returned to their seats. "Is that what your group is interested in as well?" Sabia asked.

Khadija replied before she even realized what she was saying. "Children can be the best weapons to use against the West. The West doesn't understand that a child trained to embrace martyrdom for Allah is far more dangerous than an adult. Yes, children in Caritas will become Allah's warriors."

"Then we do have a conflict," Sabia said. "We see a different future for those children, especially the orphans. Unlike you, we don't see dead children having any value. Living ones, however, have great value—to the right buyers, that is."

No one spoke, and Khadija knew that what she said next would be critical, perhaps even to her own survival. She thought of stalling by taking another sip of tea, but she knew her hands would shake. Instead, she offered a silent prayer and tried, once again, to calm her breathing.

"Clearly, you do not honor Allah or seek to do His will," she said and waited for those words to have an effect. "However, we are not opposed to being practical. We kill you, you kill us. What is gained? My superiors have heard everything we have said," she said, tapping her chest where the fake wire was pinned. "I must discuss with them. When I hear their decision, we meet again, yes?"

For a moment, Khadija wondered if Sabia saw through her ruse. When the young woman translated what Khadija had said, the man from the Mafia looked as if he would prefer to kill her.

Finally, Sabia said, "Developments are moving fast. We give you twenty-four hours."

Swallowing hard, Khadija rested her palms on the table. "Agreed. Now, I think it is time I return to Caritas."

The Italian, however, was not satisfied with the meeting ending there. Turning to Sabia, he said in Italian, "Show her the photo."

Khadija pretended ignorance and waited for Sabia to translate his command, but Sabia didn't say a word. Instead, she opened her cellphone and hit a few buttons before turning the screen around for Khadija to see. "Our friend wants you to see what we do to those who oppose us."

Khadija was glad she wasn't standing, for what she was looking at—Chaz and a blond woman shackled to chairs—made blood rush to her head and then drain in a second.

Despite feeling faint, she reminded herself of the role she was playing and tried to show no reaction to the photo. "You do not know my group if you think we are afraid of death. And we have known much torture," she said.

"Good, then we understand each other," Sabia said with a knowing smile.

As Khadija walked toward the door, she glanced at the young woman who'd let Sabia do most of the talking. In that moment, she realized why the woman was familiar to her.

"You have family in the camp, maybe a sister, yes? She has the same gold watch and rings as you," Khadija said.

The young woman nodded. "I'm Jameela. You must have seen Asha. Don't expect to see her in Caritas. She won't be there."

CHAPTER THIRTY-SEVEN

August 12
Rome's CIA Headquarters

LATER THAT MORNING, KHADIJA arrived at the Agency for a debriefing. Her lack of sleep left her with an alertness that felt brittle. In the conference room were Morgan, Allyson, and one of the men whom she'd met at the U.S. Embassy only days before.

Before she could say anything, Morgan said, "I have bad news, Khadija." Khadija's stomach tightened as she feared that Chaz and Manners had been executed.

"Chaz and Manners have been captured. We're not sure where they are or what condition they're in."

"Oh," Khadija said. "I feared something worse. Sabia and Jameela showed me a picture of them last night."

"Alive?" Allyson asked.

"I could see that they were bound by their ankles and wrists. They might have been beaten."

"You didn't mean to say Jameela, did you?" Morgan asked. "Chaz was supposed to rendezvous with her in Milan."

"That's what I thought too, but it was Jameela."

Allyson groaned. "Jameela was never in Milan, which means there was never going to be a meeting."

"Chaz was taken in from the very beginning," Morgan said.

The man tapped on the table with his pen. "Damn it, we've been played."

"Let's focus on what else Khadija learned," Morgan said.

After describing the others who'd been in the room last night, Khadija shared that the meeting confirmed the Agency's fear that crime in Caritas was connected to the Italian underworld. She also explained how a percentage of funds coming into the camp was being siphoned off by the group.

"It's what they're planning that's terrifying. They're ready to begin trafficking children, especially orphans, in the camp. That's what Hasan and the professor must have found out about, and that's what got them killed," she said.

Nobody said anything until the man spoke. "How did you play that?"

"I let them think I'm part of Al-Nusra and that my group has a different interest in the children."

"I assume you meant training jihadists," the man said.

"Yes, and because that competes with their plans, they agreed to give my organization twenty-four hours to offer a way to avoid a turf war."

"Well-played," Morgan said, looking at the man. "If we arrest Jameela and Sabia now, we can offer a trade for Chaz and Manners."

"The Agency is leery of making deals," the man replied.

"Are you saying the Agency won't try to rescue two of its agents?" Allyson asked, her voice shrill to Khadija's ear.

"Take it easy, Allyson," Morgan said. "Of course, we'll do everything we can to get them back. However, if we make a trade, our cover will be compromised. Asha, Jameela, and Sabia will leave Caritas, but they'll just move on to somewhere else. We'd be back at square one."

"Every agent knows . . ." the man began.

Khadija cleared her throat. "I think there might be another way. They bought the cover story that I'm a jihadist intent on training children in the camp for something big in Rome. I talked about Al-Nusra wanting revenge on the West for meddling in the Middle East."

She paused a moment to catch her breath. "We could propose a different trade. What if I—as a member of Al-Nusra, I mean—offered them unrestricted access to orphans in Caritas in exchange for Chaz and Manners?"

No one responded, and for a moment Khadija wondered if what she said made no sense, coming from someone who hadn't slept at all.

The man leaned forward, a look of interest on his face. "Why would they think Al-Nusra would want our agents?"

Khadija tried to tap into the calm she'd projected in the night meeting with Sabia, Jameela, and the Mafia representative. "I told them my group's mission was to hit at the West, meaning a bombing or some such attack in Rome. Wouldn't executing two CIA officers on the internet be an even better and more immediate way to hurt the West? Think about it from my . . . from Al-Nusra's perspective. No long months training children; instead, a quick execution that can be viewed around the world on the internet."

Morgan nodded. "Instead it would be a trap."

The man exhaled deeply as he looked from Morgan to Khadija. "We get our agents back, and we arrest whoever brings them to the exchange. Not just the Malik sisters and Sabia, but a Mafia boss as well. What do you think, Morgan?"

"If it works, Khadija will turn a disaster into a victory."

"And she'll have saved two lives," Allyson said.

"Do you think it will work, Morgan?" the man pressed.

Morgan smiled at Khadija. "Yes, I think it's our best chance. I say you text Sabia immediately and leave the trade offer for them to consider. It's about time for us to take the initiative."

Caritas Refugee Camp

Seppe reread the text he received from Allyson that morning. "I can't go to Caritas with you today as I'm involved in a serious problem at work. No more deception; just the truth."

As he walked into Caritas, Seppe assumed that Allyson's "serious problem" had to be connected to the camp. Otherwise, why would she be involved? The only thing he remembered Allyson telling him was that her organization had arranged for Fatima to have additional security now that she was back in the camp. Did that mean that the serious problem in Caritas was connected with Fatima?

Instead of walking to the administration building, Seppe headed for the school. He offered a quick prayer for Allyson and for Fatima, whom he hoped to find safe at her job with the children.

Inside the school, Seppe presented his ID and asked to speak with Fatima, first in Italian before switching to speak slowly in his basic Arabic. The woman at the reception desk pointed at the clock at the wall to indicate that Fatima's morning shift would end in fifteen minutes.

Knowing that Fatima was in her classroom did not totally dampen Seppe's worry. After all, the murders of Hasan and Professor Napolitano and the attack on Fatima remained unsolved. He glanced out the window at the playground and the other buildings in the camp. *What must it be like for someone like Fatima to survive a war, only to be in danger again in a place that promises safety?* Seppe wondered.

He looked up to see Fatima coming down the hallway toward him, her gait slow until she recognized him. Her smile was shy, and he wondered if she remembered when she'd been one of the camp's most assertive and energetic residents.

As Seppe rose, Fatima stopped and greeted him in Italian, reminding him of the language classes that Fatima had taken before her attack.

"Italiano o Inglese?" he asked, pointing to two chairs in the lobby.

"My English is better," she replied, taking the seat.

Speaking slowly, he asked how she was feeling.

"I am good," she said.

"Not too tired?"

"I rest after my shift."

"Good, good. I wanted to make sure you feel safe," he said.

Fatima looked down at her hands. "I think everything is okay. Your friend, Allyson, she is not with you?"

Seppe noted the quick change of topic. Before responding, he reminded himself that as far as he knew, Fatima didn't know Allyson's true identity. "Something came up at work, some problem."

Fatima's face went pale. "What problem? Please, tell me."

"Actually, I was worried that the problem might have something to do with you. That's why I came to check on you. You're sure you're okay?"

Fatima stole a look over her shoulder and, seeing that the receptionist was gone, gave Seppe a searching look.

After a long pause, she whispered, "You know Khadija?"

Seppe frowned. "Should I?"

"I think maybe Allyson tell you. Allyson bring me Khadija."

"Are you talking about your security?" Seppe guessed.

Fatima nodded. "Khadija and me, we watch out for each other."

"Tell me about Khadija."

"Khadija is strong," Fatima said.

"I think I should talk to her," Seppe said.

"She is not here," she replied, the tears flowing down her cheeks.

"Then who's protecting you?"

"Khadija come back. Yes, she come back soon. I should not say more."

Seppe sat forward and looked into Fatima's eyes. "As God is my witness, you can trust me. Please tell me, is Khadija meeting with Allyson?"

Pressing her lips together and looking out at the children playing, Fatima nodded. "I think so."

All the more reason why you shouldn't be unprotected, Seppe thought. Then another frightening thought came to his mind. "Is Allyson in danger?"

Fatima looked shocked. "Allyson? No, not Allyson. Khadija say someone else is missing."

"From Allyson's organization?"

"Sorry, I do not know."

He tried to assemble the pieces of the puzzle, suspecting that even together, Fatima and he didn't know it all. Europa Spec was obviously a front for an American agency, which he suspected was the CIA, the FBI, or some other intelligence organization. Now someone else in Allyson's and Khadija's group appeared to be in trouble.

"Fatima, does Khadija know who in Caritas was involved in the attacks?"

Exhaling slowly, Fatima nodded. "Khadija pointed out a woman. I knew her from before . . . before the attack. Before Khadija left this morning, she tell me to keep an eye on this person."

"Do you know her name?" Seppe asked.

Fatima leaned forward as she whispered, "Sabia."

The name meant nothing to Seppe. "Fatima, I'm not going to leave you until Khadija returns."

Fatima sighed softly. "Thank you."

After waiting an hour in the dining hall, Fatima whispered, "Sabia, she's not coming."

Seppe could hear the relief in her voice. "Is that unusual?" he asked.

"She not always comes for meals. Khadija thinks she has own source of food."

Outside, Seppe asked in a low voice, "Do you know where Sabia lives in the camp?"

"No, why?" Fatima said, sounding worried again.

"I just thought Khadija might want you . . . want us, I mean, to have a look. Just a look, I promise, to see if she's there."

Fatima sat down heavily on a bench. "Even if I know that, I can't do that. I . . . can't," she pled. "Anyway, Khadija, she be back soon."

"Okay, we don't have to do that. Until Khadija comes back, let's go to where you do feel safe."

"Safe?" she whispered as she looked around.

"How about you telling me what you usually do in the afternoon?"

"After Khadija and I eat together, we go back to dormitory. I get books, and Khadija walk me to class—my English class."

"Good, then let me take Khadija's place. I'll walk you to your dormitory, and then we'll walk over to your class."

At the entrance to Fatima's dormitory, she said, "Men can't come in. Will you wait?"

"Yes, I'll be right here."

Fatima gave him a nervous smile and walked into the dormitory. Seppe thought about Allyson's text message and Khadija leaving Fatima unprotected. *Something is up,* he thought, just as Fatima came out of the dormitory, looking more relaxed than before.

"Khadija left me note on my bed. She is back in the camp," Fatima said.

She handed the note to Seppe, who shook his head. "I can't read Arabic, Fatima."

She led Seppe away from the dormitory door. "Khadija say not go to my class. She meet me now in women's bathroom in gym. She say she has important news, good news."

"There's a gym in the camp?"

"At the back of the school, in basement. I must hurry."

"I'm going with you, Fatima."

"No, it's okay. I be okay once I see Khadija. Anyway, it is bathroom for women."

Seppe shook his head. "Until I see Khadija, I'm staying with you."

Fatima walked rapidly, covering the distance from the dormitory to the school in five minutes. After entering the empty school, they walked down a hallway until they came to a flight of stairs.

"Down here," Fatima said, leading the way.

In the basement, they came to a door with a sign in both Arabic and Italian. It read, "Women only."

Seppe listened for any sound but heard none. "No one's here, Fatima. I'm going in with you."

"No, please. If we are caught, I lose my job."

"Okay, okay. Just tell Khadija who I am and that I'm right outside. Tell her I have to see her to be sure you're safe."

Fatima opened the door of the bathroom. "This is good. I hear the shower."

In about three minutes, Seppe heard footsteps approaching from the other side of the door. The door opened slowly, Fatima coming out first. Immediately, from the look on her face, Seppe knew something was wrong. Behind Fatima was a woman of middle age, too old to be Khadija, he realized, along with two men. Each carried a pistol, one pointed at Fatima and the other at Seppe.

CHAPTER THIRTY-EIGHT

Rome, CIA Headquarters

"BEFORE THE TAXI TAKES you back to Caritas, can I get you a cup of tea?" Allyson asked Khadija.

"Just water, thanks."

When Allyson returned to her desk with two bottles of water, she said, "It must have been frightening. Being all alone with them last night."

"I didn't feel it was me who was there. I felt like a different person."

"That you really are part of a terrorist group?"

"I suppose. It's something I've never felt before. The person I pretended to be last night is strong, not afraid." She looked at Allyson. "You know that's not me."

Allyson shook her head. "I'm not so sure. When I was in college, I took a course in theatre. We were required to attend all the plays on campus and one play in a big city nearby. That's where we had a chance to interview the director. Someone in the class asked her how she knew what actor should play what role. I thought she'd say things like the actor's previous experience, appearance, that sort of thing. She said those were just the 'surface issues' when she was casting. The most important factor, she said, was what was at the core of the actor. She named directors who regularly cast inexperienced actors in lead roles. Khadija, she said they had the role in them." Pausing for a moment, Allyson added, "You could play the role of a hard-ass terrorist last night because you have that kind of strength within you."

Khadija smiled. "No one's ever called me a hard ass." Then the smile disappeared. "What I don't understand is why I'm afraid today."

Allyson reached out and rested her hand on Khadija's arm. "It's natural. Remember how you stood up to Chaz. That wasn't easy."

Khadija looked down, tears in her eyes.

Allyson patted her arm again. "Wasn't it your idea to wear the jewelry in the camp?"

Khadija answered in little more than a whisper, "I told Fatima that that was something I had to do. Even though it scared me, I knew I had to do it. I had to do it for me."

"I think you had to do it for someone else, too," Allyson said.

"Who?"

"For Fatima. You know deep down that what you did last night was something you did for her."

An Abandoned Warehouse Outside Florence

Surfacing from groggy half-consciousness, Chaz glanced over at Manners and wondered if he looked as bad as she did. While at first they were only tied up, after they were questioned and refused to answer, the punishment started. Braylen's left eye was closed where they'd hit her, and her lip was split and bloody. Gauging by the pain in his own mouth, Chaz knew he'd lost at least one tooth, even as he wondered if his jaw were broken. He couldn't hear out of his right ear either.

Chaz wondered why their confession was necessary. Asha knew that as an American, he wasn't part of the police or even Interpol. What other American agency could the two of them represent?

They'd been given a cup of water every two hours, although no food or a chance to use a bathroom. He wondered if their captors enjoyed seeing Americans humiliated and degraded. With their refusal to untie Manners and him for those necessities, Chaz was losing his earlier confidence that he'd be able to turn the tables on their captors.

The only hope he held on to was that they were still alive. Although his thinking was foggy, he remembered what Asha had said when she'd questioned Manners and him.

"For you Americans, there are two worlds—yours and ours. You look up at the sky and see fluffy clouds, no planes dropping bombs on your home. You go to a grocery store and decide whether to buy chicken or beef. Never in your life do you pick up rotten fruit from the ground and eat it. You never fight a dog for a bone with a bit of meat. You never sit in your own piss until now. You never see your little brother or sister die in your arms, the light in their eyes fading like burned out candle."

Asha turned away, as tears ran down her cheeks. After a moment, she turned back, not trying to hide her grief. "America and Syria—they are not in the same world. You Americans, you never try to imagine what life is like in Syria. If you do that, you might care. Guess what? Syria has now come to you."

She approached Chaz and jabbed a finger in his chest. "Hey, Mr. Muscle-Man, are your arms and legs numb? What if your arm or leg is blown off, and there is no one to stop the bleeding?"

CHAPTER THIRTY-NINE

Caritas Refugee Camp

KHADIJA WAITED OUTSIDE THE classroom for Fatima's English class to end, and as she waited, she thought about the trade offer that she'd texted to Sabia. She shared Morgan's hope that the offer, her own suggestion, would give her more control and confidence in tonight's meeting.

The door of the classroom opened, and the refugees taking the English class poured out. These were the smart ones, Khadija thought, the ones who realized that knowing English was as beneficial as having a passport, something that gave them a chance for a better future. She pictured Fatima being one of the lucky ones, once she recovered emotionally and physically from the attack.

Yet Fatima didn't appear, and Khadija tried to convince herself that she'd stayed behind to talk with the instructor. After a long two minutes, she looked into the classroom and saw the instructor sitting alone at her desk.

"Excuse me," Khadija said in English, "did I miss Fatima?"

The teacher, a Muslim woman in proper hijab, looked up. "Fatima? No, she didn't come to class today. I hope she hasn't had a setback."

In the grip of panic, Khadija hurried from the building, looking in all directions in the hope of spotting Fatima. She took a deep breath and told herself that there could be a logical explanation. Anyway, if Fatima were in trouble, wouldn't she have used the transmitter?

As Khadijah walked back to the dormitory, she thought of Daliyeh, her friend from the school.

Dalliyeh opened the door and looked surprised, even as she stared at Khadija's jewelry. "Khadija, I didn't expect to see you."

"Can I ask you something?"

"Of course." Coming inside, Khadija accepted the hugs of the two children.

"I'm hoping you might know where Fatima is," she said. "Was she at the school this morning?"

Daliyeh offered her a chair in the tiny kitchen and moved to boil water for tea. "I don't know if I should trust you."

"Daliyeh, this jewelry isn't mine. It's something I have to wear for now."

"Why must you wear it?"

"You have to trust me. I'm still the same person I was before. And soon, Allah willing, I'll never wear this watch and these rings again."

Daliyeh sat down and looked into Khadija's eyes. "I've been so confused, after you showed up at the school with that," she said, nodding toward the watch.

"Tomorrow, I should be able to explain everything. For now, can you tell me if Fatima was at the school this morning?"

"Yes, she was there."

"Did she appear troubled by anything?" Khadija asked.

"No, not troubled. After school, I saw her talking in the lobby to a young man."

"A young man?"

"An Italian. I think he's an aid worker."

Khadija tried to calm herself as she asked for a description of the man. All Daliyeh could tell her was that the man was taller than most of the men in Caritas.

If I'd been here, this wouldn't have happened, she thought. She begged off the cup of tea and said goodbye to the children before heading for the dining hall. Residents had to show an ID before each meal, giving her hope that she could trace where Fatima went after leaving the school with the man.

Entering the dining hall, she headed for the supervisor's office and said in Italian, "I'm hoping you can help me; I have an urgent message for a resident. Can you tell me if Fatima Rasul came to lunch today."

The computer was a challenge for the supervisor, and it took a few moments before she looked up and said, "Yes, Fatima Rasul came through the line at 12:21 pm."

Looking at her gold Rolex, Khadija saw that it was now half past two. Fatima had eaten lunch two hours before. What happened after that?

"Can you tell me if she was with someone?" she asked.

The woman looked back to the computer screen. "The next person after her in line was a visitor and paid with a voucher."

Khadija asked, "Who gets a voucher?"

"Staff members or aid workers. Maybe . . ." The woman turned in her chair and scooted over to a floor safe. Opening the safe, she drew out a cash drawer. After a minute, she said, "I have three vouchers from lunch today. One was used by a housekeeper, a second by an accountant, and the third from someone in the Sant Anselmo community."

"You said the Sant Anselmo community?"

"Yes, they're aid workers."

"Yes, I know," she said. If her guess was right, she knew who that aid worker was. Reaching into her pocket, she found the cellphone Allyson had given her and called her number.

Allyson picked up on the second ring. "Khadija, are you okay?"

"I am, but I can't find Fatima, and it looks like your friend, the aid worker, might be with her. Can you contact him?"

"Seppe? Let me put you on hold while I call."

The wait was so long that Khadija felt close to fainting. *I'm too tired to think straight,* she thought. Finally, Allyson came back on the line. "He's not answering, and he's not at Sant Anselmo's offices either. Are you sure he's not in Caritas?"

Khadija was already outside the dining hall when she replied, "I'll try security and call you back." Running to the administration building, she entered the security office where she found a young Syrian woman, hardly more than a teenager, sitting at the reception desk.

"You keep a record of everyone entering and leaving Caritas, right?"

"Yes."

"I believe a Sant Anselmo aid worker entered the camp this morning. Can you check if I'm right?"

After hitting a series of keys, she nodded. "Yes, Giuseppe D'Angelo came through the gate this morning at 11:15 a.m."

"When did he leave the camp?" she asked.

"Hmm. Unless there was some mistake, he's still here."

Khadija stepped out into the hallway and called Allyson back. When Allyson heard the news, she asked, "Doesn't that mean that they're safe in Caritas somewhere?"

"I hope you're right, yet I'm worried," Khadija said. "Last night, Jameela had no trouble sneaking into the camp and smuggling me out. If that's what happened to Fatima and your friend, then we don't know where they are."

Rome, CIA Headquarters

An hour later, Morgan remained stone-faced as Allyson, fighting panic, reported that Seppe and Fatima were definitely not in Caritas.

"All I can think is that if Sabia took Seppe and Fatima, that means that they saw through Khadija last night or that Chaz or Manners caved in under torture," Allyson said.

"Slow down, Allyson. I understand your fears, but there's a more likely explanation. Think about it. We're in a chess match. They move, we move, back and forth. Asha abducts Chaz and Manners. That's their opening gambit. Khadija texts Sabia the offer to trade Chaz and Manners for Al-Nusra's promise to not interfere in Caritas. That's our move. Doesn't it make sense, if Sabia and Asha are tempted to agree to the trade, that their next move would be to abduct Fatima and Seppe? Sabia has to know that Fatima and Khadija are close friends. Sabia took Fatima as insurance, guaranteeing that Al-Nusra won't renege on their promise."

"And Seppe?" Allyson asked.

"I have to believe he wasn't part of their plan. He was just in the wrong place at the wrong time."

Allyson sat down, her head cradled in her hands. *Except that Seppe will believe he was in the right place at the right time,* she thought. "How will we know if you're right about Sabia and Asha not seeing through Khadija's Al-Nusra connection?"

"Maybe it's not as hard to find out as you think. What if Khadija calls Sabia's number and asks why Fatima and Seppe were abducted? If Sabia says tonight's meeting is still on, then we know they still believe that Khadija represents Al-Nusra. That means we're still in the game."

AN ABANDONED BUILDING OUTSIDE ROME

WHEN SABIA'S MEN BROUGHT Fatima and Seppe into an abandoned warehouse in the outskirts of Rome, Jameela was surprised to see how much Fatima had changed since she'd last seen her. It wasn't just that Fatima was thinner. She looked years older and so weak that the man with her was holding her up for support.

Months before, when Jameela first met Fatima, she'd hoped that they would be friends. In their conversations, Jameela was struck by how much Fatima talked about her future goals, rather than the pain of the past. In those first weeks, Jameela tried to follow Fatima's example, but that was before her sister, Asha, arrived in Caritas.

Asha's arrival in the camp changed everything. The change came slowly, starting with Asha and Jameela sharing an apartment together. It wasn't just any apartment, but one of the largest in Caritas. She attributed that to Asha working in the housing office of the camp. Then Asha began to dress in new clothes, not the discarded ones from charities. Soon after, Asha began wearing a new watch and rings.

"Why be poor when you can be smart?" Asha explained when Jameela asked about her wardrobe. For several days, Asha wouldn't say more than that, just dangle her clothes and jewelry like bait in front of her sister. Finally, one morning, Asha handed a watch and dress to Jameela, saying, "Put these on. You're making me look bad."

It didn't take long for Jameela to realize that her sister knew people in the camp who had money to hand out. When she asked if the perks were legal, Asha replied, "If you don't want it, you can always live like your friend Fatima."

How Asha knew that Jameela admired Fatima was a mystery to her, although it was the truth. Even when Jameela began to wear the clothes and jewelry given her by Asha, she cared about Fatima's reaction. When Fatima pretended not to notice, it hurt.

From that point on, Jameela paid more attention to Asha than to Fatima. It wasn't long before Jameela as well as Asha had new shoes—Italian shoes. And when Asha told her that she knew where they could get better food than what was offered in the dining hall, Jameela joined in the meals of meat and fresh vegetables.

It didn't take long, however, for Jameela to realize that her change of fortune came with a price. Sabia assigned her to recruit other young women in Caritas, such as her co-worker Daliyeh. When Daliyeh resisted and clearly preferred the company of Fatima, Sabia accused Jameela of not being forceful enough.

Then came Sabia's demand that Jameela accuse Hasan of child abuse. When Jameela balked at the request, saying everyone knew that Hasan was an honorable man, Asha told her she had no choice. He was a threat and had to be dealt with.

After Jameela made the accusation against Hasan, she expected him to be removed from the school. His murder put Jameela in such a panic that she broke down and sobbed in front of Asha. That was when Sabia arranged for Jameela to be smuggled out of Caritas.

Jameela was living in this abandoned building in Rome's outskirts when she heard about the attack on Fatima. The news so troubled her that she thought of running away and contacting the police. That was until she asked herself how a refugee with little Italian could manage that.

Now, in the warehouse and watching one of Sabia's men try to calm Fatima, she asked him, "Did Sabia order you to beat her?"

"No," he said. "She's been like this since we grabbed them. You can ask Sabia."

"Where is she?"

"She's still in Caritas, waiting to see if anyone saw us take Fatima and the Italian."

"You were only supposed to grab Fatima," Jameela said. Staring at the young man, she added, "What your name?"

"Seppe D'Angelo. Please, Fatima is in shock. You can see that she's shivering."

Jameela instructed one of the men to find a blanket and bring a hot cup of tea. "I remember you," she said in her basic English. "You aid worker, yes?"

The young man nodded before asking, "Why are we here?"

Good question, Jameela thought. In her minimal English, she replied, "You soon see." She signaled for the men to keep watch while she left the room and called Asha.

"They're here," Jameela said when Asha answered.

Asha exploded in anger. "They? It was supposed to be just Fatima."

Jameela explained that an Italian aid worker had been brought in with Fatima. "What am I supposed to do with them? Fatima doesn't look well," she said.

"Why are you asking me instead of Sabia?"

"She isn't here. She stayed behind in Caritas."

She heard Asha curse in Arabic. "Don't do anything; do you hear me? I'll call you back."

"But Fatima is shaking badly."

For a moment, Asha didn't respond. Finally, she said, "Don't worry about that. The aid worker can be our backup."

"A backup for what?"

"Calm down, Jameela. Fatima and the aid worker are insurance for us. Once the meeting is over tonight, I'll call with instructions."

Jameela felt a hand on her shoulder and jumped. Turning around, she was face to face with the man who'd tried to calm Fatima. "The girl is very bad," he whispered.

Jameela hung up and ran back into the other room where Fatima was writhing uncontrollably on the floor.

"She's having a seizure," Seppe yelled. "Please, you have to do something. She could die."

Jameela knelt down and saw Fatima's eyes rolling back in her head, her lips turning blue. She reached out to stop Fatima from convulsing when Seppe raised his hand. "Don't," he said. "If you do that, she could break bones."

The seizure lasted several long minutes. Afterwards, Fatima's face was ashen, though the color in her lips was returning.

"She must go to a hospital. She could die," Seppe said.

"She looks better," Jameela said. "Yes, she is better."

Seppe shook his head. "People die of shock. Please, I'm telling you the truth."

"How do I know this not trick?" Jameela said, though not believing her own words. She knew what Asha would say. "If she dies, then she dies."

Seppe put his hand on Jameela's arm, causing one of the men to raise his weapon and yell at Seppe in Arabic. Seppe stepped back even as he kept looking at Jameela.

"You have me. Please, take Fatima to a hospital."

Jameela stood frozen. "Too dangerous," she said in a low voice. "Maybe she betray us."

Seppe put his hands on his head. "We had bags over our heads. We don't know where we are. Can't you see that she is dying?"

Jameela glanced down and saw something white seeping from one side of Fatima's mouth. Jameela hadn't known that Hasan Kadir would be killed. She hadn't known that Fatima would be attacked, and she hadn't been consulted when Professor Napolitano was killed. She'd numbed herself with the thought that others had made those decisions. However, the Italian aid worker was right; she would be responsible for Fatima, who'd once been her friend.

In rapid Arabic, she instructed one of the men to drive to the nearest hospital and leave Fatima at the door. One of the men looked questioningly at Jameela. "It's okay," she lied. "Asha said I should use my judgment. Leave her at the hospital entrance and come back."

In English, she explained to Seppe what she'd decided. "You, we tie up. Have no idea of being hero."

Seppe nodded his appreciation, even as he bent down and put his hand on Fatima's cold brow. When he offered what Jameela assumed was a prayer, she looked away. She'd prayed with her parents and sister before the war in Syria. That had been lifetimes ago.

One of the men carried Fatima from the room, and in seconds, Jameela heard a car start.

She expected to see fear on the Italian aid worker's face as one of the men bound his hands and feet to a chair. Instead, she saw his lips moving silently. He was still praying.

CHAPTER FORTY

Abandoned Warehouse Outside Florence
Where Asha is Holding Chaz and Manners

THE BLOOD ON MANNERS' and Chaz's faces was dry, and the two agents hadn't been questioned for several hours. With her head clearing, Manners remembered her training for how to handle hostile interrogation and torture. The Agency had offered various techniques to block pain and fight the greater threat of panic.

As was undoubtedly true of every agent, Manners understood that she might one day die in the line of duty. She thought she'd come to terms with that, but she wasn't prepared to accept that she would die because of another agent's hubris. The look on Chaz's face told her he'd never considered the possibility of death—until now. His jaw quivered as he looked at the shattered pieces of the fountain pen at his feet. *What good is your Navy Seal training now?* she thought.

The hours of being bound and having her legs and arms go numb left her with time to recall everything Chaz had said about Asha. He'd described Asha as a beautiful, impressionable woman. Although Asha was beautiful, she was clearly not weak. She was in charge of everything happening in the room.

It's a complete snafu, she thought, *and Chaz isn't going to get us out of this.* She took a breath as she recalled advice from the Agency's manual: "Tell them nothing essential; instead, engage your captors."

"I think we have a right to know what you intend to do with us," she said, speaking in Arabic to draw Asha's attention.

"You have no rights," Asha said, walking across the room and sitting in front of her.

"Then consider me curious. What do you hope to gain by holding us?"

Asha looked from Manners to Chaz and then back to her. "Did you know you were paired with a fool?" she asked.

"I do now," Manners replied.

Chaz, not understanding Arabic, offered no protest, his eyes still glued to the floor.

"Are all American men like Mr. Big Shot here?" Asha asked.

Manners considered the pros and cons of pursuing this topic. Shredding a fellow agent wasn't a tactic advocated in the manual. However, establishing common ground with captors was.

"Too many of them are like him," she said, as if Chaz wasn't even in the room. "Are you telling me men are better in Syria?"

Asha paused for a moment. "They're poorer, more desperate. That makes them different."

Manners licked her lips, bringing on more pain. "Any chance of getting some water?"

Asha retreated to a table on the other side of the room and brought back two bottles of water. She gave Manners a sip before offering some to Chaz. Chaz, however, declined with a shake of his head.

"You didn't answer my question. Why are you holding us?" Manners asked.

Asha sat down. "Many reasons. Most, you will never guess."

"I know you're part of a fraud scheme in the camp. I know you killed two men who found out about your scam. I know you tried to kill Fatima Rasul. Maybe you're planning to kill us as well."

Asha shook her head slowly. "Maybe, or maybe we hide you somewhere in Italy or somewhere else. Whoever you work must now know that you are our insurance. If they leave us along to do what we want in the camps, then you stay alive. I think you already realized that. You are smart, not much like Mr. Macho-Man. I think you are like me."

"Because we're both women who have to work with men like him? That doesn't make us alike."

"If you lived through what I lived through—everyone you loved bombed or shot or gassed—I am sure, yes, I am sure you would do everything I've done. When you wear clothes other people have thrown away, when you get food not fit for prisoners, when you're moved from one camp after another, you understand something. You have no future, and without a future, what is life?"

"I'm not responsible for the world being unfair," Manners said.

"Then who is responsible, if not America?"

"America is not Assad. We are not ISIS."

"No, yet I wonder if you've ever thought about this. Your satellites watch every day what is happening in my country. Then you say you cannot stop the war. When I was just a girl in school, I saw a picture of an American man on the moon." Asha pointed a finger to the ceiling before continuing. "I said to myself: 'A country that can send a man to the moon, this country can do anything.' Now you shake your head at me, and you say America cannot stop the war in Syria? That it is too complicated?"

As Asha rested her hands on her knees, Manners sensed the calm determination in the woman.

Asha exhaled slowly before speaking again. "I maybe shock you now. I think I believe in America more than you do, and that is why I am sad. Yes, I am sad. A country that can go to the moon can do anything. A country that can watch what is happening in my country from satellites and drones can do something. A country that can invade Iraq can invade Syria. I think America does not want to stop the war in my country."

"I think you confuse my country with God," Manners said.

"I don't know about Allah anymore. America, I think I know about. America must like refugee camps. America must think Syrians do not deserve a future. And now America wants to arrest me because I refuse to live and die in a camp. No, I will have a future.'"

"I'm sure you've heard of the Mafia. That's who is using you. Do you think the Mafia cares about you having a future? Do you think the Mafia cares about Syria?"

"No, they do not care about Syria. They want to make money. For future, I also must have money."

Manners thought she saw a possible point of leverage. "My government will pay for the two of us—big money."

Asha smiled. "Now, who is the fool? If we did that, would your government leave us alone in Caritas? No. Would your government stop hunting for me? No."

From next to Manners came Chaz's hoarse voice. "Are you going to kill us?"

Chaz's questions came with such a feeling of hopelessness that Manners almost felt sorry for him.

Asha let the questions hang in the air for a moment before addressing Manners. "Tell him that whether you live or die is up to your people. They don't care how many die in Syria. Maybe they let you both die as well."

Rome, CIA Headquarters

The beeping of the receiver made Allyson jerk in her chair. Calling Morgan immediately, she said, "It's Fatima. She's made contact."

"Finally, a break in our favor," Morgan said, her voice quivering before she gained control. "Okay, Alli, I'll get a rescue team ready in case our only option is to try to free Fatima and Seppe. Meet me at the front door. As soon as IT determines her location, we're off."

At the front door, Morgan said, "I don't know if this is good news or bad. Fatima is transmitting from a hospital in Rome."

What about Seppe? Allyson thought. *Is he at the hospital too?*

A transit van pulled up, its door sliding open. Morgan and Allyson had barely stepped inside before the van sped off. Allyson looked around and saw several heavily armed men and women in the back.

"What's the plan?" Allyson asked over the noise of the van and traffic.

Morgan opened her jacket to reveal a handgun. "You and I go into the hospital first. The rest wait outside. Once we evaluate the situation, we move to step two. That's either the team storming the location or letting us handle it."

Because the transit van was at the mercy of Rome's afternoon traffic, it took thirty-five tense minutes to arrive at the emergency room door of the hospital. Morgan told Allyson to take the lead, given her facility in Italian. At the reception desk in the E.R. department, Allyson asked for information on Fatima Rasul.

"Are you family?" the receptionist asked.

"No, we're colleagues from work," Allyson explained.

"I'm sorry, we can't give out information except to family."

Even before Allyson translated the message, Morgan handed Allyson a slip of paper. "Tell her to call this number," she said.

In a few minutes, the receptionist replaced the phone and, after giving them a suspicious look, told them Fatima's room number.

When they entered the room, they found a doctor studying the readings on the monitor. All that was visible of Fatima was her head and arms, and what struck Allyson immediately was Fatima's sickly pallor.

"How is she, doctor?" Allyson asked in Italian.

"Her system has been overwhelmed, completely overwhelmed. Do you know if she's been through a crisis recently?"

In the background, Allyson could hear Morgan telling the team outside to stand down. Allyson did her best to focus on Fatima as she replied to the doctor, "Until a week ago, she was in a coma in another hospital. She'd been attacked."

The doctor wrote the information down on a chart. "That sheds light on some things."

"Ask her if Fatima said anything before she lost consciousness," Morgan said.

The doctor, knowing enough English, said, "She came in unconscious."

"That's impossible. We received a communication from her a little less than an hour ago," Allyson explained.

"It wasn't from her. I've been with her since she we found her outside our emergency department. She'd turned blue by that point. I was very concerned."

Allyson looked down at Fatima as she asked, "When might she regain consciousness?"

"Maybe soon or maybe not for days. I make no promises."

Feeling dejected, Allyson turned to Morgan. "Anything else?"

"Ask the doctor where her clothes are."

The doctor nodded in the direction of a metal dresser on the far wall of the room.

Morgan opened the door and extracted a black plastic bag. She pulled out undergarments and a chador before removing Fatima's shoes. From inside one of the shoes, Morgan removed the pack of tissues.

"Lucky for us, the transmitter was jammed into the shoe. The tight fit must have triggered it."

Dejected, Allyson said, "I doubt she remembered that she even had the transmitter."

"Especially if she went into shock as soon as she and Seppe were abducted. Until she wakes up, I'll put two agents outside just to be safe," Morgan said.

CARITAS REFUGEE CAMP

ON THE BENCH OUTSIDE her dorm, Khadija looked at her Rolex watch and noted that nearly nine hours had passed since she'd last heard from Sabia.

"Tonight, midnight, meet at the same place," said a woman who didn't sound like either Sabia or Jameela.

"Who am I talking to? Is this Asha?"

"Ah, you're very smart. By now, you know we took Fatima and the aid worker for insurance. Don't try anything. Come alone."

Khadija froze. She was relieved that they hadn't seen through her cover story, which meant that they still thought she was part of Al-Nusra. Yet something was off. How did Asha not know that Fatima was safe in a hospital?

She replied quickly, "I understand. You agree to the exchange—the two Americans for our promise?"

"Let us say we will discuss that."

Khadija had hurriedly called Allyson after disconnecting and relayed the message.

"Was it Jameela or Sabia you talked to?"

"Neither. It was Asha, but here's what I don't understand. She said they were holding Fatima as well as Seppe."

"What? Are you sure?"

"Yes."

"It makes no sense. Then again, maybe I'm too tired to make sense of anything." After a moment, Allyson added, "Maybe they're messing with our heads or . . . "

"Or what?"

After a pause, Allyson said, "Or else, Fatima being in the hospital means that Asha and Sabia or Asha and Jameela aren't communicating. That would be a miracle."

An Abandoned Warehouse outside Rome Where Asha is Holding Chaz and Manners

Jameela felt the tension building between the other captors and her. When Sabia returned and saw that Fatima wasn't there, she threatened to call Asha. Once again, Jameela lied, saying that Asha had given her permission for Fatima to be taken to the hospital. The way Sabia scowled added to Jameela's unease.

With the others in the room clearly avoiding her, Jameela paid closer attention to Seppe. He reminded her of how she felt on her first day in Caritas over a year before. She'd been a nervous wreck, having been transferred to Caritas after she'd gotten into a fight with another refugee who accused her of stealing. Although Jameela was innocent of the charge, she was transferred.

On her first day in Caritas, she'd felt uneasy about the black mark on her record and was wary during her intake interviews. As she feared, a few camp officials treated her coldly. The only exception was an Italian aid worker, someone like Seppe, who offered a smile and said in broken Arabic, "Welcome to Caritas."

When Jameela allowed Fatima to be taken to the hospital, Seppe had thanked her for her kindness. It took Jameela a few moments to understand why his words brought tears to her eyes. At first, she thought it was simply that his words of gratitude contrasted sharply with the suspicious looks Sabia and the men in the room were giving her.

It took a few more minutes before Jameela realized that her tears were about something else, her months in Caritas "B.A.," before Asha. Asha's arrival was a tidal wave that washed away Jameela's previous life. It took Asha just days in Caritas to connect with Sabia, and soon after, Asha began to pressure Jameela.

Looking around the empty warehouse where she'd been hiding for the past three weeks, she thought, *And now, I'm stuck in "A.A."—after Asha.* When she'd first been smuggled out of Caritas, she believed Asha's promise that it was just a matter of time before she'd be in Milan or Paris, working in a perfume shop. As the days, then weeks dragged on, her hope faded. She realized too late that following Asha's lead would mean that she would either be pulled down deeper into crime, or she'd be imprisoned for her part in the attacks in Caritas. Either way, she knew she'd never be free.

Looking at Seppe, she said in her limited English, "You not part of plan. The plan just to take Fatima. How you know her?"

"I met Fatima in the hospital. When she returned to Caritas, I wanted to see if she was okay."

"But why you stay with her?"

Seppe hesitated before answering. "She told me her friend Khadija was in Rome for a doctor's appointment. That's why I stayed with her until Khadija returned."

Jameela decided to test how much Seppe knew. "Do you know this Khadija is part of Al-Nusra?"

"Do you mean the terrorists?"

"Yes, in Syria and Iraq."

After a pause, Seppe asked, "What interest would Al-Nusra have in the camp?"

"They have plans for children, I think."

She watched Seppe, who appeared genuinely puzzled until he looked up in alarm. "Do you mean using children for . . . for terrorist attacks?"

"Italian government, it knows nothing about what goes on in camps," Jameela said, realizing she was repeating something Asha had said several times.

AUGUST 13
ROME, CIA HEADQUARTERS

EVERYONE SITTING AROUND THE conference table at CIA headquarters looked exhausted.

"You all know by now that Khadija received a reply to her text, setting up a meeting for tonight," Bureau Chief Sanderson said before turning toward Khadija. "And you're sure you were speaking with Asha, not Sabia or Jameela, right?"

"Yes, she admitted it."

"The big question is what it means, then, that Asha thinks that they're still holding Fatima. Is that a good thing or some new game they're playing?" he asked. "I've brought in Agent Tufnell to help us unravel all the threads we're now dealing with."

Agent Tufnell, was a gray-haired man who, with his pocket protector, looked more like an accountant than a CIA agent.

"It's tempting to think that if Khadija did talk with Asha, then Asha and maybe Agents Eaton and Manners are now near Rome. However, if that were the case, then Asha would know that Fatima is in a hospital and no longer part of the equation. Ergo, we should assume that Asha, along with Chaz and Manners, are still somewhere else, probably in Tuscany. Let's call that the 'Florence cell,' led by Asha Malik. Sabia and Jameela are somewhere near here in Rome and until recently were holding Fatima Rasul and the aid worker, Seppe D'Angelo. They can be the 'Rome cell.' Everything to this point has led us to believe that Asha and Sabia are coordinating their moves. However, if Asha doesn't know that Fatima was taken to a hospital, that suggests that there could be a split in the leadership. If that's the case, that could be good news. On the other hand, if part of their organization is going rogue, that makes our adversary more unpredictable."

"Khadija, what are your thoughts?" Sanderson asked.

Khadija looked up from her notepad. "Maybe I'm just trying to find some hope, but if anyone sent Fatima to the hospital, it had to be Jameela. Yet, that doesn't make sense if, three weeks ago, Sabia and Jameela tried to kill Fatima."

"Wait a minute," Allyson said. "Three weeks ago, Jameela wasn't in Caritas. Asha and Sabia were there, which means they must be the ones who attacked Fatima and killed Hasan and the professor."

Agent Tufnell held Allyson's gaze. "It sounds like you agree that Jameela is the weak link. That would be very good news."

Bureau Chief Sanderson cleared his throat. "That leaves us this question. Is there a way to exploit this new situation before Khadija's meeting tonight?" Sanderson said.

No one said anything until Agent Tufnell cleared his throat. "If Chaz and Manners are in one location, and Seppe is in another, it will be next to impossible to free them all at the same time. Let's say we find one of the two locations and storm it. Even though we might be able to free Chaz and Manners, a phone call will doom the Italian aid worker . . . or vice versa."

"Look, everyone," Sanderson said when the room again was silent. "We took this job to fight and defeat these kinds of people. They are clever, yet I have to believe that as tired as we are, we can come up with a plan to rescue all three of them—Chaz, Manners, and Seppe D'Angelo. Don't prove me wrong."

CHAPTER FORTY-ONE

An Abandoned Warehouse outside Rome

SEPPE'S BRAIN AS WELL as his arms and legs felt numb as he tried to make sense of Jameela's claim that Khadija was part of Al-Nusra. Allyson had described Khadija as a part of her organization. What was the truth? Had Allyson's agency been taken in, or had Allyson's agency fooled Jameela and Sabia?

I have to be careful what I say, but I also have to find out all I can, he thought, before saying, "I still don't understand why Fatima was kidnapped. All she wants from Caritas is to get an education and move on with her life."

Jameela nodded. "Taking Fatima . . . not my decision. She is safe in hospital. Maybe she get her dream. Or, maybe that is another lie we are told, and Fatima will be in camp forever. You come to Caritas two, three times a week, then you leave, yes? You drive car to where you live. You live in nice house or apartment, not in camp. You never say to friends, 'Meet me in refugee camp.' No, you say, 'meet me at a bar.' You are happy to be away from us."

Seppe couldn't deny what Jameela was saying. "You have a right to be bitter," he said.

Jameela shook her head. "Bitter? You cannot imagine. You know what we want? We want a life like you have, but will Italy give this? No. Asha has friend. She learn some Italian by watching TV. She tell Asha that Italy will send us back to Syria when war is over. For what? Our cities are gone. Schools and hospitals gone. Factories, gone. All bombed. Syria, my country, is gone, but this is okay for you. You will send us back and forget us."

"Not all of us feel that way," Seppe said. "Sant Anselmo doesn't feel that way. I don't feel that way."

"You not Italian government."

"No, no I'm not."

"When Italy send us back, what you do?"

Even as he knew that Jameela was waiting for his answer, what could he say? Hadn't he already pictured a time in the future when camps like Caritas would be closed and he could move on to the next chapter of his life—his life in Italy, or maybe even a new life in the United States with Allyson?

Jameela's cellphone rang. She looked down at the screen, then rose quickly and left the room.

In his heart, Seppe knew Jameela's question must be every Syrian refugee's question, both in Caritas and in all the other refugee camps. For the first time, he didn't ask himself what the world should do when Syria's civil war ended. Instead, he asked, *What should I do?*

A Tactical Vehicle Filled with Armed Agents

Two hours after the meeting with Bureau Chief Sanderson, Allyson and Khadija knocked on Morgan's door, a tentative plan in Allyson's hand to rescue all three abductees—Chaz, Manners, and Seppe. Twenty minutes later, Allyson was explaining to the larger group the plan whose strengths were also its weaknesses. The plan assumed, far from a certainty, that Sabia and Asha would agree to Khadija's trade offer—Chaz and Manners for Al-Nusra's promise to let Sabia's group begin trafficking children in Caritas. On the phone, Asha had committed to discussing the trade proposal, nothing more.

If, however, Khadija could convince Sabia and Asha to take the deal, then the plan moved to its most critical moment. That was the moment when Khadija would try to trick Sabia and Asha into granting a concession, something that would seem a small obstacle but was a major concession.

Khadija had let Allyson present the plan to the group that would either agree or nix it. Allyson didn't try to hide the obvious unknown about the plan—that everything depended on Khadija, the least experienced agent in the room, the one agent most likely to fold under the pressure.

Khadija sat in silence for much of Allyson's presentation, even as the plan slowly gained support. Part of the support, Khadija knew, was that the only alternative was to focus on saving Chaz and Manners or Seppe, not all three.

It was only after the meeting broke up that Morgan sat down next to Khadija. "Can you do this, Khadija? If you can, it's our best chance of rescuing Chaz, Manners, and Seppe. However, I don't have to tell you that the risks are high."

Now, four hours later, as she followed Jameela to the van that would take her again to Sabia, Khadija felt oddly calm, as if she'd been waiting for this moment her whole life.

The next half-hour was a repeat of the previous night. Jameela again sat in the front of the car while Khadija was in between the two men in the back, a cloth bag over her head. The only difference was that instead of chatter tonight, there was noticeable tension in the vehicle.

Only when she was led from the vehicle into a room and the bag was removed did she realize that she was in the same room as the night before. Seeing a young man bound to a chair across the room, she recognized Seppe D'Angelo from a photo Allyson had shown her. He looked tired, although not afraid. For a moment, Khadija felt everyone looking at her before she realized that Sabia and Jameela were expecting her to be looking for another person—Fatima.

Taking a step toward Sabia, she said, "Where is Fatima? What have you done with her?"

"She is safe," Sabia answered.

"Fatima is not part of Al-Nusra. You had no reason to take her."

"We took her for the same reason that you're upset. She's your friend. We knew you wouldn't think of crossing us if we took her."

From across the room, the bound young man said, "Fatima is okay. They took her to a hospital."

"Why? What was wrong with her?"

"She was having seizures," he said.

"Enough of this chatter," Sabia said. "It's time to get down to business.

We were intrigued by the text you left for me: the trade offer, the two Americans for Al-Nusra's promise to give us free range in Caritas. Why would we give up our leverage in exchange for a promise that Al-Nusra could break at any time?"

Khadija focused solely on Sabia. "The Americans, once we put them on trial and execute them on the internet, will serve a far greater purpose in our war against the West than anything you could use them for. However, if you doubt Al-Nusra, let me point out one thing you are unaware of. From our perspective, the American hostages are a problem for you. They don't solve your problem; they are one."

Sabia jumped from her chair. "What do you mean? We have the Americans, Interpol, and the Italian government all looking for them."

As calmly as she could manage, Khadija slowly nodded. "And that's your problem. Italy is crawling with people looking for the two Americans. Al-Nusra wonders how long you can keep them hidden. It's clear you do not want to kill them. Perhaps at the beginning you thought kidnapping them would frighten the CIA—yes, Al-Nusra knows they are CIA—and make the mighty US government back down. Maybe you thought if you held on to them, the Americans would let you do what you want in the camp. You are no match for them. You would do better to trade. That way you and Al-Nusra both get what you—and we—want. Give us the Americans and we take your problem off your hands. We use their deaths for the greater goal of striking back at the West, and you get what you want in the camp."

Sabia stared at Khadija, and Khadija felt close to fainting. She uttered a brief prayer for courage.

It was Jameela, however, who broke the ice. "Wouldn't that mean that having the Italian aid worker is another problem for us?"

Khadija blinked twice. The crucial concession that she feared Sabia and Asha would balk at had been introduced by Jameela.

Sabia squared around to face Jameela. "And you're wondering why you're not in charge."

"Sorry, I was just wondering."

Khadija moved in quickly. "What she said makes sense. What good is the aid worker to you? It's obvious that you made a mistake in taking him. You intended to take only Fatima, which means he's just what she said, another problem."

Khadija knew from Sabia's silence that she understood her point. Finally, Sabia asked, "What good is he to you?"

Khadija felt that ice water, not warm blood, was coursing through her veins. This was the moment that everything depended on. The shy girl in Brixton, the one who hoped to be invisible despite being forced to wear a hijab every day to school, where was she? *Not here. She's not here,* Khadija thought. *She's not who Sabia is looking at.*

"Allah has given us a better vision of the future that you cannot see," she said.

"We make our own future," Sabia replied.

"No, you are wrong, and you insult Allah. The aid worker is Italian. His government has joined in the destruction of our country. Europe is our enemy as much as America. So yes, we will gladly take the aid worker, and we will execute him along with the Americans to amplify our message. Three will die for the whole world to see."

Although Khadija heard Jameela gasp as she looked at Seppe she, could see from the look on Sabia's face that she was still not persuaded. "Do this for us, and we will do your organization a favor in the future," Khadija added, even as she wasn't sure what she meant.

Sabia stood. "Just sit there; I'll call Asha. I want her to hear what you're offering."

Good question, Khadija thought. *What am I offering?*

Jameela watched Sabia on the other side of the room bringing Asha up to date on Khadija's new offer. She felt sick because the aid worker's fate was no longer in her hands. When she was about to leave the room, Seppe whispered to her, "What happens now?"

Jameela tried not to look at him. Knowing that the aid worker understood none of what Khadija had said, she decided to lie. "If things go well, maybe you be free. Then what? You go back to Caritas?" she asked. .

"Yes, I will."

"Why? Why you come week after week? Why you not hate the place?"

"I do hate that places like Caritas exist," he said. "I hate that most of the people in the world are poor. And I hate that you don't have the choices . . . the chances I have."

"Then why you come to camp?"

After a moment, Seppe said, "If I don't go, I'm afraid my heart will shrivel up and die."

Jameela, looking at the floor, said, "Asha, she tell me people in America and even Italy don't know where Syria is on map. Maybe some will know now."

"Yes, but . . . is this way?"

"What choice we have?"

Their whispered conversation ended when Jameela felt Sabia tap her shoulder.

"Asha wants all of us to hear what she says."

CHAPTER FORTY-TWO

In the Tactical Van

"KHADIJA HAS CROSSED OVER," Morgan said. "I wonder if she's scared herself."

"What do you mean?" Allyson asked.

"It's one thing when an agent takes on an identity and concentrates on staying in character. Rarely, an agent embodies the role. We call that 'crossing over.' Psychologists at CIA headquarters in Virginia think the shift isn't as much a conscious decision as a profound experience of dissociation. Last night, Khadija pretended to be in Al-Nusra. She'd done her homework on that group and didn't slip up. Yet, tonight in that exchange? Tonight, she is Al-Nusra."

"Crossing over doesn't sound like something that can be taught."

"It can't. Khadija tapped into something inside her, something that began long before tonight. When we put her in Caritas, she pretended to be a Syrian refugee. Tonight, she connected with some part of herself that views the world as a jihadist does. I don't think she had any idea that was in her—until it came out. Instead of playing a role, the role is now playing her."

"Doesn't that put her in more danger?" Allyson asked.

"Just the opposite. If I could give her one piece of advice, I'd tell her to trust herself and go deeper into the experience. Because right now, she could convince Asha of almost anything, and there's something else. In the future, Khadija will be even more valuable to the Agency—if she decides to stay. Having her in meetings will be like having an Al-Nusra or ISIS agent in the room."

Allyson couldn't control the tension in her voice. "Does that mean she'll be able to save Seppe as well as Chaz and Manners?"

Morgan shrugged. "All we know is that no one could have done any better."

Warehouse Outside Rome

Khadija could imagine what Morgan and Allyson were thinking as they listened in to her going off script.

What am I doing? she wondered. *Will the idea I just thought of work?*

"Your group has found a way to make money in the camp, yes?" she asked.

Sabia nodded. "We told you that last night. If this is some trick, you won't leave here alive."

Khadija didn't even blink. "Perhaps your group should think about the future. One day, Allah willing, maybe one day soon, America, Russia, and Europe will end the war in Syria. Do you not agree?"

When neither Sabia nor Asha on the phone said anything, Khadija pressed ahead. "When the war ends, Italy and other countries will throw us out. They do not want us here. They've never wanted us here. Camps will close, and then what will you do to make money? Perhaps you haven't thought of this."

The Mafia boss caught Sabia's arm, letting her know he wanted her to translate. When Sabia did, Khadija realized that the aid worker, Seppe, could now understand as well.

Asha's voice filled the room. "Who can know when the war ends? We may be in camps for ten more years."

Khadija said, "Al-Nusra can see what will happen, and we do not believe it will be long from now. This we are certain of. When the war ends, the governments of America and Europe will pour money into Syria. Out of guilt and shame, they will say that they want to rebuild our country."

She paused to let Sabia translate what she'd said for the Mafia representative. Slowly, she saw the derisive smile fall from his face. *He gets it now,* she thought.

"As I said, Al-Nusra has planned for this. We know what happened in Iraq, yes?"

Sabia smiled, although not in derision. "Billions of dollars poured in."

"America and Europe do not care how much money disappeared. Tribal leaders, government bureaucrats, the army—all became wealthy beyond their dreams." Khadija paused a second before adding, "What you are doing in the camps, we will do in Syria after the war, only on a bigger scale. You ask about the favor we can do for you? Our group will decide who gets the big contracts. We will remember your cooperation now."

Sabia's smile disappeared, and for a moment Khadija wondered if she'd overplayed her hand. After conversing with Asha further on the phone, Sabia asked, "The aid worker is worth that much to you?"

Khadija knew that what she said next could either free Seppe or bring about both his and her death. Again, she wondered what Morgan, Allyson, and the other agents who were listening in were thinking. Could they even believe that she was the one speaking?

"Yes, his death will be useful. There is something more," Khadija said. "I must speak to Asha myself."

Although Sabia looked like she didn't want to hand the phone over, she did after Asha spoke.

"What is this 'something more?'" Asha said.

Khadija turned off speaker-mode and took a breath before making her final pitch. "No one should underestimate American and Interpol's intelligence. You should assume that they are right now closing in, which means, if you agree, we have to complete the trade immediately. Asha, that means you must bring the two Americans to Rome, tonight."

Inside Waiting Tactical Van

Allyson watched as Morgan sat back in the van and sighed. "Alli, she did it. Khadija made the demand. She was brilliant. Perfect timing. If Sabia and Asha have been taken in, Chaz and Manners will be in the same room as Seppe before the night is over. That's when we storm the location and—keep your fingers crossed—we rescue the three of them. For now we stay on high alert, ready for the signal."

The more fatigued Allyson was, the more she battled anxiety and darkness. The back-and-forth chess match over the past forty-eight hours with Sabia and Asha had worn her down, so much so that she had a hard time joining Morgan in believing that victory was near.

She could imagine all kinds of ways the evening would end in disaster, not rescue. From their own sources, Sabia, Asha, or the Mafia representative might learn at any moment that Khadija is CIA, not a part of Al-Nusra—or Sabia and Asha could pause, talk over everything that Khadija had promised over the two late-night meetings, and balk at a trade, which left them without hostages and therefore without physical leverage.

"You don't look convinced," Morgan said as if she were reading Allyson's mind. "You think Sabia or Asha will reject the offer?"

"I'd say it's fifty-fifty. Please tell me that I'm missing something."

"Well, I'll try. Negotiations like this are decided on intimidation, although persuasion might be a more accurate term. Sabia and Asha taking Chaz and Manners and then abducting Fatima—remember, they never intended to hold Seppe—all that was meant to intimidate us, to force us to cut a deal. That was all a set-up, meant to make us panic, make us feel that we'd lost control."

"They did a good job, then, because it still feels that they have the upper hand," Allyson said.

Morgan shook her head. "Khadija changed all that. She's made Sabia and Asha see that taking the hostages was a bad move from the beginning. Even if they don't buy her argument completely, I'm sure the Mafia representative understands that the hostages, including Seppe, are a problem in the long term."

"Does that mean Sabia and Asha never intended to kill them?"

"Khadija called their bluff on that. She made the trade offer look like their only logical option, a good deal for them as well as Al-Nusra."

"You have no doubts?" Allyson asked.

"I didn't say that. What I'm saying is that Khadija is quite some agent. As I said before, no one could have done better."

Inside a Warehouse near Rome

As Khadija watched Sabia talk to Asha from the other side of the room, it became clear that they were disagreeing about something. Then, Sabia appeared to relent. Khadija tried to stay in her role, which meant she tried not to worry about what Morgan and Allyson, listening in, made of her change of plan. Would Morgan wonder how she'd been so convincing as an Al-Nusra agent?

She saw that Seppe was also following the conversation closely. Yet, because he didn't speak Arabic, she wondered what, if anything, he understood. What Khadija did assume was that she'd forced Seppe to make a decision about her. Knowing it wouldn't be safe, she'd given him nothing to make him doubt that she was a terrorist.

She knew that Morgan and Allyson must also be questioning her loyalties, even as she was asking herself the same question. From her schooldays In Brixton through her first months in the Agency, she was as her file described her: someone capable of being invisible, someone who said little but could be relied on to repeat what she heard word for word.

Now, as she replayed what she'd said to Sabia and Asha, she wondered if playing the part of a terrorist had been a role after all.

Her thoughts were interrupted by Sabia approaching her. Clearly not pleased, Sabia said, "Asha agrees to the deal, and she's on her way. She will be here in an hour."

"With the two Americans?"

"Yes," she replied, looking angry. "I warn you and anyone from Al-Nusra listening in on your device. Yes, we know they hear everything I'm saying. If this is some trick, you will not leave here alive."

CHAPTER FORTY-THREE

The Abandoned Warehouse Outside Rome

AN HOUR LATER, KHADIJA watched as Sabia ended another call and signaled for two of the armed men to step outside. *The welcoming committee*, she thought.

Five long minutes passed before sounds of a vehicle came from outside. Khadija braced herself, suddenly afraid it could be Morgan and other agents who would burst through the door. Instead, she heard Asha speaking loudly and angrily as she entered the room.

Khadija watched Asha as she turned to Sabia, then Jameela. "I see it was you, my own sister, who let Fatima go. And you wonder why we pulled you out of Caritas. You're soft, and you disgust me."

Jameela shook her head. "I can't be you; I can't."

Asha was no longer listening. She turned around and walked back outside. Picking up on Asha's anger, a guard slapped Seppe's face.

Khadija kept herself from glancing at Seppe. In her role, she had to treat him as a pawn, a thing, something Al-Nusra intended to execute, not as Allyson's close friend.

SOMETHING HAS TO GIVE soon, she thought. Hearing a new commotion at the door, she waited to see Chaz and Manners being brought in. That would be the moment when Morgan, listening in, would give the signal to storm the site.

Three people came into the room. First two armed men entered, then a tall, blond woman whom Khadija recognized from photos as Braylen Manners. There was no Chaz. Khadija was too stunned for a moment to say anything. Then, she remembered that Morgan was awaiting the signal. "Where's the American, the man?" she asked, noticing Sabia smile.

"I've decided to keep him," Asha replied.

Inside the CIA Tactical Van

Her phone at her ear, Morgan slammed her fist down on the metal seat. Turning to Allyson, she said. "Asha is improvising, too. She's keeping Chaz."

In the silence that followed, Allyson realized that Khadija's and her intricate plan to save everyone had just blown up. The last domino wouldn't fall. Finally, Morgan spoke to someone on the phone, "I can't see another way either."

She pocketed her phone. "We're in a holding pattern until we hear how Khadija reacts to the change."

Allyson tried to put herself in Khadija's place. "What can she do? I mean, if she pushes too hard to get Chaz, Asha will get suspicious."

"That's what the suits in Virginia think. They see no alternative to storming the room. There's an outside chance that we might, in a day or two, determine where they're keeping Chaz, although . . . well, the Agency doesn't hold out much hope."

An Abandoned Warehouse Outside Rome

Although Khadija wished that someone from the agency would tell her how to handle the new situation, she knew she was on her own. The lives of Manners, Seppe, and Chaz, wherever he was, were in her hands. Even as her mind raced as she tried to see a way forward, everything she imagined led to a dead end.

She stared at Asha as she said, "That's not what we agreed to."

Her face set, Asha said, "You get what you want—the aid worker and the American woman for you to execute. Why be greedy? I'm holding onto Mr. Big Shot American as insurance, insurance that Al-Nusra won't double-cross us."

"Once again, you insult Al-Nusra and Allah," Khadija said as a challenge.

Asha, however, didn't answer. Everyone looked where she was looking, to where Jameela was whispering with Seppe, the aid worker. "What's he saying?" Asha asked.

Jameela shook her head in Seppe's direction, but he kept nodding, as if he were prodding her to explain.

Jameela glanced at her sister. "He says, let the other American go and keep him instead."

CHAPTER FORTY-FOUR

Inside the CIA Tactical Van

When Morgan relayed what Seppe had offered, Allyson grasped her arm. "We can't let Seppe do this. He has to know that Khadija is one of us. He'll be safe if he just waits."

Morgan pulled her arm free as she spoke into the phone. After a long moment, she frowned and said, "You're sure? Langley is sure?"

"What are they saying? What are they saying?" Allyson said before sobbing.

Morgan gave Allyson a look that seemed to contain all the sadness in the world. "If Asha accepts the trade, we go with it. The Agency will do its best to rescue Seppe later . . . if we can."

"No, no, no. Look, Chaz is an agent; he knows the risks. Seppe has done nothing to deserve this. Nothing. When Manners and Chaz aren't executed online, Asha will realize that her group has been played. And Seppe . . ."

"Everything you say is right, although it's not going to change Langley's mind, Allyson. And remember, this is Seppe's decision. Although I know this won't mean anything to you now, your friend's sacrifice won't be forgotten."

As Allyson stumbled out of the van, she dialed Father Fortis' number. When he answered, she said, "Nick, I know it's the middle of the night where you are, but something horrible is about to happen."

"Of course, my dear. What can you share with me?"

"Not the details, but do you remember my telling you about Seppe?"

"Your religious friend, right?"

"That's a good way to describe him. What I can tell you is that he's been abducted by people who might kill him."

When Father Fortis didn't say anything, she asked, "Did you hear me, Nick?"

"Yes, Allyson. I was just praying for him. Is there anything else you can tell me?"

"Just that he's in the hands of terrorists."

"Oh, Allyson. I can tell that you're terrified. Do they want money?"

"It would be easier to deal with if that's all they want."

"Can I ask you a hard question?" Nick asked.

"That's all I have in my head—hard questions."

"Of course, of course. Allyson, tell me how you think Seppe is handling this situation."

Allyson broke down again and sobbed. "I'm sure he's praying, but I know he isn't panicking. He's calm. Yes, I'm sure he's calm. Nick, Seppe is the kindest person I know, outside of you. He's a compassionate aid worker. The refugees love him . . . and so do I."

She could hear Nick breathing on the line. "Allyson, what is it you're most worried about?"

"That the God Seppe and you believe in will let this good, good man die."

AN ABANDONED WAREHOUSE OUTSIDE ROME

ASHA STOOD OVER SEPPE in a completely silent room. "Why you do this?" she said in English. "You think you live by going with me? You think you escape from Al-Nusra? You forget that we kill Kadir and the professor."

Seppe shook his head. "No, it's not that."

"Then what is it?"

"You wouldn't understand if I told you."

Finally, Asha turned away from Seppe. On her phone, she gave instructions in Arabic before saying in English, "OK, I keep you and the bigshot American goes to Al-Nusra."

Seppe looked from Asha to Jameela. "Thank you."

In the CIA Tactical Vehicle

Once Sabia and Asha know they've been played, Seppe will die, and I will never understand, Allyson thought. Yet in an odd way, some part of her did understand. Morgan had said nothing to her since she relayed the Agency's decision. Instead, she told the agents in the van to stand down until she received further orders.

After a few agonizing minutes, Morgan's phone buzzed. Allyson felt hands around her neck, choking her, until Morgan relayed the message. "Khadija just gave the signal. Let's hope Asha and the others believe we're Al-Nusra coming to pick up our hostages."

Allyson was numb, wondering why Khadija was requesting something that had no bearing on Seppe's survival. In fact, Khadija acted as if she were aiding Asha. Then Allyson gasped, grabbing Morgan's arm again. "Oh, my God. Oh, my God. Don't you see? Seppe knows who Khadija is, and Khadija knows what Seppe is doing."

"Slow down, Alli," Morgan said. "What are you talking about?"

Allyson's mouth was dry, and the words felt thick in her mouth. "Asha agreed to trade Chaz for Seppe. If Chaz is somewhere nearby, that means that in a few minutes, Khadija, Chaz, Manners, and Seppe will all be together in the same room. We'll have our chance."

"Oh God, you're right," Morgan said, contacting someone on her phone. "Tell Langley we might have a new window. I'm putting one of my agents on."

She put the phone on speaker and handed it to Allyson. "Tell them," she said.

"There will be a few minutes, maybe no more than that, when Chaz, Manners, Khadija, and Seppe—the aid worker—will be in the same room together. That's when Khadija will say that other Al-Nusra agents are on their way for Chaz and Manners. That's the signal for the rescue. Don't you see?"

There was silence on the other end of the line until a voice said, "Put Agent Stamper back on the phone."

Allyson watched Morgan as she listened to someone on the phone. Turning to Allyson, she said, "They think the odds of completing the mission without a firefight are fifty-fifty. They're leaving the decision to me."

Allyson looked pleadingly at Morgan, who offered a small smile. "Let's hope Seppe has put one over on Asha," Stamper said. "And let's hope Khadija picked up on it. I say we go."

The Abandoned Warehouse Outside Rome

Khadija glanced around the room. *I have to be ready for anything that can go wrong,* she thought. While she knew that Morgan had heard everything, Khadija had no idea if Morgan had picked up on every part of Seppe's plan. She also realized that there was an even worse possibility. Any second now, Asha could see through Seppe's plan. If that happened, Khadija didn't give the four of them—Seppe, Chaz, Manners, or her—any chance of survival.

She tried to catch Seppe's eye. Seppe, however, was looking down at the floor. Manners was staring at her, and Khadija was certain that she'd guessed what was coming.

"I think it's safe to cut them free," Jameela said, breaking the silence as she sat down next to Seppe.

Everyone looked at Asha, who shrugged. "Do it yourself, if you want. It's almost over."

Accepting a knife from one of the armed guards, Jameela stood behind Manners, then Seppe, to cut the plastic ties from their wrists. Khadija was sure that she saw Jameela and Seppe's lips moving, although she heard nothing.

Asha told Jameela to hurry up, even as her phone buzzed. She listened, agreed to something, and ended the call.

"My men are on their way with the other American. Five minutes," Asha told everyone in the room. Turning to Khadija, she added, "I assume your people are listening in and will know where to come."

"Of course," Khadija replied. "My people are ready for the handover." Looking again at Seppe, he appeared to be somewhere else, and she wondered if this was part of an act. She thought he was the last person in the room capable of tricking Asha. Yet, he'd done just that, and if his plan worked, he would rightly receive the credit.

It felt like hours, not minutes, before Khadija could hear a vehicle navigate the rough road leading to the warehouse.

Khadija moved closer to Asha, who posted herself at one of the windows from where they could see a car stop ten yards short of the building, its engine turning off. "Everybody keep calm. This should be over soon," Asha said.

The door opened, and a man with a weapon led Chaz, a black bag over his head, into the room to stand before Asha. She took off the covering and said, "Remember me?"

Chaz squinted in the light, saying nothing. His face was a bloody mess, and he slumped, nearly falling to the ground.

"Put him in a chair," Asha ordered. "I want him to hear what I say."

Sitting in the chair, Chaz looked around until his eyes rested on Khadija. For a second, she feared he'd reveal who she really was. Instead, he muttered, "You filthy, ugly, traitor. You bitch. Why am I not surprised?"

Khadija breathed easier, realizing she'd fooled even him.

One of the men called Asha's name. "A van is coming."

"Remember, they're Al-Nusra, my people," Khadija said. "I don't want anybody harmed in the exchange."

"She's right," Asha said to the armed men. "Don't shoot."

Khadija held her breath, imagining Morgan and Allyson leading other agents toward the door. In the next second, the door flew open, and two canisters of tear gas were lobbed into the room. As the cloud spread, Khadija heard Asha swear and shots ring out.

Khadija dove to the floor and crawled in the direction of Manners. Manners, however, was already crab-walking toward one of the captors even as all the lights went out.

Realizing that Manners had been trained for situations like this, Khadija crawled to where she remembered Seppe sitting. Bursts of gunfire, like lightning, created a crazy pattern of light and dark as Khadija, eyes smarting, felt the legs of a chair. When she realized that the chair was empty, she reached down and felt a body lying motionless on the floor and then the warmth of blood.

The form didn't move, even as Khadija felt another body moving close by. Suddenly, the sounds of gunfire stopped as abruptly as they'd begun. Amidst the moans in the room, Khadija heard someone very close to her saying, "Ave Maria, gratia plena." She knew that only one person in the room would know a Latin prayer, and a wave of relief passed through her until she remembered the inert body between her and Seppe.

Even before the lights came back on and the tear gas began to dissipate, she knew the body she was touching was dead, and she knew the dead body was Jameela Malik's.

CHAPTER FORTY-FIVE

The Abandoned Warehouse Outside Rome

FOUR HOURS LATER, AS the sun was rising, Allyson and Morgan prepared to leave the site in the hands of the Italian forensic team. Ambulances had come and gone, taking four bodies to the mortuary and transporting the five people who were wounded to the hospital.

The dead included three of Sabia's and Asha's guards along with Jameela Malik. Among the wounded were Khadija, who couldn't straighten her leg, and Seppe, who had sustained a flesh wound to his shoulder. Chaz and Manners, with nasty head wounds, were also taken away for treatment and debriefing.

Allyson had rushed to the three on the floor: Seppe, Khadija, and a third, whom Seppe was holding in his arms. For a moment, Seppe looked as if he didn't recognize Allyson, and it was only after Khadija spoke that Allyson understood that the body Seppe was holding was Jameela's.

Once the dead and wounded were taken away, the ranking police officer verbally assaulted Morgan, accusing the United States of a violent and unlawful act on Italian soil. Allyson was pressed into translating the exchange, a duty she found more difficult as the exhaustion of the past forty-eight hours set in. Finally, Morgan declined to answer any more questions, telling the official that further inquiries should be directed to the U.S. Embassy.

Morgan's delicate position hadn't been helped by Chaz's actions in the melee. Once the lights had come back on, Allyson saw Chaz slamming the head of one of the armed guards repeatedly onto the concrete floor. After Chaz was pulled off, he lunged and grabbed Asha by the throat and had to be restrained again. The whole time, he cursed his captors and Syria as a nation, snarling like an enraged dog. It was only after Chaz took a breath that anyone could hear Seppe, on the other side of the room, praying softly.

In the van, as agents high-fived one another, Allyson couldn't stop crying. She cried out of exhaustion. She cried for Hasan Kadir, for Professor Napolitano, and for Fatima, whom she knew would never be the same. She also cried in relief, knowing that the evening's events would change Caritas for the better, even as she knew that the arrests wouldn't change enough. Wars in the Middle East and Africa would continue; more camps like Caritas would be built to handle the waves of refugees who were always arriving, and crime would resurface in the camps.

Morgan handed Allyson several tissues. "Don't hold it in. You did well, Khadija did well, and your friend Seppe did . . . well, you know how he did. Go back to your apartment and get some sleep. The recap won't begin until tomorrow at noon. Rest and spend time in a place that gives you some peace, okay?" she advised.

Allyson wiped her eyes and nodded. "I'll try," she said, wondering where that place could be.

August 16
Caritas Refugee Camp

No longer having a role in Caritas, Khadija spent the next two days resting in one the Agency's apartments. The rooms felt like a palace after the dormitory in Caritas. On the third day, she asked to visit Daliyeh and her children, a request she was finally granted, albeit with restrictions.

"I was worried about you," Daliyeh said over tea. On the other side of the room, her two children played with the toys that Khadija brought. "You just disappeared. I was told you'd left the camp. I was worried it was your cancer."

"No, not the cancer. Daliyeh, it's time I told you the truth. I was put in Caritas by an organization that's trying to stamp out crime in the camps. I'm not allowed to explain much more than that. I want you to know, however, that I never had cancer. That was just a way for me to be taken into Rome to report on what was going on here in Caritas."

Daliyeh's mouth hung open. "You were never sick? Then how come . . . oh, I'm sorry."

"How come I'm this thin? It's okay. It's an eating disorder that makes me look sick. Actually, looking sick was the main reason I was chosen for Caritas. Also, that I knew Arabic and Italian."

"I notice you're not wearing the jewelry," Daliyeh said.

Khadija laughed. "I can't tell you how heavy that watch was."

"And the criminals are gone?"

"Yes, arrested and no longer in camp."

Daliyeh didn't say anything for a moment. "Is your name really Khadija?"

Khadija smiled. "Yes, that's my real name, but I didn't come to the camp from Syria. I'm a Palestinian who grew up in England."

"You're not a refugee?"

Khadija pondered the question. "I realize now that I've always been a refugee."

Tears flooded Daliyeh's eyes. "You will leave Caritas and go back to England."

"Probably not England, but, yes, they'll send me somewhere."

Daliyeh's daughter came over to the table for another of the cookies that Khadija brought. "Mama, why are you crying?"

Daliyeh wiped tears from her cheeks. "It's okay." Putting her hand on Khadija's arm, she said, "I'm sad, because Khadija is going away."

Now the daughter began to cry, which brought the son over to the table. "You're going away? Do you get to go back home?"

Before Khadija could answer, the daughter pulled on her sleeve. "Can we go with you?"

"I wish you could. I'll never forget you, especially the way you put cookies into my mouth."

That prompted the girl to pick a cookie off the plate and repeat the action. Khadija accepted it with a smile. "Hmm. It's delicious because you gave it to me."

Khadija looked at Daliyeh and put her hand on top of hers. "I mean it; I will never forget you, and I will never forget these wonderful, wonderful children."

Crying, Daliyeh rose from her chair to hug Khadija. Khadija returned the hug, even as she felt both children tugging at her legs. Soon, they were all crying. Khadija regained control and, looking at the children, tried to smile. "Someday, you will be going back home. To Syria. And when you do, I promise to come and see you, okay?"

The children looked at their mother, who nodded. "Yes, Allah willing, someday we'll go home."

"How will you find us?" Karina asked Khadija.

"Don't worry. I'll give your mother an address where she can always reach me. When you go home, your mother will let me know where you'll be living, and I'll come. I promise."

"Will you bring cookies and toys?" Mikal asked.

"Of course, and books too. Because you will be in school, and you'll be so smart."

"Our own books?" he asked.

"Your own books. To keep."

After they put the twins to bed, the women sat together at the table. "Is it true? Will we be able to go home?" Daliyeh asked.

Khadija took her friend's hand again. "I came to Caritas to try to put an end to the crime here. Now I see that I have to do more, a lot more. I hope to do what I can to convince the people I work for that the only way to stop crime in the camps is to end the war. The war, the refugees like you and your children, and these camps—they all have to end. And, if Allah wills, the war will end soon."

CHAPTER FORTY-SIX

August 20
Rome, CIA Headquarters

Allyson spent the week after the rescue meeting with various agents to review the operation. In several of the first meetings, while Khadija was still in Rome, the four principals—Khadija, Chaz, Manners, and Allyson—were all together. Allyson kept looking at Chaz, wondering how the ordeal had affected him. She was surprised by how little Chaz said when the Agency dissected his mistaken assessment of Asha Malik.

Only once, when Manners identified "white male superiority" as a key factor in Chaz's approach to Asha, did he glare at her. Yet, even when he had a chance to respond, he admitted his surprise that Asha had fooled him completely. The memory of Chaz sneering at Allyson in the kitchen of her apartment came back to her, along with her plan to report Sally's and his indiscretion to Morgan. What had once seemed like the just and proper step to take, given the rules of the CIA, now, in the wake of Seppe's rescue, seemed something that called for mercy.

There were two other moments in those sessions when Allyson found herself sympathizing with Chaz. The first came when the Agency praised Khadija for her ability to adjust as the situation changed. The sentence "Agents Chaz Eaton and Braylen Manners owe their survival to the quick thinking of Agent Khadija Mubarak" was underlined twice in the report.

For a moment, as the sentence was read aloud, Chaz looked across the table at Khadija as if he might say something. Then he didn't.

The second time occurred when the Agency officially acknowledged its debt to the aid worker Giuseppe D'Angelo, whose clever ploy, offering to trade places with Chaz, led to the successful rescue. As that was read, Chaz looked up, letting his Navy Seal mask drop as he gave Allyson a slight nod.

Allyson wasn't surprised when, the day following, Chaz formally requested a transfer—and because he'd been given leave time until his transfer, he didn't attend the follow-up meeting when Khadija and Allyson were notified that they would receive commendations.

As the days passed, Allyson realized how the abductions and rescue attempt had changed everything. In addition to Chaz's and Khadija's departures, Fatima was still hospitalized, suffering from recurring panic attacks. Allyson had hoped that Fatima would be released from Caritas to begin her new life. Now, she saw that Fatima needed the stability and the security of the camp.

For several reasons, Allyson's own future felt equally uncertain. She had been assigned as an FBI agent to work with the CIA in Rome, and now that the case concerning Caritas was closed, she knew she would be reassigned.

The Agency, however, had a far more important issue to resolve than Allyson's future. Aware that Leo D'Angelo, Seppe's brother, had exposed Allyson Worthy, Morgan knew that the Agency's continuing presence in Caritas was in jeopardy. Allyson didn't envy Morgan, who'd been assigned to meet with Leo and agree to what he would ask for in exchange for his silence.

For Allyson, the worst development was being denied permission to return to Caritas and visit Seppe in the hospital. As Bureau Chief Sanderson explained, a visit to the hospital ran the risk of her running into Leo.

Consequently, it was a full week before Allyson and Seppe sat on a bench while the sun set over the Janiculum Hill.

"I was afraid that you'd already left the country," Seppe said.

Allyson put her hand on Seppe's good hand. "I'm sorry; my superiors told me I couldn't contact you, even by phone."

"And now it's okay?"

"Not officially. I'm being sent back to the U.S. in a couple of days. Given that, breaking the rules didn't feel like such a crime."

"I see," Seppe said before returning to silence for a moment. Finally, he said, "When I was in the hospital, I thought of how everything has changed for Fatima over the past week. Fortunately, she and I were in the same hospital, and we were able to visit most days. She is so weak. It broke my heart when I remembered how people described her when she was first brought to Caritas. She was taking all those classes, and she had a dream she was looking forward to."

"I remember. She wanted to arrange tours for Muslims coming to Italy. Is that now impossible?" Allyson asked.

Seppe shrugged. "I keep praying the doctor is right, that the mind wants to heal. Fatima's been through so much, though, first in Syria and now in Caritas. She's way down inside herself, if you know what I mean." Sighing, he added, "I've also been thinking about Jameela, especially her last words."

"Tell me. We couldn't hear her over Khadija's transmitter."

Seppe looked past Allyson to the lights blinking from houses perched on the Janiculum Hill. "As she cut the ties around my wrist, she whispered, 'Forgive me.'"

After a moment of silence, Allyson asked, "What did she mean?"

Seppe closed his eyes. "Jameela wasn't like her sister. She saved Fatima's life by getting her to a hospital, and after I offered to exchange places with your agent, Jameela was worried about . . . about me. She was sure I'd be killed, and it would be her fault."

Allyson was quiet for a moment before saying, "My organization believes you offered to trade places with Chaz as part of your plan to get everyone rescued." Taking a deep breath, Allyson added, "That's not why you did it, is it?"

Seppe opened his eyes and held Allyson's gaze. "No, I remembered that you told me that Khadija was Fatima's protection. I knew she couldn't be a terrorist. So, yes, I knew I'd be safe if I did nothing, but I had to do what I did. It wasn't me who saw my decision as a way to rescue all of us. It was you, Alli. Given how things turned out, I just pray Jameela heard what I said back to her."

"What was that?"

"I asked her to forgive me."

"Forgive you for what?"

Seppe looked down, his brow furrowed. "I wonder if I'll ever be able to explain what happened to me when I was with Jameela for those hours. I saw how much everyone, including me, has failed and will continue to fail the refugees."

"No, no, Seppe. I don't believe that. I know how committed you are."

Seppe shook his head. "Don't you see, Alli? Crime is always going to be in places like Caritas, as long as we use camps as holding tanks. We feed refugees, house them, give them shots so they won't spread disease and offer them a few classes. Yet every day, more of their country is destroyed, and with that destruction, so go their hopes for the future. Crime in the camps at least offers that—the dream of a better future."

Allyson sighed. "It's not as if any of us can stop the war."

Closing his eyes again, Seppe shook his head. Finally, he said, "It's no secret that I've been struggling about my future. Am I supposed to be a priest? Am I supposed to continue working in Caritas? Are you and I . . . are we supposed to be together? All those questions kept swirling around in my mind, but when l listened to Jameela, I realized something. We have to give refugees a future worth living for. When I realized that, I knew what I have to do."

Allyson felt her throat tighten. "Which is?"

"Even cynics believe the war in Syria has to end someday, and everyone knows it will take decades to rebuild their country. Yet, what are we doing in the camps to get refugees ready for that? My family's business is banking, but where are the classes in the camps on how to set up a bank, on how to structure a loan? Think of how much Italians and others know about basic carpentry, masonry, sanitation and electricity. When Syria reopens, won't that country require thousands of returning refugees with those skills as well as those who know how to operate computers and high-tech machinery? Yet, where are the classes to teach those skills?"

Allyson could hear the change in Seppe's voice, the new energy.

"That's what I have to do—no, what I want to do. I'm not saying that there won't always be refugees like Asha who will cheat the system. In my heart, however, I believe that if refugees were given the skills to help rebuild their country, most wouldn't turn to crime." His voice wavered when he added, "If Caritas had offered those kinds of classes, Jameela would be alive today."

The sun had set, and although the air was still warm, Allyson felt a chill. Underlying Seppe's words, his vision, she knew he was pulling away.

"I've already met with the leaders of Sant Anselmo," he said. "I've told them what I hope to do, either with them or on my own. Either way, I know my family will support me, and I'll use every one of my family's connections to raise funds." Seppe looked at Allyson. "What I'm talking about is going to Turkey, living in one of the camps near the border with Syria, and setting up training classes. Practical skills, all geared to a real future." Smiling, he added, "Do you think I can convince Leo to join me?"

Not knowing what to say, Allyson said nothing.

"It feels right, Alli. It just feels right. All except the one piece . . . you."

Allyson's eyes filled with tears. "When you were abducted, I hated God, and I told Him so. Your God seemed so weak. He couldn't even keep you safe. And when you volunteered to trade places with Chaz, I knew you were thinking if that was what your God wanted—you to die—you'd do that. And that made me hate your God even more. I'm not sure I've forgiven him or if I ever will. What I do know is that if your God is like fire."

"Fire?"

Allyson nodded. "The closer I got to you, the more I've been burned." She found his hand and squeezed it. "Although I can quit my job, I don't want to do that. Maybe working for the agency is my way of trying to make the world a bit better; then again, maybe it's just me liking to solve puzzles. And down the road, who knows? My future is as uncertain as yours. I might show up someday in Turkey or . . . or, we might never meet again."

They sat quietly, holding hands. "You said you felt burned," Seppe said. "Maybe what I'm going to say next will hurt you even more, but I have to say it. Alli, I owe you. I owe you for your questions, for your doubts, for all the ways you pushed me. Father Sal told me once that it takes a long time for what a person believes to move from the head to the heart. I thought I had all the answers. Then when I thought you betrayed me and your love for me was an act, my whole world fell apart, and I realized how little faith I have in here," he said, tapping his chest.

Seppe offered a weak smile even as tears streamed down his cheeks. "When I was tied up and thought I could die, I didn't feel afraid, but I did have a wish. I hoped, if I died, that somehow you'd understand . . ."

"Understand what?"

"That I died knowing that we love each other. Will I become a priest? Maybe, maybe not. I can't see any further into the future than Turkey. I might be there two years, three years, I just don't know. And I certainly can't ask you to wait, and I won't ask you to go with me. But can I ask you this? One year from now, I promise to write you a letter. I'll need to send it to the CIA, won't I?"

Allyson sniffled. "Actually, send it to the FBI. What will you write about in the letter?"

"I promise to let you know what my feelings are for you. I think I already know what I'll write. Maybe you'll agree to write me about the same time and let me know what your feelings are for me."

"Of course, I will. Where should I send my letter?"

"To my parents here in Rome. Everyone in my family knows what you mean to me."

As they kissed one another goodbye, Seppe whispered, "You said that you've felt burned. I'm so sorry about that."

Allyson whispered back. "I'm not sorry one bit."

ALLYSON'S APARTMENT

LATER THAT NIGHT, ALLYSON sat on her bed and looked at her partially-filled suitcases. Because Sally was out clubbing, she had time to be by herself and accept that Seppe was right. Weeks before, when she'd first arrived in Rome, she'd felt stuck and, even worse, she'd felt old. Everything that had happened between Seppe and her had burned her, yet that burning had left in ashes the wall she'd hidden behind since her parents' divorce.

Welcome to my new life, she thought. *I'm more exposed now, but the past is finally over.*

David Carlson is Professor Emeritus (Religious Studies) at Franklin College where he served for forty-two years. With the study of religious violence being one of his specialties, David has lectured and given radio and television interviews on ISIS, Al-Qaeda, as well as religious extremists in the US.

Now retired, David enjoys writing non-fiction related to interfaith efforts; a weekly newspaper column on religion, politics, and culture; the Christopher Worthy and Father Fortis mystery series; and now the Allyson Worthy mystery series.

His wife, Kathy, is a retired English professor, an award-winning artist, and his best editor. Their two sons took parental advice to follow their passions. Leif is a visual artist, and Marten is a screenwriter and filmmaker.